P9-CCX-651

Praise for *Lovers & Players*

"Collins is back with another sexy page-turner."
—*New York Post*

"A fast-paced, glamour-heavy Collins extravaganza . . . Another page-turning tale packed with intrigue, revenge, and romance."
—*Publishers Weekly*

"Vintage Collins here: sex, love, betrayal, and deception. Her fans will certainly enjoy."
—*Booklist*

"A decadent concoction sure to appeal . . . A fast-lane take on the lives of the rich and fabulous."
—*Kirkus Reviews*

"A totally delicious read."
—*Complete Woman*

DROP DEAD
Beautiful

Lucky Santangelo Novels by Jackie Collins

Dangerous Kiss

Vendetta: Lucky's Revenge

Lady Boss

Lucky

Chances

Also by Jackie Collins

Lovers & Players

Hollywood Divorces

Deadly Embrace

Hollywood Wives—The New Generation

Lethal Seduction

L.A. Connections—Power, Obsession, Murder, Revenge

Thrill!

Hollywood Kids

American Star

Rock Star

Hollywood Husbands

Lovers & Gamblers

Hollywood Wives

The World Is Full of Divorced Women

The Love Killers

Sinners

The Bitch

The Stud

The World Is Full of Married Men

DROP DEAD
Beautiful

Jackie Collins

ST. MARTIN'S PRESS ☙ NEW YORK

This is a work of fiction. All of the characters, organizations, and events portrayed in this novel are either products of the author's imagination or are used fictitiously.

 For information, address St. Martin's Press, 175 Fifth Avenue, New York, N.Y. 10010.

www.stmartins.com

Library of Congress Cataloging-in-Publication Data

Collins, Jackie.
Drop dead beautiful / Jackie Collins. — 1st ed.
p. cm.
ISBN-13: 978-0-312-34179-4
ISBN-10: 0-312-34179-2
1. Santangelo, Lucky (Fictitious character)—Fiction. 2. Businesswomen—Fiction. 3. Las Vegas (Nev.)—Fiction. I. Title.

PR6053.O425D76 2007
823'.914—dc22

2007009831

First Edition: June 2007

10 9 8 7 6 5 4 3 2 1

For my family, who are a constant
source of love and encouragement
And
For my friends, whom I often write about,
only I change the names to protect the
not so innocent!

DROP DEAD
Beautiful

Prologue

The house in Pasadena was grand by anyone's standards. Large and imposing. An impressive Colonial mansion that reeked of money, nothing flashy.

Penelope Whitfield-Simmons and her son, Henry, lived in the mansion. Penelope was the widow of the powerful newspaper magnate Logan Whitfield-Simmons, who died at the age of seventy-two from a massive heart attack while out on a fishing trip with his only son. Henry, twenty-two at the time of his father's death, was now thirty, but he still lived at home, because in Logan's will, Henry received nothing until the death of his mother, and Penelope—a healthy seventy—had no intention of going anywhere.

Henry had no drive, no ambition. When he was younger he'd decided he wanted to be an actor. "Acting is for pansies," his father had roared. "Your place is in the newspaper business with me."

Henry had appealed to his mother. "Listen to your father," Penelope had said. "Everyone knows that people in the film business are all drug addicts, sexual deviants, and perverts. Not our kind, dear."

Ha! *Henry had thought.* As if she would know.

Behind their backs he tried his best. He'd secretly taken acting classes and found himself an agent.

One day a fellow student in his acting class mentioned that Alex Woods, the renowned Oscar-winning director, was auditioning young actors for the lead role opposite the very famous Venus Maria in his new movie, Seduction.

Henry was excited. He set about finding out everything he could regarding the upcoming film, even going so far as to bribe his agent's assistant to get him a copy of the script. He studied the script religiously, practicing his dialogue and moves in front of a mirror. When he considered himself fully prepared, he instructed his agent to get him in for an audition.

His agent had looked at him as if he were a mental case, and informed him that getting an audition for an Alex Woods film was virtually impossible for an actor who had no prior experience.

Henry came from a world of extreme wealth and privilege. At an early age he'd learned from his father that in their world nothing *was impossible.*

With a great deal of manipulating he'd arranged to get himself in for an audition.

The day he arrived for his appointment there were fifteen other young actors sitting around in the cramped waiting room. Henry proceeded to stare them down. They might be good, but Henry was confident that he was better.

The Asian girl behind the desk handed him sides.

Sitting, fidgeting, waiting, he'd imagined his future. He would land the role, tell his parents, and there would be nothing they could do about it.

He, Henry Whitfield-Simmons, was about to become a famous movie star, with or without their approval.

It never happened.

And why not?

Because of one woman.

Her name was Lucky Santangelo.

1

Drop Dead Beautiful. The three little words were scrawled on the Cartier card Lucky Santangelo had just opened. Hand-delivered, the note had been brought up to the house in Bel Air by Philippe, her houseman, who'd discovered it in the mailbox at the end of the driveway.

Drop Dead Beautiful. No signature, no return address.

Was it an invitation to an upcoming event too clever for its own good?

Whatever. One quick glance at the card, and Lucky tossed it in the trash.

Lucky Santangelo. A dangerously seductive woman with blacker-than-night eyes, full sensuous lips, a tangle of long jet-black hair, deep olive skin, and a lithe body. Wherever she went, Lucky still brought a room to a standstill, for not only was she wildly beautiful, she was also a powerhouse—a woman to be reckoned with, a force of nature. Street-smart and forever savvy—Lucky Santangelo had it all.

In her past, she'd built hotels in Vegas, owned a major movie studio, and been married three times. She'd also survived much heartache. Her mother, Maria, had been murdered when she was five years old. Her brother, Dario, was shot to death and tossed from a moving car. Then finally her fiancé, Marco, was gunned down in the parking lot of her Vegas hotel.

Eventually Lucky had found out that the man who'd ordered the brutal killings was her godfather, Enzio Bonnatti, a man she had always respected and trusted.

The information devastated her. Filled with vengeance, she'd lured Enzio into a carefully planned trap at his home, and shot him dead with his own gun, claiming that he'd tried to rape her. It was deemed a clear-cut case of self-defense.

Self-defense. *Sure.* She'd made it *look* like Bonnatti had been about to rape her, and the D.A. had bought it all the way. No surprise there. Her father, Gino, had major connections.

The real truth was that she'd shot the son of a bitch because he'd deserved to die, and she'd never regretted doing so. Justice had taken place. *Santangelo* justice.

Don't fuck with a Santangelo—the family motto.

Grabbing her purse from a shelf in the luxurious dressing room, Lucky headed for the door. Everything was large and luxurious in Bel-Air—the privileged enclave of the very rich and famous. The house she and her husband, Lennie, were living in was a short-term rental. Recent storms had wreaked havoc on their home in Malibu and they'd been forced to leave while repairs were being made.

The beach was more her style. Bel-Air was too cut off from real life with its winding hillside streets and enormous mansions hidden behind vast gates and high walls of impenetrable greenery. People existed as if they were living under siege, surrounded by multiple security guards and vicious attack dogs. That way of living was not for her. She enjoyed feeling unprotected and free, which was one of the reasons she'd opted out of running Panther Studios several years earlier.

Being the head of a Hollywood studio was no nine-to-five job. She'd found herself working seventeen-hour days, leaving no time for family and friends. One morning she'd woken up and thought, *That's it, I'm out.* She'd had enough of dealing with ego-inflated stars, nervous-for-their-jobs executives, fast-talking agents, neurotic directors, fat-assed producers, and anyone else who thought they could make it in the movie business—which was most people in L.A.

So she'd quit running Panther, and after producing one movie, *Seduction*, starring Venus Maria, and her new discovery, Billy Melina, she'd sold the studio and gotten out of the film business altogether.

Lennie was in the movie industry. That was enough for one family.

Besides, Lucky had other plans. She was getting back into the hotel business in Vegas—the place where it had all begun for her. Several years ago she'd put together a syndicate of interesting and colorful investors to develop a huge multibillion-dollar complex called the Keys. She'd been working with architects and planners for the last five years, and in less than a month they were about to celebrate the grand opening. Since the hotel project was her baby, she was beyond excited.

"Mom!" Max burst into the dressing room without knocking. Max, her sixteen-year-old wild child. Tall and coltlike with smooth olive skin green eyes, an unruly tangle of black curls, and a killer bod, Max was a showstopper. She was also a rebel, playing truant from school on a regular basis.

"Here's the thing," Max announced, bouncing up and down on the balls of her feet. "There's no *way* I can go to Grandpa's party."

"Excuse me?" Lucky questioned, attempting to remain calm.

"Y'see, there's this big blowout for one of Cookie's best friends up in Big Bear," Max blurted, speaking too fast. "A whole crowd of us wanna go, so like I can't let Cookie down."

"You can't, huh?" Lucky said coolly.

"Nope," Max answered, tugging on a stray curl. "Cookie's my best friend an' this is like *essential*."

"You are *not* missing Gino's birthday," Lucky said firmly. "No way."

Max stared balefully at her mom. "Huh?"

"You heard me," Lucky said, heading for the door.

"I can't believe you'd be this *mean*," Max complained, trailing behind her.

"Mean?" Lucky sighed. This was major déjà vu. It reminded her of all the times she and Gino had gone head to head, and there were too many to remember.

"*Why* do I have to stay for Gino's stupid party?" Max demanded. "It's not as if he'll *miss* me."

"Of *course* he'll miss you," Lucky insisted, hurrying down the stairs.

"He'll like *so* not," Max grumbled, right behind her.

Lucky turned around, shooting her daughter a warning look. "You're getting on my bad side, so stop it."

"But—"

"*No,* Max," Lucky said, walking out the front door. "I'm not interested, don't want to hear it."

And with those words she got into her red Ferrari and roared off down the driveway.

"*Crap!*" Max shrieked as her mother's car vanished into the distance.

"Whassup?" questioned her younger brother, Gino Junior, rounding the corner from the tennis court.

"Mom sucks!" Max complained, ignoring Gino Junior's two leering friends, both of whom she knew had a total crush on her.

"What she do now?" Gino asked. He was only fifteen, but he was already six feet tall and built like a football player.

"She won't let me get out of Grandpa's lame party. That's *so pathetic.*"

Ignoring her, Gino Junior raced into the house, followed by his two friends, who couldn't take their eyes off her.

"Horny little pricks," she muttered under her breath. "Go jerk off someplace else. Like *Siberia.*"

~ ~ ~

Lucky drove like a race car driver, skillfully weaving in and out of traffic. She turned the CD player on full volume—Usher blasting.

Lately Max's behavior was becoming quite a challenge. Everything seemed to turn into an argument. Lucky sighed. It wasn't easy being a parent, especially when in your head you were hardly any older than your own child.

A frosted and Botoxed blonde in a shiny new Mercedes cut in front of her, causing her to hit the brakes. "Shit, lady!" Lucky yelled. "Whyn't you learn to fuckin' *drive*."

Not that anyone could hear her, but shouting at other drivers eased the tension, although if Lennie happened to be in the car, it made him crazy. "One of these days someone's gonna get out their car and shoot your ass," he was always warning her.

"Yeah, sure," she would reply. "I *dare* them to."

At which point Lennie would shake his head. In his eyes there was no taming Lucky Santangelo. She walked her own path, and that's exactly the way he liked her.

2

Movie star Billy Melina was over six feet tall, tanned, with shaggy, bleached-by-the-sun hair, and a body straight out of an Abercrombie & Fitch catalog. At twenty-eight Billy was in spectacular shape, with sharply defined abs that rippled as the starstruck young girl kneeling in front of him bobbed her head up and down, servicing him with sticky lips and a busy tongue.

"Suck it!" Billy commanded, pressing his hands down on top of her head. "Suck it, suck it *hard!*"

She was doing the best she could. What more did he expect?

"Aarghh . . ." He let out a long, agonized groan. "That's it, sweet thing, that's *it!* I'm coming . . . I'm coming."

The girl attempted to pull away.

"No! No!" Billy yelled, pressing down even harder on the back of her head. "*Swallow* it, suck it all *down*." He groaned again, then mumbled, "Go, baby. Go. That's it! *Yeeeah!*"

For a moment there was silence while the girl tried to decide if it was now okay to release his massive dick from the confines of her mouth.

He decided for her, pulling away with a sudden jerk, immediately stuffing himself back into his tight white Calvin's and pulling up his jeans.

They were standing next to the pool in Billy's Hollywood Hills house—a house that the Realtor had assured him had once been rented by Charlie Sheen. A house that had cost him three million dollars, and who the fuck had ever thought he would be able to afford to buy such a house?

Certainly not his old man, Ed, who'd laughed in his face when Billy had informed him, eight years ago, that he was off to Hollywood to become a famous actor. Certainly not his alcoholic stepmother, Millie, whose parting words had been, "Good riddance, Billy boy. Doncha bother comin' back anytime soon."

He'd shown them, hadn't he? Oh yeah, he'd certainly shown them. He was Billy Melina. Hot-shot twenty-something movie star. Yeah—a freakin' *movie star.* He was on a very exclusive list of young actors who had the clout to open a movie. DiCaprio, Depp, Pitt—although Brad wasn't so young anymore. And then there was Billy Melina.

Yeah! Get off on *that* old Ed and Millie pissface.

The girl, clad in denim cut-offs and a skimpy yellow tank, got off her knees and stood up. "Was that okay?" she asked matter-of-factly, as if she'd just served him an omelette.

"Sweet," he replied, wondering how fast he could get rid of her.

Earlier in the day he'd picked her up at Tower Records on Sunset. When the girl had spotted him, she'd sidled over and requested his autograph. He'd noticed her nipples, pushing to escape her barely-there tank top. Then he'd noticed her legs, long and tanned. Her face was pretty—nothing special, but he was feeling major horny, and since his call to the set was not until three that afternoon, he'd invited her up to his house for lunch and a fast blow job. Not that he'd actually mentioned that a blow job was part of the deal—but they'd both known what would happen.

Quivering with excitement, she'd jumped in her truck and followed his sleek Maserati up the winding streets to his house, barely keeping up in her beat-up old truck with a broken taillight—a truck similar to the one he'd driven to Hollywood eight years earlier with two hundred bucks in his pocket and no prospects.

"Hey," he suggested as they stood beside the pool. "How about I give you an autographed picture so you can tell your friends you met me?"

"That'd be cool," she said, acting shy—as if his cock hadn't been in her mouth minutes before.

"Wait here," he instructed sternly. "I'll be right back."

When Billy had first arrived in Hollywood, he'd called women "ma'am," and been full of respect and good manners. Stardom had gotten him over *that* particular hump, although he still had a chivalrous streak.

He darted into his house through sliding glass doors, feeling ever so slightly guilty on account of the fact that he had a girlfriend—a gorgeous, famous movie star thirteen years his senior—and if she ever found out that he wasn't exactly Joe-faithful, she'd be well and truly pissed. But hey, a blow job wasn't cheating—everyone knew that. Jeez—President Clinton had declared it wasn't sex on national TV. How could anyone argue with *that*?

Ramona, his Hispanic housekeeper, was singing to herself in the kitchen, quite oblivious to the goings-on out by the pool. Kev, his assistant/best friend from the old days, was on the loose somewhere, running errands or picking up girls. He'd certainly get off on this one.

Billy rifled through the stuff on the coffee table in his den and located a stack of glossy eight-by-tens mixed up with unopened bills, pornographic fan mail, a half-smoked joint, well-thumbed car magazines, and an empty candy box. He grabbed a pen, hurriedly scrawled his signature on the photo, and raced back outside, eager to get her off the premises.

The young girl had divested herself of her cut-offs and tank, and was swimming bare-assed naked in his pool.

Shit! What was he supposed to do now?

"Hey," he said, chewing on his thumbnail.

"Didn't think you'd mind," she responded nonchalantly.

Well, I do, he thought sourly.

"Uh . . . okay," he said, still chewing. "But I gotta take off any minute, so you're gonna hafta haul your hot little ass outta there."

"How about *you* getting in?" she suggested, becoming bolder by the minute. "It's all *warm* an' *wet*, you won't be disappointed."

She flipped onto her back, floating in his azure pool, her small nipples erect and disturbingly tempting.

He contemplated this juicy prize, there for the taking. She had a flat stomach, a huge bush of wiry pubic hair—which he found quite sexy because shaved pussy was all the rage in Hollywood—and those long, sexy legs.

Familiar stirrings down below, even though only moments before he'd experienced an extremely satisfactory orgasm.

What the hell, he'd nail her in the pool, then hustle her out of there before she knew it.

After all, what Venus didn't know . . .

~ ~ ~

"Where's Billy?" Alex Woods demanded of Maggie, his personal assistant, a tall woman of Native American descent with long black hair scraped back into a ponytail and strong, almost manly features.

They were standing next to a wooded area several miles outside of L.A. shooting Alex's current movie, *Kill,* a violent thriller.

Maggie sensed an outburst coming on. She was well aware that as a director Alex Woods was an Oscar-winning genius, and yet as a man he could be a nightmare. When things were not to his liking, everyone had to watch out—including her. She often wondered how his Asian lawyer girlfriend, Ling, put up with him.

"He's on his way," she assured him in a calm voice.

"What the fuck is *that* supposed to mean?" Alex snapped, rubbing his hands together. "His call was for three, and it's now three forty-five."

"I know," Maggie said, remaining calm.

"So get in touch with his driver and tell the asshole to put his foot down."

"Billy refused to use his driver," Maggie explained. "He insisted on driving himself."

"What kind of *shit* is that?" Alex screamed, suddenly losing it. "The insurance forbade it. D'you hear me, Maggie? They *forbade* that he drove himself to any of the locations. You *know* that."

"Yes, I do," Maggie responded in a quiet voice, because having worked with Alex for quite a few years, she also knew there was absolutely no point in provoking a screaming match.

"She knows!" Alex yelled, mimicking her. "She fucking *knows*, and yet she does nothing."

Maggie shrugged.

"Shit!" Alex screamed. "Goddamn actors. They should all go fuckin' Tom Cruise themselves out of the business."

"What does *that* mean?"

"Wait a few years," Alex said ominously, "you'll find out."

"No panic," Maggie said, relieved. "Here he comes now."

An Electra Glide fully restored Harley roared into sight, Billy Melina astride in all his glory, black-leathered up to the eyebrows.

Alex strode toward the young actor as Billy jumped off his bike. "You're fucking *late!*" he yelled.

"Traffic," Billy countered, his voice filled with the arrogance of an actor who knows there is no way he can get fired.

"Unprofessional," Alex growled.

"Not my fault, man," Billy said, casually removing his helmet.

"Of course not," Alex drawled sarcastically. "Why would it be *your* fault? Nothing's your fucking fault, is it?"

Maggie quickly attempted to defuse the situation. "Billy," she said. "Come with me. They're waiting for you in the makeup trailer."

"Hey, Mags," Billy said, turning on the charm. "You're lookin' hot. How's about you an' me—"

"Move your punk ass," Alex interrupted.

"Sure, old man," Billy said, grinning.

Infuriated, Alex stomped off toward his crew busy setting up across the street. Old man indeed. There was nothing worse than some two-bit actor with a handful of box-office hits who considered himself the second coming of Steve McQueen.

Fuck all actors. And *definitely* fuck Billy Melina.

Alex had seen them come, and he'd seen them go. At fifty-something he was a veteran producer/writer/director who'd been through the Hollywood wars countless times. He knew all the games, all the shenanigans. He'd seen studio heads ousted at a moment's notice, and a staggering lack of honesty and loyalty. The only studio head Alex had enjoyed working with was Lucky Santangelo when she'd owned and run Panther Studios. They'd had a connection that was more than business, and although Alex had always gone for Asian women, there was something about Lucky that had immediately drawn him in.

Unfortunately, she was married and in love with her husband, although there'd been a moment in time when they *had* gotten together. One crazy, insane night of love and lust when Lennie was gone, and Lucky had thought he was dead. Christ! The memory of that one night in a cheap motel in the middle of nowheresville was always there. It was a night he would never forget.

Lucky had never mentioned their one night together again. He knew that in her mind it was something she preferred to think had not taken place. But it had, and he would always have strong feelings for her. There was nothing he could do about it.

Since that time they'd remained friends, had even produced a very successful movie together, and now he was a major investor in her Vegas hotel project.

Maggie returned from depositing Billy in the makeup trailer.

"Five minutes," Alex growled. "I want that punk kid on the set in five minutes. You got that, Maggie?"

"Yes, Alex, five minutes."

"And no more turning up on his fucking Harley. I want his skinny ass in a *car* with a *driver*. It's in his contract. Make sure he honors it or get on the phone to his agent."

"Yes, Alex."

"Okay. Now let's go make a fuckin' movie."

3

Anthony Bonar—formerly Anthony Bonnatti—had it all. A well-appointed luxurious villa twenty-five minutes outside of Mexico City, a duplex penthouse in New York, a vacation home in Acapulco on the bay, and a rambling waterfront estate in Miami. He also had an American wife, Irma, to whom he'd been married for fifteen years; two children—a boy and a girl; two mistresses, his own plane, a helicopter, and a lucrative business. When asked—and not many dared—he would inform them that he was in the import/export business, which wasn't exactly a lie, because running a vast drug empire was exactly that—import from here, export to there.

For the first twelve years of his life Anthony had been raised in Italy by his mother, Mia, a hardworking maid who'd toiled in a beachfront hotel in Naples. The same hotel the Bonnatti family had stayed at on vacation when young Santino Bonnatti was a constantly horny teenager. The same hotel where Santino had knocked twenty-two-year-old Mia up one balmy night while making out with her on the beach under the stars.

After the Bonnatti family checked out and returned to America, Mia had no idea she was pregnant. When she found out, she was unable to summon the courage to get in touch with the family. It wasn't until twelve years later, when she was diagnosed with cancer and given only a few months to live, that she'd contacted the Bonnattis.

A few weeks later Santino's formidable mother, Francesca Bonnatti, flew to Italy to investigate the girl's story. Upon arrival she'd taken one look at young Anthony with his big brown eyes and cocky attitude and realized that Mia was speaking the truth, for Anthony looked nothing like her son, Santino, nor did he resemble his birth mother, Mia. No, Anthony was the mirror image of Francesca. A male version. He was *definitely* a Bonnatti.

Francesca flew her illegitimate grandson back to the States to live with Enzio and herself.

Anthony flourished. He was an exceptionally smart boy who quickly learned to speak English without an accent. Raised on the streets of Naples for the first twelve years of his life by a mother who barely had time for him, he'd learned how to survive on his wits. His grandfather soon took a shine to his ballsy illegitimate grandson. Before long Enzio began taking Anthony on business trips to Colombia and Mexico City, proudly introducing the boy to all his main contacts.

When Santino, outraged that his father had taken such a liking to his so-called son, moved his family and his own business interests—mainly the distribution of pornographic movies and magazines—to California, Enzio wasn't bothered, for Santino was certainly not the son he'd hoped for.

When Enzio was shot, it was sixteen-year-old Anthony who'd comforted Francesca and stayed by her side. Santino and his brother, Carlos, attended the lavish funeral, but neither of them stayed around. *Fuck Santino Bonnatti,* Anthony had thought. *And fuck his fat wife and asshole kids.* He wanted nothing to do with any of them, just as they had wanted nothing to do with him.

After Enzio's death, Francesca encouraged Anthony to put everything Enzio had taught him to good use. He didn't let her down.

Six years later when Santino himself was killed, Anthony hadn't felt one shred of emotion. Why would he? His so-called father had treated him as if he didn't exist, so there was no reason for him to care.

By the time Anthony reached his early twenties, he'd forged major contacts with the biggest drug overlords in Mexico City, Colombia, and Bolivia.

Anthony got off on having money and power, realizing early on how attractive those two things were to women. Plus he was not bad-looking in a darkly brooding way. Unfortunately, though, he was only five feet seven, not as tall as he'd like to be, and his lack of height pissed him off, but it didn't stop him from sleeping his way through most of the models, would-be actresses, and young socialites in New York and Miami.

Francesca was proud of his success, but she was also wary of his playboy ways, so one day she informed him that it was time he found himself a *nice* girl, got married, settled down, and started a family.

A family he would start, but settling down was for old men with nowhere left to go.

After a few months of Francesca's nagging, he decided he'd better do as she suggested and start looking for The One.

It wasn't long before he met Irma at a party in Miami. She was seventeen and he was twenty-four.

He'd taken one look at the well-endowed, pretty teenager and come to the conclusion that she might be the one—*especially* when she confided she was still a virgin.

After obtaining Francesca's approval, Anthony and Irma were married in a church in Mexico City where Anthony was negotiating to buy a large estate outside the city.

Irma—virginal in a white lace dress—made a delightful bride. They honeymooned in Europe, and shortly after their honeymoon Irma became pregnant.

Their son, Eduardo, was born the day before Irma's eighteenth birthday. A year later she gave birth to a girl, Carolina.

Anthony *and* his grandma were satisfied. Irma had delivered the perfect family, and Anthony decided that she should now concentrate all her energy on being a nurturing mother, while *he* continued to build up his business, travel the world, and whore around.

Grandmother Francesca had taught him well. Women, she'd assured him in an authoritative tone when she'd first brought him to America, were either mothers, wives, sisters, or daughters—other than that they were *puttanas*, whores and sluts.

After the birth of his two children, Anthony decided that sex with Irma was over; he didn't care to stick it in the same place his precious children had emerged from.

Although Anthony's main residence was in Mexico City, he also spent plenty of time in Miami and New York, with twice-yearly trips to Colombia and Bolivia. The drug trade he'd fallen into was already making him more money than he'd ever imagined, but in spite of his wealth and good fortune, Anthony was not completely at ease. Francesca expected *him* to be the one to avenge the murder of his grandfather and his piece-of-shit father. And she never let him forget it.

"The Bonnatti name must be avenged," she was always telling him. "You *know* the history only too well."

Oh yeah, he knew the history, and even though he'd legally changed his surname to Bonar, he was a Bonnatti by birth.

Francesca often regaled him with stories of the bad blood between the Bonnattis and the Santangelos. It was a feud that went way back.

According to Francesca, Gino Santangelo and Enzio Bonnatti were once close boyhood pals, going into business together, scoring huge amounts of money. Both teenage sons of immigrants, they'd been quick to seize all the opportunities America had to offer, from running numbers to loan-sharking, gambling, and hijacking trucks loaded with illegal booze. They'd stayed together several years, until Enzio had begun to pursue a different line of business—drugs and prostitution, two areas Gino Santangelo refused to be involved with.

Gino Santangelo must've been some dumb fuck, Anthony often thought. *What kind of man turns his back on making mega bucks?*

Apparently Gino did, because instead of continuing his partnership with Enzio, he'd built hotels in Vegas, legitimizing his business to a degree, and then allowing his daughter, Lucky, to move in and run things.

Although Enzio and Gino had parted on cordial terms, over the years they'd become dire enemies, creating a feud between the two families that had festered and only gotten worse throughout the years.

Frankly, Anthony wasn't interested in vendettas and revenge; that kind of thing was for old-timers, mustache Petes, men of his late grandfather's generation. But he knew Francesca would never quit until he did something about the Santangelos.

The Bonnattis and the Santangelos. Not a match.

4

The Heavenly Spa in Pasadena was the one place Lucky felt that she could truly relax. She and Venus, her closest friend, always made the effort to meet there at least a couple of times a month. It wasn't easy, as they both balanced hectic schedules, but somehow or other they managed it.

Lucky rushed in aware that she was late, still pissed about Max mouthing off, although she couldn't be *too* mad, for at sixteen she'd had exactly the same bad-ass attitude.

Ha! Like mother like daughter. And there wasn't much she could do about it except keep a watchful eye out.

"How's Billy?" she asked once she and Venus were settled in the mud-wrap treatment room while two formidable-looking Russian women slathered thick mud all over their bodies.

"You think I'm crazy, don't you?" Venus sighed, lying back totally naked except for an animal-print thong.

"Hey, whatever turns you on," Lucky remarked, stretching out her leg as one of the large Russian women applied a healthy coating of mud to her well-toned thighs. "If you're still into Billy, that's your prerogative. Believe me, I'm the *last* person to judge anyone—*especially* a major diva like you."

"Major diva, my ass," Venus retorted, laughing.

"Go ahead, deny it," Lucky teased. "Everyone's got your number."

"Look," Venus said, suddenly serious, "I know how fond you were of Cooper—"

"Still am," Lucky interrupted, choosing her words carefully. "Only just 'cause *I* liked him doesn't mean that you had to do time in a marriage that wasn't working."

"*I'm* not the one to blame," Venus said, shifting onto her side. "The man screwed around on me, and if that wasn't enough, Mister Life and Soul of the Party turned into Mister Boring—a man who insisted on being in bed every night by *nine!* I mean, can you imagine?" she added, rolling her eyes.

"Men get that way," Lucky said sagely, enjoying the sensation of the cold mud on her body. "It's on account of a little something called marriage."

"*Lennie's* not like that," Venus pointed out.

"Doesn't mean we haven't had our differences," Lucky retorted.

"Which you've always managed to work out."

"This is true."

"So . . . what did *I* do wrong?"

"Nothing," Lucky said, shrugging. "Except that you became a bigger star than him."

"You think?"

"C'*mon,* Venus, you *know* you did. Shit happens. Egos go trippin'. Cooper has a *giant* ego—surely you noticed?"

"Believe me," Venus said with a secret smile, "that's not all Cooper had. . . ."

"No details," Lucky said, quickly interrupting. "I do *not* get off on details."

"Not that I miss it," Venus mused. "Because I can assure you, Billy is *certainly* a member of the well-hung club. In fact—"

"Goddammit!" Lucky exclaimed. "Didn't I just say no details? Other people's sex lives bore me shitless!"

"Aren't *I* the fortunate one," Venus boasted, laughing. "Got me two in a row."

"Yeah, and let's not forget the other half-dozen in between," Lucky murmured, sotto voce.

"Ha!" Venus said vehemently. "Jealous?"

Lucky raised an eyebrow. "Have you *met* Lennie?"

"Yeah, yeah, I *know*, Lennie is the greatest everything, and you're both ecstatically happy, and neither of you cheats. But I must say, if *Cooper* had turned up with an illegitimate kid, I'm not sure I could've—"

"Don't go there," Lucky said in a warning voice. "Ancient history isn't my thing."

Much as she loved Venus, sometimes the platinum-blond superstar overstepped certain boundaries. The truth was that Lennie had fathered a child under extreme circumstances—he'd been kidnapped, trapped in an underground cave in Sicily, and made love to a woman, Claudia, who'd helped him escape. It was a onetime thing, and he'd never seen the woman again until she'd turned up on their doorstep in Malibu with Leonardo, a boy she'd claimed Lennie had fathered.

It was a difficult time to get through, but they'd done so, and when Claudia was killed, Lucky had adopted Leonardo as if he were her own. Somehow it had made their marriage stronger, bonding them even closer.

"So," Lucky said, moving on. "Will you be bringing Billy to Gino's party on Sunday?"

"Why wouldn't I?" Venus said, narrowing her eyes.

"'Cause I had to invite Cooper," Lucky explained. "Y'know how close he is to Lennie."

"Fine with me." Venus sniffed. "I suppose he'll be with that coke-snorting *child* he's been banging."

"You sound bothered," Lucky said.

"Are you *kidding* me? The only thing that bothers me is that he takes her out with Chyna, and that's not right."

"Chyna's a smart kid," Lucky said, thinking about Venus's young daughter. "She can handle it."

"She shouldn't have to," Venus said adamantly. "Cooper's latest girlfriend is a drug- and sex-addicted nineteen-year-old wannabe actress *whore*. What the hell is Cooper *thinking?* He's old enough to be her *grandfather*."

"Hey, maybe we should hook her up with Billy," Lucky joked. "They're almost the same age."

"Fuck you," Venus drawled.

"I leave that chore to my husband," Lucky murmured dryly.

"For God's sake," Venus said, "I have to take enough shit from the press, don't *you* get on my case."

"It was a bad joke. Sorry."

"Billy might be only twenty-eight, but he's an old soul," Venus felt obliged to explain. "The age difference doesn't bother either of us. The only people who seem to care are the goddamn tabloids—and oh yeah, the nighttime talk-show hosts who make a living ragging on us 'cause their dumb writers can't come up with anything more original."

"Okay, I get it."

"I love Billy, and I *know* he loves me."

"As long as you're sure. I wouldn't want to see you get hurt."

"Why?" Venus said suspiciously. "What've you heard?"

"Nothing."

"You're sure?"

"Positive."

"You'd tell me if you heard anything."

"Stop obsessing."

"I can't help it. Billy gives me chills. I feel as if I'm sixteen!"

Lucky's cell rang. She reached for it and exchanged a few sentences with Lennie, finishing off with, "I miss you—love you. See you later."

"Exactly how long is it since you two have seen each other?" Venus asked, raising an eyebrow. "Fifteen minutes?"

"Not my fault if he's crazy in love," Lucky said, hardly able to wipe the smile off her face because it was true, they were still crazy in love.

"Goddammit!" Venus exclaimed. "You and Lennie make me sick you're so damn *happy*."

"I gotta tell you, when it works, it *really* works," Lucky said. "And believe me, I am *not* complaining."

"Nor should you," Venus sighed. "Everyone knows that Lennie's the greatest."

Lucky nodded and smiled. "And *nobody* knows it better than me."

5

Francesca Bonnatti was a wise and canny woman. She'd observed much in her life, both good and bad. Now, at eighty-four, she was not at all ready to give up her vendetta against the Santangelo family. Sicilian by birth, Francesca had come to America with her parents, a hardworking immigrant couple, when she was eleven. Sent straight to school, Francesca soon found she was the odd one out—the Italian girl with the fancy name who could barely speak English. She applied herself, diligently learning the language, and by the time she was thirteen, she'd succeeded in absorbing herself into the American way of life.

At fifteen she left school and started training as a bookkeeper.

"A bookkeeper is a good job for a girl to have," her father assured her. "With that skill you will always find work."

Fifteen, smart, and quite a beauty—it wasn't long before boys came flocking around.

When she was sixteen she met Enzio Bonnatti, a man eleven years older than her. At the time she was working for a grizzled old accountant who looked after some of Enzio's accounts.

Enzio Bonnatti was tall and dangerous-looking. He was also of Italian origin, which she knew would please her father. The eleven-year age difference would not.

Enzio started visiting the cramped office where she worked on a regular basis. He always had a pretty girl hanging on to his arm. He got a big kick out of teasing Francesca, showing off as he swaggered around the office.

One day he brought his friend Gino Santangelo with him. Gino was shorter than Enzio, but he was full of charisma, with his thick, black curly hair and intense dark eyes.

Francesca began flirting with Gino to make Enzio jealous. The more she flirted, the more Enzio appeared with different girls. It was a game they both played. Teenage girl and older man. When was he going to ask her out?

Eventually he did, and she started seeing him secretly, not daring to tell her parents.

Enzio was very demanding; a kiss on the cheek did not do it for him. Every time he tried to go further, Francesca demurred, telling him she was a virgin and had no intention of changing that status until she was a married woman.

On her seventeenth birthday she told her parents she'd met a boy who wanted to take her out. She wondered what they would do if they discovered that she was really seeing the notorious Enzio Bonnatti, a man who had quite a reputation in the neighborhood. It would not sit well with her hardworking parents, so to appease them she bribed one of the boys she worked with to pretend to be her date. The boy picked her up at her house, then delivered her to Enzio's apartment. When she arrived, Enzio said, "You gotta look older 'cause we're goin' to a nightclub. I got you a dress, go put it on."

"What kind of dress?" she asked.

"You could call it a fancy dress," he joked. "It fell off the back of a truck."

Enzio wasn't shy about what he did, he never tried to hide it from her, and even though she knew his activities were not exactly legal, she couldn't help enjoying the sense of excitement he brought into her mundane life.

The dress was red and tight. It clung to her teenage curves, emphasizing her breasts and butt, making her appear older than her years. It obviously had a positive effect on Enzio, for later that night he proposed.

She told him she'd think about it. Although she liked Enzio, she'd grown to like his friend, Gino, even more. But Gino never gave her the time of day, which infuriated her. She couldn't understand it. Most men paid her plenty of attention.

One day she asked Gino why he chose to ignore her.

"You're my best friend's girlfriend," he answered. "That's why."

"I'm not his girlfriend," she objected. "Enzio's always running around with other women."

"You're the one he's gonna marry," Gino replied. "You can be sure of that."

"My father won't allow me to marry him."

"Wanna bet?" Gino said. "You'll see."

It frustrated her that Gino never responded to her beauty. She tried on many occasions to get him to change his mind but he was steadfast. His friendship with Enzio came first. Loyalty meant everything to Gino Santangelo.

Without her knowledge, Enzio went to her father and obtained his permission for them to get married. She suspected he either bribed or threatened her father to agree.

They were married two days before her eighteenth birthday. Gino was Enzio's best man.

Now, all these years later, she still thought about Gino and what might have been.

Gino Santangelo was the one she should've married. He was the one who got away.

Now all she could think about was that Gino Santangelo was alive and Enzio was dead—murdered by Gino's bitch daughter.

Retribution was a necessity for the Bonnatti family name, and Anthony had to resolve the situation. The Bonnatti honor was at stake.

For quite a while now Francesca had been muttering about the six-billion-dollar hotel complex in Vegas Lucky Santangelo was building. "You cannot let this happen," she'd informed her grandson over and over. "Gino and Lucky Santangelo tried to take everything from us. Now we take our revenge."

Anthony had many connections in Vegas. If he kept the Keys from opening, it would shut his grandmother up once and for all. After all, if it wasn't for Francesca, he would've had nothing. And since she never stopped insisting that it was time the Santangelo family paid for their sins against the Bonnatti family, it would satisfy her. Anthony had a plan. A deadly plan. Costly and explosive. If it worked out, then Grandma would be one very happy woman indeed.

It was the least he could do.

6

Max Santangelo Golden had a secret. A big one. She'd met this boy—well, man really—on the Internet, and every night for the past six weeks they'd exchanged all kinds of information online. His name was Grant and he was twenty-two. From his e-mails he sounded smart and interesting. He lived in San Diego, drove a jeep, and didn't have a girlfriend. Best of all, he'd posted his picture and he was a hottie—kind of like a younger Brad Pitt. The point was he did not fall into the category of sex-obsessed, lame teenage boy, and that was a major plus, because she was *so* over stupid boys. She wanted a real man, and Grant sounded like he might be the one.

So Max had lied, told him she was eighteen, that she worked for a fashion designer and had recently broken up with her boyfriend—which sounded way cooler than saying she was sixteen and still in high school. Actually, she *had* just broken up with her boyfriend, so that wasn't exactly a lie. She'd broken up with Donny because she'd caught him making out with some bleached-blond skank at Houston's in Century City of all places. He'd said he had to go somewhere with his parents and she'd said she was staying home. But later she'd changed her mind, called up her posse, Harry and Cookie, and the three of them had gone to Houston's for the mind-blowing ribs. And there he was, Donny Leventon—seventeen and a hunk—slobbering all over said skank, who could've been his *mother* she was so old. At least *thirty*. It was *so* utterly gross!

Cookie had spotted him first. "Whoa! Major disaster about to happen!" she'd gasped, nudging Max. "We gotta split like *now!*"

Whereupon Max had taken in the scene and being her mother's daughter, acted accordingly. Without a moment's hesitation she'd marched over to Donny's table, picked up a glass filled with Coca-Cola and ice, and tossed the contents into his lying scumbag face. Before he could react, she was out of there, Cookie and Harry right behind her.

After what she termed "the Houston Incident," she'd refused to ever speak to him again. The real truth was that Donny had broken her heart—just a tiny bit. He was her first real love, and he'd let her down.

Rejection was not something Max had ever had to deal with before, and it was hard, but eventually, when Donny came begging for her to take him back, she'd given him all the rejection she could muster. Let him see how *he* liked it.

Anyway, the point was Internet Dude had asked her if she wanted to get together and impulsively she'd said yes.

Two days later he'd announced that he'd hired a cabin up in Big Bear for the following weekend, and she'd promised to meet him there.

This was her move to make Donny sorry he'd ever cheated on her. Not that they'd been having sex, but they *had* been pretty intimate without going all the way. Now she would go all the way with Internet Dude, and *then* she would make sure Donny found out. *That* was the ass-wipe's big punishment.

Donny should've waited, she thought sadly. *I would've given it up—eventually.*

Her plans were all in place, but unfortunately her crappy mom was putting up roadblocks, which pissed her off, because why *shouldn't* she do exactly as she pleased? Her mom *always* had—everyone knew about Lucky Santangelo and *her* notorious past—so why was *she* expected to be such a little lamb?

She had *no* intention of *not* going to Big Bear and missing out on an exciting experience, but how to pull it off without getting grounded for weeks on end, *that* was the problem.

She wasn't exactly losing sleep over it, because if there was one thing she excelled at, it was solving problems. And with the help of her two best friends—Cookie, a pretty black girl, and Harry, an in-the-closet gay teenager—she'd somehow work it out.

Cookie and Harry were the best, always up to support an adventure, and meeting some hot guy in Big Bear was a *major* adventure. Not that they were going to get to meet him, but they'd back her up all the way. That's what true friends were for.

Later that afternoon, Cookie and Harry came over to lie out by the pool and mull over the situation.

"*I* wanna *meet* your Internet perv," Cookie insisted, swigging from a can of Red Bull. She was a curvaceous girl in a young Janet Jackson kind of way. Chocolate-brown dreadlocks framed her heart-shaped face, and her lips were full and pink. Her father was Gerald M., the forty-nine-year-old smooth-soul-singing icon. Cookie had chosen to live with him in Beverly Hills because her mom was a prescription-drug whore who'd moved over the hill to the Valley with a twenty-five-year-old sometime musician, and Cookie couldn't stand either of them. Her mom and boyfriend cohabited in stoned bliss, while Cookie enjoyed the good life with her famous father.

"Yeah, an' *I* wouldn't mind giving him a blow job," Harry leered, huddling under a huge sun umbrella, hiding from the sun. Harry was skinny and alarmingly pale, with dyed black hair worn spiked, as if he'd recently stuck his finger in a power socket. *His* mogul-type dad worked late hours at the TV network he ran, while his mom, a born-again, spent most evenings at her church or meeting with her pastor, a man Harry was convinced she was sleeping with.

"Bet you both *wish* you were coming with me," Max said, tossing back her long mane of dark curls. "But hey, *I'm* the one that's gonna be screwing him, *that* privilege is *all* mine, so try not to turn into jealous wrecks."

"*If* your mom lets you go," Cookie pointed out, adjusting the top of her bikini.

"I'm workin' on it," Max said confidently, knowing that she was taking off to Big Bear whether Lucky agreed or not.

"I *so* hope this dude's like *not* a *perv*," Cookie offered, wriggling around on her sun lounger, her brief pink bikini showing off every curve.

"And *I* hope he is," Harry said excitably, his skinny body fully covered in a faded black T-shirt and baggy black pants worn half-mast. " 'Cause then you can give us all the sicko details when you get back."

"*If* she gets back," Cookie interrupted, rolling her eyes for emphasis. " 'Cause he could cut her up into itty-bitty pieces an' bury her under the mountain."

"Thanks for the thought," Max said, biting down on her lower lip. "But hey, I know how to kick ass, so any cutting goin' on will be coming from *me*. *Get it?*"

"Bad shit happens," Cookie said, nodding wisely. "I read where this woman met this dude on the Internet and he like *strangled* her, 'cause that's what she told him she was into. How psycho is *that*?"

"Grant's cool," Max said airily. "I can tell."

"How?" Cookie demanded.

"I got good instincts."

"You'd better answer your cell at all times 'cause we'll be on red alert," Harry said sternly.

"Should I pick up my cell even when we're doin' it?" Max teased.

"What?" Harry said, his face reddening.

"Don't go getting all prudish on me," Max said, giggling as she reached for a tube of suntan cream. "I gotta do it *sometime*, and Grant's the perfect victim."

"He is?" Cookie asked. "How's that?"

"Well," Max said, "he's like an out-of-towner who can't go around blabbing about me. Oh yeah, an' he's older, so he'll be like an *expert* at it."

"You *go* for it, girl," Cookie said, making a victory sign. "Only try not to get slashed along the way."

"Oh, so now he's a *slasher*," Max drawled, reaching for a bobby pin and piling her hair on top of her head. "Anyone ever mention that your imagination *sucks?*"

"Could be he's straight out of a Wes Craven horrorfest," Harry said, making a spooky face. "Girl alone with strange dude equals she'll like *definitely* get her throat slit."

"It's so *encouraging* to have friends like you two losers," Max said, jumping up and making a running dive into the pool.

She didn't care what anyone said—she was going to Big Bear. No doubt about it.

7

For some time Irma Bonar had been thinking about taking a lover. At thirty-two, she'd finally decided to do something about her empty life stuck outside Mexico City in an enormous villa surrounded by servants and bodyguards. This was the place her husband, Anthony, had decided she should live, while *he* traveled anywhere he wanted doing God knew what.

Anthony Bonar was a difficult man. Difficult, arrogant, and most of all controlling.

The fact that he no longer wished to have sex with her did not please Irma at all. Over the years she'd gotten used to her husband's ferocious style of lovemaking, and now she could not understand why their once-active sex life had ground to a sudden halt.

Whenever she mentioned it to him, Anthony always managed to come up with a variety of reasons. Reason number one: he had a lesion on his penis and he wasn't sure what it was.

Irma had carefully inspected his limp manhood and found nothing.

"It's there," Anthony had insisted, "an' if you don't wanna catch nothin', you'd better listen t'me for once."

This frightened her off for a while, until one night he'd shoved his supposedly damaged cock into her mouth for a late-night blow job because he'd had a fight with one of his mistresses and the *puttana* had sent him home horny.

After that incident the lesion excuse didn't work anymore, so he'd announced that his doctor had warned him that his testosterone level was dangerously low, and that he had to lay off sex for a while.

Gradually Irma had grown to understand that her dear husband did not wish to have sex with her, and galling as she found it, she was forced to settle for the occasional jump in the dark when *he* felt like it, usually late at night or early in the morning when she was half asleep. Anthony always made sure to pull out before coming. He had no desire to make more babies—two was definitely enough.

Irma did exactly as Anthony expected of her. She concentrated on their children, making sure Carolina and Eduardo received the best of everything. She also absorbed herself in decorating their various homes, although once each place was finished, Anthony sent her back to Mexico, where he insisted she live. Anthony professed to love their home. *If he loves it so much,* Irma often thought, *why doesn't he live here permanently?* He came and went whenever it suited him, while she was stuck there with no friends and no one to talk to.

Anthony did not encourage her to make friends, although *he* certainly entertained an adoring entourage when he deigned to spend time at home. There were several couples he invited over when he was there. One of the women was American, but Anthony had warned Irma not to have any contact with the woman when he wasn't around.

"Why not?" she'd wanted to know.

"'Cause I don't want nobody findin' out nothin' 'bout my business," he'd said. "You'd better keep to yourself, Irma. That's an order."

When the children were old enough, Anthony had decided that they should continue their education in America. This delighted Irma, because she was desperate to move back to the States.

"*You're* not comin'," Anthony had said, brooking no argument. "You'll stay in Mexico—it's our main home, it's where you should be."

"No," Irma had protested. "Where I *should* be is with our children. They're still young, they need me."

"Forget it," Anthony had answered harshly. "The kids are growin' up. I'm hirin' a housekeeper to take care of 'em, make sure they do their homework an' eat properly. Oh yeah, an' Francesca will be around. They'll come to you for vacations."

Irma was livid. Anthony's witch of a grandma got to live in America while *she* had to stay in Mexico. It wasn't fair. But she knew better than to argue. Anthony had a fierce temper, and early on she'd learned that the wise way was to shy away from his uncontrollable wrath.

Anthony Bonar was not only difficult and controlling, he was a screamer of mammoth proportions. Loud, frequent outbursts were not unusual; he even screamed at his grandmother when the mood took him. The old woman screamed back, giving as good as she got. In a twisted way they both seemed to enjoy their verbal battles.

Irma didn't. She had never gotten used to their upsetting dance over the years.

Once the screaming stopped there were profuse apologies and overly affectionate *I love yous* from both of them.

Irma thought the interaction between the two of them was sick, but she never interfered for fear of repercussions. Irma had learned over the years that it was best to keep quiet.

~ ~ ~

Sometimes Anthony Bonar thought that if it wasn't for his children he would divorce Irma and marry his outstandingly sexy mistress, Emmanuelle. She was so hot that sometimes he couldn't believe she was his. Twenty years old with a body any red-blooded male would kill for, she was one of the most sought-after models in Miami. Not one of those snooty bitches who strutted the runways, no, Emmanuelle was featured on the covers of *Stuff* and *Maxim*—a popular cover girl with her sexy blond curls and the best fake tits this side of Rio, the city where she was born.

Anthony had met her in a club six months earlier. She'd been snorting coke with a hard-living male movie star who swung both ways. Anthony had taken one look at her and proceeded to move in big-time. Within weeks he'd set her up in an apartment, bought her a new Mercedes, showered her with jewelry and designer clothes.

Anthony got off on collecting beautiful, sexy women, and Emmanuelle was a prize. But as much as he reveled in his power over females, business always came first. Business, followed by his two children, then his grandmother, and trailing way behind was Irma. Truth was he didn't really like his wife; she was boring and a nag—always on his case about moving back to America. Most women would be thrilled to live in a twenty-five-thousand-square-foot home with servants and bodyguards. But not Irma, oh no, not *his* wife. Irma wanted to be near him so she could bug the shit out of him with her constant demands for sex.

Why did she still expect him to fuck her? He'd given her two children. Wasn't that enough? She was a *mother,* for chrissakes; he didn't fuck mothers.

Besides, he had other things on his mind, and making Grandma happy was a number-one priority.

When he'd told Francesca his plans for finally taking action against the Santangelos, her long, thin face had lit up. "At last you have the balls of your grandfather," she'd exclaimed. "You make me a very happy woman, Anthony."

"Whatever I'm doin', it's for you," he'd said. "'Cause you care so much."

"No!" she'd said sharply. "Not for me. For the Bonnatti *name.* For the Bonnatti *honor.* Your stupid half-brother couldn't do it. Nor could Donatella. Now it is *your* duty to ruin the Santangelo family once and for all."

"Hey, it's gonna happen," he'd promised.

"It better," she'd answered sharply. "You hear me, Anthony? It better."

"What? Ya don't believe me?"

"It's taken you long enough."

"Jesus Christ! I do everythin' for you, an' still you doubt me."

And so the screaming had started. Always the screaming.

Anthony was used to it. In a strange way it was his only true comfort zone.

~ ~ ~

Sitting outside under a leafy tree in the garden of their house, Irma watched the two gardeners at work. One was an older man, his lined face grizzled from the sun. The other was a much younger man, with a muscled body and brooding features. Irma stared at him, observing his dark, bushy eyebrows, thick lips, and muscular arms. He reminded her of her first boyfriend way back in Omaha when she was a mere fourteen. Andy Francis, a very possessive boy who'd slugged other boys simply for looking at her. *Well,* she thought with a slight smile, *I was the prettiest girl in school.*

Memories of Andy brought back feelings of her first sexual stirrings. Andy's hard little kisses, his fifteen-year-old tongue stuck firmly in her mouth thrusting and twisting. Andy's eager hands exploring under her sweater, unfastening her bra and clumsily fondling her breasts. Andy's frustration when she refused to allow him to go any further.

Irma found that she couldn't stop staring at the younger of the two gardeners. He was new, she'd only seen him a couple of times before.

Suddenly he glanced up and met her gaze. His eyes were full of suspicion, but he didn't look away, and neither did she.

It was a moment that set her thinking. Was this destined to be the man she had an affair with? This lowly Mexican gardener who probably stank of sweat and wine and would handle her roughly, because in his eyes he surely must see her as a beautiful blond *lonely* American princess.

She experienced a shiver of excitement, followed by a moist feeling between her legs.

Oh God, it had been so long since Anthony had touched her. Right now she was suffused with desire.

She couldn't take her eyes off the man, his rippling muscles, his stoic face. Yes, she had to have him. And why shouldn't she? Anthony thought he was so clever with his secretive ways, but she knew about his mistresses—the Italian whore he kept in a penthouse in New York, and the so-called model in Miami. Besides, he'd taken her children from her, and that wasn't right.

She also knew plenty about his business dealings. The drug shipments, the many meetings, his associates in Colombia and Bolivia whom she'd met.

Damn Anthony. He was forcing her to go elsewhere for the sexual satisfaction she craved.

The old gardener turned and began a slow trudge toward the greenhouse. The young gardener stayed where he was.

Irma couldn't stop watching him. After a few moments she acted on impulse and beckoned him over. He headed in her direction, a wary expression on his face.

What am I doing? she thought. *This is crazy.* But her heart was beating so fast she couldn't stop herself.

When the gardener arrived in front of her, she lost all sense of reason and found herself incapable of looking him in the eye.

"*Señora?*" he questioned. His smell wafted in the air, healthy sweat mixed with garlic.

"Uh . . . you're new here, aren't you?" she managed, fanning herself with a magazine. "What's your name?"

"*Perdone, señora,*" he mumbled, rubbing his thigh with a large work-worn hand. "*No hablar Engleesh.*"

"You don't?" she said, startled. Then she thought, *Why would he? He's only a gardener, probably dropped out of school early.*

She studied his lips. They fascinated her, they were so thick and tempting. Then there was the faint stubble on his chin, so manly. And his forearms, strong and muscled.

"Name," she repeated, fanning herself more vigorously. "*Nombre?*"

"Luis," he muttered in a low voice.

"*Gracias*, Luis," she said, dismissing him with a flick of her hand.

He turned and walked away, giving her ample time to study his tight ass in faded jeans.

Abruptly she stood up and headed for the house. If she couldn't have Luis, perhaps she would settle for the handheld neck massager she'd recently purchased. The small piece of machinery certainly wasn't Luis, but the results were always a ten.

~ ~ ~

Emmanuelle was a girl who liked to party, but Anthony Bonar soon convinced her that the best parties consisted of two people only—although an occasional other girl introduced into the mix did not seem to bother him. Early on in their relationship he'd threatened to fucking kill her if she ever cheated on him. Those were his exact words, and she was almost convinced that he meant it. Almost, not quite, for Emmanuelle was young and got off on enjoying herself. After all, Anthony was not always around. Early on she'd discovered that he had a wife *and* another mistress in New York, so she'd decided that if *he* was getting it elsewhere, why shouldn't she?

So far she'd only cheated on him once with a fellow model. Nobody found out. They'd done it in a dressing room halfway through a photo session. Hot, fast sex standing up.

Anthony *never* did it standing up. He wanted her flat on her back with her ankles around his neck while he pumped away like a machine. In, out. In, out. No technique whatsoever.

She'd soon realized that her new boyfriend was not the greatest lover in the world—although he obviously thought he was. Most men did.

Emmanuelle refused to disillusion him, for she'd met generous men before, but Anthony was in a class by himself and she was partial to luxury goods, especially when they came with a major price tag. This meant that although Anthony Bonar wasn't her usual type, she played him all the way.

In spite of the blond curls and fake tits, Emmanuelle had a head for business, and she knew she had Anthony hot enough to buy her almost anything she wanted. The downside was that he put nothing in her name—not the Mercedes, not the lease on the apartment he'd set her up in, not even the jewelry he'd gifted her with. If she ever left him, it all had to come back to him, he informed her. Or else.

Anthony was big with threats. Emmanuelle didn't like that, but even so she'd decided to stick it out for the time being until she could figure a way to persuade him to start putting things in her name. After all, if he broke up with her, it wasn't fair that she would walk away with nothing. And since he was enjoying the many and varied pleasures of her fabulous body, not to mention her extraordinary oral expertise, he *should* pay, there was no doubt about it.

Emmanuelle knew she was right.

8

"Baby!" Venus murmured, wrapping her well-toned arms around Billy Melina's neck and kissing him on the lips. "I missed you so much. How'd it go today?"

"Alex Woods is a workaholic freakin' *asshole,*" Billy complained, shrugging off his Chrome Hearts leather jacket and flinging it on Venus's oversized bed.

"Everyone knows that," she agreed, kneeling on top of the bed looking sexy in a barely-there black lace teddy. "However, at least he's a *talented* asshole, which so many of them aren't."

Billy was inclined to disagree. It was almost midnight and he was wiped out. He'd had a bitch of a day what with the sex session out by his pool with the girl from Tower Records, then working endless hours on the street faking tough-as-shit choreographed fight scenes. Alex Woods was king of the "Let's go for another take" school of directors, and it drove Billy nuts. How many times was he supposed to get punched in the head and thrown over the hood of a car? Oh sure, he had a stand-in, but Alex insisted that *he* be front and center for most of the action, and when he objected—even a little bit—Alex berated him in front of the entire crew. "Our *actor* doesn't want to get down 'n' dirty," Alex jeered. "Let's get a chair for our fucking actor so he can put his fucking feet up. Wouldn't want to *overwork* him."

At which point Billy had agreed to shoot the scene himself. No stand-in required.

Man, he felt totally shattered. When they'd wrapped for the night, all he'd really wanted to do was go home and soak in his hot tub. Instead he'd been obliged to rush over to Venus's palatial mansion in Beverly Hills, because she'd called him on his cell four times insisting he come by when he was finished, and he didn't want to disappoint her.

"It'll be late," he'd warned.

"I'll be waiting," she'd answered. "Keeping the bed warm for you, baby."

If anyone had told him eight years ago that Venus Maria, one of the most famous women in the world, would be keeping the bed warm for him, he would've laughed like a freakin' loon.

Venus Maria. Platinum-blond superstar. A woman so famous she was now known by only one name: Venus. Everyone knew who she was. They bought her CDs, flocked to her movies, wore the hottest jeans in town with her name emblazoned on the label, sprayed themselves with her latest signature scent, and worshipped at her live stadium performances.

Venus was a freakin' icon. And *he* was her boyfriend. Her much *younger* boyfriend—well, not *that* much younger, thirteen years. And that meant nothing. It wasn't as if he was some snot-nosed boy toy—he was a very successful movie star in his own right. He had a house, plenty of money, and a sizzling career. He didn't *need* Venus's fame to tag on to; he had his own.

Besides, if the situation were reversed and she was thirteen years younger than him, nobody would give a rat's ass. Hollywood was awash with old geezers whose wives and girlfriends were decades younger than them, and nobody said a word. Unfortunately, he and Venus got the treatment. Front page of the tabloids always carrying on about their age difference. Was she going to marry him? Was she pregnant? Were they breaking up? Was she too rich for him? Was he famous enough for her?

At first he'd got off on all the attention, then after a while it started to get to him. He was a star, too; he didn't appreciate all the trash talk he had to endure.

Venus loved him, he knew that. The big question was: Did *he* love *her?* Or did he love everything she represented? The extreme fame and superglamor. The adulation and nonstop fan worship. Sometimes he simply wasn't sure whether it was love or infatuation.

And if he *really* loved her, would he cheat on her the way he had that afternoon?

For a moment he flashed onto the young girl who'd followed him up to his house in her rundown truck with the broken taillight. She'd followed him willingly, and he'd given her exactly what she expected.

Screwing her was a trip. Her lips, so soft and sweet, not to mention the sticky tightness between her legs.

And yet . . . he couldn't help feeling guilty.

Sort of . . . because if he caught Venus screwing another man, he'd go ape shit. Venus was his girlfriend—*his* freakin' girlfriend—and if she played around on him, it would mess with his head big-time.

Not that he was possessive—at least he didn't *think* he was. Venus was the possessive one. She could be bossy, a bit of a control freak, but she could also be supportive and loving, the way she was tonight. Although . . . from the look in her eyes, he knew she expected sex, and man, tonight was not the night. After Alex's brutal workout his body was bruised, wrecked, and beaten.

"Come to bed, baby," she purred. "I'll give you a back rub, you know how you like that."

Yeah, sex was *definitely* on her agenda, and what was he supposed to do about *that?*

Nothing, because a sane man didn't turn down a superstar, not if he wanted to continue being her boyfriend.

"A back rub sounds kinda hot," he mumbled.

"Of *course* it does," she murmured, husky-voiced and ready for action. "'Cause *I'll* rub you, then *you'll* rub me. . . ."

"That's a plan," he said, pulling off his T-shirt. "Only first I gotta shower."

"Why?" she asked, reaching up and stroking the back of his neck. "Funky works for me."

"How about *skunky* funky?" he said, extracting himself from her touch. "Look at me—I'm in sweat overdrive, babe, an' I gotta hunch you won't go for that."

"Okay, take a shower," she sighed. "But hurry up, you *know* how impatient I get."

She wasn't kidding about *that.* Miss *I want it now!* Venus never let up when she had her mind set on something.

"You got it, ma'am," he said, reverting to his former self, the dumb-ass kid who'd hit Hollywood eight years ago thinking all women deserved respect.

How green was *he?*

Green and fortunate, because after several months of bumming around trying to make something happen, working as a waiter and sleeping on a friend's floor, he'd found himself an agent who'd sent him on an interview for an NBC sitcom. He'd scored the part, been in six on-air episodes, and just when he'd imagined himself as the second coming of Matthew Perry, the show was canceled and he was back where he'd started—waiting tables at the Cheesecake Factory in Brentwood.

Two months later he got a call from his agent informing him that Alex Woods wanted to see him. Alex Woods—mega producer/director/writer supreme! Holy shit!

The day of his interview with Alex was forever etched in his mind. He'd walked into an imposing office nervous as a virgin on a date with a porn star. And there she was, standing around as if she had nothing better to do. Venus. *The* freaking Venus. She of the platinum-blond hair, sexy stance, and out-of-this-world bod.

"Hi, Billy," she'd said, as if she actually *knew* him. "Thanks for coming in today. I'm a big fan of your work."

Thanks for coming in! Big fan of his work! Was she freakin' *kidding!* He would've done anything for a meeting with Venus—she was the jerk-off queen of all his fantasies.

Alex Woods was slouched behind a large untidy desk, speaking on the phone. He'd glanced up and waved distractedly in Billy's direction.

"Sit down, Billy," Venus had said, indicating a sprawling couch.

Billy sat. Venus sat.

He'd thought he was freakin' dreaming it was all so surreal.

Later he'd read a scene with her in front of Alex and Lucky Santangelo, another producer on the movie.

He was good; in fact, he was *better* than good—in his mind he'd nailed the part and then some. And why not, with Venus as his inspiration standing opposite him in dangerously low-cut yoga pants and a belly-baring top. Not only was she this freakin' worldwide superstar, she was also surprisingly friendly and nice. She actually treated him like an equal. She actually *talked* to him before he had to read. Who'd've thought?

Two weeks later his agent called with the words every actor yearns to hear. "Congratulations, Billy. You got the part."

He remembered stammering, "I got the *what?*" And then he'd hit the clubs with a few of his buddies—including his closest friend from back home, Kev, whose floor he'd been sleeping on for the past few months. He'd gotten bombed out of his mind and ended up with a forty-year-old Puerto Rican stripper who'd called him Blondie Pie, and given him a mild dose of the clap.

A week later he was on the set of Alex Woods's new movie, *Seduction*, acting opposite Venus. It was the start of his ride. And what a ride it had turned out to be.

Shower over, Billy returned to the bedroom bare-assed naked. Venus gave him an appreciative once-over and beckoned him to join her on the bed.

Fortunately, the Donkey King—the name a former girlfriend had bestowed on his penis—was up and at 'em, at the ready to do whatever his master bade.

"Come here, you crazy sex maniac," Venus crooned.

Yeah, like *she* could talk.

He headed for the bed, and the soft, sexy, comforting warmth of his girlfriend. The same girlfriend he'd cheated on earlier that day.

Shit! Better make it up to her, he thought, quickly forgetting about his bruised and battered body. *Better be ready to rock and roll all night long.*

~ ~ ~

And while Billy was making out with one of the most famous women in the world, Alex Woods was drinking Jack Daniel's on the rocks at a bikers hangout somewhere in the mountains off the Pacific Coast Highway. He didn't feel like going home to his architecturally perfect house situated on a prime piece of Broad Beach property.

He didn't feel like staring out at the black ocean or switching on his movie-size TV screen.

He didn't feel like making conversation, or anything else for that matter, with Ling, his Asian girlfriend—a twenty-nine-year-old lawyer with a serene attitude and amazing sexual skills.

What *did* he feel like doing?

He felt like being by himself, getting drunk, and thinking about Lucky Santangelo.

Lucky was always on his mind. Always . . .

So that's exactly what he did.

Tomorrow was another day; he could forget about her then and resume life as he knew it.

Only that never happened. Lucky was his secret obsession, and as long as Lennie was around, he knew it had to stay that way.

9

If it wasn't for Lucky Santangelo, Henry Whitfield-Simmons might have been a big star. Or at least that's what *he* believed. He knew he was far superior to Billy Melina, the actor who had stolen his role in the Alex Woods film that Henry had been so sure he was about to get.

Henry considered Billy Melina to be an inferior human being, with no acting ability whatsoever. He'd seen his movies. He'd sneered at his movies. It was a travesty that Billy Melina had been hired in his place, and gone on to become a famous star.

Even though his failed audition had taken place many years previously, Henry brooded about it on a daily basis. He knew for a fact that if it wasn't for Lucky Santangelo, *he,* Henry Whitfield-Simmons, would have been the one up there on the screen with Venus Maria in *Seduction.* Even now, although the day of his audition was eight long years ago, Henry had never forgotten nor forgiven. Lucky Santangelo, a producer on the film, was the one to blame; *she* was the one who hadn't wanted him. He was positive of this because while auditioning, he'd observed Lucky sitting across the table with the casting people, staring at him with her black unfriendly eyes while tapping her fingertips impatiently on the table. Alex Woods wasn't present that day, nor was Venus Maria.

Henry was about to read a second scene when he'd noticed Lucky signal to the casting people that she'd seen enough. How unspeakably rude!

Henry was justifiably angry, for not only was she rude, Lucky Santangelo had ruined his future. She'd taken his one chance and thrown it away with her careless actions.

Shortly after his failed audition, Henry had been summoned to go on a fishing trip with his father. It was just the two of them on a small fishing boat out on the lake, because Logan Whitfield-Simmons truly believed that getting back to the simple things in life was the best way to bond with his uncooperative and unambitious son, whom he didn't understand at all. Logan never understood anybody who was unproductive and had no work ethic. He was determined to instill some sense into his only son.

"When are you going to join the family business?" he'd asked, bristling for the right answer.

It was a leading question that initially Henry ignored, until eventually it led all the way to a vicious argument.

"You know perfectly well I want to be an actor," Henry had yelled, filled with frustration. "It's my ambition, and *you* can't stop me."

"Can't I?" Logan had answered, his long face grim.

"No!" Henry had shouted. "Not you, not Mother, *nobody*."

"You'll be an actor over my dead body," Logan had shouted back.

Soon the yelling had escalated into a serious screaming match. Logan was very angry with his useless son, who refused to listen to reason, and Henry had no intention of giving up his dream.

They screamed insults back and forth, until the older man suddenly fell silent. His face paled and he clutched his left arm. "Jes . . . us," he'd managed, before collapsing onto the bottom of the boat. "Get . . . me . . . my . . . pills."

Henry did nothing. He merely sat and watched as his father writhed in agony for at least five minutes before dying of a massive heart attack. Only then had Henry taken the boat back to the landing dock. He wasn't sorry, not at all. It was his father's own fault—he'd caused the fatal heart attack himself by shouting at him.

Logan Whitfield-Simmons's funeral was a heavily attended and somber affair. The Whitfield-Simmonses were a well-known and respected family in Pasadena. In fact, they were a well-known family across America. Logan Whitfield-Simmons was always at the top of *Forbes* magazine's richest people in America list, while Penelope Whitfield-Simmons was lauded on the society pages for her extensive charity work, elegant clothes, and Fortune 400 friends. Great things were expected of Henry, their only son and heir. He fully intended to disappoint.

After his father's funeral Henry felt a certain freedom. Without asking anyone's permission, he borrowed his mother's credit card, went out and purchased an extremely expensive sports car. Two days later he smashed the car up in a head-on collision. Unfortunately for Henry, he emerged from the accident with a broken pelvis and hip, and since his hip never set properly, he was stuck with a permanent limp, putting paid to his dreams of becoming a famous actor.

After his accident Henry rarely left the house. Mostly he stayed in his room watching movies or hunched over his computer.

Penelope was not concerned that her son stayed at home and did nothing; having him around was company for her. "My son, the computer nerd," she would sigh to her friends. "Henry knows more about computers than anyone. He's threatened to teach me one day, although who has the time to understand all that newfangled technology?"

Henry lived a whole other life on the Internet. There were girls to visit, places to go he'd never gone before, naked girls he didn't have to talk to, because Henry had never been good with the opposite sex. Henry Whitfield-Simmons was still a virgin. As far back as he could remember, his mother had always warned him that girls would chase after him because of the family's wealth and position, and that he should always resist their advances. He'd taken note of her wise words, and never had a girlfriend.

One day while surfing the Internet, he'd come upon a site that featured young teenage girls. Somehow he'd managed to enter their private domain, a Web site where they exchanged personal messages and wrote vividly about their thoughts and dreams. Most of their thoughts and dreams concerned boys, which Henry found boring. But he liked looking at the photos the girls posted of themselves. They were pouty and pretty; young, innocent girls playing dress-up with long, flowing hair draped seductively over one eye and come-on expressions.

Henry was soon addicted. Every night he would sit at his computer checking them out. Until one night he realized there was something very familiar about one of the girls, and when he Googled her, he discovered who she was. The girl was Maria Santangelo Golden, Lucky Santangelo's daughter.

The information astounded and thrilled him.

10

Even though Lucky arose at five A.M., ready to work out with her personal trainer—so L.A. (but if she didn't have Cole to kick her butt three days a week, she'd never do it)—there were never enough hours in the day to get everything done, especially as she flew to Vegas twice a week. After a vigorous workout she usually made her East Coast phone calls—business and family. Her son Bobby had recently opened a restaurant/club in New York, and Brigette was busy designing her own jewelry line. Neither of them needed to work, as they were both descendants of Greek billionaire Dimitri Stanislopolous, Lucky's second husband, and had both inherited huge fortunes, although Bobby would not inherit the bulk of his until he hit twenty-five.

Lucky was happy about that. Bobby was smart and extremely good-looking—the burden of such a fortune was bound to influence him. She fervently hoped that in two years' time he'd be able to handle the pitfalls that came with being ultrarich.

Bobby had dropped out of college after a couple of years because he was bored and wanted to get out into the world and do something. Lucky had encouraged him; as far as she was concerned, it was more important to get a street education. Not that opening a club was exactly street, but it *was* an education.

Every few weeks Lucky took a plane into New York to check things out. Brigette was doing well. She'd given up her once-hot modeling career, and after a series of disastrous affairs and a bad marriage, at thirty-two she finally seemed to have gotten it together.

Brigette was the child of Olympia, Dimitri's daughter who'd died from a drug overdose locked in a hotel room with famous British rock star Flash.

As one of the richest heiresses in the world, she'd always lived her life in the spotlight. Constantly dogged by paparazzi, written about in all the gossip columns, and envied by most mere mortals, not only was Brigette unbelievably rich, she was also a natural blonde with a willowy figure and an extremely pretty face. Brigette was every fortune hunter's dream. Problem was she always managed to attract the wrong men. If there was a bad-boy loser around, send him in Brigette's direction—she seemed to collect them. The last disaster was Carlo Vittorio Vitti, an Italian count who'd managed to turn Brigette onto drugs, married her, then attempted to murder her so he could inherit her enormous fortune.

Ever since that fateful marriage, there'd been a lull, and for the last few years Brigette seemed at peace. All the same, Lucky kept a close eye on her.

Bobby, on the other hand, was Mr. Cool. He had a Kennedy-esque air about him—great looks and charmingly self-deprecating. Girls fell at his feet and he took his pick, working his way through the pack.

"You're my hero," Gino Senior told him every time they got together. "Screw the Stanislopolous bloodline—you're a Santangelo all the way, an' doncha forget it."

Gino, who resided in Palm Springs with his decades-younger wife, Paige, was crazy about all his grandchildren, especially Bobby, who reminded him of his own womanizing youth.

Lucky felt fortunate to have such a great family, but having a family didn't mean sitting around doing nothing. Money had never been a problem for Lucky—her name said it all, plus she was a savvy businesswoman with all the right instincts. She was totally psyched about getting back into the hotel business. The last hotel she'd built was the Santangelo in

Atlantic City—a fine hotel—but Atlantic City wasn't Vegas, so after a few years she'd sold it, garnering almost three times her investment. Now, in Las Vegas, she had created the Keys complex—a hotel casino with luxury apartments. It was her dream hotel, and she couldn't wait for opening night, which was in a few weeks' time.

In the meantime she had Gino's ninety-fifth birthday party to plan. She wanted it to be ultraspecial, so she'd hired a party planner to take care of all the details. Gino would love being the center of his own party; he lived for action. At almost ninety-five he was as active as ever, full of energy and a zest for living.

Gino the Ram was his nickname when he was a teenager running riot on the streets of Brooklyn.

As a kid, Lucky couldn't wait to hear all about Gino in his wild days—clawing his way up from nothing, making his fortune, scoring with dozens of beautiful women, until one day he'd met Maria, and she'd turned out to be the love of his life.

Maria. Lucky's mother. Brutally butchered and left for five-year-old Lucky to discover floating on a raft in the family swimming pool, the blood draining from her lifeless body.

Her mother's death had forced Lucky to be strong and independent. It had taught her how to be alone and to never be scared again.

The violent and unforgettable tragedy had taken away her childhood and all the good memories, but screw it—even after Dario was murdered and then Marco, she'd never allowed herself to get beaten down. Never.

No. Lucky's power was in her strength, and nobody could take that away from her.

Nobody dared.

~ ~ ~

Early Thursday evening Max bounced into the den where Lucky was busy working on the security list for Gino's party, and Lennie was jotting down random notes on the script of his upcoming movie.

"Hey, Mom," Max said, employing her best conciliatory tone of voice. "I just came up with a totally cool idea."

"Really?" Lucky said, hardly looking up.

"Yes," Max replied. "Y'see, I have the perfect solution."

"You do, huh?" Lucky said skeptically.

Max nodded, full of confidence. "I'll drive to Big Bear *tomorrow,* then come back Sunday morning like *way* in time for Grandpa's party. How's that?"

Lennie glanced up from his script. "You're going to Big Bear?" he said. "I used to love to ski."

"And your lovely daughter doesn't," Lucky said crisply. "Besides, Max, there's no way you can miss dinner tomorrow night. Gino's driving in from Palm Springs, and Bobby and Brigette are coming from New York. It's a big family reunion dinner, and I'm cooking."

Max groaned inwardly. Friday nights Lucky made a point of everyone sitting down for the whole family dinner thing. Why did *she* have to be there? Surely she had enough of Gino Junior and his lech friends all week?

"But Mom—" she began, working it hard.

Lucky shot her daughter a look. Friday nights were important, especially *this* Friday with everyone arriving. She'd planned on taking over the kitchen herself and making the one dish she excelled at: pasta and meatballs with her special sauce. It was Lennie's favorite meal, and preparing it was her favorite therapy. Besides, she'd always encouraged her kids to bring their friends, so why was Max so intent on giving her a hard time?

"You should be here," she said, throwing her daughter another long, steady look. "Everyone wants to see you."

Max frowned. This Friday-night family deal was totally lame, she was so not into it, even though her friends couldn't wait to come over for Friday dinner. "Damn, girl!" Cookie was always informing her. "You actually, like, *have* a family. All I've got is my dad, an' all *he* has is a different big-boobed skank like every other *second.* An' *he* gets to fuck 'em. *I* have to talk to them, so Friday night at your house rocks!"

It infuriated Max that both Cookie and Harry considered Lucky and Lennie the coolest parents ever.

"*You* don't have to live with them," she would often point out. "They're not that easy. My mom can be a total pain. When I got that tattoo on my thigh she went total ape shit."

"I'd swap 'em for mine any day," Harry would always reply. "At least they notice you're alive."

Max had to admit that on the very few occasions she'd seen them, Harry's parents were quite scary. And as for Cookie's dad, Gerald M., he was a major sex addict.

"Everyone will see me on Sunday at the big party," Max said, flashing Lennie a pleading look. "Dad . . ."

"What's the deal?" Lennie asked, finally putting down his script.

"One of Cookie's friends is having a blowout birthday thing Saturday night," Max said, words tripping over each other. "And Mom says I can't go. But if I'm back in time for Grandpa's party . . ." She trailed off, continuing to gaze pleadingly at Lennie, all intense green eyes and innocent expression.

Lennie got the message. "Hey, Lucky," he said. "Whyn't you let her go? What's the big problem?"

"No problem," Lucky responded, suddenly feeling like the uptight mother figure, a feeling she did not appreciate. "I guess as long as she's back for Gino's party it's okay."

"I, like, *so* will be," Max dutifully promised, vainly attempting to subdue her triumphant expression.

"We'll need the number where you're at," Lucky said, sensing that somehow or other she'd just lost out. It pissed her off when Lennie overruled her without even a discussion about what they should do. Parenting was supposed to be a joint venture—something Lennie didn't seem to get.

Lennie winked at his willful but quite beguiling daughter. "Happy now?" he asked.

"Thanks, Dad," she said, giving him a quick hug, then hurriedly fleeing before Lucky changed her mind.

On the way to her room Max made a mental note that the next time she wanted anything she should ask while Lennie was around; he was way easier to deal with than her mom.

Upstairs she called Cookie. "It's on!" she announced. "I'm driving up there tomorrow."

"Tomorrow?" Cookie said. "Doesn't that screw up Friday dinner at your house?"

"Dinner's a no-go," Max explained. "I told them this thing in Big Bear is for one of your friends, so natch you'll be coming with me."

"But I won't," Cookie stated blankly.

"*I* know that, and *you* know that, but *they* don't. So you've got to lay low, an' tell Harry the same."

"*Crap!*"

"What?"

"Missing dinner at your house like major sucks!"

"Oh, I'm so sorry that *my* hot date messes up *your* weekend," Max drawled sarcastically.

"Okay, I like *get* it," Cookie answered crossly. "No need to freak out."

"Who's freaking out?"

"You are."

"I am *so* not."

But inside she was, just a tiny bit.

Shutting her cell, she hurried over to her laptop and quickly logged in. "*I'll be in Big Bear Friday afternoon,*" she tapped out. "*Where shall we meet?*"

Within minutes Grant had e-mailed her back. "*Meet me in the Kmart parking lot. Stay in your car. I'll find you.*"

I'll find you! How romantic was *that.*

She rushed to her closet, desperately trying to decide what to wear. Skinny jeans or short skirt? T-shirt or sexy tank? Bra or no bra? Strappy heels or flats?

She finally decided on tight jeans and a layered T-shirt—best to go the casual route, she didn't want to look as if she'd tried too hard.

How tall was he? She'd forgotten to ask.

It didn't matter. This weekend she was doing the deed with her Internet hottie.

Oh yeah! She was doing the deed and there would be no regrets.

Sorry, Donny. You blew it.

~ ~ ~

"Remember the first time we met?" Lucky murmured later that night as she and Lennie lay in bed.

"You think I could forget?" Lennie responded. "It was Vegas, an' if I recall correctly, *you* tried to rape me."

"You thought I was a hooker," she said indignantly.

"Yeah," he agreed, laughing. "And a *very* expensive one."

"Screw you," she said, pretending to be mad. "I wanted to sleep with you and *you* turned me down."

He raised an eyebrow. "I did?"

"You *know* you did."

"Yeah, well, didn't we make a date for later and *you* failed to show?"

"As if I *would* after the way you treated me."

"*Then* you had me fired," he said, mock-frowning at the memories. "Nice. Very nice. I was out on my ass with nowhere to go but down."

Lucky smiled as she remembered. Lennie had been working stand-up in the lounge of the Magiriano, her hotel. She'd felt restless and lonely and he was there and available, so she'd invited him up to her suite, and when she'd indicated that she expected a lot more than conversation, he'd walked out on her.

"The thing is I'd heard you were such a major *playa*," she teased. "So how come you rejected *me*?"

"'Cause you came on like a guy," he said, reaching over her for a bottle of Fiji water.

"Something wrong with that?" she said, challenging him with her dark eyes.

"Whyn't you shut up an' c'mere," he said, putting the bottle down.

"Okay, mister," she said, playing along. "Take off your pants and show *me* some action."

"Thought I just did."

"Oh, *my* bad," she said, laughing softly.

"How quickly they forget," he sighed.

"Forget *you? Never,*" she said teasingly.

"Anyone ever tell you you've got a smart mouth?" he said, throwing her a quizzical look.

And before she could answer he was pressing his lips down on hers and they were starting all over again.

A long and sexy marriage suited both of them.

11

"You're the best," Emmanuelle crooned. "I've never met a man like you before. Oh my *God*, Anthony, you make me so *weak*."

She actually wanted to say *weep*, because sexually Anthony was totally inept. He was under the impression that climbing on top of her and going at it like a randy dog was enough. No foreplay, no words of desire, nothing, *nada*—just an angry hard-on and a fit of manic energy as he pumped away, heading toward his own satisfaction like an express train, not at all concerned about *her* orgasm.

"Yeah, pie-face, you sure are one lucky little girl," Anthony agreed, still vigorously thrusting back and forth.

Even though Anthony was only thirty-nine, Emmanuelle had a sneaking suspicion he took Viagra to make sure he stayed hard. One time she'd discovered a couple of the telltale blue pills in his jacket pocket, and when she'd asked about them, he'd gotten furious and informed her they were for headaches. Some headaches!

Rapidly getting bored with Anthony's lack of skill, Emmanuelle decided to fake it early, hoping it might make him come. She began her own personal ritual, a series of long, drawn-out sighs, followed by cries of "Oh, *Anthony*. Oh yes, yes, *yeeees!* You make me so *wet* and creamy. Oh, *yeeees*, baby, you're the man, the big, big *man*."

She was done, finished.

Not really, but let him think she was.

Contracting her vagina, she squeezed his cock tight.

It did the trick. He hurriedly pulled out and spurted all over her stomach.

Anthony refused to wear a condom; he also refused to come inside her. Emmanuelle knew it was because he didn't want to take the risk of getting her pregnant.

Ha! Like she would want *his* baby. All she wanted from Anthony Bonar was material goods—in *her* name. And the sooner, the better.

~ ~ ~

Two minutes later Anthony was standing in the shower scrubbing off Emmanuelle's scent. Once the sex was over he had nothing to say to her. Fact is, he had nothing to say to women period. The only woman he'd ever come across worth a dime was his formidable grandmother. Now, there was a woman who gave as good as she got. He admired her, yet at the same time he was more than a little scared of her. Ridiculous really, because Anthony was never scared of anyone or anything, but sometimes Francesca made him feel exactly like the twelve-year-old boy she'd plucked off the streets of Naples and given a life. Some life it was too. He was rich, and in *his* world extremely powerful. He could have more or less anything he wanted, and he did. Yes, he'd come a long way from his impoverished childhood with an Italian mother who'd worked as a maid, and an American father who'd never bothered to acknowledge him.

Now, if he was to satisfy his grandmother, he had to bring the Santangelo family down. And Lucky building the Keys in Vegas had given him the perfect opportunity.

~ ~ ~

Two days passed before Irma spotted the young gardener again. This time she was determined to take it a step further since a so-called friend had sent her a newspaper clipping of her husband exiting a nightclub in Miami with the piece of white trash he kept stashed in an apartment there.

Anthony had some gall to flaunt his "girlfriends" or "cheap hookers," as Irma thought of them. It infuriated her. Didn't he *give* a damn?

Apparently not.

Well, if *he* didn't care, why should *she?* She'd sleep with the gardener and to hell with her controlling husband. Let him see how *he* liked it when *she* did it back to *him*. Not that he'd ever find out, but *she* would know, and that was enough to satisfy her.

It was late afternoon and the older gardener was nowhere in sight. However, Luis was there, on his knees, tending to the rosebushes.

After a few moments of indecision, Irma approached him. "*Hola,* Luis," she said, fanning herself with a magazine.

Unfortunately, her Spanish language skills were quite limited, although she was well aware that *hola* was a familiar greeting used by friends, and Luis was *not* her friend, he was her employee, or rather Anthony's employee—which would make sleeping with the man a sweet punishment for her cheating husband.

Luis glanced up, startled. "*Señora,*" he managed, wiping a slick of sweat from his brow.

She studied his face for a moment, his thick lips and brooding features. He was rough and masculine-looking, so unlike Anthony, who was very much into grooming with the most expensive face creams and hair products, his bathroom shelves crammed full of bottles and potions. Anthony, who plastered his face with fake tan, had his eyebrows plucked professionally, and indulged in a weekly facial.

"Can you please cut some roses for me," she said. And when Luis looked up at her blankly, she pantomimed what she wanted, bending to touch a rose, allowing him to get a perfect view of her breasts as the summer shift she had on fell slightly open.

"Ah . . ." Luis said, his eyes lingering, "*Si, señora.*"

Irma experienced a flutter of excitement. Where would they do it when the moment came? Her bedroom? The very same bedroom she shared with Anthony when he honored her with his presence?

Why not?

Or perhaps they would stay outside while there was no one around to spy on them. The guards were on duty at the front of the house, and the old gardener was obviously not there.

Her heart began pounding. Merely thinking about making love with this man had her juices flowing.

So intent was Luis on surreptitiously checking out her breasts that he accidentally cut himself on a prickly thorn.

Irma watched intently as a thin line of blood trickled across his wrist.

"Oh, dear," she exclaimed, tentatively touching his forearm. "You're bleeding."

"*Non importante,*" he muttered, quickly standing up.

"Yes," Irma insisted. "It looks bad, Luis. You should come with me." Taking him by the arm, she began leading him toward the house.

Luis's eyes darted around to see if there was anyone watching. He needed this job, and the American woman obviously needed more than her roses clipped.

Irma was past caring. If Anthony was informed of her indiscretions, she didn't give a damn. Her dear husband hadn't touched her in over a year. Luis was about to be her revenge.

~ ~ ~

The Grill was Anthony's number-one bodyguard. Nobody knew where he had picked up the name, and nobody asked. As a professional bodyguard The Grill didn't need much—his fists were enough to defend himself and his boss, his fists and a complete knowledge of all martial arts. The Grill was from Slovakia. At six feet four, with muscles of steel and a plain, foreboding face with a dangerous scar carving its way across one cheek, he cut a sinister figure. Anthony liked having him around simply for the fear factor—nobody cared to mess with The Grill.

Finished with Emmanuelle for the night, Anthony headed for the airport and his plane.

"We're goin' to Vegas," he informed The Grill.

The Slovakian man barely nodded. Wherever Anthony Bonar went, he followed. He had no life of his own. Anthony Bonar was his destiny.

Checking out his flashy gold Rolex, one of his many watches, Anthony decided to call his Italian girlfriend, Carlita, a raven-haired beauty of twenty-eight. Carlita, a former model, designed overpriced handbags and belts, a business he'd financed. Anthony appreciated a woman with ambition, and Carlita certainly possessed plenty of it. He'd met her at a party two years previously, and stuck with her ever since. She was smarter than Emmanuelle, she knew what was going on in the world.

Carlita's voice mail picked up. He tried her cell and the same thing happened. Goddamn voice mail. Annoyed that he couldn't reach her, Anthony made several business calls before retiring to his private bedroom for the six-hour flight to Vegas. May as well catch some shut-eye. Making love to Emmanuelle was quite exhausting—she was young and energetic, and she expected a peak performance every time.

Naturally he delivered. In bed he was a raging bull. Oh yes, Anthony Bonar had never had any complaints.

That's the way it was. And that's the way it would stay.

~ ~ ~

Sunlight filtering through the curtains woke Irma. She lay very still for a few moments reliving the events of the previous day.

Luis. One moment he was the gardener, the next—her lover. And *what* a lover. Alternatively rough and gentle, his large hands exploring her most private parts the way Anthony never had, his lips kissing her in places Anthony had never ventured.

And then . . . he'd brought her to a climax, and she'd been overcome with a feeling of ecstasy the likes of which she'd never experienced before.

Anthony had never made her come.

Anthony had never touched her down there except with his penis—a ferocious weapon intent on nothing but its own satisfaction.

Anthony had never really cared.

Irma sat up in bed, her cheeks glowing.

Luis wasn't the answer, but she knew one thing for sure: she had to divorce Anthony.

The time had come to get away from her coldhearted husband, reclaim her children, and finally take responsibility for her own happiness.

12

Every morning Venus worked out, varying her activities, but making damn sure she did either jogging, weight training, Pilates, or yoga. Lucky and she used the same trainer, Cole de Barge, a great-looking black guy with abs of steel, fine muscle definition, and the one special thing a girl needs from a trainer—a take-charge attitude. There was no slacking off around Cole.

Venus enjoyed teasing him. "If you weren't gay, I'd sweep you off to some exotic island and marry you."

Cole simply smiled. He had perfect teeth. In fact he had perfect everything.

"Do *not* try to get around me," he said, turning stern. "Today we're takin' a hike in the Canyon, so you'd better bring your favorite bottled water, an' no complaining."

"But Cole," she protested, feigning a delicate yawn. "Last night I—"

"Hey, Miss Superstar," he interrupted, "it ain't my business what you did last night. Your *body* is my business, so move your fine ass an' let's get it on."

That's what she liked about Cole—he took no prisoners. She might be dizzily famous, but if Cole wanted her up and out, she was there. No arguing with Cole, and the results were worth it. Besides, Billy had left at some ungodly hour, and since Chyna, her daughter with Cooper, was away at summer camp, she had nothing else to do. She was between movies, between recordings, and between concert tours. It was her time to relax.

"Very well," she said grumpily. "Don't worry that I had no sleep—"

"I'm not worrying."

"Billy spent the night," she explained. "He was coming off a tough day with Alex Woods. It was up to me to console him."

"So that's what they're callin' it now—consoling."

"Oh, get a life!"

"I *got* a life, superstar, an' today it involves pushing you out there. So let's hit it. Now!"

Reluctantly she followed Cole out the front door. Today she really didn't feel like indulging in any physical activity. She was genuinely tired, so why couldn't she have stayed in bed and watched mindless morning TV? Although there was nothing mindless about Matt Lauer on *The Today Show*—he was still the hottest talking head on TV.

And thinking of hot . . . last night Billy had excelled himself. She'd always thought her ex-husband—legendary movie star/cocksman Cooper Turner—was the best she'd ever had in bed, but Billy surpassed him. Such enthusiasm, such energy, such a tongue!

If only she wasn't thirteen years older than Billy. It was a major drag. This year she'd be forty-two, and while everyone knew that forty was the new twenty—what did that make Billy? *Twelve?*

He'd assured her he didn't mind, that age was just a number. Yeah, sure, but the tabloids never let either of them forget their age difference, and she knew that it bugged Billy when the late-night comedians made jokes about them. It was all so unfair. When she'd been married to Cooper Turner nobody had said a word about Cooper being twenty years older than her. Talk about a double standard. If she was European would anyone care? European actresses were revered for getting older. American actresses were not. America was a raging youth culture, but along with Madonna and Sharon Stone, she was hanging in there, she *still* looked great, and why not? She worked like a motherfucker to make sure everything stayed in place. Hence her daily ritual with Cole, whether she felt like it or not.

"I'm right behind you, slave driver," she announced, catching up with Cole as he walked briskly to his car—a new sports Jaguar. "*Very* fancy," she remarked. "Business must be outta the park."

"It's a present," he said.

"From a grateful client?"

"Let's just say he's *very* grateful, but he's not a client."

"Name please."

"You'll get his name when we're married with a weekend house in Aspen and two adopted kids."

"Revealing as usual," Venus said dryly.

"Some of us prefer to keep our private lives private," Cole replied, not eager to discuss his personal life.

"Some of us are *able* to do that," Venus responded tartly, hiding her eyes behind blackout Dolce & Gabbana shades.

"Yeah, an' *some* of us are making millions a year, which is the price they pay for *no* privacy. Sorry, *Miz* Superstar."

"He *always* has to get the last word," she sighed, jumping into the passenger seat.

"That's *right!*" Cole said, getting behind the wheel. "An' now we're off to Franklin Canyon, so get your energy goin', girl, we're takin' an hour-long hike, *no* slackin' off allowed."

Venus slumped back in her seat and groaned. Cole was a hard taskmaster, but that's the way it had to be.

~ ~ ~

"Orange juice, Meester Billy?" Ramona inquired, invading his bedroom, standing next to his bed and peering down at him, a glass of freshly squeezed juice in one hand.

"Huh?" Billy mumbled, barely opening one eye. He'd staggered home at five A.M., telling Venus he had an early call—which was a lie—then collapsing into his own bed, totally spent. Now his housekeeper was standing over him, and how many times had he told her not to wake him? Didn't she understand that he needed his sleep?

"Jeez," he muttered. "What's the time?"

"Time for you to haul your lazy ass outta the sack," announced Kev—gofer, assistant, driver. Kev was short, with wiry brown hair and a permanently cocky expression. They'd been best friends since meeting in kindergarten at the tender age of five. They'd grown up together, closer than brothers. Kev had taken off for L.A. before Billy with a plan to somehow or other break into movies. It hadn't happened for him, Billy was the one who'd gotten the golden ticket, and once Billy made it, he'd brought Kev along for the ride.

"Get fucked," Billy groaned, reaching under the sheet to scratch his balls.

"It's past twelve," Kev said, opening the blackout blinds, flooding the room with bright sunlight. "You got an interview for that fancy mag *Manhattan Style*. The journo's comin' here at one, an' Janey's on her way over now. She told me to wake your ass, an' remind you this is important shit. It's the cover story, so she says there's no way you can blow it off."

"Crap!" Billy muttered, kicking away the sheets, revealing his naked body and a very impressive piss hard-on.

Ramona seemed oblivious to her employer's lack of clothes and his erect penis. She handed him the glass of juice and left the room.

"Why's Janey coming?" Billy inquired.

"'Cause she's your publicist, an' that's what she does," Kev replied.

"No, what she *does* is charge me a shitload of money to do fuck all," Billy grumbled.

"*You're* in a piss-poor mood."

"So would you be if Alex friggin' Woods had spent the day watching you get the bejesus whacked outta you," Billy complained. "An' how come you didn't make it to the location last night?"

"You never told me you needed me there."

"I gotta tell you everything?" Billy said, finally getting out of bed and making his way into the bathroom.

"You usually do," Kev said, trailing behind him. "If you'd wanted me there you should've said so."

"What am I supposed t'wear?" Billy asked as he finished peeing and headed for the shower.

"Janey said you'd better look hot."

"Janey wouldn't know hot if it hit her in the ass."

Kev chuckled. Ramona reappeared with two plastic dry-cleaning bags. "Meesus Janey say you wear these," she announced, handing the bags to Kev.

"What's a movie star supposed t'do t'get some kind of *privacy*," Billy grumbled. "My johnson's not a show 'n' tell, so everyone get the fuck OUT!"

Ramona and Kev hurriedly retreated, leaving Billy alone in the bathroom. He stepped into the shower, thinking that perhaps he should call Venus, tell her how great last night was.

Problem was he wasn't feeling it. Anyway, she was probably still asleep, or out with her trainer—the good-looking black guy she swore was gay, although sometimes Billy wasn't so sure. The dude didn't *act* gay. He didn't even *look* gay.

Shit! What if she was screwing her trainer and they were both laughing at him behind his back?

This thought eased his guilt about the girl in the truck with the broken taillight. If Venus could do it, so could he.

And yet . . . Once again waves of guilt swept over him. Venus wouldn't. She couldn't. Venus was a one-man woman. She'd often confided how much it had hurt her when she'd caught her husband screwing around on her. But hey, that's what guys did—*especially* movie star guys. Surely every woman was aware of that?

He got out of the shower, toweled himself dry, and ripped open the plastic cleaning bags. Black silk pants and a crisp white Armani shirt.

Screw it, he was more comfortable in jeans and an old army shirt stolen from the wardrobe department on one of his movie shoots. Janey would simply have to accept his style or get herself fired.

One of the most important lessons Billy had learned in Hollywood was that nobody was indispensable. They all thought they were, but the sad truth was that everyone was replaceable. Including himself.

~ ~ ~

"Starbucks," Venus gasped as she and Cole got back in the Jag after a long, grueling mountain hike.

"Is that so you can undo all the good work we just put in?" Cole questioned, throwing her a disapproving look.

"Please! I don't usually beg. But I would *kill* for a caramel low-fat Frappuccino."

"You'll get nailed by the paparazzi," he warned.

"I don't care."

"Okay," Cole said, starting his new Jaguar, a gift from an aging rock star who was trying to persuade Cole to work—and other things—exclusively for him. The Jag was a bribe Cole had accepted as long as there were no strings. He quite liked the guy in a casual way, but he had no intention of hooking up on a permanent basis. He'd done that once, and the memories were not good. Besides, his sister Natalie, the host of a TV entertainment show, would kill him. She considered all celebrity relationships poison, and she should know, having indulged in a few disastrous ones herself.

There was a line at Starbucks, as usual.

Venus peered out the car window. "*You* go in," she suggested. "You know what I want."

"This goes against everything you *should* be doing," Cole said sternly.

"C'mon, indulge me, babe," Venus crooned.

"Doesn't everyone, *babe*," he said sarcastically.

Venus giggled. "Yeah, for an old broad I suppose I do get everything I want."

"Including Mr. Melina."

"Ah, Billy," Venus said fondly. "He's such a sweetheart."

"Sure," Cole agreed.

He didn't want to ruin her day, but yesterday he'd spotted Billy leaving Tower Records with a young girl in tow. Hey—maybe she was his sister. Besides, Cole didn't believe in causing trouble. As a trainer of the rich and *infamous* he knew where every body was buried. He also knew he was better off keeping his mouth tightly shut.

"He is, you know," Venus added, as if she was trying to convince herself. "*And*, in case you're wondering about the age thing, Billy is an old soul, he's not like a twenty-something guy. *And* we've been friends for eight years, so it's not as if I don't *know* him."

Cole shrugged. He didn't want to get involved. No good ever came from interfering in other people's love lives.

"We have the same interests," Venus continued. "Lucky thinks we're great together, and he doesn't put up with my b.s. So . . ."

So what? Cole wanted to say. *The dude's a hot young movie star dealing with pussy overload. It's a given he'll cheat. Wise up, Venus, you're too clever to put up with his shit.*

But Cole stayed silent. It simply wasn't his business.

13

"Did you see Max before she left?" Lucky asked, sweeping into Lennie's poolside office early Friday morning.

He was on the phone and waved her away with a dismissive gesture.

"Are you *kidding* me!" she exclaimed. "Don't dismiss me like I'm a fucking fruit fly!"

"Hang on a minute," Lennie said into the phone. Choking back laughter, he pressed down hold. "Fruit fly? A fucking *fruit* fly?"

Grinning, Lucky said, "Sometimes I have to come up with something original to get your attention."

"I'm talking to the studio."

"Fuck 'em," she said, perching on the edge of his desk. "Have you seen Max?"

"Nope."

"Her car's gone, and she didn't leave a number."

"Call her cell," Lennie said, returning to his phone call.

Hmmm . . . Lucky thought, getting up and heading for the kitchen. *As if I don't have enough on my mind without Max sneaking off.*

Although what did it matter? Lennie was right: she could reach Max on her cell at any time.

Yes, but Max should have come and said good-bye. She'd wanted to make absolutely sure her wild little daughter was back in time for Gino's party. Right now unreliable was Max's middle name.

Sixteen. Some age! She remembered it well. At sixteen you thought you were invincible, you thought you owned the world, you thought you could do anything and get away with it, you thought your parents were moronic idiots.

Yeah. Sixteen. Fun memories. Until Gino had married her off to Craven "the lox" Richmond, and she'd been too young and too foolish to realize she could've said no.

Ah well . . . She had no intention of marrying Max off, but she did plan on keeping a closer eye on her. After Gino's party, after the launch of the Keys, she would spend some quality time with her daughter. She had to convince Max that not cutting school was important for getting into the right college. And even though *she'd* made it without a formal education, she wanted Max to experience all the advantages.

Philippe approached. The very precise Philippe had come with the house, and although Lucky often found his manner to be too formal, she put up with him because he was a stickler for making sure the house ran smoothly. Now, with houseguests arriving, Gino's upcoming party, and the opening of her hotel in Vegas, she was grateful to have Philippe and his organizational skills. At least she knew he was there ready and willing to take care of everything.

"Mrs. Golden," he said stiffly.

"Yes, Philippe?" she answered briskly.

"There is another hand delivery for you," he said, passing her an ecru envelope.

She ripped open the envelope and inside was a Cartier card with the same scrawled message—*Drop Dead Beautiful.*

What kind of an invite is this? she thought. *Quite stupid if it doesn't include a save-the-date.*

"Did you see who left it?" she asked, opening the fridge and reaching for a can of 7-Up.

"No, Mrs. Golden. It was in the mailbox with the rest of the mail. But I can assure you it was hand-delivered."

Drop Dead Beautiful. Sounded like a movie or maybe the opening of a happening new club. Hollywood publicists were getting much too inventive.

The phone rang, taking her mind off the latest note. Sticking it under a pile of cookbooks, she took the call. It was Alex Woods.

"Lucky," he said. "We haven't spoken in a while. Thought I'd check in."

"Alex, what's going on?" she said, always pleased to hear from him even though she knew he still harbored a mild crush.

"I'm shooting my movie."

"I know that," she said, taking a swig of 7-Up from the can. "How's it going?"

"Great. How's our hotel progressing?"

"We're on schedule. I have a fantastic team in place, and we'll be opening on time. You'll be there of course."

"Wouldn't miss it. When I invest money I want to see the results."

"Oh, you will. The Keys is going to rule Vegas, I can promise you that."

"Everything you do always works out, so I'm confident this'll be another moneymaking triumph."

"Enough with the compliments—Lennie tells me the two of you have been trading missed calls."

"*You* know what it's like when you're at the end of a shoot, no time for anything."

"Ah yes, I remember it well," she said, momentarily nostalgic for her producing days.

"We should develop another movie together."

"Oh sure," she said sarcastically. "I can do that—in my spare time."

"We'd have a blast, just like before."

"How's Billy working out?" she asked, quickly changing the subject.

"I hate goddamn actors," Alex said vehemently. "Once they make it, they're out of control."

"I know you do, but you wouldn't be able to do your job without 'em," Lucky said, wondering what Billy was up to now.

"Ever heard of animated flicks?" Alex said.

"Yeah," she said, laughing. "I can just imagine an animated Alex Woods movie. Cute little rabbits and adorable farm creatures beating the crap outta each other with machetes! Blood and severed limbs everywhere!"

"Ah . . . she knows me so well," he said dryly.

"Oh yes, Alex, I do."

"Any chance of lunch anytime soon?"

"Thought you were busy shooting."

"I am. But maybe you'll visit the set one day. I'll have them set up lunch in my trailer."

"You, me, and Lennie?"

"Just you and me was what I had in mind."

"It's good I don't take you seriously."

"Why's that?"

" 'Cause then I'd have to tell Lennie you were hitting on me, forcing him to kick your ass."

"Sounds dramatic. But I was always under the impression that *you* had the balls in the family."

"Low blow, Alex."

"Just telling it the way I see it."

"Lennie has plenty of balls, believe me."

There was a short silence while she tried to figure out what was on his mind. Every so often he made an attempt to get together without Lennie. She always laughed him out of it. She was very fond of Alex as a friend, and that's the way she wanted to keep it. Yes, she'd slept with him once and once only, but it was long ago and it didn't really count, because at the time she'd thought Lennie was gone forever. It was obviously a night Alex had never forgotten.

"You're coming to Gino's party on Sunday?" she asked, breaking the silence.

"Wouldn't miss it," Alex replied.

"Bringing Ling I hope."

"Should I?"

"*Why* are you asking *me?* She's *your* girlfriend. Isn't it about time you made it legal?"

"Gotta go," he said abruptly. "See you Sunday." And he hung up.

That's right, Alex, let's not get anywhere near your personal life, Lucky thought. She wished he'd find that special someone, because even though he'd been living with Ling for a couple of years, she obviously wasn't it.

There were times Lucky found it uncomfortable between her and Alex—especially as she'd never told Lennie about their one-night stand. The truth was she wanted Alex and Lennie to remain friends, but if Lennie ever found out . . .

It was all too complicated, she refused to think about it. There were too many other things to deal with, and right now making Gino's party perfect was number one on her agenda.

14

Friday morning Brigette and Bobby Stanislopolous met at a private airport in New York, ready to board the Stanislopolous plane to Los Angeles. Neither of them used the plane much; it was the company jet and usually flew members of the Stanislopolous board and chief executives around Europe. However, it was at their disposal whenever they needed it.

When they met up at the airport, Brigette realized she hadn't seen Bobby in almost a year. "Look at you," she exclaimed, genuinely pleased to see him. "Handsome!"

Bobby was indeed handsome. Like Lucky he was tall, with olive skin, jet-black hair, and intense black eyes. Like his late father, Dimitri, he had a Greek nose, strong chin, and dominant personality. He was a hybrid—half Santangelo, half Stanislopolous.

"Is that any way to talk to your uncle?" he teased, checking out his devastatingly pretty niece.

"Oh, sorry, *Uncle* Bobby," Brigette said with a flicker of a smile. She was naturally blond and cover-girl pretty. "I hear your club is doing great," she added. "Good for you."

"Yeah," Bobby replied, nodding his head. "We got written up in *New York* magazine last month. How come I've never seen you there?"

"I finished with the club scene after I finished with modeling," she said. "It's not for me. Too many needy people on the prowl."

"You gotta be my guest one night," Bobby said, full of enthusiasm at the thought of showing off his gorgeous niece. "I'll look after you. We'll have fun, that's a promise."

"Thank you, *Uncle* Bobby," she answered, smiling. "I shall look forward to that."

Wow! She's such a babe, Bobby thought. *What a waste. I know a dozen guys who'd give their left nut for a shot at her. And if we weren't related . . .*

"Is the plane ready for boarding?" she asked.

"All set," he said, scooping up her Fendi overnight bag and throwing it over his shoulder.

"Then let's go," Brigette said, standing up.

"You got it," he said, taking her arm.

Together they headed for the plane.

~ ~ ~

Meanwhile, Gino Senior sat in the front passenger seat of his new Cadillac, while Paige, his wife of twenty years, drove. For an old broad Paige still had it going on, or at least Gino thought so. He couldn't have asked for a more spirited, loyal, always-there-for-him wife. And attractive too, with her flaming red hair and pocket Venus figure. Even in her seventies Paige still cut a swath. He'd made a smart choice when he'd dumped his third wife, the frosty Susan Martino, and married her best friend, Paige. There'd been a few bumps along the way—nobody was perfect. He'd never forget walking in on the two women in bed together. But that was ancient news, and who was he to make judgments? After all, his past was hardly blameless.

Ah . . . So many women, so many memories . . .

Now he was old. Frigging *old*. And it didn't seem possible when in his head he was still maybe forty years of age. Christ! Looking in the mirror and seeing an old face peering back at him was not something that thrilled him. Better than the alternative, though; he was a true survivor and let no one forget it. He'd outlived them all—Enzio Bonnatti, Pinky Banana, Jake the Boy—all the old crew. He'd weathered jail, a heart attack, the death of a child, a couple of assassination attempts, the murder of his beloved first wife. Jeez! And a thousand other things.

In two days he was about to be ninety frigging five, and it wasn't so bad, apart from the fact that his body was falling to pieces. His knees were gone, arthritis had claimed his hands, his back hurt, his eyes were fading fast, and worst of all, he couldn't get it up anymore. Not that he had any desire to, sex was off the agenda—had been for a couple of years. Gino the Ram was no more. He'd had a good run, and he didn't regret one step of the way, although he did feel sorry for Paige—she must miss the action. Not that she complained; Paige would never do that.

"Can't wait t'see the kids," he said, settling back. "This should be some weekend."

"Fasten your seat belt," Paige said, sounding quite bossy. "If we have an accident, you could go through the windshield."

"Big friggin' deal," Gino replied, indulging in a vigorous coughing fit. "I'm gonna be ninety-five, woman. Ya think a goddamn seat belt's gonna save me?"

"Be sensible, Gino."

"Now, when's *that* gonna happen?" he said, shooting her a quizzical look.

~ ~ ~

"What time is everyone getting here?" Lennie asked, wandering into the den, where Lucky was busy making notes.

"Brigette and Bobby should be here at four," she said, putting down her pen and stretching her arms above her head. "And Gino and Paige are arriving around the same time."

"Full house this weekend," Lennie remarked.

"Gino wanted to stay in a hotel, but I told him he has to stay here."

"Maybe he likes hotels," Lennie said, walking over to her and starting to massage her shoulders.

"Hey, maybe *I* want him here," Lucky retorted.

"That's 'cause you're Miss Control Freak."

"I am certainly not," she objected.

"Y'know," Lennie mused, "if anyone had told me you'd turn into Earth Mother, I would've laughed in their face."

"You would, huh?" she said, turning her head.

"Lucky Santangelo Golden, former wild one—Earth Mother supreme."

"What *are* you talking about now?"

"Take a count. Three kids—well, four if you count Leonardo. One father. A stepmother. A goddaughter. A husband—"

"That would be *you*," she said, starting to smile.

"Yeah, me," he said, smiling back. "And we'll all be in the same house this weekend, getting ready for Gino's big one. And if I know you, you'll be watching out for everyone. Like I said—Earth Mother supreme."

"Who'd've thunk?" she said ruefully. "Me. The original independent woman. But I wouldn't have it any other way. Would you?"

"No, sweetheart, not for a minute. You make my life complete."

"I do?"

"Y'know," he added thoughtfully, "we've been through a hell of a lot together."

"Now, ain't *that* the truth," she said, getting up.

"So . . . I want to thank you, Mrs. Golden. And if you come over here, I'll show you how."

"Hmm . . ." she said, smiling. "Might I remind you it's the middle of the day."

"No shit?"

"And I have a thousand things to do."

"So I suppose a blow job's outta the question?" he said, only half serious.

"Lennie!" she exclaimed, taking a step back.

"I know, I know," he said, ruefully. "It's the middle of the day. But hey, I can remember the time when—"

"When *what?*"

"You know what."

"Okay, *husband,*" she said, impulsively grabbing his hand. "I think you need to come with me."

"Huh?"

"With me," she said firmly. "That's an order."

"And where are you taking me?" he asked, playing along.

"Somewhere we can lock the door. How's that for a plan?"

He grinned. "Now, *that's* the girl I married."

"You'd better believe it!"

~ ~ ~

And out on the highway Max drove too fast, just like her mother.

Today she was into rap. Loud, throbbing, ear-splitting rap played mega volume in her car—the amazing BMW sports car her parents had bought her for her sixteenth birthday. Lucky had been against her getting a sports car, but Lennie had soon persuaded her. Lennie had to be the coolest, most laid-back dad in the world. He could talk Lucky into anything—which was why Max realized she should have gone to Lennie in the first place instead of asking Lucky if she could go to Big Bear.

But hey—whatever. Here she was sitting in her BMW on her way to Big Bear heading for an adventure. No problemo. No *way.* This was major exciting!

Giggling to herself, she turned the volume even higher.

Internet guy, here I come. I hope you're good and ready!

15

"I shall be going away this weekend," Henry informed his mother. He was standing in the imposing front hallway of the Pasadena mansion wearing khaki pants and a mud-brown shirt. His prematurely thinning hair was plastered down, and he carried a large canvas hold-all. Henry was not handsome, nor was he ugly—he was merely quite ordinary-looking with no distinguishing features.

Penelope was shocked and at the same time secretly pleased, because much as she tolerated having Henry around, she realized that it was not exactly healthy for him to never leave the house, especially for a boy of his age—man really, for Henry was almost thirty.

"Where are you going?" she inquired.

"To visit friends," he answered vaguely.

Friends? Henry didn't have any friends, at least none that she knew of.

"How long will you be gone?" she asked, adjusting a tall vase of tulips perched on an antique table.

"It depends," he said evasively.

"Have you met a girl?" she asked. "Because if you have, I wish to meet her before you even *think* of getting involved. Remember what I have always told you about girls, Henry. When they look at you all they see is dollar signs. You are a Whitfield-Simmons, and do not ever forget it."

As if he could. She'd drilled it into him since he was six. He was a Whitfield-Simmons, and one day he would inherit the Whitfield-Simmons fortune.

"Maybe," he replied, refusing to look her in the eye. "I'll phone you, Mother, and let you know when I'll be back."

"Very well, Henry, I certainly hope you have a pleasant time."

"I think I will," he said, limping toward the door. "As a matter of fact, I'm sure I will."

"Look after yourself, dear," Penelope said, her attention drifting back to the tulips, which seemed in dire need of fresh water.

"I always do," Henry muttered, aware that his mother was no longer listening to him.

He exited the house and stood for a few minutes in the circular driveway.

Markus, his mother's chauffeur, appeared. "Can I help you, Mr. Henry?" Markus asked. He was black and subservient, and had been with the Whitfield-Simmons family since before Henry was born. Shades of *Driving Miss Daisy*, Henry thought. He knew plenty about movies, because apart from his time spent hunched over his computer, he was a movie buff, fascinated by old movies, and especially horror classics such as *The Texas Chainsaw Massacre*, and every one of the Freddy films.

"No help needed, thank you, Markus," he said. "I shall be away for the weekend."

Markus's bushy eyebrows shot up. "That's nice, Mr. Henry, a nice change for you."

"Yes, it is," Henry agreed.

"What car will you be wanting to take?" Markus inquired.

"Mother's Bentley."

"Oh, no, Mr. Henry," Markus said, looking dismayed and beginning to sweat. "Mrs. Penelope won't allow that. She's given me strict orders—"

"I understand, Markus. I was merely joking."

"Yes, Mr. Henry, I knew that," Markus said, thoroughly relieved. "You was joking with me."

"I'll take the Volvo."

"Certainly, Mr. Henry, I'll bring it round to the front."

"That's okay, I'll get it myself."

"If you're sure . . ."

"I'm sure."

Henry walked around the side of the house where the cars were lined up in a row of garages. There was his mother's shiny royal blue Bentley, also a pristine black Cadillac she used when she considered the Bentley too flashy to take on one of her charity jaunts downtown, and next to the Cadillac, a gray Mercedes SUV for shopping trips.

The dark brown Volvo lurked in a corner spot. It was the car out-of-town guests used when they came to stay, and sometimes Markus was allowed to take it out. Ever since his accident Henry had not wanted a car of his own; there was no point since he wasn't going anywhere.

But today he was. Oh yes, today he was off on a mission, and he had to admit that getting out of the house was quite exhilarating.

Opening the trunk of the Volvo, he carefully placed his canvas holdall inside. It contained everything he needed for a very interesting weekend indeed.

16

Vegas and Anthony Bonar were a good match. *What's not to like?* Anthony thought whenever he visited the desert city. *Gambling, spectacular shows, fine restaurants, and beautiful women—plenty of hot, sexy, ready-to-do-anything babes.*

Not that he was looking, he had enough to deal with juggling Emmanuelle and Carlita—Irma didn't count. But even though he wasn't on the hunt, Vegas was Vegas, and if some ready-to-rock piece of ass took his fancy, why turn it down? Viagra meant never having to say you were too tired.

He didn't need the damn blue pills, but after trying Viagra a couple of times he'd become addicted to the major hard-on that never quit. Emmanuelle and Carlita did not object, in fact quite the opposite—the two of them begged him for more. *Insatiable bitches,* he thought with a self-satisfied smirk.

The first woman he'd ever screwed was a whore plying her trade on the streets of Naples. It had happened a few weeks before his twelfth birthday and he was already ragingly horny. The whore had beckoned him into an alley—snatched his money, which he'd stolen from his mother's purse, and screwed him standing up. Fast and furious, that was the way she'd liked it. He'd realized then and there that was the way *all* women liked it.

He'd never changed his sexual style. Fuck 'em hard and fuck 'em long. The story of his success with women.

Renee Falcon Esposito, joint owner of the Cavendish Hotel, had sent a limousine to the airport. Renee and he went way back to the days she was married to Oscar Esposito, the Colombian billionaire politician, a man who'd met his fate by being tossed from a moving plane after trying to pull a double cross on an extremely powerful and vengeful drug lord. Since Anthony had been banging Renee on the side, she'd immediately turned to him for help. He'd never revealed to her that he was part of the plot to get rid of Oscar, but he *had* helped her flee Colombia with the money she'd inherited from her deceased husband—not to mention several safe-deposit boxes stuffed with illegal cash, which he'd persuaded her she had to split with him.

He'd moved Renee back to her hometown, Las Vegas, where she'd eventually hooked up with another mega-bucks female, Susie Rae Young, the widow of famous country singer Cyrus Rae Young. The two of them had formed a life partnership *and* built their dream hotel in which Anthony had declared himself a silent partner.

That was over ten years ago, and business was excellent, so Renee had not taken much convincing that the Keys was a direct threat, and could pull away many of their best customers. Anthony insisted they had to do something drastic to stop the Keys from opening. He'd come up with an idea of how to do this. It was a costly plan, but it would be totally effective. Anthony had agreed to pay half of the million bucks it would cost them to have an expert blow up the complex—one building at a time. He had no intention of paying his half. Let Renee foot the entire bill. She owed him.

The hotel limo was waiting on the tarmac alongside his plane. The driver was a tall Swedish blonde dressed in black leather from her knee-high boots to the jaunty cap sitting on top of her head.

"Welcome back to Vegas, Mr. Bonar," she said in a throaty, accented voice. "I will be your driver while you are here."

He barely glanced in her direction.

"My name is Britt," she continued, handing him a small silver cell phone. "All my numbers are programmed in. I'm on duty twenty-four hours a day. Call whenever you need me, I'm at your disposal."

Anthony tossed the phone to The Grill, a move not lost on the blonde, who pretended not to notice.

"Straight to the hotel, Mr. Bonar?" she inquired, holding open the door.

"Yeah," he said, climbing in the back. "An' no conversation."

The Cavendish was a small—by Vegas standards—boutique membership-only luxury hotel catering to extreme high rollers, sports and movie stars, plus high-powered moguls and executives. Very few of the general public were allowed in. The gambling was exclusive, as was the hotel, which had a reputation for supplying all services a guest required. "The best of everything" was the hotel's motto, and that included any known drug, and the highest-priced call girls in the city. Renee ran a tight operation, with major security all around.

Renee herself was standing in the cool marble lobby of her hotel waiting to greet him. Every time he saw her, Anthony couldn't help marveling at the woman's transformation. When he'd first met her Renee had been Oscar Esposito's American trophy wife, a curvaceous former showgirl with teased blond hair, long legs, and large breasts. Definitely fuckable. Definitely a babe. Now she weighed well over two hundred pounds, wore her hair in a severely cropped dark brown bob, and her implants were long gone. Renee was a different woman. A tough dyke who'd carved a niche for herself in Vegas as a canny businesswoman with a life partner who was even richer than her. All she and Anthony had between them now was business, and that's the way it suited both of them.

"Anthony," Renee greeted. "My favorite bad boy."

"Renee," Anthony responded. "My favorite dyke."

Renee had stones, an admirable quality in a woman, although Anthony wasn't too sure about the lesbian thing. Surely she missed cock?

"Smooth flight?" Renee inquired.

"Not bad," Anthony replied, his eyes flicking around the lobby, checking things out.

"I've put you in Bungalow One. I thought we'd meet for dinner, Susie's excited to see you."

"I ain't here to socialize, Renee," he reminded her gruffly. "I'm here to make certain everythin's in place."

"I can assure you it is," Renee replied, irritated that he would doubt her. "You told me to hire Tucker Bond, and I did. We're paying for the best, Anthony. Half up front, and the rest when the job is done."

"I don't want no fuckups," Anthony growled.

"I don't allow for fuckups," Renee responded.

"Yeah?"

"I'm as concerned as you are," she said, annoyed that Anthony had a way of speaking down to her that she did not appreciate.

~ ~ ~

Once Anthony was settled into the luxurious bungalow with its own private swimming pool and a bar stocked with the finest brands of liquor and wine, he placed another call to Carlita.

This time his sexy Italian mistress picked up.

"Where the fuck ya bin?" he demanded, drumming his fingers impatiently on the table.

She made up some excuse about visiting a sick relative.

"So sick ya couldn't pick up ya fuckin' cell?" Anthony said, frowning.

Once again Carlita had an answer, telling him that her phone had a low battery or some such shit.

He said nothing. He was pleasant, affectionate even, although he had a strong gut feeling that the douche bag was cheating on him.

As soon as he put the phone down, he called one of his minions in New York and issued an order to have Carlita followed. "Whatever she's doin' I wanna know 'bout it," he instructed. "An' if you find her doin' anythin' she shouldn't, get me photos, proof. Do whatever you gotta do t'bring me the goods."

If she was innocent of screwing around on him, nothing lost.

And if the *puttana* was guilty . . .

Well, if she was guilty, it was her funeral.

~ ~ ~

Irma's second session with Luis was all she had hoped for and more. It was late afternoon, she'd sent the housekeeper out, the old gardener was still away, and the guards were stationed at the front of the house with Anthony's two ferocious Dobermans.

"I need you to look at my indoor plants. Follow me," she'd informed Luis, who still hadn't understood a word she'd said, although he'd certainly understood what "Follow me" meant.

As soon as they'd reached the privacy of her bedroom, she'd locked the door behind them. Luis hadn't hesitated. He'd ripped the clothes from her body with feverish haste, then he'd begun divesting his own garments as fast as he could get them off.

Words were not spoken.

Words were not needed.

Once she was naked, he'd leaned her back against the wall, spread-eagling her legs.

Propped against the wall with her legs apart, she'd felt exposed, vulnerable, and unbelievably sexually excited.

Luis had stroked her nipples, fingered her crotch, then dropped to his knees and started going down on her, his tongue forcing its way through her wiry bush of pubic hair, darting into her most secret place—a place Anthony had *never* visited with his tongue.

After a few minutes of indescribable ectasy, she'd shuddered to an earth-shattering climax, moaning with passion as Luis stood up. He'd then gathered her into his strong arms and carried her over to the bed, whereupon he'd laid her down, once more spread her legs, and mounted her, slowly and surely moving back and forth inside her.

Words were still not spoken.

Words were still not needed.

For once, Irma had been totally satisfied.

~ ~ ~

Being married to a corrupt politician had taught Renee the ways of the world—the world that Anthony and his business associates inhabited. She knew how to please the men she had to deal with, and not in a sexual way. Renee had turned herself into one of the boys—a tough broad who ran a tight operation and could dole out punishment with the best of them.

A few months after opening the Cavendish, Renee had caught one of her dealers cheating. Two days later his bullet-riddled body had turned up in a used-car lot. Renee had wanted his body to be found. The message was clear enough: *Don't think you can fuck with me simply because I'm a woman.*

The message worked until an L.A.-based madam decided to have a few of her best girls work the high rollers at the Cavendish. The madam moved them in big time under the guise of actresses and models, but Renee soon caught on. She had invitations printed inviting half a dozen of the girls to a very exclusive lingerie party given by a Saudi prince. She also put the word out that each girl who attended would receive a large cash bonus.

Saudi prince and *cash bonus* were the four key words. The girls arrived wearing nothing much at all. At the door of the penthouse suite where the party was to take place, they were relieved of their purses as a security measure.

While the girls—clad in nothing more than revealing underwear—waited in the plush suite for the Arab prince to appear, Renee had her people visit all their rooms and gather together every item of the girls' expensive clothes and accessories. When this was done, Renee supervised a huge bonfire in the parking lot, and the girls were herded together and forced to watch as everything they'd arrived in Vegas with was burned—including the contents of their purses.

After the bonfire ceremony they were driven into the desert and left there half naked with no money, no airline tickets, no cell phones—nothing.

Somehow or other they all made it back to L.A. And sure enough, their madam got the message.

Nobody sued.

Nobody came back.

Point made.

Since that time Renee had dealt with several other employees who had caused her trouble. She was relentless when it came to protecting her territory, which was why she'd agreed with Anthony when he'd come up with his plan to destroy the Keys. He was right, the new hotel complex was a direct threat to the Cavendish, especially as the building was so close. The Keys would be targeting all of the Cavendish's best customers, and as the building progressed, Renee was just as determined as Anthony to do something about it.

Anthony had come up with the idea of hiring Tucker Bond to take care of their problem, and Renee had put it together, speaking to the man herself.

It was an expensive undertaking, but Anthony was splitting the cost, and he'd assured her it would be worth it to get rid of their direct competition.

The Keys project opening in Vegas was bad business for everyone. That's all there was to it.

17

"Billy Melina," the female journalist singsonged in a raspy voice. "Billy Melina in the flesh."

Florence Harbinger was fiftyish, fat, and frumpy with a digital recorder clutched in one hand and a verging-on-sarcastic attitude.

Instinctively Billy knew he'd have to work hard to win this one over. Female journalists. A breed unto themselves. They needed care and attention, otherwise they'd destroy you in print. Billy had learned the hard way.

Rule number one: Compliment.

Rule number two: Flirt.

Rule number three: Ask about their family.

Rule number four: More flirting and make it stick.

Florence Harbinger had a reputation. She ate actors for breakfast and spit 'em out all over the pages of the high-profile magazine she worked for. And because the magazine was so high profile, every publicist in town was hot to get their star clients on the cover and getting the cover meant sitting down with the lovely Florence. Billy was *so* not into it.

Where was Janey when he needed her? His so-called publicist was a total flake. If she didn't put in an appearance in the next five minutes, he was definitely firing her skinny ass.

"Billy, Billy, Billy," Florence repeated, chanting his name. "So tell me, dear, how's it working out with you and the older woman? Is it difficult? Are we having fun? Or do you think being with the multitalented Venus diminishes *your* fame?"

Oh yeah, this was going to be a bumpy ride. Grin and flirt with the dried-up old hag who probably hadn't gotten laid in years. Give her a taste of the old hick-seed charm he'd possessed when he'd first hit Hollywood.

"You know, Florence," he said, speaking slowly, "I never thought of that." As he spoke he gave her the famous Billy Melina blue-eyed stare. Kev called it the "panties off" stare, hard for any female young or old to resist. "By the way, have you lost weight? You're lookin' *very* good," Billy continued.

Florence was too old and seasoned to fall for it completely, but her attitude toward him noticeably softened, and by the time Janey arrived, the interview was well on course.

Janey, a sallow-faced girl with wispy yellow hair and an out-of-control overbite, allowed the interview to run over, which infuriated Billy. How many times had he told her that if a journalist couldn't get what they wanted in an hour, it was over?

Billy was incensed, trapped, and pissed off. This wasn't right. He was talking too much and probably saying things he shouldn't, and dumb Janey was hanging in the kitchen with Kev as if he, Billy, was perfectly fine with *two freaking hours* of interrogation. SHIT!

Finally his cell rang and he took the opportunity to make a quick escape. "Gotta take this," he informed Florence, who looked like she was all set for another two hours of scintillating conversation. "I'll be right back."

He raced into the kitchen and blasted Janey, who managed to look forlorn and hard-done-by—as if *he* was the one at fault.

"Two minutes," he hissed. "Two more freakin' minutes, then you come in and break it up."

"HELLOOO." Whoever was on his cell was yelling for attention.

"Sorry," he said, realizing it was Venus.

"*What* is going on?" Venus wanted to know.

"Oh, hey, it's nothing," he said vaguely. "I'll tell you later."

"Why not now?"

"Uh . . . I gotta call you back."

"Why? What are you doing?"

Another interrogator. What was it with women and their questions?

"I'm in the middle of an interview, so I'll—"

"Who with?"

"Some magazine."

"*What* magazine?"

"Really, babe, I gotta call you back."

"Fine," she said in her best *you're an asshole* and *I hate you* voice. "You do that."

Oh crap. Now he had Venus on his case and that wasn't a good thing.

"Billy," Florence called out from the living room. "Where are you, dear? I need to verify a couple of facts."

He was *not* having a great day.

~ ~ ~

Venus clicked off her cell and frowned. What was up with Billy? He wasn't himself, he was edgy, and—dare she even think it—distant.

Oh God, he was distant. Did that mean he was having second thoughts about their relationship? Did distant mean he was looking for an out?

This was ridiculous. They'd been together almost a year, and as far as she was concerned they were blissfully happy. Well . . . about as blissfully happy as two movie stars can be considering their every move was dogged by the paparazzi, not to mention the false rumors that appeared in print or on the Internet every single day. She couldn't count how many times she was supposedly pregnant, or how many times they'd secretly gotten married, or how many times they'd broken up. All lies. All hurtful. All damaging to their relationship.

Venus sighed as she realized she'd done something extremely foolish. She'd fallen in love with Billy, and how dumb was *that?* Now she was experiencing all the pangs of teenage rejection, because surely if he didn't have time to talk to her—that was rejection?

Dammit! Love was a pain in the ass. Love made you weak and vulnerable and open to getting hurt. This was not her M.O. at all. Venus was strong and invincible and an icon. That's why her fans loved her so much. Now she'd gone and fallen in love with a boy—not a man like Cooper, a boy—a movie star boy who however hard he worked would never be as famous as she was.

Or as rich.

And yet . . . it didn't matter to her, she was cool with it.

But if he rejected her, dumped her . . .

No, it simply couldn't happen.

Stop being needy, she told herself. *Everything's fine. Billy loves you. He tells you all the time.*

Billy Melina. Who would've ever thought *he'd* be the one when he'd walked into Alex Woods's office eight years ago? She certainly hadn't. All she'd seen then was an apprehensive, fidgety twenty-year-old boy who, when he'd read a scene with her, had exhibited a fierce and endearing talent.

She'd kind of steered him through his first important role, and he'd given a dynamic performance, launching a highly successful career.

They'd become friends. She was married to Cooper and had a small child. Billy was on the road to stardom with a pretty new girl on his arm—or in his bed—every other day. Occasionally they spoke on the phone, or ran into each other at big events such as superagent Ed Limato's Oscar party or one of the endless award ceremonies.

When Billy made the cover of *People* magazine as "The Sexiest Man Alive," she'd sent him a life-sized inflatable doll with a funny note attached. And when she'd won two Emmys, a People's Choice Award, and three Grammys all in one year, he'd sent her a Harry Winston diamond star pendant with a sweet letter praising her achievements.

After that they'd started meeting for lunch on a regular basis. She'd teased him about his parade of nubile girlfriends; he'd listened when she'd found herself confiding her marital woes.

He was understanding and an excellent listener.

When she finally left Cooper, Billy was there to hold her hand and help her through it.

One memorable night their friendship developed into a full-blown love affair. She hadn't planned it, hadn't wanted it, but somehow it was inevitable.

The gossip rags went into overdrive. Venus and Billy Melina—what a tabloid-headline-making duo! It was all too irresistible.

Now they'd been together almost a year, but she wasn't sure how it was going. She knew she should be happy—Billy hadn't said anything or done anything that would make her feel otherwise—but deep down she had a nagging feeling that something was amiss, and one of the keys of Venus's huge success had been to always follow her instincts.

What were her instincts telling her now?

She wasn't sure. She didn't know.

But hey, she had to believe it would all work out in the end. Everything always did.

~ ~ ~

"You drink too much," Ling scolded.

"What now?" Alex Woods said, emerging from the shower, knotting a towel around his waist.

"Last night you came home drunk," Ling continued in a sanctimonious tone. "And you were driving, Alex, that's extremely stupid. If you had been stopped and Breathalyzed, it could have turned out very badly."

Was his exquisitely beautiful Asian lawyer girlfriend calling him stupid?

No. It wasn't possible.

Or was it? Because if it was, it was time for her to go. Nobody called

Alex Woods stupid and got away with it. If she was working on one of his movies, he would fire her ass. But she wasn't working on his movie, she was living in his architecturally modern beach house, sharing his oversized water bed, and sometimes driving his Porsche. Plenty of perks. More than enough. And he did not need criticism coming out of her perfectly formed mouth. Oh no. Her mouth was for other purposes.

"What if you'd been arrested?" Ling droned on. "Then what, Alex? Headlines you do not care for. Publicity you hate."

"Spoken like a true lawyer," he said, dropping his towel.

"I'm sorry if you do not like to hear the truth," Ling said, all pissy-faced. "But it is only for your own good."

Yeah. Sure.

"Did you have your gun on you, Alex?" Ling continued. "Because I continually remind you that you do not have a license to carry a firearm, and were you stopped and the gun was found, that would constitute a far greater problem."

"Okay, okay," he said impatiently. "I'm listening. Next time I go on a bender I'll leave my gun at home. Does that make you happy?"

"Yes, Alex, that makes me happy. Although why you need a gun at all—"

"I get threats, Ling," he said, reaching for his pants and pulling them on. "How many times I gotta tell you?"

Over the years he'd grown to realize that there wasn't a woman in existence who knew when to shut the fuck up. Except perhaps Lucky Santangelo. When it came to Lucky, she could talk all night and he'd listen to every word. But then Lucky was unique, a one-of-a-kind woman who possessed the three B's in abundance—Brains, Beauty, and Balls.

Thinking about Lucky made him smile.

"Why are you smiling, Alex, it is not funny," Ling scolded, as if she was speaking to a naughty child.

"Give it a rest," he said. "I don't *want* to hear it and I don't *have* to hear it, so shut the fuck up."

"Do not speak to me like that," Ling said, tilting her chin.

Oh Jesus. She wasn't his *wife*, why was she lecturing him as if she was?

He stared at his five-feet-two-inches-tall girlfriend with the slim, toned body and ridiculously large fake tits—too big for her slender shape. Her tits had always bothered him. What was she thinking when she'd had them done? *I want to be a lawyer, but maybe I'll moonlight as a stripper on the side*?

It didn't make sense.

"I have a major fucking hangover," he said, feeling the throb in his head. "So I suggest we drop this conversation before you get yourself in trouble."

"Very well, Alex," she said, tight-lipped. "But I tell you only because I care."

"I'm sure you do," he sighed.

End of dialogue.

Cut.

Print.

18

Hugging her father felt so damn good. Gino the survivor, a real character. Lately Lucky had come to the conclusion that the older she got, the more she understood him. Now she realized why he'd married her off at sixteen. He'd thought he was protecting her, saving her from her wild ways, and his mind was set that way because he'd been raised during a time when women were not considered smart, independent human beings; women were considered soft and obedient, they were supposed to get married, have kids, and shut the fuck up.

Wow! What a shocker she must have been to him—a girl who craved freedom and power; a girl who was sexually free; a girl who did things her way and turned out to be exactly like daddy.

The two of them could laugh about it now, for Lucky considered Gino to be not just her father, but also her best friend. She loved hearing him reminisce about the early days when he was living on the streets of New York struggling to make a buck. He often spoke about the time he was involved with the very elegant and very married Clementine Duke, the nightclub he opened way back, his long stretch in prison, and the excitement and challenge of building his first hotel in Vegas.

Oh yes, Gino had stories like nobody else.

Her kids adored him and he them. Gino Junior called him Mister

Cool, and Bobby had always looked up to him. Max—not so much. "He's like *major old*," Max always grumbled whenever Gino visited, as if being old was a bad thing. "Why do I have to kiss him every time I see him? He smells of fish, like a decrepit trout."

"Your grandfather believes in taking a lot of vitamins," Lucky had explained. "Sometimes they leave an odor."

"It's utterly *gross!*" Max would complain.

Perhaps it's just as well that Max is not here for dinner, Lucky thought, ushering Gino and Paige upstairs to their room. She gave Gino another hug, and left them to unpack.

Downstairs Lennie was about to get to work on his script. "Good thing we made out before they got here," he remarked.

"Glad you're pleased."

"And it wasn't just sex, it was fantastic sex, an' not even make-up sex!"

"You're such a romantic."

"I try."

"Try harder," Lucky quipped.

A short while later Bobby and Brigette arrived.

Is it possible that this tall handsome guy is my son? Lucky thought proudly. *Wow, I must've done something right.*

"Where's Max?" Bobby asked, exchanging a series of playful punches with Gino Junior, who was excited to see his big brother.

"She went to a party up in Big Bear," Lucky explained. "She'll be back in time for Gino's celebration."

"*Great*," Bobby complained, pulling a face. "I come into town and she takes off. I gotta have a serious talk with that girl."

"I wish somebody would," Lucky muttered.

"What does *that* mean?"

"It means she's exactly like her mom was when Lucky was her age," Lennie interjected.

"Who's exactly like their mom?" Brigette asked, entering the house, followed by a red-faced driver attempting to balance several large Fendi bags.

"There you are," Lennie said, grabbing her in a bear hug. "How's my girl?"

Brigette smiled. She had special feelings for Lennie, who'd once been married to her mother, Olympia. Lennie had always treated her with kindness, unlike so many other people she'd had to deal with. "I'm doing okay, Lennie."

"You look fantastic," he said, thinking how fresh and pretty she was for a girl who'd been through so much.

"Max is on the missing list," Bobby announced. "She took off to some party," he added, shaking his head as if he couldn't quite believe that his half-sister hadn't stayed around to greet him. "How about that? Wait till I get hold of her, she's in for major punishment."

"You can phone her later," Lucky said. "Lay a guilt trip on her, especially as she left without saying good-bye this morning."

"*Bad* little girl," Bobby said. "Hey, Mom, you're looking as beautiful as ever."

"Thanks, Bobby, you always know what to say."

"Don't thank me, thank the good genes you got from your old man. Is Gino here yet? Can't wait to see him."

"They arrived ten minutes ago, they're settling in."

"We could've all stayed at a hotel," Bobby said. "Wouldn't that've been easier for you?"

"Not at all," Lucky replied. "In case you haven't noticed, this house is huge—there's plenty of room for everyone. Besides, us all being here together is kind of nice. We should make the most of it."

"How soon do you get your Malibu house back?"

"Another couple of months. But it's not so bad, 'cause Lennie's going to be shooting his movie in Canada, and I'll be spending most of my time in Vegas."

"Oh yeah!" Bobby said enthusiastically. "The Keys. Can we talk about me opening a club there?"

"We already have a club, Bobby. You know that."

"Yeah, but you don't have *my* club. It's taken off big time."

"I'll keep you in mind if we decide to open another one. Maybe sometime in the future if you're really serious."

"It's great to have connections," Bobby muttered. "Gets me exactly nowhere."

"Who's coming tonight?" Brigette asked.

"Family only," Lucky replied. "I'm cooking pasta, so you'd all better be ravenously hungry or else."

"Did you invite Venus?" Bobby ventured.

"Still got a crush?" Lennie interjected with a sly grin. "'Cause if you do, I hear she's into younger men."

"Be quiet," Lucky said, trying not to smile. "Bobby never had a crush, did you?"

"No *way*," Bobby said, a touch too emphatically.

"She'll be at the party Sunday," Lucky offered. "You can catch up then."

"The Santangelo clan," Brigette said with a sunny smile. "I'm so glad I'm part of it."

"And we're glad to have you," Lucky said warmly.

"Yeah," Lennie agreed. "Especially without some deadbeat trailing along behind you."

"Hey, don't be so hard on her," Bobby objected. "That's my niece you're talking to, and she's one hot number."

"Thanks, Uncle," Brigette said, still smiling. "You're not so bad yourself."

"Okay," Lucky said. "Why don't I take you upstairs to your rooms, and you can unpack."

"Great idea," Bobby said. "Then later we'll talk about my future club in your hotel. It's not like I come cheap, y'know, you'll have to pay for the privilege."

"Really?" Lucky drawled. "Can't wait to negotiate with you, Bobby. I'm sure you're a regular hard-ass."

"I want to be around for *that* meeting," Lennie said, joining in.

"I'll make sure you are," Bobby said, full of confidence.

"Yes, Lennie," Lucky said. "You can take notes, see who wins."

"I think I already know the answer to that one," Lennie said, grinning.

"Don't be so sure," Bobby responded. "I'm a Santangelo crossed with a Stanislopolous. That means you can never count me out."

~ ~ ~

Big Bear was unfamiliar territory to Max. She drove around getting lost, stopping to ask directions to Kmart, which turned out to be on the main street.

All of a sudden she was nervous. How would she recognize Grant? How would he recognize her? Had she mentioned what car she was driving? She must have told him she had a BMW—then again maybe she hadn't.

Crap! This was nerve-racking, and she was not feeling as cool about it as she'd thought she would. What if she hated him? What if he was a major jerk? Or even worse—a major perv like Cookie had suggested he might be?

Oh great! This could end up being a no-win situation.

Desperate to find a bathroom and dying of thirst, she parked her car, hurriedly glanced around the parking lot, and went inside the store thinking that maybe Grant was already there, looking for her.

She spotted a lanky-looking guy in a Lakers sweatshirt and faded Levi's lounging near the check-out. He didn't seem to be buying anything, and even though he looked nothing like the photo Grant had posted, she wondered if it could possibly be him. After walking by him a couple of times she finally swooped in for an approach. "You wouldn't be Grant, would you?" she asked, giving him the green-eyed stare that most boys seemed to find irresistible—most boys except Donny, the cheater, and he'd turned out to be the biggest asswipe ever.

The lounger checked her out. He saw an incredibly pretty girl with clouds of dark curls and a killer bod. "That a new pickup line?" he said, looking her up and down.

"Excuse me?" she said, frowning.

"You trying to pick me up?" he repeated, groping in his Levi's for a stick of gum.

"No," she said defensively. "If I was *trying* to pick you up, you'd know it."

"Would I?" he said, peeling off the gum wrapper.

"Bet on it," she answered, using one of her mom's favorite sayings.

Crumpling the wrapper, he tossed it on the ground. "I'm not Grant," he said. "Who is he anyway?"

"My friend."

"Some friend," he said derisively. "You're not even sure what the dude looks like."

She shrugged, attempting to appear casual. "I wondered if you were him, that's all."

"I'm not."

"*Okay*," she said, irritated. "I so get it."

"Right."

"Yes, right."

Boys! They were like *such* a major pain. This one couldn't have been more than eighteen, so he obviously wasn't Grant, although she had to admit he was a real hottie, even if he *was* wearing a Lakers sweatshirt and she was a Clippers fan.

She wandered off, trying to remember whether Grant had said she should wait in her car or not. After a few minutes she glanced at her watch. It was almost one. Crap! Why hadn't they fixed a time? She'd snuck out of the house early in case Lucky changed her mind, and now here she was wandering around a dumb-ass Kmart wasting precious time, because all they had together was two days.

Hmm . . . two days with a perfect stranger.

And what if he wasn't perfect? What if he was some looney dork she hated on sight?

Oh no, that couldn't happen, she'd informed Cookie and Harry she was going to have sex with her Internet dude. But what if she *hated* him?

Grant was twenty-two. She'd told him she was eighteen. He'd probably expect her to be experienced—especially as she'd said she'd recently broken up with her boyfriend. It was one thing communicating with someone via the Internet, but actually meeting them was way different.

Oh double crap! This was turning out to be *so* not such a clever idea. She'd embarked on this adventure full of bravado. Now all that bravado was beginning to crumble.

Maybe she should make a run for it and drive home before Grant appeared.

But how could she? Losing face with Cookie and Harry was *definitely* not on her agenda.

She had to go through with it and that, unfortunately, was that.

19

Getting bored easily was a state of mind, and Anthony Bonar often found himself in that state of mind. He craved action at all times, and after a long meeting with Renee he did not feel like sitting alone with her and Susie for dinner. Susie was a pain in the ass. There was something about her he didn't like and he had a strong hunch the feeling was mutual. He needed some excitement. He was in the mood for a one-night stand—a girl who was sexier than Emmanuelle and more exciting than Carlita. His two mistresses were adequate, but occasionally he desired a new body to play with. Tonight he decided that body should be black.

His requirements were specific. She had to be a knockout, in her twenties, not a whore, and smart.

He informed Renee of his requirements. She nodded, as if finding such a girl was no problem.

He retired to his suite, took a nap, and when he awoke there was a message from Renee that she'd found just the girl for him.

Renee never disappointed.

He joined Renee and Susie for dinner in one of the hotel's restaurants. Susie was a fragile blonde in her forties with birdlike features and a slight facial tic. Her famous country singer husband, Cyrus, had choked to death on a chicken bone six months after their wedding, which was fortunate for Susie, who'd always preferred female company. A year after Cyrus's demise she'd met Renee and true love had bloomed. Anthony was uneasy in their company—the whole dyke thing disturbed him.

The girl Renee had set him up with was half Ethiopian and half Portuguese. She was twenty-nine, six feet tall, and striking in a regal ethnic way. Her name was Tasmin, and according to Renee, she was not a whore, although Anthony wasn't too sure about that. He trusted Renee—but not completely. How had she come up with this exotic creature on such short notice if the girl wasn't a professional?

"Where'd you dig this one up?" he asked Renee when, after dinner, Tasmin excused herself and went off to the ladies' room.

"You said you wanted smart," Renee replied, sipping a hefty brandy. "She's a bank manager, works at the bank I use."

"You gotta be shittin' me?" Anthony spluttered.

"Would I do that to you?" Renee said calmly. "She's very astute and a genius with numbers. I'd love to steal her away to work for me."

"Oh, no no *no!*" interrupted Susie. "I'm not having *her* around you all day."

"Surely you trust me, Susie?" Renee asked.

"Not with *her,*" Susie answered, pouting.

"C'mon, sweetie, don't be like that," Renee said, putting her arm around her girlfriend's shoulders. "You *know* you can trust me."

"I do?" Susie responded, batting her eyelashes. "Perhaps you should try to convince me."

"Christ!" Anthony complained. "Can't you two dykes give it a rest?"

"So *sorry* if we've offended your macho sensibilities," Renee said bitingly as Tasmin returned to the table.

Anthony decided he'd been social for long enough. He leaned toward Tasmin, placing his hand over hers. "Tas, baby," he said, as if they were the oldest of friends. "I hear ya good with numbers. Wanna count how many steps it takes t'get to my suite?"

~ ~ ~

Regal, ethnic Tasmin turned out to be a freak in the bedroom. Anthony had expected hot, but this one was a total fucking maniac, and strong with it. She practically *raped* him.

He was taken by surprise. They arrived in his suite, he opened a bottle of champagne, and suddenly, like a wild tiger, Tasmin sprung into action, ripping off her clothes, grabbing his pants and pulling them down, fastening her mouth on him until he was so hard he thought he might explode.

Then she pushed him—with a great deal of unexpected strength—onto the bed, leapt aboard, and straddled him, going at it like an athlete on their way to the finishing line.

He was too shocked to object. This was a whole new experience for a man who was always on top and always in charge. And come to think of it, it wasn't a bad experience at that. Tasmin certainly knew what she was doing—that is, until she produced a set of gold-plated handcuffs from her purse and attempted to fasten them around his wrists.

"What the fuck ya doin'?" he demanded, hurriedly rolling away from her.

"Relax," she said calmly. "I can promise you'll enjoy the experience. Surely you've tried it before?"

"Not me, honey," he growled. "Enough is enough."

Tasmin was a woman of few words. "Handcuff *me*, then," she ordered. "Handcuff me to the bed and go down on me."

"What?" Anthony spluttered. He was an Italian American macho man with standards, there was no way he'd go down on a woman, that was *their* job, oral sex was all about the woman giving the *man* pleasure. Who did this douche bag think she was dealing with?

"If that's what you're lookin' for, you're outta luck, honey," he said, thinking it was time he got rid of her.

"Why?" she asked boldly. "The taste of pussy frighten you?"

This one was definitely trying his patience. He'd fucked her—or rather, she'd fucked him. Now he wanted her out.

"This little party is over," he said, getting up, walking to the bathroom door and reaching for a bathrobe.

"You think?" Tasmin said, squatting on the bed—all erect nipples and satiny milk chocolate skin.

"I know."

She laughed.

Was she laughing at him?

Would she dare?

"Somethin' funny?" he snarled, giving her a cold-eyed glare.

"You," she replied, coolly swinging her handcuffs back and forth as she knelt on the bed.

"Me, huh?" he said, a slow anger beginning to build within him. "I'm funny, huh?"

"You so-called macho guys from New York and Miami, you're all the same when it comes to sex. Scared little mommy's boys. Mustn't get too down 'n' dirty. Mustn't do bad things or Mommy will spank your little bottom."

Was she talking to *him,* Anthony Bonar? Was this smart-mouthed *puttana* disrespecting *him?*

Hadn't Renee told her who he was? Hadn't Renee warned her to treat him nice?

"Get the fuck out," he said, his voice hard.

"My pleasure, Mr. Nothing," she answered. "I'll go, and you can run on back to Mommy, I'm sure she's waiting for you."

Something snapped. Something bad. He'd had a long day and he didn't need this shit.

Without thinking about the consequences, he went for her, slapping her across the face with the back of his hand, his pinky ring cutting open her cheek.

"You dumb cunt, nobody talks t'me like that," he shouted. "Now GET OUT."

Tasmin had some moves of her own. She'd taken self-defense classes and did not take kindly to being assaulted. She made a fatal mistake. She slapped him back.

That a woman would dare to attack him was beyond his comprehension. The last person who'd physically attacked him had ended up in a ditch with his throat slit.

She must be insane, he thought as he whacked her across the face again, getting blood on the sleeve of his bathrobe.

She was angry too. She fought back, leaping upon him until the two of them fell on the bed, wrestling for the power position.

This woman was one strong motherfucker; she almost had him pinned down.

Bringing his knee up he jammed it into her stomach, grabbed a handful of her hair, and sharply jerked her head back, snapping her neck.

"You fucking *bitch!*" he screamed. "You think you can talk to me like that an' get away with it. You get the fuck outta here *now.*" And he shoved her away from him with all his strength.

She fell onto the floor next to the bed.

Muttering to himself, he went into the bathroom. "You better be outta here by the time I come out," he yelled over his shoulder.

Shrugging off the bathrobe, he stepped into the shower and stood under the cold stinging water, reaching for the soap and thoroughly lathering his cock and balls.

What if she had AIDS? He hadn't used a condom, she hadn't given him time to even think about using one.

JESUS CHRIST! Wait until he got hold of Renee and told her about this. She should be more careful about who she recommended, he was getting too old for this shit. He had Emmanuelle, and Carlita, and he had a wife sitting on her fat ass in Mexico City. So what did he need other whores for? And although Renee had assured him that this one *wasn't* a whore, she'd certainly acted like one.

Now that he got to thinking about it, she was even worse than a whore.

She was supposed to be so smart and intelligent, but in his mind he decided she was nothing but a cheap nympho slut with a bad attitude.

After toweling off, he went back into the bedroom and was surprised to see that she was still there. He couldn't believe it: there she was, lying on the floor exactly where he'd left her.

"I thought I told you to get out," he said harshly.

She didn't reply.

He walked over to her and prodded her in the stomach with the tip of his foot.

She didn't move.

He prodded her again.

Goddamm it! Slowly realization dawned.

The bitch had gone and died on him.

20

"I was thinking we could go out for a quiet dinner, just the two of us," Venus suggested to Billy when he finally called her back.

"Sounds like a plan. Where d'you wanna go?"

"You choose."

"No," he countered, "*you* pick a place. We always end up going where you want anyway."

"That's not true," she said quickly.

"Yes it is."

"No, Billy, it's not."

There was a short silence while they both decided whether they wanted this to turn into a fight or not.

Venus decided not. "How about the Ivy?" she said.

"Paparazzi frenzy," he groaned, not relishing the thought of being chased down the street by a crazed pack of jackal-like photographers intent on getting the worst photos.

"Spago?"

"Not feeling it tonight."

"Where, then?"

"Dunno. Surprise me."

She put down the phone, annoyed. Billy was the man in the relationship; why did *she* have to make all the decisions? Surely *he* was supposed to surprise *her?* Her former husband, the legendary cocksman Cooper Turner, had spent half of their marriage surprising her, until one memorable day *she'd* surprised him banging her stand-in while he was visiting the set of one of her movies.

Cooper had suffered from that well-known male affliction, the zipper problem. What a disappointment he'd turned out to be.

That was one of the things she liked about Billy: he didn't have the zipper problem. Oh yes, when they were out and about at various events and he was surrounded by beautiful, sexy women, he looked, but as far as she knew, he never took it any further. Nor did she for that matter, and she had plenty of opportunities. There were always hunky backup dancers around, hot male costars, horny producers and directors—they were all within her radar, but she was never tempted.

Venus was a one-man woman, and right now Billy was her man.

~ ~ ~

"*What* sounds like a plan?" Kev asked, wandering into the kitchen.

"You listening in on my phone conversations?" Billy responded, shoving his cell phone into the back pocket of his jeans.

"If it's a private deal, you'll tell me to bug off," Kev said, helping himself to a cold beer from the fridge.

"Dinner with Venus, that's the plan."

"Didn't you say you wanted to stay home tonight and watch the game on that frickin' giant-screen TV you had delivered yesterday?"

"Yeah, that was the original plan," Billy said, stifling a yawn. "But now Venus wants to go out to dinner."

"How come?"

"Waddya mean, how come?" Billy said, frowning. "She's my girlfriend, for chrissakes. Gotta do what the girlfriend wants."

"How come?" Kev repeated.

"What's *up* with you? Stop repeatin' yourself like a freakin' parrot."

"Nothin's up with me."

"There's something on your mind."

"Maybe."

"Spit it out, asshole."

"It's just that it gets on my tits seein' it, that's all," Kev blurted.

"Seeing *what?*" Billy asked, exasperated.

"Y'know, seein' you turning into one of those pussy-whipped dudes," Kev said, taking a swig of beer from the can, then wiping his mouth with the back of his hand.

"Me?" Billy said, outraged. "Pussy-whipped? You gotta be jerking me off."

"Venus calls, you cancel everything an' run. It's all wrong."

"So I'm missing the game, big freakin' deal," Billy said, walking into the living room.

"S' not the point," Kev said, following him. "Guys gotta be in charge, otherwise girls trample all over 'em."

"Since when did *you* become an expert on relationships?" Billy said, flopping down on the couch.

"I know what I see."

"Screw you, Kev. I *am* in charge."

"Yeah?" Kev said disbelievingly.

"Yeah," Billy responded, wishing Kev would shut his big mouth.

"Then if you're in charge, why doncha stay home an' watch the game? Y'know it's what you wanna do."

"No, Kev, it's what *you* wanna do."

"Not me," Kev said, shrugging. "I got a date. But if I *did* want to see the game, I'd cancel her ass so fast she wouldn't know what hit her."

"You would, huh?"

"'Course."

"Then do it."

"Do what?"

"Cancel her. I'll do the same."

"Yeah?"

"Pussy-whipped my ass," Billy muttered.

"You really want me to cancel my hot date?" Kev said, not quite sure he believed him.

Billy threw him a long, cool stare. "Do I look like I'm lyin'?"

~ ~ ~

First Venus tried on a slinky black Dolce & Gabbana dress, then she decided it was way too fancy for a casual dinner with her boyfriend. Jeans were more Billy's style, tight low-slung jeans worn with high boots and a plain white tee. She put the outfit together and paraded in front of the mirror, immediately realizing it was too casual—more suitable for lunch at the beach. She'd had her assistant book a table at Giorgio's, and although the Italian restaurant was near the ocean, it wasn't beach style. Last time she'd been there she'd run into Tom Hanks, Charlie Dollar, and Steven Spielberg, so she had to look her best. That was one of the major setbacks of being a star: everyone was ready to criticize.

How was she looking, they all wanted to know. Old? Fat? Lifted? Botoxed? If she looked good she got accused of all of the above. And if she looked like crap she was accused of letting herself go.

It was a no-win situation. The perils of being a superstar.

She finally decided on black matador pants, suede boots, a red cashmere shell, and a short black Armani jacket. Casual but chic. Sexy but not over the top. Billy would like it.

Her cell rang. Private line. Billy.

"Hey," he said.

"Hey," she responded.

"Uh . . . would you be mad if we didn't go out tonight?"

"What?" she said, shocked that he was obviously about to cancel.

"I'm still kinda beat up from that session with Alex, an' I just got an early call for tomorrow, so . . ." He trailed off, waiting for her to say something.

She summoned her pride and put on an okay voice, although inside she was seething. “Fine,” she said, and then because she couldn’t help herself she added, “Do you want me to come over?” *Oh God! How needy!*

“That’s okay,” he said. “I’m gonna get an early night, catch up on sleep.”

“Then I guess we’ll talk later?” she said, realizing that begging him to call back was even more needy.

“You got it, babe.”

She put down the phone and let out a primal scream. “Son of a *bitch!*” she yelled. “How dare you treat me like this! How fucking dare you!”

And then a little voice in her head whispered, *He’s treating you like this because you’re allowing him to. Cut your losses and end it while you can.*

But she didn’t want to end it.

She was in love, and how sad was *that*?

21

The Volvo broke down in the middle of nowhere. The engine spluttered and after a few moments the car shuddered to a halting stop.

Henry was nonplussed—he didn't know what to do. First he checked the gas gauge. Almost a full tank. Next he got out of the car and inspected the tires. They were all in good shape. Gingerly he popped the hood to take a look. Not that he knew what he was searching for, the mechanics of how a car ran had never interested him.

Damn! This was not the way he'd planned it. After a smooth and uneventful drive he was supposed to arrive in Big Bear, find the girl, and take her to the old family cabin nobody had used since his father died. Nobody except him. Over the last month he'd made two daytime trips there. Best to be prepared, and once they reached the cabin he certainly was. After that it was anyone's guess what would happen.

This was an exploratory trip to meet her, find out more information about her mother, and decide how best to pay back Lucky Santangelo for depriving him of the career he should've had—the career Billy Melina had stolen from him.

Now this unexpected setback.

He reached for his cell to summon the Automobile Club roadside assistance.

His phone flashed a *No Service* message.

Henry kicked the side of his car. He was filled with a burning sense of frustration.

It was fast becoming apparent that he was stranded and there was absolutely nothing he could do about it.

~ ~ ~

By three P.M. Max was thoroughly fed up. She'd explored the Kmart aisle by aisle, perused countless magazines, bought a couple of CDs, lingered by the makeup shelves, and now she was seriously thinking of getting in her car and driving back to L.A. because what was the point of being stuck in Big Bear with nothing to do and no Internet guy in sight?

How stupid they both were, she and Grant. They had not fixed an exact time and they had not exchanged cell phone numbers, so how were they supposed to communicate?

She tried to recall their last exchange of words. *Meet me in the Kmart parking lot,* he'd written. *Stay in your car, I'll find you.*

Like exactly *how* was he supposed to find her when he probably didn't even remember what car she was driving?

Dumb! Dumb! Dumb!

He'd mentioned that he drove a jeep, and she'd told him she would be arriving in Big Bear in the afternoon. Maybe he wasn't expecting her until four or five, and that's why he hadn't appeared yet.

She wandered outside and ran straight into Mister Hottie—the dude in the Lakers sweatshirt.

"Whoa!" he said, coming to a stop. "Still lookin' for Grant?"

"Do you *know* Grant?" she asked suspiciously.

"No. But he's gotta be some kinda dumb-ass if he's standing *you* up."

"Who said he's standing me up?" she demanded, green eyes flashing.

"Gimme a break. He's not here, is he? So the dude's gotta be a loser."

"No way," she said, jutting out her chin. "He'll be here soon."

"Where'd you hook up with him anyway?"

"We met on the Internet," she blurted. "We're supposed to get together today. It's my fault—I must've messed up on the time."

"Are you tellin' me you don't even *know* this loser?"

"Yes, I know him," she answered defensively.

"Seems like you don't."

"Yes, I *do*," she said, checking out Mister Hottie for the second time that day. He was annoyingly argumentative, with dazzling blue eyes and an appealing cleft in the middle of his chin. Tall too, and major cute.

Once again she wished he was Grant. But no such luck, he obviously wasn't.

"So," he said, squinting at her. "While you're waiting for loser of the year, wanna go get an ice cream?"

"Ice cream!" she exclaimed. "What are you, *eight?*"

He threw back his head and laughed, giving her a chance to admire his very white teeth. "Never too old for ice cream," he said, "an' you look like you could swallow something sweet."

Was he talking dirty to her? She wasn't sure, boys were always coming out with stuff that sounded vaguely rude.

"I suppose I wouldn't mind a coffee," she said guardedly, realizing that she hadn't eaten all day, and coffee was hardly going to do it. She required a big, fat, juicy burger and a double-thick shake.

"I'll buy you a coffee if you tell me your name," he said, kicking a stray leaf into the gutter.

"Max," she said, still sizing him up. "What's yours?"

"Ace," he replied, still checking her out.

"That's an odd name."

"An' Max isn't?" he said, rubbing his chin.

"Max is a perfectly normal name," she said tartly.

"For a guy."

"Well, here's the thing," she confessed. "I used to be Maria. Changed it to Max when I was nine."

"How come?"

"Who wants to be reminded of *The Sound of Music* every time they hear their name? Not me. Changed it, and refused to answer if anyone called me anything else."

"Your parents have anythin' to say 'bout that?"

"They got the message."

"So even at nine you had it goin' on."

She giggled. "I guess."

He started to walk. "There's a Starbucks down the street," he said. "I'll buy you that coffee."

"Cool," she said, following him because she had nothing better to do. Besides, there was something likable about him, and it wasn't just that he was hot. He had a quirky attitude and plenty of confidence. In a way he reminded her of herself.

Hmm . . . maybe she should dump Mr. Internet and stick with this one.

She wondered if he had a girlfriend, if he was out of school, and what he was doing hanging around Kmart all day.

He walked fast on long legs, and she had to hop and skip to keep up. "You like the Lakers?" she asked.

"Somebody gave me the shirt. I'm not into following teams."

"You're not?" she said, slightly breathless.

"It's a fat waste of time unless I'm playing."

"What *do* you play?"

"Soccer."

"Are you brilliant?"

"When I want t'be."

"When's that?"

"Jeez," he said, shaking his head. "You sure ask a shitload of questions."

"Oh, like *you* don't," she responded.

"Here's a question for you," he said, stopping for a moment. "How old are you?"

"Eighteen," she lied. "How about you?"

"Nineteen."

"So you're out of school?"

"You too, right?"

"Oh yeah," she said, adding another lie while staring at the cleft in his chin wondering what it would be like to kiss him.

"I'm guessing you don't live around here," he said, starting to walk again.

"Do you?" she countered.

"Why d'you answer a question with another question?" he said, looking perplexed.

" 'Cause I'm naturally curious."

"*Nosy* is the word you're searchin' for."

"How rude!"

"No, honest."

"What are you doing anyway? I know why *I'm* hanging around. How about you?"

He stopped again, turning to face her. "You see that bank over there," he said matter-of-factly.

She glanced across the street. "Yes."

"Well . . . here's the deal," he said, taking a long beat. "I'm plannin' on robbing it."

~ ~ ~

"This is what I like t'do," Gino announced, clearing his throat. "Haul my ass outta bed real late, take an afternoon nap, watch a coupla those cop shows on TV, suck down a few inches of Jack, have a fine meal with my old lady, an' hit the sack nice 'n' early."

"It's all about your bed," Lucky observed.

"Yeah, kiddo, an' when you're ninety somethin' it'll be all 'bout yours."

She smiled. "There's a bottle of Jack Daniel's in your room. And guess what? I'm cooking dinner myself—pasta and meatballs, your favorite."

"What a girl!" he exclaimed, grinning. "If only your mother had lived to see how you turned out."

Inexplicably her eyes filled with tears. She wasn't a crier, but how often did she get a one-on-one with Gino, and how often did he talk about her mom? Practically never. She'd always figured it was too upsetting for him to reminisce about Maria, but since *he* was the one who'd brought it up, maybe now was the time to pursue it.

"I guess you've never stopped missing her," she said softly.

"I miss her every single day," he sighed. "My Maria was the best. Y'know, kiddo, I still think about her all the time."

"So do I," Lucky murmured. "I remember her skin, it was so smooth, and she always smelled like rose petals."

"That she did," Gino said, nodding.

"Every night she would read to me and Dario. She loved this English author—Enid Blyton—and she'd read these crazy stories about a magic faraway tree with special powers and strange lands at the top of the tree where you could run around doing anything."

"Gave you ideas, huh?" Gino chuckled.

"Mama always told me girls can do anything."

"An' boy, did you follow her advice!"

"I was five when she was murdered," Lucky said sadly. "Only five . . . but I've never forgotten her."

"I know, sweetheart, I know . . ." he said, opening his arms.

Suddenly she found herself nestling close to the man she'd spent so many years feuding with, and now he was old—although he was still sharp. But she knew that one of these days in the not-so-distant future she'd have to say good-bye and it broke her heart.

Gino Junior came barging into the room, interrupting their moment of closeness. "When's dinner?" he asked. "Let's go, Mom, I'm starving."

Lucky broke away from her father and composed herself. "You're not starving," she admonished. "And since I'm heading for the kitchen, I could do with some help."

"Mom . . ." Gino Junior groaned.

"You can learn to roll meatballs the Italian way. You'll enjoy it, trust me."

"Grandpa . . ." Gino Junior said, appealing to his grandfather to save him.

Gino Senior obliged. "Give the kid a break," he rasped. "Paige'll help you. She's always bin pretty adept at rollin' balls."

Lucky shook her head and tried not to smile. Gino was an original, no doubt about that.

~ ~ ~

Henry waved down a truck and slipped the driver a hundred bucks to find out what was wrong with his car.

He'd been attempting to wave cars down for two hours, and this was the first driver who'd stopped. Henry hadn't given him much choice, he'd practically flung himself in front of the oncoming truck.

After the driver had finished bitching and complaining about Henry forcing him to pull up so abruptly, Henry had handed him the hundred-dollar bill, and the truck driver had done a full inspection. Finding nothing mechanical, he'd eventually discovered that the gas gauge was faulty—stuck on half-full, while the gas tank was actually empty.

"You're outta gas," the truck driver announced, scratching his hairy belly under an I DIG FAT CHICKS T-shirt.

Henry frowned. Damn Markus. The man was lazy. Surely he must have known the gas gauge was faulty? After all, it was his *job* to know.

Henry glared at the truck driver as if *he* was to blame. "What am I supposed to do?" he whined.

"For another hundred I can fix ya up with a can of gas," the truck driver offered. "My emergency supply."

Well aware he was being taken advantage of, Henry agreed. He had no choice.

22

Anthony and Renee stood over Tasmin's lifeless body, both of them gazing down at the naked girl, Renee in disbelief and shock, Anthony full of anger that this had happened.

"You broke her neck," Renee stated.

"She fuckin' attacked me," Anthony responded. "For a moment there I thought she was gonna pull a piece on me."

"The woman is naked, and *you* thought she had a gun?" Renee said, shaking her head in disgust.

"What the *fuck* was I supposed t'do?" he said, impatient to get the hell out of Vegas and far away from this situation, which was bugging the shit out of him. "Jesus *Christ*, Renee, this is *your* fuckin' fault, you set me up with her."

"You kill a girl and it's *my* fault," Renee said, stoney-faced.

"You'd better arrange to dispose of the body," Anthony said flatly. "No way can I be involved in this."

"Damn you, Anthony," Renee said, her voice rising. "This isn't some bimbo we're talking about. This is a respectable woman with a high-powered job and a kid at home. How am I supposed to cover *this* up? You're in big trouble, Anthony."

He turned to her, his eyes like two pieces of cold steel. "*I'm* in trouble? You think *I'm* responsible for this shit?"

"If you're not, who is?"

"She acted like a fuckin' lunatic," he said, starting to yell. "An' she ended up gettin' what she deserved."

"Sure," Renee muttered, "and you're just an innocent party."

"What's your fuckin' problem?" he shouted, his face darkening.

"You were too rough with her, any fool can see that."

"You gotta be fuckin' *shittin'* me!" he exploded. "The broad was a sex freak."

"You're a big boy, you could've handled yourself without killing her."

"Let me tell you somethin', Renee," Anthony said, outraged that he was being forced to explain himself. "She wanted me to lick her fuckin' pussy. Ya think there's any way in hell I'd lower myself an' do that shit?"

"Going down on a woman is a normal sex act," Renee said, hating the very sight of him.

"Maybe to you," he spat. "But there's nothin' fuckin' normal 'bout you."

"Is that why you broke her neck—because of some macho Italian code of ethics?"

"How many times I gotta tell ya—she fuckin' attacked me for no reason," he said harshly, wondering why he was bothering to continue this conversation. "I hadda defend myself, she's six feet tall an' strong as a fuckin' horse. You take care of it, Renee, like I took care of you when you had to get outta Colombia in a hurry. Remember?"

Yes, she remembered all right. He'd helped her leave, and he'd also helped himself to half the cash Oscar had stashed. Then when she and Susie had put together the money to build the Cavendish, he'd declared himself a silent partner. No paperwork involved, simply a monthly payout in cash.

"I take care of this and we're even," Renee said flatly. "Score settled."

"What the fuck *you* so uptight about?" he demanded.

"Tasmin was a smart, beautiful woman. Look what you've done to her. Don't you have any remorse?"

"For chrissakes!" he roared. "She was nothin' but a crazy freak."

"Your idea of a freak and mine differ," Renee snapped.

"I bet," he sneered. "You'd feast on pussy all day long if you had your way."

"Nice," Renee said coldly. "Real nice."

"Don't you forget who helped you when you needed it," he warned. "Take care of this mess, use your most trusted people. I'm gettin' outta here—deal with it."

Anthony left the problem of Tasmin's lifeless body with Renee and took off. He had no feelings of guilt. Renee owed him and now it was payback time.

The Grill drove him to the airport in one of the hotel's cars. Even though he still had things to take care of in Vegas, he knew this wasn't the time to linger. Best to distance himself and get out quickly.

Once he was safely on his plane and it had taken off for New York, he called his wife.

"What's goin' on?" he said gruffly.

"Where are you, Anthony?" Irma asked. "When will you be home?"

"I'll let you know." A long beat. "You miss me?"

Irma was shocked; it was so unlike her husband to ask her such a question. "Yes," she said stiffly, hesitating for only a second or two.

He decided she didn't sound like she meant it, and after he hung up, he got to wondering what Irma did all day. The kids were in Miami with their nanny and Francesca; the house in Mexico City was taken care of by his coterie of servants; so how *did* Irma keep herself occupied?

She probably went shopping, spent his money, and indulged in massages and manicures. Womanly pastimes, that's all she was capable of.

For a moment he felt sorry for her. At least she was a normal woman who'd never requested any depraved sexual acts from him. Goddammit, she was his wife, she'd better not.

Next he phoned Emmanuelle. "What's goin' on, sweet-ass?" he asked, thinking of her undulating sun-kissed body and luscious lips, and wondering why he'd gone elsewhere when Emmanuelle was always available.

"I just finished shooting the cover for *Crude Oil* magazine," Emmanuelle said excitedly. "Isn't that the *best!*"

"Yeah?" he questioned, not so sure he liked her posing for magazine covers where every asshole on the street could ogle her spectacular body. "What didja wear?"

"*Veree* short Daisy Dukes and kind of a skimpy bra," she said, her voice low and seductive. "*Veree* sexy. You'll *love* the photos."

"You'd better not love the photographer," Anthony warned. "It better be a woman."

"No, honey bunch," Emmanuelle cooed, purposely pissing him off because she got a kick out of making him jealous. "It was a super-sexy Latin *man*."

"Don't fuck with me, Emmanuelle," Anthony growled. "I ain't in the mood."

He put the phone down and thought briefly about Carlita before calling his man in New York. "Any news?"

"Too soon, boss. Nothin' to report."

Could it be that he was wrong about Carlita?

Maybe.

Maybe not.

Now he had to think about what he was going to tell Francesca. She'd expect to hear that everything was in line to sabotage the opening of Lucky Santangelo's hotel, only in view of what had taken place he wasn't so sure about Renee. She was pissed because he'd accidentally killed some freaky bitch, and even worse—she'd refused to admit that it was all her fault for putting them together in the first place.

Too fuckin' bad. She'd better get over it and fast, because once the body was taken care of he would be back in Vegas calling *all* the shots.

And that's exactly the way it should be.

~ ~ ~

After speaking to her husband, Irma experienced a moment of sheer panic. Did Anthony suspect something? Did Anthony *know?*

She assured herself that she was being paranoid—there was no chance of Anthony suspecting anything. How could he? She was beyond discreet, never bringing Luis in the house when any of the servants were around, always making sure to lock the bedroom door so no one could accidentally intrude.

The only way for Anthony to find out would be if he walked in on them, and that could never happen because Anthony always informed her in advance when he was coming home. He did this because he expected her to have everything ready for him. He insisted that the kitchen was fully stocked with all his favorite foods; his two Dobermans had to be sent to the vet to be bathed and groomed; plus he expected her to put together a series of fancy dinner parties for his friends.

Well, Anthony called them friends. Irma called them a bunch of suck-up freeloaders who laughed at Anthony's jokes and sat around watching him admiringly whenever he decided to entertain them with his not-so-brilliant karaoke skills. Karaoke was his favorite way of amusing himself, but only as long as he had an adoring audience fawning all over him.

No, Anthony would *never* surprise her. He wanted everyone on alert when *he* came home.

She walked to the window and glanced outside.

Luis was busy working on the grounds.

Immediately she experienced a rush of excitement. Just looking at the man made her heart beat faster.

Luis was her savior.

Luis made every day worth living.

Later she would invite him up to the house.

She could hardly wait.

~ ~ ~

When Anthony was eleven and more or less existing on the streets of Naples, he'd stabbed a man. He wasn't sure whether he'd killed the man or not, but he'd certainly experienced an overpowering rush of adrenaline—especially when he'd bent over the fallen man and extracted his wallet from his jacket pocket.

Stuffing the wallet down his pants, Anthony had raced off down the street like a deer. *Run fast, never let 'em catch you,* that was his motto.

Most of the time he hung out with a gang of kids who all came from one-parent families. They watched out for each other, sometimes robbing tourists and other unsuspecting civilians. Anthony led the pack; even at such a young age he was a born leader.

Arriving in America at the age of twelve, and spending time with his grandfather, Anthony had soon realized that in America anything was possible. Enzio Bonnatti had taught him a lot, and he was sad when the old man got himself shot, but he was happy Enzio had shown him a way of living that brought great rewards.

Although Tasmin's death was accidental—and nobody could prove otherwise—Anthony had no regrets. She'd been asking for it with her kinky requests.

His only problem was Renee. The old dyke better not give him any shit, because if she did, he had ways of dealing with her.

Nobody fucked with Anthony Bonar and got away with it. And if Renee was smart, she'd definitely keep that in mind.

23

"What's up?" Venus asked over the phone.

"What's up is I'm knee-deep in ground beef, tomato sauce, bread crumbs, and garlic," Lucky answered, cradling the phone under her chin.

"You are? Why's that?"

"'Cause I'm making my famous Italian-style meatballs. Remember I told you I'm cooking a big blowout dinner for Gino and everyone? They're all here, the entire family, and I'm loving every second of playing Mama. How's that for a switch?"

"Can I come over?"

"I thought you and Billy were all set for a romantic night on the town?" Lucky said, squeezing a tube of tomato paste into the bowl.

"We were," Venus said, trying to sound like she didn't care. "That is until Billy bailed on me, and now I really need to talk."

"You do?" Lucky said, because family dinner and Venus pouring her heart out was not a perfect combination.

However, she rallied, because Venus was her best friend and she knew if the situation were reversed Venus would be there for her.

"Sure, come on over," she said warmly. "Gino would love to see you, and Bobby's gonna be thrilled."

"*Little* Bobby?"

"Not so little anymore," Lucky pointed out. "And hands *off*. Remember who he is."

"Oh sure," Venus said with a dry chuckle. "Like I'm about to make a move on your son. I don't think so."

"I don't think so either, so let's keep it that way."

"Yes, *ma'am*."

"And don't dress up, it's super casual, and bring your appetite."

"Any more instructions?"

"Nope, that's it for now."

"Okay, I've got it. Hands off Bobby. Skanky old jeans. Enormous passion for meatballs."

Lucky laughed. "We'll talk, but it'll have to be later, okay?"

"Sounds like a plan," Venus said, then after a long beat she added, "It's just that I don't think I can be alone tonight."

"I understand."

Venus put down the phone. She felt as if she was thirteen and her big high-school crush was crapping all over her. Why, oh why, had she allowed herself to fall in love with Billy? They hadn't even been together a year and he was pulling away, she sensed it, and it was driving her nuts.

Well, screw him, she thought, attempting to pull herself together. She was Venus Maria, superstar. She would *never* let him see her crumble, however much it hurt.

~ ~ ~

"This is freakin' great!" Billy exclaimed, lounging on the couch in his underwear and a T-shirt in front of his new big-screen high-definition TV munching popcorn and scratching his crotch.

"Told ya," Kevin boasted. "You can pick your nose, hang a fart, change channels, do whatever the fuck ya want. An' no little lady gettin' on your case."

"It rocks."

"Sure it does. And . . ." Kev paused for a moment before continuing. "If ya start feelin' horny later, I got a number I can call that'll send a coupla girls over to do anything your dick desires. No questions asked."

"Hookers?"

"Highly paid young ladies."

Billy hesitated, then: "I'm not into paying for it, Kev. That's not my bag."

"I know that, an' everyone knows you don't have to. But sometimes it's the convenient way. They come. They go. No hassles."

"Look, just 'cause I'm takin' a night off doesn't mean Venus and me are through. We're very much together."

"Yeah, I get it. But sometimes banging a girl you paid for can be a kick."

"Thanks, but I'm not into cheating."

Kev shrugged. "Whatever swings your balls."

For a moment Billy flashed on the girl he'd picked up at Tower Records. He felt guilty, but the good news was that no one knew, and he wasn't about to tell. The girl was a one-off, a lack of judgment on his part.

He redirected his attention to the TV, stuffed his face with a handful of popcorn, and settled back to enjoy the game.

~ ~ ~

Venus liked to drive herself whenever she could dodge the paparazzi who lurked outside her gates day and night waiting for her to emerge. A few months ago she'd come up with the perfect escape plan, eliciting the help of a friendly neighbor—a stoned record producer who'd allowed her to build an illegal underground tunnel into his garage, where she kept a dark blue Phaeton with blacked-out windows. Whenever she didn't feel like being followed she used the tunnel and took out the anonymous Phaeton, zooming past the hapless paparazzi who had no clue that it was her in the car.

Tonight she hurried through her escape tunnel, got in the car, and revved up the Phaeton—her low-key luxury vehicle. Outsmarting the paparazzi gave her a big charge. Fuck 'em. Oh sure, they had a job to do, but did they have to do it 24/7? It made her especially mad when Chyna was with her, and they stuck cameras in her child's face.

Cooper didn't seem to care. He was always allowing himself to be photographed with his cute and somewhat precocious little daughter. There they were in *People* and *Us* strolling down Rodeo eating ice cream, sitting courtside at the Lakers game, picking up shells on the beach in Malibu. Recently he'd added Mandy—his teenage girlfriend—to his family outings. Mandy was a publicity-crazy nineteen-year-old wannabe singer/actress/model, and Venus did not want her daughter being around the girl.

"It's not healthy for Chyna to be exposed to so much media," she'd complained to Cooper, carefully not mentioning Mandy's name.

"Look who's talking," Cooper had responded. "You're *queen* of the media, running around all over town with your young stud. Were you banging him when we were together?"

"No, Cooper—*you* were the one out getting laid. Remember?"

Another nasty verbal battle had then taken place, which was exactly what Venus didn't want. There was nothing worse for Chyna than having to watch her divorced parents fight.

At least their daughter was safely away at summer camp, and according to her e-mails and phone calls, she was having a fantastic time.

~ ~ ~

"Shit!" Billy exclaimed.

"What?" Kev responded.

"I think I got a problem."

Kev burped and loped into the kitchen to fetch another beer.

Billy rolled off the couch and followed him. "Aren't you listening to me?" he said, scratching his crotch. "You're supposed to listen to me."

"I'm listening," Kev said, popping the top off a bottle of imported Carlsberg. "You got a freakin' problem. Spit it out."

"Like *you* care."

Kev took a swig of beer before giving his full attention to his best friend and employer. "Spill. What's the problem?"

"I think," Billy said, vigorously scratching away, "I got me a case of the freakin' crabs."

24

"You're joking, aren't you?" Max said, staring at Ace wide-eyed.

"What do *you* think?" he answered with a sly grin.

"I think you're putting me on," she said, struggling to remain cool in the face of his confession.

"Why's that?" he asked, staring her down.

" 'Cause if you *were* planning on robbing a bank for real," she said, narrowing her eyes, "there's no way you'd tell me."

"Why not?" he said, shrugging. "It's not as if there's anything you can do about it."

"I could go to the cops," she answered boldly.

"An' tell 'em *what*?" he said, full of bravado.

"That . . . y'know . . ." She trailed off, aware that if she went to the cops she'd probably sound like a crazy person. And why *would* she go to the cops anyway? It wasn't her business what he planned to do.

"Yeah, go on," he said, encouraging her.

"You're like eff-ing with me," she said.

"If that's what you think."

She didn't know what to think. But at least he was keeping her occupied until Internet Guy put in an appearance—that's if the jerk ever showed up.

They were standing outside Starbucks, and Ace made a move to go inside.

Max stood her ground. "I've decided I don't want a coffee," she said petulantly. "I'm incredibly hungry. I need like real food."

"Am I stopping you from eating?" he said, giving her a quizzical look.

"Y'know what?" she said boldly. "There's no need to sweat it, I can buy my own burger. All you have to do is point me in the direction of someplace that serves food, then go rob your bank."

"Oh, Miss Cool," he said, grinning, "doesn't give a fast crap."

"It's not as if I believe you," she said, tossing back her long hair.

"Nobody said you had to," he answered. "An' by the way, how long you planning on waitin' around for your loser friend? 'Cause it looks t'me like he's a no-show."

"He'll be here," she said stubbornly.

"I sure hope so—otherwise it seems *I'm* stuck with you."

"Wow!" she said, green eyes flashing danger. "You certainly have a high opinion of yourself."

"How's that?"

"What makes you think you're *stuck* with me? I'm getting something to eat, then driving back to L.A."

"You can't do that," he said, straight-faced.

"Why not?"

"'Cause I might wanna use your car as my getaway vehicle. Y'know, after I rob the bank an' all."

"*Whaaat?*"

"Hey—idea," he said, laughing. "Maybe you could be my getaway *driver*."

"You're looney-tunes," she said, shaking her head in exasperation.

"You're not exactly sane," he countered.

"*Excuse* me?" she said, thinking that although she hardly knew him, she was beginning to like him. A lot.

"Picking up some whacked-out loser on the Internet," he continued. "Whaddya gonna *do* with him if he does appear?"

"You don't want to know," she said in what she hoped was a mysterious tone.

"I get it," Ace said, "you're gonna make out with this dude."

"None of your business."

"I'm guessin'. Boyfriend dumps you, an' this is your way of gettin' back at him. Am I on the right track?"

Max glared at him, deciding she didn't like him after all. How dare he be such a smart-ass. And how dare he figure out exactly what she was up to.

~ ~ ~

The dinner was great; everyone cleaned their plates. Lucky caught Lennie's eye across the table and he winked at her, assuring her that the family reunion was progressing smoothly. Lennie was her rock, always there, always positive.

Gino sat at the head of the table flanked by Venus on one side and Brigette on the other. Gino might be almost ninety-five, but he could still appreciate a beautiful woman, and Venus and Brigette were the cream.

Bobby was on the other side of Venus, then Lucky, and next to her sat her half-brother, Steven, his wife, Lina—the vivacious English ex-supermodel—and their exquisite little daughter, Carioca. Paige was next to Carioca, then Gino Junior and Lennie.

The family were all present except for Leonardo who was at the same summer camp as Chyna, and Max—who Lucky realized had not bothered to check in. Two black marks against Max. First one for leaving without saying good-bye. Second one for not calling.

Lucky decided that when her daughter got back—and it had better be in time for Gino's party—they were due for a major sitdown.

"I'd like to propose a toast," Gino said, tapping the side of his wineglass with a fork. The table fell silent. "My daughter," he continued, "is not only beautiful, smart, an' one hell of a wife an' mother—she could get herself a job in an Italian restaurant any day. These friggin' meatballs." He kissed the tips of his fingers and made a sucking noise. "*Bellissimo! Fantastico!*" He raised his glass, and his dark eyes met Lucky's. "To my daughter. Always remember, kiddo, girls can do anything. An' I do mean you."

Lucky felt a sudden rush of emotion. For Gino to be so open with his feelings—especially in front of everyone—was not an everyday occurrence.

"Uh . . . thanks, Gino," she managed, then lightening up she added, "Didn't know my meatballs would have such an effect."

There was much laughter, then Bobby raised his glass to toast his grandfather. Soon everyone was adding comments and having fun.

Lucky looked around the table and felt fortunate to be part of such an interesting and sometime loving family. They were all individuals, but tonight everyone seemed to fit.

Later the family gathered in the large living room, catching up. Steven was talking away to Gino. Brigette and Lina, who'd once modeled together, were exchanging horror stories from their past. Carioca fell asleep with her head on Paige's knee, while Lennie, Bobby, and Gino Junior went outside onto the terrace and started up a challenging game of table tennis.

Finally Lucky had a chance to talk to Venus, who'd been quiet all night, which was so unlike her.

"What's up?" Lucky asked, pouring her friend a liqueur glass of limoncello, Venus's favorite after-dinner drink.

"Instinct. A feeling," Venus replied, gesturing vaguely. "Nothing concrete."

"Instinct about *what*?"

"Billy, of course," Venus sighed.

"I thought the two of you were blissfully happy—what with his big cock and old soul."

"Don't remind me," Venus said, rolling her eyes.

"Well, c'mon, what happened?" Lucky pressed. "Did you have a fight?"

"No, nothing like that."

"Then *what?*"

"Like I said, instinct."

"That's not enough for me to comment on," Lucky said, pouring herself a shot of limoncello. "You've got to give me more than that."

"Okay," Venus said patiently. "Here's the deal. We were supposed to go out tonight, have a quiet dinner together, then just as I was getting dressed, he called to cancel."

"What did he say?"

"He told me he was tired, and that Alex had given him an early call for tomorrow. That's it."

"Hey, if he has an early call, it's understandable, right?"

"I guess," Venus said unsurely. "But then I offered to come over to his place, and he said no."

"That's understandable too. Would you want someone coming over when you've got an early call? You of all people should know what it's like."

"I'm getting the distinct impression you're on his side," Venus said irritably.

"No way," Lucky responded. "But I get it."

"I wish I did," Venus said, downing her limoncello in one swift gulp.

"You've got to give him space," Lucky said, willing her friend to snap out of the ridiculous girly funk she was obviously in. This wasn't like the Venus she knew.

"Why's that?"

" 'Cause if you don't, he's gonna feel crowded. And if you understand anything about men, they're all shit-scared of any hint of commitment. That's when they run. You know, 'It's not you, it's me,' and all that crap they come out with."

"I think I know why he's acting like this," Venus mused. "It's all this press stuff that never stops. Morons writing trash about us, delving into our innermost thoughts. We need to get away to some unreachable island."

"Nowhere's unreachable today," Lucky pointed out. "They'll follow you with their long-range lenses and there'll be even more photos."

"I'm just . . . I dunno," Venus said, gesturing helplessly. "I guess I'm depressed."

"Billy cancels one dinner and you're depressed," Lucky said. "This isn't like you, Venus. Where's the kick-ass girl I used to know?"

"It's not just him backing out of one dinner. He's pulling away, I can feel it."

"Oh, for God's sake, you're not a kid," Lucky snapped, fast running out of sympathy. "Why don't you *ask* him what's going on."

" 'Cause if I ask, he might say he doesn't want to be with me anymore. Then what?"

"Then you'll hook up with somebody else," Lucky said patiently.

"It's not that easy."

"You've never had a problem before."

"I know, but this time I've done something really foolish."

"C'mon, let's hear it, what now?"

"I've gone and fallen in love."

~ ~ ~

Finally Henry made it to Big Bear. He drove directly to the Kmart parking lot, got out of his car, and looked around. He seemed to remember that Max said she drove a BMW, but he couldn't recall if she'd mentioned what color it was. He knew he'd recognize her once he saw her, because she'd posted her picture and he had a copy in his wallet. She resembled a very young version of Lucky Santangelo, the woman who'd stolen his future.

Oh yes, he was about to make sure that Lucky's daughter paid dearly for her mother's mistake.

He limped into the store cursing his bad leg, for there were times he yearned to move faster. He'd been dealt a bad hand, although not quite as bad as his dearly departed father.

He moved slowly, checking out the aisles one by one, realizing that they hadn't fixed a time, and since it was now late afternoon, would she have waited for him to arrive?

Why not? he reasoned. After all, she'd come all this way.

A large black woman brushed against him. He hissed an insult under his breath.

The woman heard him and stopped abruptly. "*What* you say?" she demanded, several wobbly chins quivering with indignation. "What you *damn* say?"

"I wasn't talking to you," he muttered.

"You'd better watch your mouth," she snorted, marching away.

Watch his mouth? All he'd said was, "Don't touch me, you fat bag of lard."

He hated being out amongst the common people; it was beneath him. He was Henry Whitfield-Simmons, a special man, a privileged man. He could not abide crowds—they made him feel insecure. Not that the Kmart store was crowded. There were very few people walking around, and that was good.

So where was she? Max Maria Santangelo Golden. Where the hell was she?

He limped to the front of the store and stood outside, his eyes scanning the street.

She was there, somewhere. He knew it.

Now all he had to do was find her.

25

Halfway to New York, Anthony changed his mind. "Tell the pilot to reroute, we're flying to Miami," he informed The Grill.

The big man didn't argue—even though they'd been in Miami less than twenty-four hours earlier. Whatever Anthony Bonar wanted, he got.

The Grill informed the pilot of their change in destination. The pilot, who had a wife and two kids waiting in New York, was disgruntled. He carried on about air-traffic control and landing permission.

The Grill told him to work it out.

Anthony owned a luxurious waterfront home in Miami where his two teenage kids lived with their English nanny, while Francesca resided on the property in a guesthouse he'd had specially built to her specifications. Emmanuelle lived nearby in a magnificent Ocean Drive penthouse—*his* penthouse, because he'd never put anything in her name. If Emmanuelle ever decided to leave him, she left with nothing. He was no fool. He'd even made Irma sign a postmarriage prenuptial giving her practically nothing should they ever divorce—which was unlikely, because having a wife was excellent insurance as far as protecting himself from other women.

Anthony never did anything without thinking about it first. He was smart that way; his grandfather had taught him well. "When it comes to women, ya gotta use your head," Enzio had often lectured. "Your dick is for fuckin' 'em, an' your head is for fuckin' 'em in a different way. Don't never forget that."

For a brief moment Anthony thought about Tasmin. He hoped that by this time Renee had disposed of the girl way out in the desert, buried where nobody would find her. The authorities could add her name to the hundreds of people who went missing every day in America. She was a bank manager, for chrissakes. Who gave a damn? It wasn't like he'd fucked a movie star and snapped her neck.

Renee was upset with him, but that wouldn't last. She was smart enough not to piss him off. And if she was *really* smart, she'd never mention Tasmin again. It was over, done with, there was no going back.

By the time his plane landed in Miami, it was late morning. He had a choice: Should he go to his home, or should he go straight to Emmanuelle's apartment? He decided to surprise Emmanuelle.

His number-one mistress lived in a white Art Deco building right in the middle of Ocean Drive. The doorman knew him. Unbeknownst to Emmanuelle, Anthony paid both the night and day porters to give him a full report of her activities.

The day porter, a Hispanic man with bad teeth and an unruly mass of frizzy hair, greeted him with an ingratiating leer. "Señor Bonar, eez pleasure to see you back so soon."

"Anything to report?" Anthony said, not in the mood for pleasantries.

"Nothing, *señor,* all is quiet." The day porter lowered his voice to a conspiratorial whisper. "She's had no visitors. I watch. I see."

Anthony gave a curt nod and moved away from the man who never failed to annoy him. He stepped into the elevator with The Grill right behind him. He always kept The Grill in close proximity since he never knew what dangers were lurking. His connections were varied, and sometimes not so trustworthy. He also had to be on the alert for undercover cops who often attempted to infiltrate his business. Fortunately, he had a nose for smelling them out, and when he did, he either added them to his extensive payroll, or their careers turned out to be short-lived.

He entered Emmanuelle's apartment with his key and discovered her asleep in the bedroom, naked beneath peach-colored satin sheets. Emmanuelle was a true diva in training—she went for all the trimmings: satin sheets, sumptuous cushions, and huge fur throws. It always surprised Anthony that she was able to sleep on the slick satin sheets, because whenever *he* lay down on them, he had the distinct sensation that his ass was about to slide right off the bed. Damn sheets! But if they made her happy . . .

Stripping off his clothes, he dumped them on the floor before climbing into bed beside her. No Viagra today, with Emmanuelle he didn't always need it.

Smoothing his hand over her bare ass, he began sliding his fingers into the crack.

"Honey bunch, it's you," she murmured, rapidly waking up. "What're you doing here?"

"I'm back," he announced, as if she wasn't already aware of his presence.

"You only just left," she said, yawning. "Are you checking up on me?"

"I check up on you all the time," he said with a smug smile. "Only you don't know it."

"You do?" she responded, thinking to herself, *I might look like a bimbo, but I'm well aware he pays people to watch me. I would never be dumb enough to bring a guy here for that reason. I'd go to their place or we'd check into a hotel.*

It was actually quite fortunate she was back in her own bed, because the previous night she'd gone out dancing and a couple of smokin' guys had definitely caught her attention. She'd flirted a lot, been tempted, then decided she was too tired from her photo shoot to do anything about it, so she'd come home. Alone. Thank God! Because here was Anthony, back again, and she hadn't been expecting him for another couple of weeks.

"How come you're back so soon?" she asked, her delicate fingers fluttering over his chest, twirling his coarse black chest hairs around her fingers. She knew he liked it when she touched him there.

"Must've missed you," he said, his hand diving between her legs.

"Oooh," she murmured, wriggling away from him. "Baby's gotta take a shower."

"You don't wanna do that," he said. " 'Cause I wanna fuck you just the way you are."

~ ~ ~

Back in Las Vegas, Renee Falcon was crazed with fury—a cold, hard, hopeless fury she knew she had to keep to herself, because what else could she do? Anthony Bonar had come into town, she'd fixed him up with a date, and he'd left her with a dead body that he expected *her* to dispose of.

He'd given her no choice. She couldn't report him to the cops, and she certainly couldn't allow a body to be discovered on the premises of her hotel.

She'd known Tasmin from her dealings with the bank, and although they were not exactly friends—more casual acquaintances—she'd always liked her. Tasmin was smart, a hard worker, and the mother of a ten-year-old boy. She was also—according to rumors—a swinger. So Renee had thought that fixing her up with Anthony might work for both of them. Now this horrible tragedy.

Jesus Christ! It wasn't as if Tasmin was some out-of-town runaway whose body could be disposed of and nobody would ask any questions. There'd be plenty of questions about Tasmin.

Renee was acutely aware that they'd all been seen together at the hotel restaurant, which meant there were probably witnesses who would have observed Tasmin leaving with Anthony.

Damn Anthony Bonar. Underneath the relentless grooming and five-thousand-dollar suits lurked a murderous blackmailing chauvinist greedy thug. Yes, that's what he was. A dangerous killer with absolutely no conscience.

Renee realized she'd have to pay a great many people off to make this go away. And would Anthony recompense her? No. He was a cheap motherfucker on top of everything else. He was supposed to pay half of Tucker Bond's astronomical fee, and so far, every time she asked him for it, he stonewalled her. Maybe she should cancel the whole damn thing.

Right now she had to concentrate on the task at hand. Job number one was disposing of the body—a costly undertaking, but one she could make happen. After the body was gone she had to arrange for the room to be thoroughly cleaned, the sheets disposed of, fingerprints removed from everything. As far as anyone was concerned, Anthony had not spent any time at the hotel. He'd flown in for a meeting, had dinner, and left immediately after.

Yes, that was it. Tasmin had driven away from the hotel and that was the last anybody had seen of her.

Fortunately, Renee had surrounded herself with employees she could trust—that is, as long as they were well compensated.

By the time she'd taken care of everything, she was worn out and still very angry.

Susie was half asleep when she finally got back to their house.

"Where have you been?" Susie asked, removing her powder-pink sleep mask. "Anthony calls and you go running. What did he *want*? That man is so classless and dumb, it's beyond me why we have to entertain him every time he comes to town. Isn't it enough that he takes money from us every month?"

"Don't ever let him hear you call him dumb," Renee said, shrugging off her jacket. "You should know better than that."

"For God's sake," Susie complained, pouting. "We don't *need* someone like him in our lives. I hated dinner, I hated that you acted as his pimp. Surely he can find his own girls?"

"Listen, Susie," Renee said, sitting down on the edge of the bed, her face grim. "Something bad happened. I can't tell you what it is because I don't want you involved, but I *can* tell you that we won't be seeing Tasmin again."

"Why?" Susie said tartly. "Has she run off with Anthony?"

"Please—no questions," Renee said wearily. "And if the police come around asking anything, all you know is that we had dinner with Anthony, he was *not* staying here, and Tasmin was not his date. That's it. Nothing more."

"What *is* going on?" Susie asked, sitting up in bed.

"Tasmin was dining with us," Renee continued. "Anthony just happened to join us. It's important. Do you understand?"

"No, I don't," Susie said, looking alarmed.

"I've told you enough," Renee sighed.

Susie put her hand on her partner's arm. "Renee, whatever it is, it's *you* who mustn't get involved. You have to distance yourself from that horrible man."

"I already *am* involved," Renee answered, wearily shaking her head. "There's nothing I can do about it, Susie, so please leave it alone."

~ ~ ~

"Hey, kids," Anthony said, entering his house and greeting his two teenage children.

Fourteen-year-old Eduardo was on his way out. He attempted to push past his father mumbling that he'd see him later.

"Where ya goin'?" Anthony demanded, grabbing his son's arm. "Why ya runnin' out on me?"

"He has basketball practice, Mr. Bonar," their English nanny announced. "His friend's father is picking him up."

"Okay, so go," Anthony said, releasing Eduardo. "Have a ball. Shoot one for me."

Thirteen-year-old Carolina was sitting cross-legged on the couch watching a dating game on MTV. Next to her perched Dee Dee, her bubble-gum-chewing best friend.

"Anybody need money?" Anthony offered. Oh yes, he knew how to attract his pretty daughter's attention.

Carolina didn't disappoint him. Jumping off the couch, she flung her arms around his neck. "*Please*, Papa," she cooed. "My credit card is over the limit, and Dee Dee and me want to go to the mall, so we need *plenty*. I have to buy a new outfit for the school dance and lots of other stuff."

"You girls *always* need money," Anthony said, smiling expansively at his daughter and her friend. Carolina was blond and cute and in his eyes could do no wrong. She was as pretty as Irma had been when he'd first met her, and that was saying something.

Eduardo was another case, surly and not quite the son Anthony had hoped for. All Eduardo wanted to do was play sports. He wasn't even interested in girls, and he certainly wasn't interested in learning about the family business, which in the long run was probably wise, because Eduardo did not exhibit any sign of the Bonnatti balls.

Fishing in his back pocket, Anthony handed Carolina a fistload of hundred-dollar bills. She grabbed them out of his hands with an excited "*Whoopee!* Thanks, Papa."

Their English nanny, an older woman with iron gray hair worn in a no-nonsense bun, and a fierce expression, didn't say a word, although her disapproving look indicated more than words.

Anthony took no notice. Like he gave a shit what some uptight English twat thought.

"Gimme a big kiss, Princess," he said, hugging his daughter again.

Carolina kissed him full on the lips.

He chuckled, and smacked her lightly on the ass. "No talkin' to boys at the mall. No talkin' to boys period. You're too young. Understand me?"

"Yes, Papa," she said obediently.

"I mean it," he said sternly. "I'm the only boy you can talk to. Ain't that so, Princess?"

"I know, Papa," Carolina said, rolling her eyes.

"Okay," he said, giving her another brisk pat on the ass. "I'm gonna look in on my grandma. Wanna come with?"

"I saw her yesterday," Carolina replied, counting out her money while giggling with her friend.

"You're sure?"

"Very sure, Papa."

"I'll take a shower first. You remember what I told you."

Upstairs in his bedroom, he stripped off his clothes yet again. He hadn't showered at Emmanuelle's; as soon as he'd fucked her, he'd wanted out. But now, once again he had an urge to get her smell off him.

After a quick shower, he marched naked into his bedroom, clicked on the large-screen TV, and sat on the end of the bed. The bedroom was modern and masculine—all brown leather and chrome furniture, with touches of orange cushions and throws here and there. He had to admit that Irma had done an excellent job of decorating the Miami mansion. It had taken her several months and plenty of money. Once she was finished he'd sent her back to Mexico City, he didn't want her hanging around in Miami. It was better that they didn't live in the same city. A nonstop diet of Irma could drive a man loco. The kids didn't seem to miss her—truth was they barely mentioned her.

Flicking through the channels and finding nothing to attract his attention apart from an endless offering of mind-numbing soaps, he dressed and headed for Francesca's. His grandmother would want to know everything. She always did.

He'd only tell her what he thought she should know, and that was it.

He certainly wasn't telling her about Tasmin. She'd have plenty to say about *that*.

Too much information could sometimes be a bad thing. The less she knew, the better.

26

Max was just about to get into her car when she heard a voice behind her.

"You must be Max," the voice said.

"Huh?" she gasped, turning around, totally startled. A man was standing there. He was at least thirty, not very tall, slight of build, with thinning hair and a weaselly face. He was carrying a large canvas hold-all. "How do you know who I am?" she asked suspiciously.

"I recognized you from your photo."

"What photo?" she said, glancing quickly around the car park. It was dusk, the light fading fast, and unfortunately there was no one else in sight.

"The one you posted on the Internet," he said, taking a moment to study her face. So very pretty. So very young. Full, pouty lips and innocent green eyes. The clouds of black curly hair reminded him that she was a younger version of her mother. Lucky Santangelo—the woman who'd ruined his life, the woman who'd taken away his moment of triumph and handed it to Billy Melina. "I'm Grant," he said, unable to take his eyes off her.

"*You're* Grant?" she questioned, hardly able to conceal her surprise, because he looked nothing like the photo he'd posted. He was way older and way creepy. Ugh!

"I'm late because my car ran out of gas," he explained, shuffling awkwardly from one foot to the other. "Sorry about that, but at least I'm here now."

"Uh . . . you're like *very* late," she pointed out, wishing she hadn't blown Ace off with a casual "Go rob your bank. See ya." She could sure use him now.

"You can leave your car," Weasel Face said. "We'll take mine."

This must be a joke. There was no way she was getting into a car with this guy—he was hardly the Internet dude of her dreams. Cookie must've had a premonition—this dude was most likely a serial killer who planned on chopping her up and eating her for his dinner. He was a definite creep. Ha-ha! The joke was on her.

"I enjoyed your e-mails," he continued in a conversational tone. "We have so much in common."

"We do?" she gulped, glancing quickly around the car park.

"Yes, we do," he said, moving closer and placing his hand on her arm, a move that totally freaked her out. "It seems we both enjoy the same things."

Oh crap! If she kicked him in the balls, would it give her enough time to jump in her car and take off?

"You don't look like your picture," she said accusingly. "That photo wasn't you, was it?"

His grip tightened on her arm. Her stomach experienced some kind of crazy cartwheel, this was not a good scene.

Then all of a sudden, like some kind of Superman, Ace appeared out of nowhere. "Hey, little cous'," he said, stepping between them, forcing Henry to let go of her arm. "Is this the dude we were waitin' for?"

Wow! Ace was no slouch in the "getting it" department. She was impressed.

"Who's this?" Henry said, glaring at Ace, a ferocious scowl covering his face.

"This . . . uh . . . this is my cousin Ace," she said, thinking fast. "He uh . . . drove me here today."

"He came *with* you?" Henry said, his thin lips tightening. "Why?"

"'Cause, uh . . . my mom didn't want me meeting someone I didn't know by myself," she said, biting into her lower lip.

Henry was silent for a moment, digesting this new information. He was extremely upset that she was with a male companion, even if the boy *was* her cousin. This was a complication he had not expected.

"You'll be fine with me," Henry said, attempting to recover his composure. "Your cousin can go home."

"You're not listenin', man," Ace said, still standing between them. "Max's mom asked me to stay with her. We're like on this weekend trip together. So, uh . . . you got a plan?"

"I've hired a cabin," Henry said, furious that this boy would dare to interfere.

"Like for the three of us?" Ace asked, exchanging a quick glance with Max.

"I was not aware there were going to be three of us," Henry said stiffly.

"Hey, look," Ace said. "Max's mother doesn't want her staying over anyway, so we kinda thought we'd say hello, then take off." He threw Max a meaningful look. "Right?"

"Yes," she said, thinking how fortunate it was that she'd bumped into Ace, and what a relief that he was there to extract her from such a weird and uncomfortable situation. Not because he was the greatest protector in the world—because according to him he was a would-be bank robber—but having him around was certainly better than nothing. "We have to get back to L.A. My mom's giving a family dinner."

"But we made an arrangement," Henry said, a muscle in his cheek twitching. "A firm arrangement."

"Not so firm," Max said quickly. "And if I'd had your cell number, I would've called and told you I wouldn't be able to stay."

Henry glared at her. Pretty as she was, she was not behaving in the way he had expected.

Wow! Max thought. This was turning out to be even more of an adventure than she'd anticipated. She would have major stories to tell Cookie and Harry when she got back.

"I was expecting to spend the weekend with you," Henry said, still glaring. "I organized everything. I hired a cabin, bought supplies. This was supposed to be our time to get to know each other."

Eeww! Max thought. *This guy takes creepy to new heights.*

"Sorry, dude," Ace said, cracking his knuckles. "It's not as if you *know* Max."

"I *do* know her," Henry corrected, a slow rage beginning to build inside him. "And she knows me. We have—"

"Hey," Max interrupted. "That's not true. It's not like I exactly *know* you. I mean, it's not as if we ever *met* or anything."

"Listen, we gotta go," Ace said, nudging Max in the ribs. "Gimme the keys, Max, I'll drive."

"Sure," she said, handing Ace her car keys, quite excited at the thought of a fast getaway from this creepo freak.

And then everything happened very quickly, although later, when she looked back, Max decided it was more like a slow-motion sequence from a movie than an actual real-life event.

Grant produced a gun. Just like that he pulled it out of his pocket and pointed it straight at the two of them.

"Get in the car," he said, his voice flat and devoid of any emotion. "You first," he said, waving the gun in Ace's face. "Behind the wheel. One wrong move and I blow this pretty little girl's head off. Do you understand me?"

Yes. Ace understood him.

27

Saturday morning Lucky was awakened by an early-morning phone call from Mooney Sharp, the general contractor in charge of everything to do with the Keys. The call came through on her private phone, a line she had asked Mooney to use only in emergencies.

"What's going on, Mooney?" she asked, struggling to wake up.

"You gotta get yourself up here, Lucky," Mooney informed her.

"Why's that?"

"The cosigner from the bank hasn't turned up. We usually do the check signing every Friday afternoon, but she was busy last night, asked if we could postpone to this morning. I said sure. Now she's not here."

"Where is she?"

"Called her house—the babysitter said she never made it home last night. I guess she must've gotten laid or somethin'."

"What's this got to do with me, Mooney?"

"There's checks gotta be signed today. I need a cosigner—an' you're it."

"Why am *I* it?" she asked irritably.

"'Cause I haven't been able to reach anyone else."

"Great!"

"I was thinkin' you could fly in for a couple of hours."

"Jeez, Mooney, this is not an easy weekend for me. I'm throwing a big party tomorrow for Gino."

"This is urgent, Lucky. Some of the contractors don't get their checks today, they'll walk. We can't afford for that to happen, not at this final stage."

"Fine," Lucky said, making a quick decision. "I'll be there as soon as I can."

Lennie was still asleep. Lucky leaned toward him. "Hey, sleepyhead, wake up," she said, nudging his shoulder.

"It's too early," he groaned.

"Gotta go, they need me in Vegas," she said briskly. "Thought I might score a good-bye kiss."

He opened one eye. "You're going today?"

"Yup. I gotta cosign checks."

"Why d'*you* have to do it?"

"Don't even ask."

"Jesus, Lucky—"

"I know," she interrupted. "But I'll only be gone a few hours, and I was hoping you'd hold it together here. That's unless you feel like coming with me."

"No, I don't feel like coming with you," he said, stretching out his arms. "Rome, maybe. Paris, yes. Vegas—no way."

"So you'll entertain Gino, Paige, and the others?"

"Me?"

"Yes, you, and they'll be erecting the party tent today, plus the caterers will be setting up, but Philippe will take care of that side of things. You're in charge of family."

"Gee, thanks," he said, pushing his hand through his hair. "Just how I wanna spend my weekend when I should be working on my script."

"Please, Lennie," she cajoled. "It's not often I ask you to do something for me."

"You're *always* asking me," he said, reaching out for her.

"I am?" she said softly, falling into his arms.

"Yes, you are," he teased, pulling her close for a long, slow kiss.

"You'd better let me go or I'll never get out of here," she murmured.

"So stay."

"You know I can't," she said, wishing she could.

"Okay, okay," he said, releasing her from his arms. "Go make your trip. I'll hold it together here."

"And please call Max. I left a message on her cell yesterday and she never called back. I'm so pissed, but I don't have time to get involved in a fight. That's why *you* should call her, make sure she's back in time for the party."

"Yes, *ma'am*," he mocked. "Anything else?"

"You're the best and I love you," she said, kissing him.

"Keep on tellin' me that an' we'll live happily ever after."

"Oh, we will," she promised, kissing him again.

Downstairs in the kitchen Brigette and Bobby were sitting at the counter drinking coffee.

"How come you two are up?" Lucky asked.

"We're operating on a different time zone," Bobby reminded her. "Three hours ahead."

"I have to fly to Vegas today," Lucky said, pouring a cup of coffee for herself.

"Can I come too?" Bobby asked. "Haven't been to Vegas since I was a kid."

"If you want to."

"Definitely. Can't wait to see what kind of a club you've put together. I'll be your adviser."

"Gee, thanks Bobby," Lucky said caustically, "just what I need."

"Hey, I do have one of the hottest clubs in New York, as I keep on telling you."

"I know," she said patiently. "You do keep on telling me, don't you."

"You've been there, you've seen for yourself."

"It's great."

"So?"

"So, as I am constantly reminding you, you weren't in the club biz when I put together this complex. Who knew you wanted to run clubs? Certainly not me."

"If you're all flying to Vegas," Brigette said brightly, "can I come too?"

"Yeah!" Bobby said enthusiastically. "We can make a day of it. Blackjack, twenty-one, craps—maybe time for a quick dive into a strip club somewhere along the way. A lap dance will suit me just *fine!*"

"Absolutely not!" Brigette said, starting to laugh. "I'm thinking shopping."

"What?" Bobby said, straight-faced. "You're not into lap dances?"

"You can both come," Lucky decided. "As long as you remember this is a fast trip—no time for gambling, strip clubs, *or* shopping."

"C'mon, Mom," Bobby said, winking at Brigette. "A little lap dance never did anyone any harm."

Ignoring her son, Lucky headed for the door. "Be ready in one hour. Do *not* keep me waiting."

On their way out Lucky left Gino a note.

I know you understand—Vegas calls.
We'll be back in time for dinner.

If anybody understood business it was Gino.

As they were getting in the limo to take them to the airport, Philippe hurried over to the window and handed her an envelope. She opened it in the car.

"Who's that from?" Bobby wanted to know.

"I keep on getting these cards dropped off at the house," Lucky said, tapping the card on her knees. "All they say is 'Drop Dead Beautiful.' "

"That's weird," Brigette said.

Bobby grabbed the card from her and inspected it. "You shown this to anyone?" he asked.

"Why would I? It's probably an invitation to an event, and eventually I'll find out what it's for."

"How many of these have you gotten?"

"Um . . . maybe this is the third one."

"Where are the other two?"

"Guess I must've thrown them away."

"And they were all put in the mailbox?"

"What are you, a district attorney?" Lucky joked.

"Seriously, Mom," Bobby said, "we should have someone check out the security cameras, get a look at who's delivering them."

"Why are you so concerned?"

" 'Cause you never know."

"Never know *what?*" Lucky asked, amused that Bobby was taking some frivolous invite so seriously.

"You must have enemies, y'know, people from your past."

Lucky wondered exactly how much Bobby knew about her past. Too much from the sound of him.

"What *are* you talking about?" she said lightly. "I do not have any enemies."

"Your son Googled you," Brigette said, joining in. "He knows plenty about both of us."

"I grew *up* knowing about our family," Bobby said. "I didn't have to Google anyone. And hey, Mom, you think I don't *remember* what happened to me and Brigette when we were kids? That whole kidnapping thing which you refuse to talk about."

"I never talk about it, Bobby, because bringing it up is bad karma. It all happened a long time ago, so leave it alone."

"I was *molested,* Mom, in case you've forgotten. I was five years old and molested by some crazy old mobster. You think I can forget that?"

"I don't expect you to forget it," Lucky said carefully. "But we've all moved on."

"Yes, Bobby," Brigette said. "If *I* can move on after what happened, so can you."

"Hey," Bobby said. "Without you, Brig, I probably wouldn't even be here. You were the one who shot the old pervert. I'll never forget you picking up that gun and—"

"Enough," Brigette interrupted, her blue eyes clouding over. "Now *I'm* the one who doesn't want to start taking a trip down memory lane."

"Okay, I get it," Bobby said. "Sorry I brought it up."

~ ~ ~

Mooney Sharp met them at the airport. A big man in his late fifties, Mooney was over six feet, with a halo of bushy red hair, matching eyebrows, and a huge gut. His favored outfit was cowboy boots, pressed jeans, and a low-slung belt with an enormous silver buckle—all the better to exhibit his massive stomach. At seventeen all his front teeth had gotten knocked out in a bar fight, and now his party trick was to remove his row of yellowing false teeth and horrify everyone with a manic toothless grin.

"Hey, Mooney," Lucky said. "As you can see, I'm here. Happy?"

"Morning, boss," Mooney answered, tipping his well-worn Stetson. "Lookin' great as usual."

"Compliments are going to get you nowhere," Lucky said. "I had to leave all my houseguests and jump on a plane, not my favorite way to spend Saturday morning."

"Sorry, Lucky, like I told you, I couldn't reach anyone else with signing privileges, an' this *is* an emergency."

"It better be."

"Oh, it is. We're in the final stages, wouldn't want anything holding us up."

"You remember my son, Bobby, don't you?"

"Sure do," Mooney said, giving Bobby a hearty handshake. "You was just a little tyke last time I saw you."

"And this is Brigette, my godchild."

"See you made it a family party," Mooney remarked, escorting them to his mud-splattered SUV. "I'm big on family. Trouble is I never get to see 'em."

"How come?"

"'Cause I'm busy workin' for you twenty-four-seven," he said with a hearty guffaw.

"Wanna quit?" Lucky asked jokingly, sitting up front.

"If I quit, I die," Mooney said, getting behind the wheel.

In the backseat Bobby leaned across to Brigette who was sitting beside him. "Sorry about earlier," he said. "Y'know, bringing up the whole kidnapping deal. I didn't mean to—it kinda slipped out."

"That's okay, Bobby," she said quietly. "It's just bad memories."

"I'm sure."

"It was my fault for getting us into it in the first place," she continued. "I was so young and naive, and you were just a helpless little kid. I knew I had to do something to protect you, and the gun was right there."

"You did the right thing, Brig. You saved us both."

"Y'know, Bobby," she said thoughtfully. "Maybe we *should* talk about it. I saw a shrink. You never did."

"No, shrinks aren't my style. I've moved on—it's the way to go."

"Okay," Brigette said, her pretty face serious. "But any time you feel the need . . ."

"Thanks. If I ever do, I'll call you."

The moment they hit the Strip, Lucky turned her head, feeling the old familiar surge of arenaline. "Well," she said, "we're back in Vegas."

"I think I love it," Bobby said enthusiastically. "Gambling and girls—my two favorite things. Maybe I should build my own hotel—blow you out the water!"

"You're a Santangelo, all right," Lucky said, smiling.

"Yeah," he agreed with a sly grin. "A Santangelo loaded with Stanislopolous money. Pretty cool combination, huh, Mom?"

For a moment she thought she was talking to Gino, which made her smile even more.

"Yes, Bobby," she said. "Pretty damn cool."

28

Lying is never a good thing. Lying always has a way of coming back and kicking you in the ass, or so Billy discovered. He'd lied to Venus, told her he had an early call. The truth was that he didn't have to work again until Monday, so when Venus called him on his cell Saturday morning, he was still happily asleep.

"Mmm . . . yeah?" he mumbled.

"Billy?" she said, sounding surprised. "Are you asleep?"

Without thinking, he said, "Uh, yeah, somethin' wrong with that?"

"You told me you had an early call," she said accusingly.

"Shit . . . yeah, um . . . that got canceled."

"It did?" she said coldly. "What time was it canceled?"

"Uh, sometime last night. Late. Kev took the call. I was, uh, trying to get to sleep early, like I told you."

"You never called me last night," she sighed. "You promised you'd call before you went to bed." Oh God! Was that a needy whine she detected in her voice?

"Sorry, V," he said. "I was watching the game, must've passed out in front of the TV 'cause I don't remember anything till I woke up at three an' hauled myself into bed."

"I see," she said, hating the way she sounded, like an uptight school marm questioning a badly behaved student. Lucky was right—this was so unlike her, she had to get it together.

"How're you doing?" he ventured, well aware that she was way pissed at him.

"I'm doing great, Billy, if you care."

"What does *that* mean?"

"It means that I don't know what's going on between us, and I think it's time we sat down and talked."

Oh shit, he thought. *She wants to have the "We need to talk" conversation.* When women wanted *that* conversation, it was always a no-win situation.

"Whatever," he said vaguely.

"Don't you think we should?" she persisted. "Surely you sense that something's going on between us?"

"Like what?" he said, following the "I'm just a dumb guy, what do I know" tactic.

"We shouldn't discuss it over the phone."

"You wanna come by?" he suggested, immediately wishing he hadn't.

"If you'd like me to," she said cautiously.

"Why wouldn't I? I'm not working today. I got a free pass."

"Okay, I'll be over soon."

Billy put down the phone and groaned. His crotch was still itching like crazy, even though last night he'd sent Kev out to the drugstore to buy some special cream to kill the little fuckers. Kev had questioned him into the ground about where he'd gotten them from. But he'd stayed firm, and come out with the old toilet-seat story.

Of course, he knew where he'd gotten them. It must've been from the girl he'd picked up at Tower Records. She'd infected him, dirty little groupie.

More important—what if he'd passed on the disgusting bugs to Venus? How the hell could he explain *that*?

Hey, Miss Superstar Girlfriend. I might have given you a dose of the crabs. How about we discuss it?

Running his hand through his hair, he got out of bed. "Kev!" he yelled. "Where the frig are you?"

Then he remembered that Kev had gone home last night after bringing him the medication from the drugstore. Rubbing it into his crotch was a laugh a minute, and even worse, it didn't seem to be working.

Devoid of clothes, he made his way into the kitchen. Ramona did not come in on Saturday or Sunday. He'd decided privacy was on the top of his hit list for the weekends; he didn't want his housekeeper hanging around. Besides, she needed time off too.

Removing a carton of orange juice from the fridge, he drank straight from the carton and burped. Ah, yes—not being polite was one of the advantages of living alone. Discovering a California Pizza box in the fridge, he opened it and devoured half a cold barbecue chicken pizza. It tasted great, better than cereal any day, and he had to build up his strength: Venus was in the "We've got to talk" mode, so he'd better be prepared.

It suddenly occurred to him: Was breaking up on her mind? Is that where they were heading?

Yeah, probably. It was time. He was so over being referred to as Venus's boy toy. Goddammit, he was a big star in his own right, he didn't have to put up with that crap any longer.

If they *did* decide to break up, he had to make sure that Venus knew it wasn't anything she'd done. She was an amazing woman, and yeah, he loved her in his own way. But he needed to be free of all the garbage that went along with being Miz Superstar's boyfriend.

Problem was he didn't have the balls to come right out and tell her, so he was hoping *she'd* be the one who'd break up with him.

Yes, that would be very convenient.

Or would it?

~ ~ ~

Venus was mad as she listened to herself turning into the kind of woman she couldn't stand. The kind of woman who hung around waiting for the phone to ring, holding her breath for some guy to validate her very existence.

Billy Melina had her hooked, and she hated it. She, who was usually so in control, was now out of control because of a man. *Billy* was calling all the shots, and *fuck him!*

Lucky was right. If Billy wanted out, she should be the one to move on, get out first. Why allow *him* the pleasure of doing it?

Oh God, I'll miss him, she thought. *Those abs, that face, that beautiful dick. My Billy. My gorgeous guy. I can't help it. I love him.*

What would people say? Would they think he'd dumped her because she was an older woman? Or would she be able to spin it and announce that *she'd* dumped *him?*

Yeah, that was it. She'd tell her friends that she'd let him go because he was too young and immature, and he wanted to move in. The press would go to town on that one.

Statement from her publicist to the hungry media:

> *Billy Melina is a wonderful and spiritual man and we'll always be close friends. Unfortunately, the timing is not right for either of us.*

She thought about who she might start seeing next. There were always opportunities, always men panting to go out with her. There was the black TV entertainment reporter with the dazzling smile and flirtatious manner. There was the successful movie producer who was constantly inviting her out. There was the Bad Boy movie star—one of Billy's main rivals—who kept on phoning to inquire whether she'd gotten rid of Billy yet. And then there were the fans—legions of them. Only she'd never date a fan; too risky.

What was she going to do? She wasn't ready to break up with Billy. She didn't want to, she was perfectly happy, *he* was the one causing waves.

Oh God! The thought of dating again. No! No! No! It was too horrific to even contemplate.

The first date, the first kiss, the first fuck. A *nightmare*. Not to mention the dumb conversations that had to take place.

Where do you live?

What's your star sign?

You like dogs or cats?

Sushi or steak?

Missionary or tantric?

No. She was not allowing Billy to break up with her. No way.

~ ~ ~

The paparazzi were lying in wait outside Billy's house.

Don't they have anything better to do? Venus thought, ducking her head and driving past. She didn't want them to see her in the Phaeton, it was her secret getaway car, and if they saw her in it, her clever ruse would be over.

She called Billy on her cell. "What shall I do?" she wailed.

Oh, great! She'd gone from needy girlfriend to helpless one. Dammit! If she didn't get it together soon, she'd be forced to slit her wrists.

"Uh . . . drive home, I'll come pick you up," Billy suggested. "Or maybe we should hang out at your place."

She didn't want him at her house. If he was there, he could leave whenever he felt like it, and that gave *him* the power position. Today that position was going to be strictly hers.

"Not to worry," she said. "I know exactly what to do. See you soon."

Hitting the gas pedal, she raced down the hill and along Sunset until she reached the Beverly Hills Hotel, where she gave her car to the parking valet and asked him to call her a cab. The parking valet, a would-be actor, was in awe. Especially when she slipped him a fifty-dollar tip.

Ten minutes later she was paying off the cabdriver outside Billy's house, while the assembled paparazzi launched into a photo-taking frenzy. They were not shy about yelling out questions:

"How come you're in a cab?"

"When are you and Billy getting married?"

"Any babies in your future?"

"Over here, Venus, gimme that dazzling smile."

Ignoring them, and a gaggle of girl fans hovering near the bushes, she rang the doorbell. Billy had never offered to give her a key, and since she hardly ever came to his house, she'd never asked for one.

On the other hand, he had the code to get into *her* house, so maybe she *should* have a key.

Billy came to the door himself, causing the girl fans to dissolve into moans and shrieks of ecstatic joy, and the paparazzi to blind everyone with their continuous flashbulbs.

Billy grabbed her by the arm, yanking her inside, slamming the door behind them.

"Jesus, Billy, isn't it time you put up gates?" she said, trying to catch her breath. "It's a circus out there."

"You think I should?" Billy asked, managing to sound as if he'd just ambled into Hollywood straight off the farm.

"Of course you should. And not for my sake. You're famous. You need protection. What if one of those crazy fans had a gun?"

"Oh, c'*mon*, don't go gettin' all dramatic on me."

"I suppose you've never heard of Rebecca Schaeffer or John Lennon?"

"Who's Rebecca Schaeffer?"

"It doesn't matter, Billy," she sighed. "What does matter is that it's essential you get security gates put up around your house. Why don't you have what's-his-name arrange it."

He knew exactly who she meant by "what's-his-name." Kev. She had a thing about Kev. Early on in their relationship she'd pronounced that Kev was a hanger-on and incompetent. She was always trying to persuade him to hire a "real assistant."

Well, too bad. Apart from being his gofer, Kev was his best friend from way back. Besides, the underlying reason she wanted Kev gone was because she considered him a bad influence.

"I'll think about it," he mumbled, trailing her into his living room, hoping he'd remembered to hide Kev's latest stash of porno tapes that he insisted on bringing over.

She zeroed in on his coffee table, picking up photos of girls in various stages of undress. "Who are these?" she asked.

"Fans," he said sheepishly. "They send me this crap all the time."

"To your house?"

"Some. Or the studio forwards them over."

"Are you telling me you don't have anyone organizing your fan club?"

Man, she was in a pissy mood, bossy too. "Uh . . . when I'm on a movie the production office hires someone to take care of it," he said.

"Billy, we've got to get you organized. This is ridiculous."

"Yeah, I guess," he said lamely.

"So," she said, moving a pile of newspapers and magazines out of the way before sitting down on the couch. "Where's your housekeeper today?"

"Jeez, Venus, relax, we're here by ourselves. We don't need a bunch of people looking after us, do we?"

Realizing she was being picky, she shut up. If he wanted to live in a state of disarray, it was his problem.

"Actually you're right," she said, performing a catlike stretch. "It's kind of nice not having anyone around except us."

"You see?" he said triumphantly. "No one to spy on us, check out what we're doing. We can walk around naked if we feel like it."

"Or swim naked in the pool," she said, glancing out the full-length glass doors to the inviting pool. "I haven't done that since I bought my first house."

He immediately flashed onto the girl who'd given him crabs. She'd been naked in his pool. Oh shit! Did the little buggers swim?

His crotch itched at the memory. He scratched himself vigorously, silently cursing.

"What's the matter?" Venus asked.

Should he tell her? Well, at least he'd better make up a cover story in case he'd infected her.

"Got a slight problem," he said sheepishly.

"What problem?"

"One of the stuntmen on the movie had crabs. *My* stunt double, believe it or not. Wardrobe got our pants mixed up, and since I was going commando—"

"No!"

"Sorry, babe. I only just found out. Hope I haven't passed them on to you. I've got the cream to treat 'em. . . ."

"I don't believe this!"

"Yeah. I know. I could kill the son of a bitch."

"So *that's* why you've been in such a strange mood."

Whew! He was off the hook. All she was worried about was his mood.

"Uh . . . yeah . . . guess so."

"You should've told me before."

"I should've?"

"Well, yes. It's unfortunate, but these things happen."

"They do?"

"Oh Billy, you're such a baby," she said affectionately.

If he'd had a hard-on, it would've deflated on the spot.

29

After spending time with Francesca and assuring her that everything was on track to bring down the Keys and the Santangelo family once and for all, Anthony realized there was nothing for him to do in Miami. Sure, he had Emmanuelle, and he had his kids, but he'd been neglecting business, and since the crux of his business operations was in Mexico City he decided he should get back.

He instructed The Grill to have the plane ready. "We're going to Mexico City," he informed him.

The Grill nodded, a man of few words, always ready to move at a moment's notice.

Anthony had promised to take Emmanuelle out to dinner, but he didn't bother informing her that he would not be doing so. Emmanuelle getting all dressed up and sitting around waiting for him gave him a sense of extreme power and control. Women needed to be controlled at all times, and any man who didn't realize that was a foolish man indeed.

The thing with Tasmin had disturbed him, and even though it was Tasmin's own fault, Renee's reaction had put a damper on his weekend. Fuck Renee Falcon. How dare she criticize him. It wasn't as if he'd experienced a rush of adrenaline knowing that he'd accidentally killed a woman. Now, if Tasmin had been a man . . .

He called Renee on his way to the airport.

"Everything taken care of?" he said roughly.

"What do *you* think," she replied, sounding distant and cold.

Lesbian *bitch!* When she'd dealt with the Vegas business it was time to set her straight and let her know who was boss.

Give a woman too much power and it always came back to bite you in the ass.

~ ~ ~

Sometimes Irma felt as if she was living in a prison—a luxurious, magnificent prison, but a prison all the same. Oh yes, the house was grand, the grounds lush and green, there were servants to do anything she wished.

She had everything anyone could possibly ask for, and yet there were guards at the gates.

Anthony had informed her that he employed the guards to protect them from kidnappers and robbers. But she knew the real truth. Her husband was a drug dealer—and as such he had to surround himself with all the protection he could pay for.

When she'd first met Anthony, he'd told her he was in the import/export business, and that's what she'd always tried to convince herself was the truth. But she'd always known it wasn't so. Anthony was a major dealer, that was a plain and simple fact. She'd met several of the men he did business with when he'd taken her to Colombia to attend a drug lord's daughter's wedding. And she'd witnessed many meetings at the house, and mysterious helicopter arrivals late at night.

Now that Luis had made her feel desirable and confident again, thoughts of leaving Anthony were constantly on her mind. She could not communicate this to Luis, but what did it matter? She wasn't planning on running off with him, although sometimes she daydreamed it might be possible.

Every night she tossed restlessly in bed, her mind racing in many different directions, thinking about what to do. She had a lot of burning questions. Since she had no money of her own, no bank account, no savings, how would she survive without Anthony to support her? Anthony had never allowed her to have her own checking account; he gave her a fistful of charge cards and cash whenever she asked. His office in Mexico City paid all the bills.

She had her clothes and jewelry, but what about her children? Could she simply abandon them?

It really didn't make any difference because she wasn't allowed to see them anyway, not unless Anthony said so.

I need a lawyer, she thought. *And not a Mexican lawyer who will automatically be on Anthony's side—an American lawyer. I have to get away from this place I am imprisoned in. My life is seeping away and I am kept here like a caged animal.*

She wondered what Anthony would do if she asked him for a divorce.

Silly question—she knew exactly what he'd do. He'd go berserk, he'd start screaming the way he screamed at his grandmother, he'd refuse to believe that she wanted to leave him. Anthony had a very high opinion of himself, especially sexually. Not that he'd touched her in almost a year, but he still regarded himself as King Stud.

Being Mrs. Anthony Bonar was a huge burden to carry around, and the time had come to shed that burden.

Luis was the perfect lover for her. He was young and available, and conveniently he was allowed on the property at all times since he was one of the estate's gardeners. Who would ever suspect him? Who would ever guess that she had personal knowledge of the rippling muscles beneath his workshirt, that he was built like an Adonis, that his kisses were so sweet and tender? Who would ever suspect that she would fall in lust with this man?

Most of the staff had Saturday off, unless Anthony was in residence. Only Marta, the cook, remained, and she was half deaf anyway. As usual the guards were stationed at the front of the house with the dogs, and the old gardener never came in on weekends—there was only Luis.

Irma glanced out the window, making sure he was there, before taking a leisurely bath, then putting on a simple white dress. She felt like being virginal today. Virginal, so Luis could rip the dress from her body. She knew that once her bedroom door was locked, the lowly gardener turned into a sensuous animal, and frankly she couldn't wait.

After putting on the white dress, she dabbed perfume behind her ears, between her breasts, and on her thighs. Then she hurried downstairs, making a detour through the kitchen.

Marta was sitting in front of the kitchen TV engrossed in a dramatic Spanish telenovella with the sound turned up.

"Marta," Irma said, startling the woman. "I won't be needing anything else today. I'm on a diet, so no dinner for me. You can go home now."

"*Gracias, señora,*" Marta said, quickly standing up and gathering her purse before Señora Bonar changed her mind.

"Enjoy your weekend," Irma said, walking outside into the garden.

Luis spotted her and quickly looked away. He never indicated anything intimate between them; it was only in the privacy of her bedroom that he became this erotic and sensual creature.

"Luis," she said, approaching him in a formal manner. "I'd like you to come look at my houseplants."

She kept up this charade because she never knew who might be watching them. There were many cameras on the property, so it was possible they could be observed without them knowing.

"*Sí, señora,*" Luis said, keeping his eyes fixed firmly on the ground.

"I'll see you in the house," she said.

He didn't understand the words she was speaking, but he did understand exactly what she meant.

She turned and headed back toward the house.

He waited a few minutes, then casually made his own way across the lawn and into the big house.

Luis always got a thrill entering the cool tiled hallway with the massive chandeliers hanging from the fifty-foot ceiling. It was such a magnificent mansion, so different from the squalid two-bedroom house he lived in with his sickly mother, three argumentative sisters, and pregnant wife. Obviously Señora Bonar was unaware that he had a wife, and he was not about to tell her. Not that he could, since he didn't speak her language.

He climbed the marble staircase two steps at a time. How fortunate was he? He had a job, a frustrated American woman who wanted sex every day, and a wife at home who would shortly give birth to his first son.

Irma's bedroom door was open. He walked in, closing and locking the door behind him.

Irma was lying on the bed in her white virginal dress, waiting for him.

Luis didn't hesitate, he hurriedly unzipped his pants and fell on top of her. He was hot and horny and he took her fast.

Irma was dismayed—fast sex reminded her of Anthony. She expected Luis to take his time like he usually did.

"Luis," she objected, making a vain attempt to push him off her, "what are you doing? Slow down."

"*Qué?*" he muttered. But it was too late—he'd already come.

Irma was disappointed and a little angry. If she wanted fast sex with someone rough, she would hardly have chosen Luis.

She got off the bed and stalked into her bathroom, near tears.

Luis could tell she was upset, so he followed her.

"No, Luis," she said, shaking her head. "Not like that, never like that."

"*Ah, cara,*" he said, and very slowly he moved toward her and began peeling down the straps of her white dress, exposing her full breasts.

"No, Luis," she repeated, holding up her hand. "No more."

Ignoring her, he started touching her nipples with the tips of his fingers. Fondling, squeezing, then bending his mouth down and sucking, kissing . . .

She was immediately filled with a fierce and overwhelming desire for this man.

Oh yes, Luis knew how to turn her on. They might not speak the same language, but he certainly knew how to fulfill every one of her fantasies.

30

It was morning, Max knew that. She knew because she could hear birds singing outside the small room she was locked inside. The one window in the room was boarded up, but light filtered through the cracks.

Her head ached, her shoulders hurt, her stomach rumbled, and she had a desperate need to pee. She'd slept fitfully, experiencing hideous nightmares about Cookie's predictions that Internet Dude could turn out to be some kind of maniac serial killer. Was this person who'd held a gun on them and brought them to the cabin a serial killer? Were her worst nightmares about to come true?

She was lying on a hard bed, her left ankle chained to the sturdy wooden leg of the bed. Ace was nowhere in sight.

Pulling her thoughts together she started going over the events of yesterday in her head. The drive to Big Bear, the waiting around for her Internet guy to show, hooking up with Ace, and finally the weasel-faced stranger approaching her and telling her he was Grant, although he looked nothing like the picture he'd posted. What a liar! What a creep!

Fortunately, Ace had reappeared all set to rescue her, but the man had pulled a gun on them, then forced them both into her car. He'd made Ace drive while he'd sat in the back next to her.

She was horrified at what was happening. Then she'd started thinking that maybe it was a hoax, some kind of weirdo TV show that Cookie and Harry had set up.

But no, they wouldn't be so nuts.

I'm not frightened, she'd told herself. *I refuse to be scared.*

But when the man had leaned over and forced a blindfold around her eyes, she'd finally felt the cold grip of fear.

"Where're we headin'?" Ace had asked at one point.

"Be quiet and drive," Grant had replied in a low, even voice. "Follow my instructions and do not say another word."

"You'll never get away with this," Ace had muttered.

"That's for me to decide."

Scrunched in the backseat, she'd stayed as far away from the Internet Freak as possible, managing somehow or other to remain calm. She'd thought about her mom. What would Lucky do?

Oh man, Lucky would probably kick his ass big time. Her mom was known for taking no prisoners, and although they had their differences, under it all Max really admired her.

They must have driven for at least half an hour before finally stopping. When the car came to a halt, Internet Freak had ripped the blindfold from her eyes, and she'd seen that they were parked outside a cabin in a heavily wooded and seemingly remote area.

"Both of you—get out of the car," he'd ordered.

Ace had slid out of the driver's seat and stationed himself next to the car.

"And you," he'd said to Max. "Tie his hands behind his back."

"With what?" she'd answered, staring him down, letting him know she wasn't intimidated, not her.

"Use your blindfold for now."

She'd tied Ace's hands, making the knot as loose as possible.

"Stay cool," Ace had whispered when she was close to him. "We'll get out of this."

"I know," she'd whispered back.

"Tighter," Internet Freak had said, watching her closely.

She'd redone the knot, her heart beating fast, her mind reliving every horror movie she'd ever seen. Those kinds of films were always set in some backwoods area, and there was always a teen couple who inevitably ended up dead on arrival. Oh, great! Was that their destiny?

"What do you want?" she'd asked, turning to face him. "Money? 'Cause my mom will pay you."

"Your mom," Internet Freak had sneered. "I don't want your mom's money, I have plenty of my own."

"Then what *do* you want?" she'd asked, keeping her voice firm.

"I'll tell you when I'm ready to tell you," he'd said. "And stop asking questions."

He'd then instructed Ace to get in the trunk of the car. When Ace objected, he'd threatened to shoot her, so Ace had complied.

After that was done he'd commanded her to enter the house. Once inside he'd shoved her into the small room and manacled her ankle to the leg of the bed. Then he'd left her there without saying another word.

Now it was morning and she had no idea what was going on.

Where was Ace? Was he all right?

Where was Internet Freak? What were his intentions?

He'd taken away her purse with her cell phone, but surely by this time someone would've called her and realized she was missing? Her mom, Cookie, Harry—they'd all been so adamant she had to check in.

The room smelled musty, as if it hadn't been used in years. Her eyes ached to match her relentless headache. She was desperately hungry and thirsty.

After a few minutes of getting acclimatized, she half fell off the bed, attempting to drag it toward the window.

The bed was too heavy, it wouldn't budge.

She reached down to her ankle. It was beginning to chafe and swell.

"Hey!" she yelled loudly, refusing to panic. "Anyone out there? Anyone at all?"

There was no response.

31

Giving Brigette and Bobby a tour of the Keys was a thrill for Lucky. She flew to Vegas every week, so nothing was new to her, but seeing the enormous development through Brigette's and Bobby's eyes was exciting, and they seemed fully impressed, as so they should be. Even if she said so herself, the Keys was awesome.

"This is probably the best hotel I've created," she said proudly. "What do you think?"

"Oh my God," Brigette gasped. "It's amazing. I want to buy one of those apartments today! They're incredible."

"Yes, and I'm happy to say they're nearly all presold, although I think there might be a couple of penthouses still available."

"We'll take 'em," Bobby quipped. "I'll buy one, Brig can have the other."

"I thought you were going to build your own hotel, Bobby," Lucky said, teasing him.

"Maybe I will," he answered. "Put you out of business."

"So that's your ambition, is it?" she asked, hands on hips. "To put your poor old mom out of business."

"Poor old Mom my ass!"

They grinned at each other, shadowboxing.

She'd given them the grand tour, making their way through an army of workmen finishing up various areas. Finally they'd reached the private rooftop nightclub where the final touch-ups were taking place.

"Well?" she asked both of them. "Opinions please."

"It's okay," Bobby said, surveying the premises with a critical eye. "I could've done better for you."

"Really," she said coolly, making it more of a statement than a question.

"It's . . . y'know, nothing special."

"Nothing special!" she exclaimed. "Are you kidding me? How about the illuminated staircase? The one-hundred-and-eighty-degree view over the Strip? The indoor fountains? The VIP rooms? The paintings—all originals I might add."

"That's not what makes a great club, Mom. A really cool club is all about the vibe."

"And what vibe would that be?"

"The people, the mix—now, *that's* what makes a club a happening place."

"And what makes you think we won't attract the right people?"

He shrugged.

"Hey, Bobby," she said lightly. "I *do* have major connections. I've built hotels before, I ran Panther Studios, Lennie is one of the most respected directors in Hollywood, so between us we know just about everyone."

"You gotta get 'em young," Bobby explained. "It's all about the youth culture. Hot sexy girls in hot sexy outfits. Rich dudes with their Ferraris and cool dude attitudes. All under thirty-five and horny."

"Thanks, Bobby. Are you trying to make me feel old?"

"You? You'll *never* be old. Look at you, you're the best-looking mom *I've* ever seen."

"And you've seen a lot of them, have you?"

"I get around," Bobby said, laughing.

"Let's get positive here. What's your favorite part of the hotel?"

"The different decors on each floor are amazing," Brigette said. "And

I love the way the main swimming pool is built so that it's half underground. It's pretty cool that people can swim right into an underground grotto."

"Yeah, that's hot," Bobby agreed. "But you've still gotta make it exciting—like stage a topless wet thong competition, stuff like that."

"Very classy, Bobby," Lucky said dryly. "May I suggest you save that kind of stunt for *your* hotel?"

"How about *guys* in thongs?" Brigette suggested, winking at Lucky. "I'd judge that one!"

"I'm glad to see you're heading back to the real world," Lucky said. "Isn't this better than locking yourself up in your New York apartment and never going out?"

"I guess," Brigette said, quite enjoying herself.

"The golf course is pretty spectacular," Bobby said.

"And great shops," Brigette added. "Gucci, Cartier, Chanel—excellent choices."

Lucky nodded. "The Keys will have the premier shopping mall in Vegas. This is just the beginning."

"Gotta give you props," Bobby said. "When you do it, you *really* do it."

"So I've been told," Lucky said, smiling. "Now, if you two want to go off and play for a couple of hours, I have to sit with Mooney and take care of business. We'll meet back here at three."

"Sounds like a plan," Bobby said. "Come on, Brig, we got us a sexy lap dance waiting."

"Bobby!" Brigette objected. "I told you—no lap dances."

"You know you want it."

"I do not," she said indignantly.

"You gotta stop fighting your impulses," he said, grinning at her.

"For God's sake," Brigette said, breaking out in a smile in spite of herself. "Will you give it a rest?"

"*What?*" Bobby said innocently.

"You know what," she said, linking her arm through his.

The two of them left Lucky surveying her latest kingdom. She wished she'd thought of bringing Gino with them today—it would've been the perfect opportunity for her to give him the grand tour. He and Paige were coming to the big opening ceremony, but that was a major event; she would have preferred giving him a private look.

Her thoughts turned to his party. Thank God she had Philippe on the case. Today he'd be coping with the caterers, the company erecting the huge outdoor tent, the flower deliveries, and security. Everything had to be ready for Gino's party—she wanted it to be the most special day of his extremely eventful life.

She called Lennie to make sure everything was on schedule.

"It's a madhouse here," he complained.

"Where's Gino?"

"Junior's playing tennis. Senior's watching college football on TV."

"Did you call Max?"

"Left a message on her cell."

"And she hasn't called you back?"

"Not yet."

"That kid—"

"Don't go getting excited, I'll talk to her. How's everything there?"

"I'm signing checks and heading right home."

"That's very good news, sweetheart, 'cause I miss you."

32

Breaking up was not on the agenda after all. Venus was thoroughly relieved; all her worries that Billy was cooling off had turned out to be nothing but a dumb case of the crabs. Like who hadn't experienced *them?*

After Billy confided his problem, she led him into the bathroom, made him drop his pants, sat him on the side of the tub, picked up his razor, and shaved his pubic area clean as an eight-year-old boy.

"There! All fixed," she announced. "Now we have matching Brazilians!"

They both broke up laughing.

"Come on," Billy said, grabbing a fresh pair of Levi's. "I'm taking you out to lunch."

"What about the paparazzi?"

"Fuck 'em. We're going to the beach."

Soon Venus was perched on the back of his motorcycle, arms clasped firmly around his waist, a crash helmet covering her platinum curls, a dozen paparazzi in hot pursuit.

They didn't notice. They were both up for an adventure. Things were definitely getting better.

~ ~ ~

When Alex Woods was working, he was content. Making movies was his sole reason for getting up in the morning. Not only did he write and direct all his own films, but he sometimes produced, usually with a partner. His best producing partner had been Lucky. They'd worked together so well, a perfect fit. No hassles, no useless fights about the budget, everything was cool with Lucky. *Seduction* was one of his favorite movies. It had made Billy Melina into a star, while Venus had given the best performance of her career.

After they wrapped production, Alex was shattered when Lucky informed him she'd decided not to produce any more movies. He'd argued with her, tried to convince her, but she was adamant.

Lucky was a challenging woman, always pursuing new ideas, always doing exactly what she felt like doing whenever she had the urge. Now she was back in the hotel business in Vegas and he was a major investor in the Keys. He wasn't worried about his money—with Lucky in charge it was all good. Besides, he enjoyed spending time in Vegas. It was a kick-ass city with plenty going on. There were times when he jumped on a plane, flew to Vegas, gambled for a couple of hours, then made it back to L.A. before midnight. It was relaxing—the perfect quick getaway for a workaholic.

He felt like doing just that on Saturday when he awoke fighting a massive hangover. He had no desire to bring Ling along—her nagging about his drinking turned him off. Who did she think she was, giving her opinion on whether he should drink or not? If she didn't like it, she should pack up and leave.

The truth was he couldn't care less *what* she did. They'd been living together for almost two years—it was long enough. Besides, having a woman living in his house was not an appealing situation. Women were always trying to add feminine touches. Who needed fresh flowers and a fridge full of food? He ate out most of the time—it wasn't his style to indulge in housekeeping.

Without telling Ling, he left his house, drove to the airport, and hopped a plane to Vegas. As long as he had his laptop with him he could work, gamble, maybe get laid if he felt like it, then fly home. He needed the quick break—then he'd resume work on Monday feeling refreshed. Working with Billy Melina was a pain—stardom had gone to the kid's head, not to mention his sure-to-be-disastrous affair with Venus. Alex liked actors to do exactly what he told them to do. Billy wasn't pliable anymore—he had ideas of his own. It pissed Alex off.

The plane was late taking off and packed. Alex didn't care, he'd never lusted after things like private planes or two-hundred-foot yachts. Cars were his deal—he owned several. Three classic Ferraris, a Porsche, and a vintage Bentley. Ling had taken over driving his Porsche, which didn't thrill him. When she'd first moved in she'd had her own car, but when the lease expired she'd started driving his Porsche. It annoyed him, but he wasn't about to buy her a car. Generosity was not high on his list of things to do for the woman in his life.

In Vegas he usually stayed at the Cavendish. They always took care of him, and the owner, Renee Falcon, was quite a colorful character.

After checking in, he took a cab over to the Keys to take a look at how things were progressing. He'd visited several times during construction, and the place was unbelievable. Lucky had the touch, but that was no surprise since Lucky always did things with class and style.

The Keys complex was surrounded by high-security fences with guards stationed at key points.

Alex flashed his pass at one of the guards. "Mooney around?" he asked.

"He's up in the main communication offices meeting with Ms. Santangelo."

Had he heard right? Was Lucky in town? She hadn't mentioned she was flying in. This was very welcome news indeed.

He strode across the property, past the two huge swimming pools, past the private poker rooms, through the casino, and upstairs to the main office. Everywhere he looked people were busy working toward getting ready for the grand opening.

Since the office door was ajar, he walked right in.

"Mr. Woods," Mooney said, standing up, "this *is* a surprise."

Lucky was sitting in front of a big circular console surrounded by dozens of in-house TV monitors. "Alex," she exclaimed. "What are *you* doing here?"

"The question is, what are *you* doing here?" he responded, happy to see her.

"Check signing," Mooney explained. "Couldn't find anyone else."

"Now this I don't get," Alex said, perplexed. "Lucky Santangelo has to fly to Vegas to sign checks. Are you kidding me?"

"You know how hands-on I am," she said. "There are only four people who can countersign with Mooney, and I happen to be one of them. The other three weren't available, so here I am."

"My friend the control freak," Alex said, shaking his head. "You never fail to amaze me."

"Well, it takes one to know one," she said, grinning. "And how come *you're* here?"

"Working with that asshole Billy Melina, I found myself in desperate need of some R 'n' R."

"Is Billy being difficult?"

"You know what it's like with actors—give 'em a taste of success an' they think they walk on water."

"I never imagined Billy would go that route."

"He has. They all do."

"Lennie never did."

"Lennie's an exception."

"So . . . Billy Melina drove you to Vegas. Hmm . . ."

"Not exactly. I figured that while I'm in town, I'd check out my investment."

"Don't trust me, huh?" Lucky said.

"You're the only one I do trust," Alex responded, quite seriously.

"That's nice," she said, keeping it light.

"Aren't you supposed to be throwing a party tomorrow?"

"This is true, which is why I'm flying back to L.A. this afternoon."

"You here by yourself?" he asked, wondering if Lennie was about to appear and ruin everything.

"Bobby and Brigette came along for the ride."

"Where are they?"

"I'm not sure," she said vaguely. "I think they went off to get a lap dance or something. Perhaps you should join them."

"Lap dances aren't my scene."

"Really?"

"Yes, really."

They exchanged a long slow look.

Sometimes, Lucky thought, if it weren't for Lennie . . .

~ ~ ~

Lunch at Geoffrey's, a restaurant perched on a cliff overlooking the Pacific Ocean, was suitably romantic. Venus devoured a huge dish of lobster and shrimp. She held hands with Billy across the table and wondered why she'd been feeling so insecure. Everything was perfect. A perfect morning, followed by an exhilarating ride on his motorcycle all the way to the beach, clinging to his back as he broke a few speed records while attempting to ditch the pursuing paparazzi. And now lunch.

She felt as if she was sixteen and in love for the first time. There was certainly something to be said for the joys of a younger man. She tried to imagine Cooper on a bike flying through the mountains at eighty miles an hour. That would never happen. Cooper was into drivers and limos and bodyguards. Cooper lived the life of a big star to the hilt. She'd heard a rumor lately that he was even thinking of stepping into the political arena. Hmm . . . lots of luck with *his* reputation.

Now that things were back on track with Billy, she could start concentrating on her career again. The following month she was in the recording studio laying down final tracks for her upcoming CD, due to be released the same week her fifteen-city concert tour began. After that she had two movies lined up, the launch of her new fragrance, and a line of upmarket sports clothes. Plus she'd promised Lucky that she would make a surprise appearance at the opening of the Keys. Which meant that somewhere along the way she would have to fit in rehearsals with her backup dancers and, since it was a new theater, a serious sound check at the Keys venue.

"You're off on a mind trip," Billy remarked, leaning across the table. "Where you at?"

"Right now I'm here with you," she said affectionately. "I'm thinking how great it would be if we could get to do this every weekend."

"You'd soon be bored."

"No I wouldn't."

An overbearing woman in a lilac pantsuit interrupted them by storming the table and thrusting a slip of paper under Billy's nose.

"My daughter'll never forgive me if I don't ask you to do this," she gushed. "My daughter simply adores you, thinks you're wonderful. Would you mind signing? Oh my! This'll make her year."

Billy graciously scrawled his signature on the slip of paper, then passed it over to Venus.

The woman started to object—that is, until she recognized Venus, whereupon she launched into fan overdrive.

Venus signed, not so graciously, and told Billy to get the check.

Somehow or other the spell of being two almost normal people out on a lunch date was broken.

Still . . . it was nice while it lasted.

33

The offices Anthony Bonar kept in Mexico City were merely a front. Beneath the facade of a thriving import/export business most of his dealings in the drug trade took place.

He entered his private office, nodding at a couple of trusted associates he'd summoned from his plane. It was time to make sure everything was on track—shipments, deliveries, cash payments.

Privacy and secrecy were of paramount importance to Anthony—every morning he had a surveillance expert sweep his office for bugging devices. In his business it was imperative to always be careful and alert. One mistake and it could all be over.

His office was spacious, the focal point being an oversized partners desk. In front of the desk stood a big leather couch along with several matching chairs. A fully stocked bar was over in the corner, while one wall consisted of floor-to-ceiling bookcases. This wall featured a concealed door that led into an inner office where Anthony took care of private business. A sophisticated entry code scanned his fingerprints before the concealed door would open, and he was the only person with access. He kept three safes in his second office, all of them stuffed with cash. There was also a private exit to the street should he ever have to get out fast.

After a couple of hours going over the latest business transactions with his associates, he instructed The Grill to bring the car around. It was time to go home.

"You want I call Mrs. Bonar, tell her you're coming?" The Grill inquired.

"No," Anthony said. "I'll surprise her."

This was a first. Usually he told Irma well in advance when he was coming, but since he planned on only staying overnight he didn't bother. Tomorrow they'd move on to their Acapulco home. He felt like taking a break—the unpleasant experience in Vegas still had him on edge.

Irma would be pleased to see him, especially when he told her they were going to Acapulco, and as an extra surprise he was flying in the children.

On the drive to his house he called the Miami mansion and spoke to the nanny. "Pack everyone up, you're all comin' to Acapulco," he informed her. "My secretary's gonna contact you with flight details. Be there tomorrow."

"The children will not be very happy about this, Mr. Bonar," sniffed the nanny. "They have arrangements with their friends."

"Cancel whatever *arrangements* they got. Tell 'em to bring their friends if it'll keep 'em happy. Make it happen, Nanny, or get your uptight ass fired."

~ ~ ~

Irma glanced at the bedside clock, noting that it was almost five. Luis was asleep beside her, sprawled across the bed. Since the gardeners' hours were eight until four, she realized that she had to get him out of there before the guards became suspicious. It was one thing Luis being there all day, but all night? She didn't think so. Too risky.

Gently she leaned over and stroked his muscled back. "You have to go," she whispered. "It's getting late."

"*Qué?*" he muttered, turning over and stretching.

"You have to go, Luis," she repeated. "Get up."

"*Ah, sí,* Missus Bonar," he said, leaning on one elbow. "*Veree* good."

"You're starting to speak English," she exclaimed.

"Engleesh," he repeated, a shy smile spreading across his craggy face.

She put her hand against his cheek. "I'm going to teach you a word every time we're together," she promised. "Love. Can you say love?"

"Love," he repeated, rolling off the bed.

She watched him as he picked up his clothes and began pulling on his worn jeans and frayed work shirt. He was certainly what her sister back in Omaha would call a hunk.

She moved close to him, placed her arms around his neck, and impulsively kissed him. "*Adiós,* Luis," she said softly. "*Mañana?*"

"Tomorrow," he agreed, nodding his head.

It pleased her that he'd obviously been trying to learn a few words of English; it proved that he cared. She wished he could spend the night, but how could she outthink the guards? It was impossible. If Luis stayed, they'd know.

Once he left she was faced with a long lonely night by herself. What did Anthony imagine she got up to? He refused to allow her any friends, nor could she entertain when he wasn't in residence.

Well, she was *definitely* entertaining the thought of leaving him, and *that* was one reality he couldn't stop.

~ ~ ~

Luis lingered in the vast marble hallway on his way out. To think that all this belonged to one man, the house, the grounds, the woman . . .

Ah, the woman. Señor Bonar might own a lot of things, but he sure as hell did not own the woman.

Luis experienced a moment of sheer satisfaction as he let himself out the front door. The woman was his whenever he wanted her. That was a fact.

He walked around to the back of the house and climbed into his battered truck, then he drove toward the entrance gates of the Bonar mansion.

As he drew his truck up to the wrought-iron gates, one of the guards stepped forward and waved him to stop.

Cursing under his breath, Luis recognized Cesar, the guard, the sometime boyfriend of his slutty sister, Lucia. Luis disliked Cesar intensely.

"Hello, Luis," the man said in Spanish. "What's goin' on?"

Luis shrugged and told him that nothing much was going on.

"You're working late today," Cesar said, consulting his watch. "It's past five."

"I had things to do," Luis said.

"What things?" Cesar asked.

"Things in the house for Señora Bonar," Luis said evasively.

"You seem to be spending a lot of time in the house," Cesar said.

"When Señora Bonar wants something, it is my job to take care of it."

"I'm sure," Cesar sneered.

Luis held his temper in check. Was Cesar insinuating something?

"How's your lovely wife?" Cesar asked.

"Very well," Luis replied.

"Give her my regards. Tell her I drop by for supper one night, your sister asks me all the time."

"You'd be very welcome," Luis lied, experiencing a sick feeling in the pit of his stomach. Maybe he was taking too many risks spending so much time in the house with Señora Bonar. But then again why shouldn't he? There was nobody around to stop him.

"Can you open the gate?" he said.

"You know who's on their way home?" Cesar said, in no hurry to do anything.

"Who?" Luis asked, impatient to get out.

"Señor Bonar."

"*Sí?*"

"Ah," Cesar said, stroking his small black mustache, "here comes his car now."

A sleek silver Mercedes drove into view.

"Pull over, allow him to pass," Cesar ordered Luis in his most officious security guard voice.

Luis did so, staring out of his window at the approaching car. He'd never seen Señor Bonar; all the months he'd worked at the house the master had never appeared.

As the heavy gates opened, Anthony rolled down the back window of his Mercedes, glanced over at Luis, still behind the wheel of his truck, and signaled the guard.

"Who's that?" he snapped, forever suspicious.

"One of the gardeners, Señor Bonar," Cesar replied, standing at attention. "He's leaving now."

"Any problems here?" Anthony inquired.

"No problems, *señor.*"

"Keep it that way."

Anthony took another look at Luis. Their eyes met for a fleeting second.

Luis experienced a full-body shiver of sheer dread. Anthony Bonar had the coldest eyes he'd ever seen.

34

Things were not progressing the way Henry had planned. He'd wanted the girl, not the girl plus one. And the plus one could present problems he'd never even considered.

After locking Maria—or Max, as she was known—into the secure room, he'd had to decide what to do about her so-called cousin. He'd felt a strong urge to shoot him and bury him out in the woods. But that would be wrong, wouldn't it? And Henry had no intention of ending up in jail punished for a crime he'd never meant to commit. So he'd left him in the trunk of Max's car for a while, then later he'd driven to the out-house in the back of the cabin, and once there he'd opened the trunk. He had not expected the cousin to hurl himself at him screaming expletives, almost knocking him to the ground.

Not quite. Henry recovered quickly, held on to his gun, and waved it in the boy's face. That shut him up.

Henry had never realized before how powerful the threat of shooting someone could be. The gun came from his father's collection. It was not too small, not too big, perfect for threatening purposes. He was quite familiar with guns, for when he was twelve his father had taken him on a hunting trip with several of his rich cronies. They'd flown to Canada on a private plane, then gone on an all-out killing expedition in the wilderness where his father had forced him to shoot wild boar and any other animal that moved. Henry had hated the experience, he'd hated firing the gun, then dealing with the blood and guts of the dead and wounded animals, but at least he'd learned how to handle a gun.

Once he had her cousin securely locked in the windowless outhouse with the solid oak door, he had not felt like starting his relationship with Maria. Yes, Maria—he did not care for the name Max, it was a most unsuitable name for a pretty young girl to adopt as her own. And she *was* pretty. Oh yes, she was very pretty indeed. Prettier than her mother, who had more of an exotic look about her. Maria's face was softer, her lips fuller, and she had the most exquisite emerald green eyes he'd ever seen.

Henry had expected none of this—he'd anticipated that the girl would be a bitch like her mother. The surprise was that this girl could never be a bitch, he'd immediately sensed that she was very special indeed.

He knew he should go to her, assure her that everything would be all right, but somehow he couldn't bring himself to do so. Best to let things lie until the morning. Best not to rush her.

Besides, now that he had her in his power, he was strangely nervous. He wanted her to like him, and he realized that locking her up was not a good start.

He had to think of ways to change the circumstances of their first meeting. Ways to make her like him.

~ ~ ~

Saturday morning Henry heard her yelling. He was the only one to hear her, for when his father had built the out-of-the-way log cabin, he'd bought up all the surrounding land, guaranteeing complete privacy for miles around.

After his father's unfortunate death, nobody had visited the cabin except him. Henry had a feeling that somehow or other everyone had forgotten it existed, which was fine with him because when his mother passed on it would be his anyway, and he'd been thinking that maybe he'd sell the Pasadena mansion and move to the cabin where nobody could bother him.

It occurred to him that if he was able to gain Maria's trust and convince her what a witch Lucky Santangelo was, perhaps she would come with him—willingly the next time.

Things could have been so different if she hadn't brought her cousin with her. Damn him! This was an inconvenience he hadn't expected. If the cousin hadn't been present she would have come with him quietly, exactly as they'd planned. Hadn't they corresponded nicely on the Internet? Didn't she know plenty about him? The fact that he didn't look like the photo he'd posted meant nothing—she would have soon gotten used to him. He'd posted a photo of an obscure model, knowing if he'd put up a photo of himself she probably wouldn't have come.

Henry was aware that he was not the best-looking man in the world. However, that did not mean he wasn't a talented and accomplished actor, unlike Billy Melina, who was nothing but a pretty boy with no substance.

Henry hated Billy Melina, just as he hated Lucky Santangelo. But he didn't hate Maria. Oh no, one look into those hypnotizing emerald green eyes and he didn't hate Maria. Quite the reverse in fact.

During the night he'd taken Maria's car and driven back to Big Bear, where he'd left it in the Kmart parking lot. Before doing so he'd wiped it clean of prints, feeling like a criminal, which was stupid since he was certainly no criminal. He'd also taken her laptop, which he'd discovered under the passenger seat. After that he'd driven his Volvo back to the cabin and unloaded the supplies he'd stocked up with on his way to Big Bear before the car had run out of gas.

He'd filled the fridge with food, lit a fire, and made the place as comfortable as possible. Then he'd gone to sleep on the foldaway bed in the main room. Now it was morning and he could hear Maria yelling to be let out.

The anticipation of seeing her again filled him with excitement. What would she say to him this morning? How would she feel? She was probably hungry and thirsty, so before unlocking the bedroom door where she was held captive, he prepared a tray with something for her to eat. A dish of cut-up fruit, a glass of orange juice, and two pieces of wheat toast. He wished he'd thought of bringing flowers, even a single rose would've been a nice touch.

When he opened the door he found her sitting on the floor, her ankle still manacled to the leg of the sturdy bed. He immediately noticed her ankle was red and swollen and he felt bad.

"Who *are* you?" she shouted, glaring at him, her expression wild and furious. "What the hell do you want with me? I *hate* you, you freak! Let me out of here!"

He was shocked. He hadn't expected her to hate him. His feelings were hurt.

"I thought you might be hungry," he said, carefully placing the tray on the end of the bed, determined to stay polite in spite of her nasty attitude. "Do you like fruit?"

"What am I supposed to do, grovel and thank you?" she yelled, shooting him another furious look. "I need to use the bathroom."

"I can't let you do that unless you promise to behave," he said, wishing she would stop shouting.

"If you don't let me go to the bathroom," she threatened, "I'll pee all over the floor."

He didn't appreciate vulgarity, it wasn't right. But he had to remember that she'd been raised by Lucky Santangelo, so she obviously didn't know any better.

"I'm trusting you," he said, reaching in his pocket for the key to the shackle on her ankle.

"Trusting me?" she shouted. "Are you out of your fucking *mind?*"

Now she was using foul language, another habit she'd probably picked up from her mother.

He bent down and unlocked the shackle.

She stood up, quite unsteady. He took her arm and led her to the small bathroom his father had added on when he'd found the outhouse was not to his liking.

"Well," she demanded when they reached the bathroom, "are you going to stand there *watching* me? Is that how you get your sick kicks?"

"I'll wait outside," he said stiffly.

She slammed the door in his face and he heard running water.

This was not the way he had planned things at all. His original plan was very clear. They would come to the cabin together, spend a pleasant time talking about all the things they'd e-mailed to each other, and he would have found out plenty about her mother. Only then would he have decided what his next move would be. The way things were turning out was a completely different scenario.

He wasn't happy, and yet he wasn't exactly sad. The girl was his. They were alone together. She was in his power, and Henry had never had anyone in his power before. It felt quite invigorating.

Then he remembered her cousin locked in the outhouse. What was he supposed to do about him? He couldn't let him starve to death.

Perhaps he should drug him, but he hadn't brought any drugs. Who'd have thought it would come to this?

Kill him, a little voice whispered in his head. *It's the only way.*

~ ~ ~

Desperately trying not to panic, Max checked out the bathroom. There was a rusty old tub, a shallow sink, and a wooden toilet. That was it. High up was one tiny window, too small to wriggle through.

This was a crazy situation, completely insane. She'd actually been abducted! Was she dreaming? Was this some kind of out-of-control nightmare? If it was, she hoped she'd wake up soon.

Once again she wondered if Cookie and Harry had anything to do with this. Then she thought no, it was impossible.

Gingerly she climbed on top of the wooden toilet making a vain attempt to pry open the tiny window.

It wouldn't shift, the window was totally jammed.

"Crap," she muttered, jumping down, running the tap, and quickly peeing.

He knocked on the door. "Are you coming out?" he asked.

"I'm never coming out, you pervert," she yelled back, pulling up her jeans.

"Then I shall have to come in," he said, opening the door and walking in. "I should look at your ankle," he said. "Is it sore?"

"You're only going to manacle me again, so why bother?" she said, tossing back her long dark hair.

"Not if you make me a promise that you won't go anywhere," he replied, marveling at her beauty.

"You put a fucking *leg iron* on me," she said accusingly. "How could you do that?"

"Kindly control your language, young lady," he said, thinking how pleasant it would be if she would only stop swearing.

"I ain't no lady, mister," she answered, staring at him defiantly. "And you ain't no gentleman."

Taking her arm he led her back into the bedroom.

"Do you *realize* what you're doing?" she said, her voice rising. "You've *kidnapped* me, forced me to come here with you at gunpoint. That's a federal offense, mister, and when they catch you they'll lock you up and throw away the key."

"They'll never catch me," Henry said confidently, quite enjoying this exchange of words.

"Where's Ace?" she demanded, changing tactics. "What have you done with my cousin?"

"He's perfectly safe," Henry said, once more shackling her ankle to the leg of the bed.

"How do I know that?"

"Because I'm telling you."

"Ha! Big deal. I bet my family is looking for me *and* him, so you'd better let us go, otherwise you're gonna be in *major* fucking trouble."

"You're a very pretty girl with a very dirty mouth," Henry remarked, pursing his thin lips. "Your mother should wash it out with soap."

"What're you, from another century?" she said scornfully.

He didn't like the fact that she was so aggressively verbal. Surely she could sense that he wasn't about to hurt her?

Surely she knew they were destined to be together?

35

After an hour of sitting at the roulette table Brigette was up several thousand dollars. There was nothing like a winning streak to make a girl smile. Bobby kept running off to the crap table, then coming back to check on how she was doing.

"Roulette's an idiot's game—how come you're winning?" he asked, hovering over her shoulder.

"I know," she said, blue eyes gleaming. "I keep on putting a stack of chips on eleven, and can you believe it's come up three times!"

"Way to go, Brig."

"Oh, *yes*."

"Didn't realize you were such a gambler."

"I'm not."

"You could've fooled me."

"Do you mind?" she said, placing more chips across the table. "You're disturbing my concentration."

"Don't go losing it all."

"No intention of doing that."

"And don't pick up any guys," he added, observing that quite a few men lurking around the table had their eyes on her. It was a given. She was undeniably hot.

"Why not, Bobby?" she asked innocently, as if she were totally unaware of the kind of attention she was attracting.

" 'Cause *I'm* the one who's watching out for you today—after all, I *am* your big, bad uncle."

"Surely you mean my *little* uncle," she contradicted, grinning at him. "Let's not forget you're nine years younger than me, Bobby."

"Okay, so I'm your little uncle who's keeping a close eye on his smokin' niece."

"Shh . . . you're messing with my luck," she said, busily placing even more chips around the table.

The wheel started spinning. Once again her number came up. She let out a whoop of delight.

"Wow!" Bobby whispered in her ear. "A few thousand dollars certainly turns *you* on."

"You're right," she said, excitedly scooping in her winning stack of chips. " 'Cause this is *my* money, Bobby. I didn't inherit it from anybody. Made it all myself."

"How about cashing in and we go get a drink?"

"I'd sooner have something to eat."

"We can do that too," he said. "Go on, Brig, make a move before you lose it all back."

"If you insist," she sighed, reluctantly pushing her stacks of chips back toward the croupier.

~ ~ ~

"I was thinking I could take you for a pizza at Spago," Alex suggested, willing her to say yes, because how often did he get a chance to be alone with Lucky?

"Is that what you were thinking?" Lucky said, shuffling through a pile of change orders from various contractors.

"You're finished signing, aren't you?"

"I guess, but there's other things I should go over," she answered vaguely.

"Now?"

"Well . . ." she said, hesitating for a moment. "I suppose I *could* do everything on Monday when I come back."

"Go eat," Mooney encouraged, letting out a discreet burp. "Have fun while you're here. Go toss a few coins in a slot machine."

"Do I *look* like a slot machine kind of girl?" Lucky said dryly.

Mooney roared with laughter.

"Okay, Alex," Lucky said. "I can always find time for a pizza." She turned to Mooney. "Why don't you take a break and come with us?"

"Gonna pass," Mooney said. "Too much to do, but I'll drive you over."

Ten minutes later Mooney dropped them off at Caesars, where they made their way to the outside patio at Spago.

"This is a quite a coincidence," Lucky said after they were seated. "Both of us in Vegas at the same time." She took a long beat before adding, "You wouldn't be stalking me, would you, Alex?"

"Sure," he answered, quite amused. "I'm stalking you, Lucky. Got nothing better to do with my time."

"Sending me notes too?"

"Notes?"

" 'Drop Dead Beautiful.' "

"What the hell are you talking about?"

"I've been getting a series of notes delivered to my house. Could be an invitation to something, but Bobby thinks I should have someone look into it."

"Wanna tell me about it?"

"I just did."

A young waiter came over, handed them both menus, and took their drink orders.

"What exactly do the notes say?" Alex asked, after ordering a Bloody Mary.

"That's it," Lucky said. "Short and simple—'Drop Dead Beautiful.'"

"Sounds like a movie. In fact, I think there *was* a movie with that title."

"The thing that's a bit odd is that the notes are hand-delivered to my house," Lucky said, picking up a glass of water and taking a sip.

"What does your security guard say?"

"I gave up guards a couple of years ago. Didn't want to live like that, nor do I want my children thinking they have to be protected."

"No?"

"*Definitely* no. I've hired security for Gino's party, but other than that I want to be able to get in my car and go places without being followed and watched."

"Y'know, Lucky," Alex said thoughtfully, "you have a big reputation and a ton of money. You *should* have security."

"Don't need it, Alex."

"Okay," he said, picking up the menu. "Let's talk pizza. What you got in mind?"

"I'm thinking smoked salmon," she said, relieved he was dropping it.

"I'm thinking I'll join you," he said, snapping his fingers for their waiter.

After they'd ordered, Lucky sat back and took a long look at Alex. He was aging well—in fact, he looked better now in his late fifties than ever. He was super smart, very attractive, and extraordinarily talented. She wondered why no woman had been able to lure him into marriage.

"Where's Ling?" she asked casually.

"Ling doesn't fly well," he responded.

"You know, Alex," she said, fingering the rim of her water glass, "you should get married. You need a woman to look after you."

"Yeah," he answered, giving her a look. "And who do you think that woman should be?"

"Haven't given it any thought," she said offhandedly.

"Apparently you have."

"No."

"No?" he said disbelievingly.

"I do have a few things on my mind other than your marital status," she said, fishing her sunglasses out of her purse and putting them on.

"Yeah," Alex drawled sarcastically. "It's bright in here, isn't it?"

"Fuck you," Lucky responded, trying not to smile, because she had to admit that Alex knew her so well. He even knew that whenever she felt uncomfortable she hid behind her shades.

"Anytime," he said, half smiling. "All you have to do is name a time and a place."

"Oh, shut up," she said, finally laughing.

"And she finds me an object of amusement," he said dryly.

The waiter delivered their drinks to the table—a Bloody Mary for Alex, Perrier for Lucky.

"This is nice," Alex said, picking up his drink.

"What's nice?"

"You and me sitting here enjoying some time together, just the two of us."

"This is hardly a date," Lucky pointed out. "So don't try making it into one. We're good friends who happened to run into each other."

"Good friends who are never alone anymore."

"Any*more*, Alex?" Lucky said, raising an eyebrow.

"When we were making *Seduction* we had plenty of alone time," Alex reminded her. "I remember it well."

"Sure," Lucky said lightly. "Us and a crew of hundreds."

"I guess you're choosing to forget all the time we spent in the editing rooms?"

"Why do you think I wasn't prepared to make another movie with you?" she said flippantly.

"Don't be like that."

"Like *what?*"

"Like you don't feel that there's anything between us."

"Alex," Lucky said impatiently. "I've told you this before, there can't be anything between us."

"Because of Lennie?"

"I love Lennie, you *know* that. How many times do I have to tell you?"

He sighed. "There's something I've always wanted to say to you."

"Please don't," she said, drumming her fingers on the table. "I don't want to hear it."

"I'm going to."

"No, Alex, you're not," she said firmly.

Before he could reply, Bobby and Brigette strolled into view.

Lucky immediately waved them over to the table, delighted to create a distraction.

"Alex," Brigette exclaimed, flushed from her recent win. "Haven't seen *you* in ages."

"It's been a long time," Alex agreed, standing up. "And look at you, Bobby, I hear you're running the hottest club in New York."

"Tell my mom," Bobby said wryly. "I'm not sure she believes me."

"Sit down, join us," Lucky said quickly. "We're about to have smoked salmon pizza."

"Delicious!" Brigette exclaimed. "I'm starving!"

"Then we shall order two more," Lucky said, signaling their waiter.

Alex threw her a look. "Of all the joints in Vegas they had to pick this one," he murmured ruefully. "Timing's everything, huh?"

Lucky nodded. "It sure is."

And once again they exchanged an oh-so-intimate smile.

36

When Internet Freak returned later that day with a tray of food and a bottle of water, Max was ready for him. She'd had all afternoon to think about what she was going to say.

"You should know that I'm only sixteen," she announced, making a desperate attempt to let the creep know how young she was. Maybe, just maybe, it might convince him to release her. "When I told you I was eighteen," she continued, "I was lying. And another thing, I never mentioned to my mom that I was meeting some strange guy, and when she finds out I'm missing, she'll major *freak*!"

"But you're not missing," Henry said patiently. "You're here with me. You're perfectly safe."

Unexpected tears filled her eyes. This dude was a looney and she couldn't take much more of this insane situation. "I'm *not* safe," she shouted, forcing her tears to go away. "I'm your fucking *prisoner*. You've kept me locked up here since last night. YOU'VE GOT TO LET ME GO!"

"Eventually," Henry said, quite composed.

Eventually. What did *that* mean?

Gotta stay strong, she told herself. *It's not smart to show weakness*. Ever since she was a little girl, Lucky had drilled into her that girls can do anything. Lucky's mantras: *Be strong. Kick ass when necessary. Never give in.*

Well, there was no way she was giving in to this creepo loser with his weaselly face and psycho lifeless eyes.

Taking a deep breath, she glared angrily at her captor. "Where's Ace?" she demanded. "Why are you keeping us apart?"

"That is not your concern," he said.

"Yes it *is*," she argued, still glaring at him. "Where is he?"

"I sent him away."

"No you didn't."

"Yes I did."

It suddenly occurred to her that Ace and Internet Freak might be in cahoots. It was very possible that Ace was part of the plan and *that's* why he wasn't around. Of course. It was all so obvious. He'd sent Ace to soften her up and then pounced. How stupid was she to fall for it?

She shivered uncontrollably.

"Are you cold?" Henry asked, sounding concerned.

"I'm uncomfortable," she complained. "You'd better undo this thing on my ankle 'cause it really hurts."

"If I do, you'll try to run. But I should warn you that there is nowhere to run to. We are in an isolated spot surrounded by woods, and you would be very foolish to attempt to leave."

"I won't run," she lied.

"Can I trust you?"

"Do I look like an idiot?"

He produced the key and undid the shackle.

She rubbed her ankle, which was blistered and red. "I need disinfectant," she said. "I can barely walk."

"I'll see what I have," he said, leaving the room, locking the sturdy door behind him.

Immediately after he was gone, she jumped off the bed and made it to the window. It was boarded up with strips of plywood on the outside. A quick exploration of the room did not give up anything that looked even remotely useful.

Crap! She'd been hoping for something—anything that she could use as a weapon when he returned. Smash him over the head and run. He wasn't holding his gun, and he looked like a weakling with his gimpy leg and scrawny build. She was sure she could take him.

Yes. She didn't need a weapon. She was strong, she'd taken self-defense classes.

Her plan was to catch him off guard, kick him hard in the balls—and run like hell.

37

The villa in Acapulco was Anthony's favorite home. He'd designed every detail of the three-story waterfront villa himself, from the Italian marble bathrooms (six) to the sunken black-bottomed infinity swimming pool overlooking Acapulco Bay.

The grounds consisted of a magnificent landscape of coconut trees, giant palms, and fragrant walls of many different colors of bougainvillea. There were several areas for dining alfresco. Anthony's favorite part of the outdoor design was an all-glass elevator that descended from the top floor of the house to the lower-level entertainment area. He'd been inspired by the movie *Scarface*.

Another feature Anthony was particularly pleased with was his own personal boat dock and heliport, where a select few of his business acquaintances could come and go without the outside world checking on their activities. It was a very convenient way of conducting business.

Anthony kept a full staff in residence, including Manuel and Rosa Sousa, a married couple who ran the estate when he was not there. Rosa was a magnificent cook, while Manuel oversaw everything else. They had worked for Anthony since he'd built the villa ten years previously.

One day Emmanuelle had seen pictures of the villa and begged him to take her there. "It's so beautiful," she'd sighed longingly. "And very *sexy*. We could make love in every room." A seductive pause. "Maybe even in the elevator. What do you think, honeybun? Will you take me there?"

He'd thought it was quite an appealing idea, but he had yet to invite her. It was one thing entertaining his mistresses in other cities, but to bring them into one of his homes . . . maybe not. Even Anthony observed *some* boundaries.

Irma had been startled to see him, even more startled when he'd informed her they were flying to Acapulco the following morning.

"Why didn't you let me know you were coming?" she'd asked. "Nobody is prepared."

"What? You don't like surprises?" he'd responded, fondling his two large dogs, and deciding that his wife looked as if she'd lost weight. Not that Irma was ever fat—quite the contrary—but she was looking particularly sleek and attractive. Hardly Emmanuelle-style attractive, nor Carlita, but for the mother of two children, she wasn't bad.

That night he'd given her the pleasure of blowing him, and the next morning they were on their way to Acapulco, accompanied by two other couples he didn't mind spending time with. Fanta and Emilio Guerra were rich Mexicans in the clothing business. And Innes and Ralph Masters were Americans who lived in Mexico City. The two men greatly admired Anthony, while their wives lusted after him. It amused Anthony the way the two couples glorified him. They laughed at his jokes, took full advantage of his generous hospitality, and clapped at his singing prowess.

All in all they were an adoring entourage, and who didn't enjoy being adored?

~ ~ ~

Irma shuddered when she realized how close she'd come to getting caught. God! What if Anthony had walked in on her and Luis? It was scary and unthinkable. She'd had a narrow escape, and it had shaken her, made her think about the risks she was taking.

Anthony turning up unannounced was most unusual—in fact, she could not recall it ever happening before. There were always the calls to warn her of his imminent arrival, and then much activity would take place in the house as everything was cleaned and scrubbed to a spotless finish, the dogs were groomed, the friends were alerted, and by the time Anthony arrived everything was in place.

This time not only had he arrived home unexpectedly, but he'd announced that they were leaving for Acapulco the next day. Irma had no wish to go to Acapulco with her husband, but she could hardly say no, especially when he informed her that the children were meeting them there. At least that was some kind of consolation.

Later that night, lying in bed, he'd started pawing her for a few seconds before pushing her head down until it was on a level with his penis. She knew what he wanted, and she was forced to oblige, for the consequences of *not* doing what Anthony wanted were not pretty. So she'd shut her eyes and pretended it was Luis she was servicing, and somehow or other she'd managed to get through it.

In the morning they'd boarded the plane with his friends in tow.

Under different circumstances she might have quite liked Fanta and Innes—they seemed to be pleasant enough women. But circumstances were such that all they did was buzz around Anthony, hanging on to his every word.

Ralph Masters was a lecherous creep. Whenever Anthony's attention was elsewhere, Ralph managed to make suggestive remarks toward Irma—remarks she would never dare repeat to Anthony. Emilio Guerra, on the other hand, chose to totally ignore her, treating her as if she didn't exist. As far as Emilio was concerned, she was just a wife, and therefore hardly worth his attention.

The plane ride was excruciating. Champagne and caviar flowed, while Anthony's sycophants agreed with everything he said.

It wasn't where Irma wanted to be. She'd allowed her thoughts to drift, wondering how Luis would feel when he came to work and found she wasn't there. Someone would probably mention that the master of the house had arrived home, and Señora and Señor Bonar had left for the Acapulco house.

She'd asked Anthony how long they would be staying in Acapulco. "What does it matter?" he'd said. "We stay as long as I wanna stay."

That was Anthony Bonar. He never told anyone what he was doing from one day to the next.

Anthony's two large Dobermans traveled on the plane with them. The dogs always made Irma nervous, so much so that when Anthony was not in residence she insisted that they stay outside with the guards. When he was home, Anthony allowed them to sleep on the bed, and it terrified her, but when she complained, her husband simply laughed at her fears.

The Acapulco villa was Anthony's domain. The couple who worked for him, Manuel and Rosa, kissed his ass big time.

Upon their arrival Anthony picked Rosa up and swung her around for the benefit of his friends. She was a short woman, and quite plump. Placing a fake smile on her face she tolerated the manhandling, but Irma sensed she loathed the way Anthony treated her.

"How's my Rosa, huh?" he'd crowed, pinching her cheek with a not-too-gentle touch. "Rosa's worked for me ten years, but I could fire her tomorrow, huh, Rosa? Would I do that? No, 'cause you're the best little cook in the whole of Acapulco."

Anthony was showing off in front of his friends, flexing his control.

"Okay, Manuel," he'd said. "Get your lazy ass to the airport, go meet my kids. They're coming. It's good, huh?"

Yes, Irma thought, *it's very good.* At least she would get to see her children.

~ ~ ~

And back in Las Vegas, an investigation was about to take place concerning Tasmin Garland's disappearance. Her babysitter reported to the police that Tasmin had not returned home on Friday night. Her ex-husband, a croupier at one of the hotels, followed the babysitter's concerns by filing a missing-persons report. He was about to get remarried, and much as he loved his son, he did not plan on having the boy live with him.

Where was Tasmin Garland? Forty-eight hours had passed since she was last seen; it was question time. Diane Franklin, a tenacious, twice-divorced black detective in her mid-forties, was assigned the case.

After talking to the babysitter and the ex-husband, the next person she had on her list to question was Renee Falcon.

38

Playing with Billy on his home turf was a revelation for Venus. Instead of staying in her fortresslike mansion, where she felt safe away from the adulation of her rabid fans, she and Billy were out and about. First the ride on his motorcycle, which she'd never done before, then the delightful lunch at Geoffrey's, and after that they'd stopped at the Cross Creek shopping center in Malibu, where she'd purchased a shady sun hat, a pair of blackout sunglasses, and a nondescript track suit.

"Disguise time," he'd informed her.

"I have plenty of disguises at home," she'd assured him.

"I know, but you're not at home, are you?"

"We'll never fool the paparazzi, they're out in droves."

"Trust me," Billy had said, grinning. "I got a plan."

Carrying her purchases, she'd hopped on the back of his bike and they'd taken off again.

There was something very sexy about riding on the back of a motorcycle. It had to do with contact—the way her breasts felt pressed up against his back, the wind in her face, the warmth of his body. She'd held on tightly as they'd sped down the Pacific Coast Highway, several paparazzi still in hot pursuit.

"Why can't they leave us alone?" she'd breathed in his ear.

"'Cause they got a job to do, an' *my* job is losing 'em," he'd answered, before making an illegal U-turn and roaring off in the opposite direction.

Venus couldn't help laughing. It was highly dangerous but unbelievably exciting—it made her realize just how much she'd been missing out on the fun side of life.

Being married to Cooper could do that to a girl. Cooper Turner, legendary movie star, legendary cocksman, and very boring when one was married to him. That's why their marriage had failed, because Cooper had forgotten how to have fun. He'd turned into the reformed playboy. Marriage had changed him, but it hadn't changed her. She'd always had a rebellious streak, and just because she was a few years older than Billy, it didn't mean that he couldn't bring it out in her.

"I think you've lost the paparazzi," she said breathlessly. "I think they're history."

"You just gotta have the moves," Billy boasted, making a sharp left turn toward Paradise Cove. "I want you to go to the ladies' room an' put on your disguise."

"That's a bit pointless, isn't it, since everyone will still recognize you?"

"Not unless I want 'em to," Billy said. "I got the kinda face that blends in."

"No you don't," she said, laughing.

"Yes, I do," he insisted.

"How about the woman who came up to you in Geoffrey's? It wasn't *me* she recognized, it was *you*."

"I have that effect on women," he joked. "If they look me in the eyes, they got me."

"You can be such a punk."

"Think so?"

"Apparently Alex does."

"How do *you* know *that?*"

"'Cause he complained about you to Lucky."

"Oh, that's great. What did he say?"

"He thinks all your success has gone to your head."

"Maybe Alex should move with the times," Billy said irritably. "I'm not about to be his puppet an' jump every time he tells me to. I have my own ideas. I'm gonna direct one of these days."

"I'm sure you will."

"I *know* I will."

The rest of the day was equally blissful. They'd walked along the beach holding hands, fooled around on the sand, and paddled in the surf. It had been a long time since she'd felt so totally carefree—that is, until the paparazzi discovered them again, and then it was over.

On the ride home she said, "I think I'll stay at your house tonight."

"That'll be a first," Billy shouted, roaring down the fast lane. "You've never wanted to stay there before."

"Tonight I do," she answered, hugging him even tighter.

Arriving back at Billy's, they discovered Kev stretched out on the couch with a bottle of beer in one hand and a carton of popcorn in the other. He was busy watching motor racing on TV.

"Venus," he exclaimed, abruptly sitting up and brushing popcorn off his jeans.

"Kev," she responded. "How's it hangin'?"

"No complaints," he said, hurriedly getting off the couch.

Billy threw him a look. Kev was no slouch in the getting-the-hint department. "Guess we won't be watchin' the game tonight," he said.

"That's right," Billy replied.

"*Okay*," Kev said, sliding toward the door. "Think I'll be movin' on."

"See ya, dude," Billy said. "Come to the location Monday."

"I'll do that," Kev replied, and then he was gone.

"Doesn't it bother you, him coming and going as he pleases?" Venus asked once Kev had left.

"'Course not," Billy said, grabbing a handful of popcorn. "Kev's like my brother."

"We could be making love, and he could walk right in on us."

"Lucky him."

"Seriously, Billy."

"Stop bitchin' and come over here, babe," Billy said affectionately, dropping down onto the still warm couch and holding out his arms.

So she did, and everything was great.

~ ~ ~

Sunday morning they awoke late, read the papers, and lounged around the house. Billy put on college football, while Venus attempted to make scrambled eggs in the kitchen. She hadn't cooked in a while, and they turned out mushy, but at least she'd tried.

"Do we *have* to go to that party tonight?" Billy asked, trying to pretend he was enjoying the eggs. "I'm not in a party mood, and I have a real early call tomorrow."

"Yes, we have to go," Venus said. "It's for Lucky's father, and since she's my best friend, I can't *not* go. Anyway, Gino's a great character."

"He is?"

"You've met him, haven't you?"

"I might've, but that would've bin a few years ago when we were making *Seduction*."

"Then tonight you'll see him again," she said, standing up and ruffling his hair. "Here's a thought—how about developing a movie about Gino's life? It would make quite a story. Way back his nickname was Gino the Ram—seems he was quite a stud in his day."

"Would I get to play Gino?" Billy asked, stifling a yawn.

"Are you five-foot-eight, dark-haired, and an Italian American?" Venus said, smiling.

"No, but I'm a stud, aren't I?"

"Oh, yes!"

"Well . . ."

"Billy, this party is important to me. Don't give me a hard time."

"Okay, babe, we'll go."

She hugged him. "That's my Billy."

Later, when it was time for her to go home and get ready for the party, she'd called a cab, taken it to the Beverly Hills Hotel, then waited five minutes before coming out and getting in her car.

Fooling the paparazzi was a full-time job.

~ ~ ~

Ling wasn't talking to Alex, and he didn't give a shit. She was annoyed that he'd gone to Vegas without her. It didn't seem to matter that he'd come back the same night—she was in full nagging mode.

"You know, Ling, I don't need this," he said, giving her a warning look as he walked into his study overlooking the ocean. "I got work to do."

"I don't need it either," she responded, following him. "You're very cold toward me, Alex. You never pay any attention to me. I sit in your house all day—"

"Don't give me that," he interrupted. "You're a lawyer. You go to work."

"And then I come home and cook dinner and you're never here. You show up anytime you want, usually drunk."

"Then why do you stay?"

"Because"—her voice quavered—"I love you, Alex."

Love. The *L* word. Christ! What had he done to deserve this?

"I'm sorry, Ling," he said, not really sorry at all. "This isn't working out for me."

"And don't think I don't know why," Ling said spitefully. "It's because of Lucky, isn't it? Every time you see her you're like a different person. You turn into a puppy dog. If you had a tail it would wag."

"Quit saying such ridiculous crap," he said, sitting down in front of his computer.

"I can see it, and I'm sure everyone else can too," Ling insisted. "*Especially* Lennie."

"You're full of it."

"Look in the mirror, Alex. Look in the mirror and see a man who's in love with another man's wife."

"What do you want from me, Ling?" he said, losing his temper. "I'm not about to marry you. I'm not about to commit to a long-term relationship. *What* the fuck do you want from me?"

"Nothing," she said sulkily.

"Okay, now we've established that, are you staying or going?"

"I'll stay," she said. "Because I know you'll realize in time that I *am* the right woman for you."

Why was it so damned difficult getting a woman to leave?

39

Sunday morning Internet Freak unlocked the door and entered the room where Max had spent a second miserable night with her ankle shackled to the leg of the bed.

Her clever plan of instant freedom had not worked. Yesterday, when he'd returned with a bottle of disinfectant, she'd been all primed and ready to kick him in the balls and make a swift run for it. Unfortunately he'd turned out to be stronger than she'd thought. The moment she'd attempted to jump him, he'd grabbed her arms in a steel lock behind her back, and forced her onto the bed.

She was shocked at his strength. Shocked and horrified. Was he going to rape her? Was that why he'd kidnapped her?

But no, he didn't attempt that. He'd shackled her ankle again, informed her he was most disappointed that she was not to be trusted, and stormed out of the room, not returning until now.

"Call your mother and leave a message," he said, thrusting her cell phone into her hands.

"What'm I supposed to say?" she muttered, glaring at him.

"Tell her you're with friends and you've decided to stay longer."

"You must be like super *crazy!*" she yelled, still desperately trying to bury her fear. "I keep on telling you—my mom's expecting me home today for a big party. If I don't get there she'll have *everyone* out looking for me, and believe me, when she finds out what you've done, you'll be *major* sorry. Nobody messes with my mom. Nobody. She *kills* people who do."

Henry shoved the phone into her hands. "Do it," he said. "People keep leaving you messages wondering why you're not calling them back."

"My friends have probably gone to the cops already," she said, sure that Cookie and Harry must be freaking out because they hadn't heard from her.

"Why would they do that?"

"'Cause you're holding me here, a prisoner."

"They don't know that."

"Oh yes they *do!* You're screwed, mister."

"That's why you'll make a call, to put everyone's mind at rest," he said, determined to ignore her rudeness because he was sure that deep down she couldn't possibly mean it.

"I'm hungry," she said. "Give me something to eat and I'll make the call."

"You will?"

"Yes," she said sulkily, thinking that perhaps there was a way to convey that she was in serious trouble.

Henry nodded and shuffled his feet. His original plan had been to get back at Lucky Santangelo, but plans change, and now he wanted to make Maria see just how good he could be for her. Why not? He had plenty of money, or at least he would have when his mother died, which hopefully might be soon. He was not a gambler or a cheat. He was a nice guy. A regular guy. He was the same person she'd corresponded with online and liked enough to meet.

The truth was he was enamored with this girl. Right now she was all that mattered to him, and given more time he was certain he could convince her to like him back.

"I'll get you something to eat," he said. "Then you'll make the call?"

She nodded.

He left the room thinking that his immediate problem was what to do about Ace. Since locking him in the outhouse, he had not ventured back. He was hoping that when he finally opened the door the boy would be in too weak a state to attack him.

How long could someone live without food and water?

It wouldn't be his fault if Ace expired in there. That would not be murder. That would just be unfortunate.

40

"She's sixteen," Lucky pointed out. "Sixteen, Lennie. She should have *some* sense of responsibility."

"How responsible were you at sixteen?" Lennie questioned.

Sometimes Lennie drove her crazy with his laid-back attitude. "I was fucking *married* for chrissakes," she pointed out. "It's Sunday, and there's absolutely *no* excuse for her not returning our calls. You've left two messages. I've left three. She ran out of here without saying good-bye, and I don't mind telling you I'm major pissed."

"No? Really?" he said in a lightly mocking tone. "Whyn't you tell me how you *really* feel."

"Don't do this, Lennie," she warned, flashing him a deadly look. "Do not piss me off even more."

"Listen," he said encouragingly. "Max will be home in time for Gino's party, so try and hold off the big mother/daughter fight until tomorrow."

"What fight?" Bobby asked, bouncing into the room.

"Your little sister," Lucky said.

"Yeah, what about my little sister?"

"We haven't been able to reach her," Lucky said, fuming. "And if she doesn't get home in time for Gino's party, that's *it*—she's grounded for the rest of the year."

"I'm kinda pissed at her too," Bobby remarked. "I was looking forward to us hanging out. Max is *the* best."

"She's not the best at all," Lucky said sharply. "She's a brat."

"No way, Mom."

"She is, Bobby," Lucky insisted. "You don't have to live with her. Everything I say she turns into an argument."

"I know I keep repeating myself," Lennie said. "But face it, Lucky, she's *exactly* like you were at her age. The kid's a rebel, does things her way. You should understand that better than anyone."

"Oh God," Lucky said, shaking her head. "You two, one look at a pretty face and that's it, you both turn to mush."

"Yeah, Mom," Bobby said. "That's why we've always done exactly what *you* want us to do. And talking about that—what *do* you want us to do today? There's people everywhere, so is there anything I can do to help with the party?"

"Yes—stay out of the way."

"Is that it?"

"I don't know, Bobby, I'm so mad right now."

"I could take everyone out to lunch."

"Great idea. Take them to the Hotel Bel-Air and get a table on the patio. Gino will like that."

"Here's a thought," Lennie said.

"What?" Lucky sighed.

"If you're so upset with Max, call her girlfriend Cookie, the one she was going to Big Bear with. When she answers, have her put Max on."

"Are you saying that Max is *purposely* avoiding speaking to us?" Lucky said, frowning.

"You know your daughter, she's not into lectures."

"I don't have Cookie's phone number."

"Isn't her father that soul singer, Gerald M.?" Bobby inquired. "I can get you his number from our computer at the club—everybody who's anybody's listed. One call and the number's yours."

"Do it," Lucky said. "Before I run out of patience."

"When you speak to Max, no fighting," Lennie said. "Just make sure she'll be back in time for the party."

"Any other instructions?" Lucky asked, shooting him an "I do not appreciate being told what to do" look.

"Y'know, on second thought, *I* should be the one to call Cookie," Lennie decided. "Go get the number, Bobby."

"Like I don't have enough with the hotel opening and the party for Gino," Lucky grumbled as Bobby left the room. "This is a joke. I'm wiped out."

"Who was it that insisted on flying to Vegas yesterday?" Lennie said. "I think that might've been you. You should've had Mooney bring *you* the checks."

"There was a whole stack of them."

"What happened to the woman from the bank who was supposed to cosign?"

"Who the fuck knows—Mooney's trying to locate her. I refuse to deal with that bank again. I instructed Mooney to switch our accounts."

"That's pretty harsh, isn't it?"

"No. If the woman can't be bothered to cosign the checks, I refuse to keep someone so unreliable around. We're a huge account, she should be more responsible."

Bobby returned with Gerald M.'s private number.

Lucky started to punch the number into her cell phone. Lennie grabbed it from her. "I said *I'll* do it."

The phone rang. Finally somebody picked up. "Gerald?"

"Who's askin'?"

"Lennie Golden, Max's Dad."

"Great t'hear from you, Lennie," Gerald said, sounding stoned. "How ya doin', man?"

"Not bad," Lennie responded. "I need Cookie's cell phone number."

"How's that?"

"The girls are in Big Bear and Max is having a problem with her phone, so we thought we'd reach her on Cookie's."

"Yeah, yeah," Gerald M. said. "Cookie can give it to you herself, she's standing right here."

"She is?" Lennie said.

"Cookie," Gerald M. called out. "Baby girl, get over here."

Lennie turned to Lucky. "Cookie's in L.A.," he said. "She's coming to the phone."

"You've *got* to be kidding me," Lucky said, snatching the phone out of his hand. "Cookie?"

"Oh, uh, hi, Mrs. Golden."

"Where are you?"

"I'm, uh, at my dad's house."

"I thought you were going to a party in Big Bear with Max."

"Uh, y-yes," Cookie stammered. "Well, um . . . I was like *there*, but then I had to get back early."

"Didn't you and Max drive up to Big Bear together?"

"No, we, um . . . took separate cars, so, uh . . . that's why I'm like home, 'cause I had my own car."

"Cookie," Lucky said, smelling trouble, "what *is* going on?"

"Nothing, Mrs. Golden," Cookie said, brimming with fake innocence.

"Whose party was it?" Lucky demanded.

"Um, this friend of mine. Like she's this girl I know."

"Give me the house phone number."

"The party was on Saturday, it's way over."

"I understand that, but I'd like to speak to your friend's mother."

"You can't do that, they've flown back to Aspen."

"Back to Aspen," Lucky repeated. "Y'know, Cookie, do me a favor, get your ass in your car and drive over here. I need to talk to you face-to-face."

"But Mrs. Golden—"

"Cookie, this is not up for discussion. Do it, and do it now."

41

On the way over to the Santangelo/Golden house, Cookie frantically punched out Harry's number. He finally answered after three attempts.

"Where have you *been*?" she screeched. "I'm in major crap city."

"With my dad," Harry answered. "We're on a TV set. The reception on my phone sucks."

"Did you reach Max yet?"

"No. I've left messages."

"So have I," Cookie said. "And listen to this—I've been summoned to her house by Lucky."

"*Whaaat?*"

"Yeah, she tracked me down, and now I like have to go to her house and explain where Max is."

"This is bad," Harry said. "What are you going to say?"

"I dunno," Cookie said. "I mean, Lucky's gonna ask me all these questions about where the party was an' like who the people were an' was Max staying there. What *am* I gonna *say*?"

"Don't sweat it," Harry said, annoyingly unconcerned. "It's Sunday, Max'll be back soon."

"I hope so," Cookie wailed. "'Cause truthfully I'm kinda freaked that she hasn't answered our calls."

"Me too."

"She goes off with some Internet asshole an' we hear nothing. It's like too *weird*."

"Maybe you'd better tell her mom."

"Maybe *you'd* better meet me at her house an' we'll tell her together."

"Can't," Harry said flatly. "I'm in Pasadena."

"Awesome, Harry, you're a big freakin' help," Cookie complained, pulling her car up behind a row of party trucks. "Okay, I'm here now," she said, parking her Corvette, jumping out and making her way to the front door.

Gino Junior was sitting on the steps with an acne-encrusted friend. "What're *you* doing here?" he asked.

"Yeah, what're you doing here?" his friend echoed.

The two boys were checking her out. Gino Junior and his friends were always doing that, horny little jerk-offs.

"Max isn't back yet," Gino Junior offered. "She's gonna be in *way* shit with Mom when she gets here."

"Where is your mom?" Cookie asked, agitatedly twirling her sunglasses and wondering what she was going to say to Lucky.

"In the kitchen," Gino Junior said. "Screaming at everyone."

"See ya," Cookie said.

"Yeah," Gino Junior said. "At the party. It's gonna be full of old farts, so let's sneak off somewhere an' kill a bottle of vodka."

"Grow up, Gino," she said over her shoulder, making her way into the house and through to the kitchen.

Lucky was talking to the caterers, waving her arms in the air. It did not look like she was in a pleasant mood. As soon as she saw Cookie she stopped, marched over to her, took her arm, and steered her out of the room. "Come with me," she said, black eyes flashing danger signals.

"Uh, Lucky, uh . . . nice to see you too," Cookie stammered.

"Don't give me that 'nice to see you' crap," Lucky snapped, narrowing her eyes. "I was your age once, I do know what goes on. Has Max got some boy she's meeting? Is that it?"

"Uh . . . I told you, they—"

"Enough with the bullshit, I want the truth," Lucky said, maneuvering Cookie into her study where she slammed the door shut. "Now sit down and tell me *exactly* what's going on. You didn't go to Big Bear with her, did you?"

"I, uh, yeah . . ."

"I'm telling you, Cookie," Lucky warned, "this is no joke, so don't fucking lie."

"Mrs. Golden—"

"And don't start calling me Mrs. Golden. You've always called me Lucky before, so stop with the innocent friend act 'cause I'm not buying it. Let's get it clear here—I want to know where Max is, and when she's coming home."

"Well . . ." Cookie stammered. "I . . . I tried calling her a few times. I—"

"We've all tried calling her," Lucky interrupted. "And since she's not answering her phone, I suggest you quit stalling and start giving me information."

"Max . . . uh . . . she met this guy," Cookie blurted, because she realized they were at a point where she was forced to tell a few semitruths, and if Max didn't like it, that was her problem because she should've checked in instead of leaving everyone hanging.

"What guy?" Lucky asked through clenched teeth.

"He's like this really cool guy," Cookie lied. "And Max . . . uh . . . wanted to spend time with him."

"'Spend time with him,'" Lucky repeated, raising an eyebrow. "What exactly does *that* mean?"

"She, uh . . . wanted to, uh, I dunno," Cookie mumbled, trailing off.

"And you're her alibi, right?"

Cookie slumped back in the chair, feeling out of her depth. "There's no way I can rat Max out. You'll have to ask her yourself."

"If she was here, I'd love to ask her," Lucky said coldly. "So since she's not, it's up to you to tell me who the boy is, and what's his phone number?"

"I don't know much," Cookie said, blinking rapidly, wondering why *she* was the one getting all the shit. "She kind of hooked up with him on the Internet."

"Are you *serious?*"

"They've been, y'know, like e-mailing for a while. And, um, like I mentioned before, he's a really cool guy."

"You've met him, have you?"

"Uh . . . no."

"Has Max met him?"

"She has now."

"Oh my God! Save me from stupid fucking girls!" Lucky exploded. "Jesus Christ! You're telling me Max went to Big Bear to meet up with a guy she found on the Internet, and now we can't reach her, and *you* think that's okay?"

"Max can look after herself," Cookie muttered.

Lucky shook her head. This was the worst news she'd heard in a long time.

"What's his name?" she demanded.

"Uh . . . I dunno," Cookie mumbled.

"You must know."

"It's uh, like Grant, yeah—that's it. Grant."

"Grant who?"

"Max never said."

"Perfect!"

An hour later Lucky and Lennie were still trying to figure out what to do. Max had taken her laptop with her, so it wasn't as if they could find out anything there. And a brief search of her room revealed nothing. If it wasn't for the party, Lucky would've jumped in her car and driven to Big Bear herself, although she was sure that by this time Max was on her way home. And boy, when Max finally got home she was in for a major lecture.

Lucky had to admit that Lennie was right: in a way she understood Max's rebellious behavior. At sixteen she'd been the original wild one, she'd taken off for weeks at a time before Gino had managed to track her down. But that was then and this was now, and the world was a far more dangerous place.

Max was a smart kid, but unfortunately she thought she knew it all. She was also a beauty in a heartbreakingly young way, and that could get her in big trouble.

Lucky couldn't help thinking back to Lennie's kidnapping ordeal. And the time Santino Bonnatti had abducted Brigette and Bobby when they were both so young.

Surely the nightmare couldn't be happening all over again?

No. It was impossible. Any minute now Max would come walking through the door.

42

Roasted pig was one of Anthony's favorite meals. He got a big kick out of seeing the succulent animal—head and all—right in the center of his buffet table. Rosa didn't disappoint. Sunday brunch she delivered a baby roasted pig with the traditional apple stuffed firmly in its mouth.

"*Eeww!* Gross, Papa," Carolina complained, skipping away from the buffet table.

Anthony chased his daughter, caught her, and pinched her bottom. "It's a tasty treat, Princess," he assured her. "You're gonna love it."

"No, Papa, I won't love it," she protested, scampering back to her table where she was sitting with two girlfriends who'd flown to Acapulco with her. Eduardo was also at the table, but he'd elected to come alone. The adults were at their own table, where in addition to the Guerras and the Masterses, Anthony had invited half a dozen other friends who lived locally.

Irma sat stiffly among them, daydreaming about Luis and the quite exceptional sex they'd experienced together. She couldn't get the young, muscled gardener out of her head. Her thoughts drifted to his tongue between her legs, and his fingertips moving so expertly over her nipples.

"What *you* thinking about, little lady?" Ralph Masters asked, edging nearer, his meaty hand drifting onto her thigh under the cover of the fiesta-style tablecloth.

"Excuse me?" Irma replied, quickly brushing his unwelcome hand away.

"Did you and my friend do it last night?" Ralph whispered in her ear with a salacious leer.

"Ralph, please do not talk to me like that," she said, shifting in her chair. "It's most inappropriate."

Ralph licked his fleshy lips. He was a big man with small eyes and dyed black hair that resembled a bad wig—although it wasn't. Innes, a woman twenty years his junior, was his third wife.

"Don't be like that, I meant it as a compliment," he said in a low voice. "When a woman's getting the right kind of action I can always tell. My specialty is the tongue." Suggestively he flicked his tongue at her. "Most men aren't into oral, but I'm an expert."

"Good for you," Irma said, turning her back on Ralph and concentrating on the Mexican businessman sitting on her other side.

Anthony was in his element. Entertaining an admiring group of friends was his favorite way of relaxing, especially with his children present. Carolina was such a ripe little peach, if he wasn't her father he would pluck her for himself. Thirteen and sweet as pie. Woe-betide any boy who came sniffing around Carolina. Anthony would make sure she stayed a virgin until she was twenty-one, then he would personally select a match for her—a male who lived up to his expectations in every way. He beamed at the thought of watching Carolina develop into a young woman, although come to think of it she was already quite well developed. She had breasts and a cute little ass, she probably even had her period. He reminded himself to ask Nanny.

Eduardo had not brought any friends with him. He was a surly boy with nothing to say for himself. What a disappointment he'd turned out to be, but fortunately Carolina made up for her taciturn brother.

After a long and leisurely lunch, Anthony regaled his guests with several off-color jokes, then out came the karaoke equipment, set up by Manuel.

"Anyone for a song?" Anthony asked, puffing on an expensive Cuban cigar.

"Anthony, please, you sing for us," begged Fanta Guerra, a comely Latina woman with huge breasts and shoulder-length honey blond curls.

"Yes, Anthony," Innes, Ralph's American wife, said, puckering her silicone-enhanced lips. "We've missed you so."

Irma was well aware that both women would make love to her husband given half a chance. She didn't care; they were welcome to him. Now that she was mentally prepared to move on, she felt a lot stronger.

Anthony took his position near the karaoke machine, microphone in hand. "And what am I singing for you lovely people tonight?" he asked.

"Oh please, sing 'My Way,'" pleaded Fanta.

Innes, not to be outdone, gushed, "I love it too. You sing it so well, Anthony. You sing it better than Sinatra."

Their husbands chuckled, while Anthony basked in the praise, and the other guests clapped enthusiastically as they settled into chairs set out in a semicircle.

"So," Anthony said, playing with the microphone, "what does my little Carolina want to hear?"

Little Carolina didn't want to hear anything. Little Carolina wanted to run off to a disco with her friends, but she knew that her papa would never allow her to do that. "Whatever you want to sing, Papa," she said demurely.

"I'm singin' 'My Way.' After that you an' I gonna perform a duet."

"No, Papa! Please, no!" she squeaked.

"Yes, Princess, the two of us will make beautiful music," Anthony said, oblivious to her embarrassment.

Irma had not had a chance to interact with her children. The sad thing was they treated her like a distant relative—it seemed that Anthony and Francesca had managed to completely alienate them. Irma was sad because it wasn't as if Carolina and Eduardo didn't love her. Truth was they hardly knew her.

Anthony lifted the mike and began singing. He didn't have a bad voice, but it was hardly in the Sinatra category.

As he crooned, giving the song his all, he moved amongst his guests, leaning down to serenade and caress the women, a lascivious twinkle in his eye.

He should have been an entertainer, Irma thought. *Instead of a drug lord, a controller, a son of a bitch.*

Soon she wouldn't have to put up with him any longer.

Soon she was moving on.

43

Henry was filled with excitement and a sense of freedom coupled with power, although he was shocked that Maria had tried to escape. She obviously did not appreciate all the trouble he'd gone to.

After her failed attack on him he'd been forced to shackle her ankle once more. He hadn't wanted to, but in view of her behavior it was necessary.

At least he'd persuaded her to call her mother, which was a wise move, because it wouldn't do to have Lucky out searching for her daughter. Not that she'd ever find her. They were isolated and perfectly safe where they were.

Muttering under his breath, he made his way around the back of the cabin to the outhouse where he'd imprisoned Ace approximately thirty-six hours earlier.

He'd been putting it off, but he'd known that eventually he'd have to do *something*.

It infuriated him that this boy had come along and interfered with his plans. Without him, everything could've been so clean and simple. Now he had to deal with the situation, and he had no clear idea of how to manage it.

A voice kept screaming in his head:

Shoot him.

Bury him in the woods.

It's the only way.

But that would be murder, wouldn't it?

Not if the boy is already dead.

Standing outside the door of Ace's prison, he strained to hear if there was any movement inside.

Not a sound. Total silence.

This was good. This meant he wouldn't have to deal with the cousin. This meant that he didn't have to open the door if he chose not to. He was out of the Pasadena mausoleum and living an adventure. He was not shut in his room watching endless horror movies and pornographic images on his computer. He was the star of his own movie, and this was one role Billy Melina could *never* steal from him.

AN ADVENTURE
Starring
HENRY WHITFIELD-SIMMONS
and
MARIA GOLDEN

It should be a love story.

It *would* be a love story.

Now that the cousin was taken care of, he would make it happen.

44

The enormous white tent set up on the grounds of Lucky and Lennie's Bel-Air house was an impressive structure, no expense spared. The tent was ablaze with hundreds of twinkling fairy lights, crystal chandeliers, and garlands of white calla lilies winding around Roman columns. Exotic orchid arrangements were the magnificent centerpieces on each table, along with musk-scented candles in tall sterling-silver holders. The theme was white and silver from the long flowing tablecloths to the pristine place settings.

Before reaching the tent where dinner was to be served, guests gathered around the two Art Deco bars, one on each end of the shimmering blue pool. Sensual Brazilian music played over loudspeakers, while attractive waiters and waitresses circulated holding aloft trays of champagne, wine, and sparkling water.

Venus and Billy were amongst the first to arrive. Bobby was playing host for his mother who was still upstairs dressing. He raced over to Venus, his former boyhood crush, and greeted her with an enthusiastic kiss on both cheeks. "You are looking spectacular," he said admiringly.

"Doesn't she," Billy agreed, claiming possession.

"You know Bobby, Lucky's son," Venus said, introducing the two men.

"Oh yeah, you're the dude with the club in New York, right?" Billy said.

"A *hot* club in New York plus a billion dollars when he hits twenty-five," Venus added, smiling. "And you *know* how I like young men. You'd better watch out, Billy."

"Hey, baby," Billy said, taking her arm. "*I'm* the *only* young man in your life, an' don't you forget it."

"As if I could," she said, hugging him.

"I had a crush on her when I was twelve," Bobby admitted. "Posters on my wall, CDs on my mind, the whole ten yards."

"Didn't we all," Billy said with a knowing grin. "I can remember—"

"Hey!" Venus objected. "You're making me feel as if I'm ninety years old!"

Bobby lifted a glass of champagne from a passing waiter and surveyed the arriving guests.

"Got a hunch I'm not gonna be getting much action here tonight," he said. "It's like couples' city. I knew I should've imported a date."

"Sorry, bro," Billy said, holding on to Venus. "But this one is definitely taken."

"I can see that."

"There's Gino," Venus said, gesturing across the pool. "C'mon, Billy, let's go say hello."

"For an old guy, he looks pretty damn great," Billy said, squinting.

"Yeah," Bobby agreed. "For an old geezer, Gino is amazing."

"Y'know," Venus ventured, "Billy and I were thinking of maybe developing a movie about his life."

"No shit?" Bobby said, looking interested. "Have you run it by Lucky?"

"Not yet, but wouldn't it make an incredible movie?"

"It sure would," Bobby said. "Gino stories are legendary in our family. When I was growing up, Uncle Costa had tales to tell nobody would believe."

"Maybe we should sign Uncle Costa up as creative consultant," Billy suggested. "Is he here tonight?"

"If he is it's a miracle," Bobby said with a wry grin. "Costa's long gone. If he was still around he'd be about a hundred years old."

"Oh," Venus murmured dryly as they all headed toward Gino. "The same age as me!"

Gino was delighted to see everyone. All dressed up in a pinstriped suit, white shirt, and red tie, he did not look anywhere near ninety-five—he was still an impressive-looking man with all his own teeth, a healthy head of gray hair, and a ribald sense of humor. He sat in a chair next to the bar, holding court.

"An' here she comes," he exclaimed as soon as he spotted Venus. "Lucky's hot little friend. How ya doin', kiddo?"

"I'm doing great, Gino," Venus responded, bending down and kissing him on both cheeks. "Even better for seeing you."

"Always noticed you was a sexy-lookin' broad," Gino said, clearing his throat. "Ah . . . if only I was a coupla years younger, what I wouldn't do to you!"

Everyone laughed. Venus introduced Billy.

"Paige," Gino said, grabbing his wife's arm. "Y'see this kid, he's a big friggin' movie star. We saw him in somethin' last week, am I right?"

"Indeed we did," Paige agreed.

"Yeah, you played a psycho killer. Nice job, kid, you got it down."

"Tell that to Alex Woods," Billy said, still smarting from Venus's earlier comments about Alex's opinion of him. "Anyone seen him around?"

Venus gave Billy a sharp nudge in the ribs. "Now don't get all wound up over nothing," she cautioned. "I shouldn't've told you what he said."

"Well, you did, babe, an' now I'm pissed."

A few minutes later Lucky made her entrance wearing a red column of a Valentino dress that set off her smooth olive skin and unruly cascades of jet black hair. She wore diamond hoops in her ears and a stack of antique diamond bracelets up both arms. As usual she looked incredible.

Lennie was by her side. He'd been trying to calm her down about Max all afternoon. The good news was that they'd recently received a message from their daughter on Lucky's cell phone, which had made her feel better, although she was still furious at her errant daughter. "I'm gonna bust her too-smart-for-her-own-good ass when she finally makes it home," she'd threatened, after listening to Max's message a third time.

The message was Max saying, "Mom, sorry to miss Granddad's party. I'll be home tomorrow. Love ya."

Hmm . . . *love ya*. That wasn't Max's usual greeting, and she always called Gino by his name, never Granddad. Lucky had her misgivings. What the hell was Max up to now? And how come Cookie didn't know anything?

Glancing around at the clusters of guests, Lucky noticed Cookie over in a corner with Max's other friend, Harry. The two of them looked like they were in deep conversation. Distracted, she waved a quick greeting at everyone, said, "I'll be right back," and hurried over to Cookie and Harry.

"Did you hear from Max?" was her first question.

"No," Cookie answered, wishing Lucky would stay out of her face. Why was *she* the one getting all the flack? "Did you?"

"She left a message on my cell," Lucky said. "I'm wondering why she didn't call on the main line."

"So like what did she *say*?" Cookie asked, most put out that Max hadn't called her, she'd left enough frantic messages.

"Just that she's coming home tomorrow."

"Tomorrow?" Harry questioned.

"I'm mad as hell," Lucky said. "And you two—what were you thinking, letting her go off to Big Bear to meet a stranger? I thought you were her friends."

"You know what Max is like," Cookie said, shrugging. "We couldn't stop her even if we wanted to. Max does things her way."

"I understand that," Lucky said coldly. "But did you have to encourage her?"

"We're real sorry, Mrs. Golden," Harry muttered.

"Don't call me Mrs. Golden," Lucky snapped. "It makes me feel ancient. You know my name—use it."

"You're like *so* right," Cookie said, biting her lower lip. "We should've tried to stop her."

"Yeah," Harry agreed, his black hair spiked higher than ever.

"Thing is, I *did* tell her," Cookie said, getting into it. "I like *so* warned her that the Internet dude could turn out to be a pervert freako who could chop her up into little pieces." Harry shot her a warning look. "Uh . . . just joking," she finished lamely.

Shaking her head, Lucky walked back to join Venus and Billy. "You look fantastic," she said to Venus, still distracted. "And Billy—always a star."

"Oh, just what I need," Venus muttered. "Here comes Cooper." And as she finished saying it, Cooper strolled over with his very young girlfriend, Mandy, whom Billy seemed to know.

"Hey, Mandy!" Billy exclaimed, giving her a friendly hug. "How ya doin'?"

"Billy!" Mandy squealed. "You're here! How fab! I thought it would be all old people!"

Venus gave Cooper a cool look. "Hello," she said.

"Good evening, Venus," he replied.

"I see you went trolling outside the school yard for a date," she said, indicating Mandy, who was all over Billy.

"You too," Cooper said, glancing at Billy. "Must run in the family, huh?"

~ ~ ~

"Alex, you drive like a maniac," Ling complained, sitting stiffly in the passenger seat.

"I drive the way I've always driven," Alex replied, maneuvering his Porsche into a line of cars waiting to enter the Bel-Air driveway of Lucky's house. "Never had an accident."

"Your driving makes me nervous."

"Then shut your eyes."

"Why can't you be nice to me?"

"I *am* nice to you," he said. "You live in my house, isn't that being nice to you?"

"Is it because of your mother that you're the way you are?"

"I have no problem with my mother," he said, reaching for a cigarette.

"I think you're wrong. Your mother is a *very* domineering woman."

"No she's not," he said shortly, lighting up. "And do not discuss my mother, she's off limits. Try to remember you're a lawyer, not a shrink."

"That's right," Ling said, holding tightly on to her clutch purse resting on her knees. "I'm a divorce lawyer, so I know plenty about relationships."

"Good," Alex said, exhaling smoke. "'Cause I'm not planning on getting married, which means you won't have to represent me."

"I represent women, only women," Ling said.

"Of course you do," Alex said, taking another drag on his cigarette. "When the fuck is this line of cars getting to the goddamn house?"

Ling gazed out of the window and hoped that maybe tonight she would meet somebody more to her liking than Alex Woods. He was an extraordinarily talented man, but he treated her with no respect, and that wasn't right. But then again, as she'd recently confessed, she was in love with him, which made things complicated.

Soon they reached the front of the line where parking valets jumped forward to take the Porsche.

Alex got out and strode into the house. Ling tagged along behind him, finding it difficult to keep up in her ultrahigh heels.

Waiters holding trays of champagne were circulating. Alex grabbed a glass and downed it quickly. "Let's go find the bar," he said. "I need a proper drink."

"Please don't drink too much," Ling begged.

"For God's sake, quit with the nagging."

~ ~ ~

Venus loved being out with Billy, especially amongst her peers. She knew they made an amazing couple—he didn't look too young and she didn't look too old. They looked like contemporaries. She also liked that he was getting plenty of attention as well as her. Billy was an excellent actor, and a well-respected one too. It wasn't like she was out with some boy toy; Billy had his own high profile.

Holding on to his arm, she proudly introduced him to people he hadn't met before, enjoying the compliments bestowed upon him.

Billy was enjoying himself too, although his crotch itched like crazy. Venus might have gotten rid of his crabs, but the stubble burn from her shaving skills was driving him nuts.

"Gotta go to the men's room, babe," he said, slipping away from her.

As he walked toward the house, a tray-carrying waitress stepped in front of him, blocking his way.

"Billy?" she said.

He gave her a puzzled look. "Do I know you?"

"You should know me," she retorted. "It was you who gave me the crabs."

Holy shit! It was the waif from Tower Records. Miss Broken Taillight herself. And here she was all neat and clean in a waitress uniform with her hair piled on top of her head, looking quite respectable.

"What do you mean, *I* gave *you* crabs," he said, outraged. "I got them from *you*."

"You certainly did not!" she replied, equally outraged. "You were the one who had them."

Jesus! He motioned her over to the side of the room. "People can hear," he said, keeping his voice low. "Don't talk to me about this here."

"When *should* I talk to you?" she retorted. "You gave me crabs and I had to spend a ton of money I didn't have visiting the doctor and finding out what it was. You're disgusting!"

"Hey," he said, scowling, "you didn't get them from me 'cause the only person I sleep with is my girlfriend."

"Really?" she said. "Then what does that make me? A one-afternoon stand?"

"I didn't mean that," he said, steering her over to a quieter corner. "What I meant was that when we did it, I was broken up with my girlfriend."

"Is Venus your girlfriend?"

"Yes," he admitted.

"And you hooked up with me? Wow! I'm flattered. I hope you didn't give *her* crabs too."

"Jesus Christ," he muttered, "will you shut the frig up? What do you want from me?"

"I want you to remember me when you see me. We had sex, I went down on you. Doesn't that mean anything to you, Mister Big Movie Star?"

"What we had was a short encounter."

"An encounter?" she said incredulously. "Should I have gotten your autograph on my ass? If I remember correctly, all you offered me was a signed photo."

"What are you after? Money?"

"I'm an actress, not a hooker," she said huffily. "Give me a part in your movie and I'll shut up. Otherwise I'm telling Venus what a bad boy you've been. Okay?"

No. It wasn't okay at all. But what could he do?

Hurriedly he gave her his cell phone number. In the distance he saw Venus approaching.

"Get lost," he said, desperate to make a quick escape. "You got a deal, call me tomorrow. Now get the frig away from me."

45

Max wondered how long the freak was going to keep her prisoner. It disturbed her that he hadn't covered his face. She knew what he looked like, which meant if she ever got out she would be able to identify him. And that wasn't good, because in all the movies she'd ever seen involving a kidnapping, the kidnappers kept their faces covered—because if they didn't, it meant they were planning to kill their victim.

Man, this was bad. This wasn't a game.

And yet there was something about Internet Freak that gave her hope. He obviously wasn't your usual run-of-the-mill criminal. He kept on looking at her with what she could only describe as a lovesick expression—like ugh! It was as if he wanted to be her boyfriend.

Maybe she should stop yelling at him and play up that angle, find out what he was really after, 'cause it didn't seem to be money.

When he returned late in the afternoon she was all prepared with her new attitude.

"I think we got off to a bad start," she ventured.

"Excuse me?" he responded, startled that she was speaking to him without yelling.

"Well, you *are* the same guy I was communicating with via e-mail, yes?"

He nodded unsurely.

"Then what went wrong?"

"Wrong?" he repeated blankly.

"I mean the whole thing with the gun," she continued. "And this shackling me to the bed like some kind of animal. I thought we were friends."

"But we are," he said anxiously. "Friends, yes, we are certainly friends."

"Friends don't point guns at people and *kidnap* them."

"I didn't mean to. But the circumstances . . . your cousin . . . I wasn't expecting him. You said you'd come alone. I was prepared for us to spend the weekend together, just the two of us."

His words got her wondering about Ace. Could it be that they *weren't* in cahoots, and if not, what had he done with him?

"Where is Ace, Grant?" she asked, speaking slowly.

It was the first time she'd used his name. It galled her to do so because all she really wanted to do was kick him in the balls and run—which hadn't worked out so well earlier in the day.

"I told you," he said, clenching his teeth. "I let Ace go."

She knew he was lying, because why would he let Ace go? There was no way.

"Can you undo this thing around my ankle? It really hurts," she said, summoning up a tear or two for his benefit.

"Last time—"

"Forget about last time, Grant," she said, keeping her voice low and soothing. "I learned my lesson and this time I'll behave. I promise."

She watched him closely. His expression weakened, and she knew she was about to get a lot further by being nice.

He produced the key, undid the shackle, fetched her disinfectant and cotton swabs for her ankle, then allowed her into the living room where he fixed her a bowl of canned tomato soup. Wow! Why hadn't she thought of being nice before?

They talked. Or rather *he* talked while she managed to check out her surroundings, taking in every detail. She noticed there was a chain and a double lock on the front door, and no bars on the window in the combination kitchen/living room where they were sitting. In the kitchen section she spotted a knife stand and a collection of pots and pans. In the living room she noticed that he'd set up his rollaway bed under the window.

His voice droned on, horribly monotonous. He told her he was an award-winning actor, and had received many accolades.

"Would I have seen you in anything?" she asked, not believing him for a minute.

"Did you see the film *Seduction*?" he asked, nervously cracking his knuckles, thrilled that he was getting a chance to impress her with his achievements.

Of course she'd seen *Seduction*—her mom had produced the movie. She remembered visiting the set when she was just a little kid. She sure as hell didn't remember him.

"Were you in it?" she asked.

"I should've been," he said, his tone suddenly changing, becoming sharp and angry.

"Then why weren't you?" she asked, putting down her soup spoon.

"Because of—" He stopped abruptly.

Now that they were getting along so nicely, he didn't care to bring up her bitch mother.

Later, when they were really close, he'd tell her the real story.

Later, when he'd convinced her they should stay together forever.

46

Sunday night Anthony decided to throw another party. Even though it was a last-minute decision, he expected it to happen in spite of the fact that Rosa and Manuel had worked their asses off getting the roasted-pig lunch together at such short notice.

"My little Carolina's gonna be fourteen in two weeks' time, so tonight we celebrate," Anthony informed his guests. "Right, Fanta? Right, Innes?" The two women nodded enthusiastically. "C'mere, Rosa," he bellowed, summoning his cook.

Rosa appeared, wiping her hands on her apron. She was exhausted, and it showed on her heavily lined face.

"Rosa!" Anthony exclaimed, grabbing her in an overpowering bear hug. "You go make two of those chocolate cakes I like, an' a lemon birthday cake for Carolina. An' I think we have lamb tonight, an' chicken, an' those potatoes you cook so well. We have another feast," he crowed, pinching her cheek with his thumb and forefinger. "You see this woman," he boasted to his cronies. "She would do anything for me. Anything! Correct, Rosa?"

"*Sí, señor,*" Rosa muttered, enduring the humiliation of a pinched cheek.

"An' if she doesn't—I fire her ass. *Sí*, Rosa?" he said, roaring with laughter. "What you waitin' for, woman?" he added, smacking her on the ass. "Go make the cakes, oh yeah, an' some of those almond cookies you're famous for. Move it!" he added, giving her one final whack on her ass before sending her on her way.

"*Sí, señor,*" Rosa said, wondering how he expected her to have time to organize a dinner party *and* bake. The man was loco, but she and Manuel needed their jobs, and when Anthony wasn't in residence things were quite peaceful.

"She loves me," she heard him braying to his lunch guests. "I'm tellin' you, she loves me to death!"

Irma sat quietly watching Anthony strut and show off, plotting and planning her imminent escape. She knew that her husband kept cash in all his main homes, and taking some of his stash would hardly be considered stealing. After all, she was his wife, and if they lived in America half of everything he had would be legally hers.

She knew the combination of the bedroom safe in their house in Mexico City. Several months ago they'd arrived home from a big black-tie event late at night. Anthony was drunk—he'd flung his emerald cuff links and hundred-thousand-dollar diamond-encrusted watch at her and told her to put them in his safe. She'd asked him for the combination, and in his drunken state he'd given it to her.

She'd opened his safe, and was shocked to see bundles of cash piled high. After putting his watch and cuff links away, she'd written down the safe's combination and hidden it.

Yes, she was more than entitled to anything she cared to take.

~ ~ ~

Much to Luis's fury, Cesar decided to take Lucia up on her invitation to dinner. He arrived unexpectedly late Sunday afternoon, carrying a wilted bunch of flowers and a bottle of cheap sangria.

Lucia greeted him as if she was receiving a visit from the king of Spain. Lucia was desperate to get married and as far away as possible from the overcrowded family situation. She'd dated Cesar on and off for a year, and even though she'd given him what she considered memorable sex, he was not close to making any kind of permanent commitment. Cesar appearing at their house was an encouraging sign.

"Look who's here," she bragged to her two sisters and wheelchair-bound mother. "Doesn't Cesar look handsome?"

Luis was dismayed to see him. He was not sure what Cesar knew about him and Señora Bonar—if anything. But it still made him uncomfortable that Cesar was in his house, making himself at home.

Ana Cristina, Luis's seven-months-pregnant wife, followed her sister-in-law's lead and greeted Cesar as if he were royalty. Everyone was impressed with his job. "Security guard" had a special ring to it. They all hoped he'd marry Lucia or at least take her off to live with him. Their tiny house was so full, and with Ana Cristina and Luis's baby due soon, Lucia's absence would be a godsend.

Luis, the only man in the house with four women, reluctantly offered Cesar a bottle of beer.

Cesar patted Ana Cristina's swollen belly. "Do we know what we're having?" he asked, his hand lingering a little too long on his wife's stomach for Luis's liking.

"A boy," Ana Cristina replied, shyly lowering her eyes.

"A boy! Congratulations!" Cesar exclaimed.

"It's a blessing," Ana Cristina murmured.

"Indeed it is," Lucia said, hanging on to Cesar's arm while fluttering her overmascaraed eyelashes. "Babies are always such a blessing, aren't they, Cesar?"

Cesar didn't reply. "Let's sit outside," he said to Luis. "Enjoy our beers, watch the world pass by."

There was nothing Luis would like less.

"Sure, Cesar," he said.

The two men stepped outside onto the patch of sparse sun-dried grass and sat down on two mismatched plastic lawn chairs.

After a few moments of silence Cesar leaned over to Luis and muttered, "I want in."

"Excuse me?" Luis said.

"I want in," Cesar repeated.

"In what?" Luis said, twisting his beer bottle.

"Do not act as if you don't know what I'm talking about."

"I don't," Luis replied.

"You idiot!" Cesar said, becoming agitated. "I want in with the American woman. I want to sample some of that juicy American pussy you've been dipping into. And if you don't arrange it, Luis, not only do I tell your fat wife, but I tell Señor Bonar too. Do we understand each other, *amigo?*"

47

Eventually the party moved outside to the tent where dinner was to be served. An eight-piece Cuban band played on a platform next to a circular dance floor, while a voluptuous Latina woman seductively crooned "Bésame Mucho."

Lucky was trying her best to enjoy herself, but she still couldn't get over her anger at Max for not arriving home in time for the party, especially since she'd emphasized how important it was to her.

"You gotta calm down, sweetheart," Lennie said, attempting to soothe her bad mood. "You can't walk around with a pissed-off expression. This is Gino's big night—don't let Max ruin it for you."

"Nobody knows better than me what a special night this is," Lucky said, steaming. "But Lennie, I'm *so* mad at her. How could she do this to us? We have no clue where she is, or even *who* she's with. It's crazy."

"I know," he agreed.

"Trust me," Lucky said, her black eyes flashing major danger signals, "when that child gets back she is *so* grounded. I'm not allowing her out of the house. She can say good-bye to her phone *and* her car."

"We'll get into it when she comes home."

"Yes we will," Lucky said fiercely. "And you'll get into it with me, 'cause you're not playing good cop while I'm the bad one. This is something we're handling together. Her behavior is freakin' beyond."

"You got it, Lucky," he said, still trying to calm her. "Now, let's try to relax and show Gino a good time."

~ ~ ~

"*What* is going on with you?" Venus asked Billy, cornering him on the way to their table. "First I see you talking to one of the waitresses, and the next thing I know, you're all over Cooper's girlfriend like you're long-lost buddies."

"Mandy was in one of my movies," he explained. "She's a sweet kid."

"Really?" Venus said archly. "What did she play, the child?"

"She's nineteen, babe," he said, his mind still on his unfortunate encounter with Miss Broken Taillight.

"Oh wow, nineteen," Venus said sarcastically. "Just about young enough for Cooper."

"Bitchy! Bitchy!" Billy said, baiting her.

"Doesn't she get that she's fucking her *grandfather*?" Venus snapped.

"You wouldn't be jealous, would you?" Billy said, grinning.

"Me? Of course not, but a little more attention in my direction might be nice."

"You can't always be the center of attention," Billy teased. "Is Miz Superstar feeling neglected?"

"*Excuse* me?"

"You heard."

"Don't be ridiculous."

"You're the one who's carrying on about nothing."

"Stop chasing after my ex-husband's underage girlfriend and *I'll* stop carrying on."

"Who's chasing? I'm being polite."

"Your idea of being polite and mine obviously differ," she said, hating herself for sounding like a jealous shrew.

"C'mon, babe," he said, turning on the Billy Melina charm, "lighten up."

"Don't tell *me* to lighten up when you're the one doing all the chasing."

"Do you seriously think I'd do that?"

"You're sure talking to her a lot." *Oh God, Venus, stop it already!*

"Mandy doesn't know anyone here."

"And since when did that become *your* problem?"

"We'd better go sit down," he said, leading her to the table next to Gino and Lucky's.

Venus took a quick peek at the place cards. Billy was seated next to her, and on her other side was Alex. Charlie Dollar was already sitting across from them with *his* date, another juvenile delinquent.

What was it with these fifty- and sixty-something men who thought that the only date worth having was a twenty-something Twinkie? They probably imagined it made them look like a big sexy stud, when all it actually did was make them look older and kind of pathetic. Without Viagra they'd all be singing the blues.

"Hi, Charlie," Venus said, waving at her old friend.

"There's my Venus," Charlie drawled with a jaunty wink. "Queen of the tasty treats."

Charlie Dollar was a huge movie star, a stoned icon for his generation. A superlative actor and quite a man about town; whatever he did, it always involved a little bit of magic. Even at sixty-something he still managed to snag any girl who took his fancy. Slightly balding with a paunch and a maniacal grin, Charlie was up there with Nicholson and Pacino as one of the all-time movie greats.

"Say hello to Bubbles," Charlie said. "She's my latest project."

"Hi, Bubbles," Venus said, waving at his very young date, wondering if she was a stripper. Who else would walk around with a name like Bubbles? Oh yes, Michael Jackson's monkey.

"Ohmi*god*!" Bubbles trilled in total awe, flapping her hands. "I'm so thrilled and honored to meet you. I grew up watching you on TV and listening to your music. My daddy is your biggest fan!"

Christ! What *was* this? Make-Venus-feel-old night?

"Thanks, dear," Venus said, about to sit down. Before she could do so, strong arms grabbed her from behind. "Good evening, gorgeous. I'll be watching everything you put in your mouth tonight, an' that *includes* food."

"Who *is* this?" she asked, struggling to turn around.

"Your main man."

She spun around and there was Cole, her trainer. He was with Rich Morrison, a fifty-something billionaire English rock star, who favored white suits and an abundance of expensive jewelry. Rich was considered an icon, having been in the business for twenty-five years, and having scored numerous awards and more gold records than Elton John.

Cole, a black beauty, and Rich, all in white, made quite a couple.

So this is the giver of Cole's new Jag, Venus thought. She was delighted to see her old friend Rich. She'd had no idea he was Cole's latest admirer, but it made perfect sense because Cole was a black Adonis *and* smart—and those were the two qualities Rich coveted above all else.

At the next table Lucky was trying to get her people seated. Gino was at the head of the table with Paige on one side and Steven's wife, Lina, on the other.

Lina, a beautiful black supermodel, was full of personality—she lit up any room. Next to her sat her daughter, Carioca, then Gino Junior, with Lennie next to him. Lucky had Bobby on her right, then Brigette and Steven. It was the family table; the only person missing was Max.

At least Gino seems to be enjoying himself, Lucky thought. *Ninety-five years old and forever a party animal.*

She wondered how he really felt. Pretty old, no doubt, but still holding up.

Glancing over at the table next to her, she observed Venus and Billy indulging in some kind of verbal battle, while Alex was nursing a half-full glass of Scotch, and Ling didn't appear to be too happy. It was definitely time for Alex to settle down with the right girl and take himself off the market.

Was Ling the right girl? Probably not.

Lucky knew that Alex still harbored a big crush on her. She'd thought that by this time it would've faded—but no, Alex was forever hopeful.

At the last moment the party planner had switched tables, and somehow or other Cooper and his girlfriend had ended up at Venus's table, which had not been Lucky's intention. She hoped Venus wasn't too mad.

"Lucky," Steven said. "This is a wonderful evening."

"Thanks, Steven," she said. "I wanted it to be special for Gino. I mean, how often is he going to be ninety-five?"

"Take a look at him," Steven said, beaming. "The old man is in his element."

"I know." Lucky nodded. "Surrounded by beautiful women and feeling no pain. The story of his life."

"Where's Max?"

"Oh, you know Max," Lucky said vaguely. "She's off running around with her friends. Teenage girls, what can I tell you. Hopefully she'll make it later."

"I was thinking of flying up to Vegas with you next weekend," Steven said. "Thought I'd take a look at everything before the grand opening."

"I'd love that."

Lucky appreciated having Steven in her life. A half-brother was so much better than no brother at all, and since Dario had been so brutally murdered it was great having found someone she could look up to. Steven was the result of Gino's one-night affair many years ago with a black woman, Carrie. It had taken Gino a while to accept the fact that he'd fathered a black son who had not appeared in his life until he was an adult, but once Steven had shown up, Gino had rallied and eventually accepted Steven into the family.

Steven was an extremely successful lawyer. Several years previously his wife had been shot and killed in a carjacking, and sometime later he'd married Lina. They seemed to be very happy together, in spite of Lina's somewhat wild past.

After dinner was served Gino stood up and prepared to make a speech. The room hushed. Someone handed Gino a microphone—he held it gingerly.

"First time I had one of these things stuck in my face," he joked. "Plenty of guns, never one of these." Pause for laughter. "Y'know," he continued, "never thought I'd make it to ninety-five friggin' years old. It's a miracle I'm still around, an' I plan on stayin' around a lot longer for my family. My unbelievable ballsy daughter, Lucky. My son, Steven, who came into my life late and made it even better. My grandkids, I love 'em all. Then there's my wife, Paige, she's the woman who keeps an eye on my drinkin', gamblin', an' womanizing." Another big laugh from the crowd. "Paige is kinda like a prison guard," Gino continued, warming up. "An' believe me, I've crossed paths with a few of *them* in my time. Anyway, I wanna thank you all for comin' out tonight, for supportin' me and my family. An' a special toast to Lucky for makin' this party for me. So drink up an' have a good old time, 'cause me—I can't wait t'hit the dance floor."

Lennie gave Lucky a nudge. "Your turn."

"I'm not good at speaking in public," she protested.

"Do your best, sweetheart, I know you can."

"Guess I've got no choice," she said, taking a long deep breath before standing up and tapping the side of her glass until the room was silent again. A tentful of expectant eyes turned toward her. She hated being in the spotlight; keeping a low profile was much more to her liking.

"Uh, thanks, Gino," she began. "Your speech was beautiful, and this is quite an occasion." Her eyes met Lennie's. He nodded encouragingly. Taking another deep breath, she continued speaking. "So . . . y'know, ever since I was a little girl Gino never allowed me to call him Daddy, I have no idea why. Then I got to thinking it was because of the parade of women coming in and out of our house, and he didn't want some little kid running in yelling, 'Daddy! Daddy! Daddy!'" Everyone laughed.

"Well . . . after that I got used to calling him Gino, and I got used to his ways. Hey, you all know Gino, I had no choice." More laughter. "Anyway, growing up with Gino was a major pain in the ass, so to compensate I decided to become an even *bigger* pain in the ass than him. But anyone who knows us realizes that we finally got together and made our peace, and since that time Gino has been everything to me. I can't even begin to tell everybody how great he is, and I'm so *happy* that he's hitting ninety-five. Wow! Some freakin' landmark! So Gino," she said, tilting her champagne glass toward him. "I toast you and everything about you." A long slow beat. "Oh yes, and thanks . . . Daddy . . . I love you, I really do. Happy birthday!"

Glasses were raised and champagne was drunk.

Lucky sat down.

"Perfect," Lennie murmured in her ear. "You're a talented woman."

"It wasn't that good," she said modestly. "Just some hokey speech I came up with at the last minute."

"It was from your heart," Lennie assured her. "That's all that matters."

"You think?"

"I know," he said, taking her hand and squeezing it tightly. "God, I love you."

"Right back atcha!" she said, reaching up to touch his cheek.

"Let's blow this party and go make out."

"Now?"

"*Right* now. You and me in the guest bathroom. How about it? Just like old times, huh?"

"Lennie . . ." she began.

"*What?*" he said, giving her the look she could never resist.

"Nothing," she said, standing up. "So c'mon, move it, Mr. Golden, or are you all talk?"

"That's my Lucky," he said, grinning.

"Oh *yes*, mother of your children and sex maniac!" she said, pulling him to his feet. "That's your Lucky."

Laughing together they left the tent.

~ ~ ~

Nursing his fourth—or was it fifth?—tumbler of Scotch, Alex watched them go. Lucky. *His* Lucky. Without her existence things could have been so simple. But with her around nothing was simple, and nothing was ever enough. Not the endless women, the expensive possessions, his successful career. Three fucking Oscars, and he'd give them up tomorrow for just one night with Lucky. She was his ultimate woman, and yet she belonged to Lennie. And what could he do about that?

Nothing.

Exactly nothing. And the pain of not having her never left him.

"Alex," Billy said, breaking into his thoughts.

"What?" Alex growled.

"I heard tell you think success has gone to my head?" Billy said, taking a belligerent stance.

"Huh?" Alex questioned, standing up. He hated it when punk actors got in his face—this wasn't the first time.

"Yeah, you told Lucky an' she told Venus who told me," Billy said, determined to force a confrontation.

"What the fuck is this, grade school?" Alex spluttered.

"No. Reality," Billy said. "I'm not that green kid you put in his first movie. It's time you gave me some respect."

"Respect!" Alex chortled. "You'll get my respect when you do somethin' to deserve it."

Billy's handsome face darkened. "What?"

"You heard."

"Fuck you, Alex," Billy said in a loud voice. "You're yesterday's news, an old guy who's losin' it. So whyn't you wake up an' smell the retirement hittin' you smack in the face."

Alex took a step forward and spewed a litany of insults. "You dumb, no-talent, ass-kissin', fuckin' boy toy prick. You—"

Before Alex could utter one more insult, Billy hit him square on the jaw. Pow! A direct shot that took Alex by surprise, but not enough to stop him from retaliating. As a Vietnam vet, Alex had a few moves of his own, and he came back at Billy with a vengeance. Suddenly it was on, a full-out fistfight.

Venus, who'd been deep in conversation with Cole and Rich, jumped to attention. "Oh *my God!*" she screeched. "Somebody stop them!"

And Gino, sitting at the next table, looked on admiringly. "Now *this* is what I call a *party!*" he crowed to Paige. "Trust my Lucky to come up with the right friggin' mix! This is the best damn party of the year!"

48

Max was asleep, once more locked in her prison, when she thought she heard a scratching sound coming from the outside of the boarded-up window.

The sound awoke her instantly. She quickly sat up, got off the bed, and padded toward the window, her heart beating fast. She'd persuaded the freak to keep the shackle off her ankle—the sense of freedom it gave her was quite liberating.

"Anyone there?" she whispered, attempting to peer out, but all she could see was pitch blackness.

"It's Ace," a voice whispered back. "Is that you, Max? You in there?"

Relief flooded her whole being. Ace had come to rescue her. Thank God!

"Yes, it's me," she answered excitedly. "I'm locked up here."

"I'm gonna try getting you out," he promised.

"How?"

"Who knows," he said in a low voice. "Where's the freak?"

"I think he's asleep, but he's right next door so you'd better be quiet."

"I'm gonna attempt to pry the boards off the window."

"What if he wakes up?" she asked, panicking. "He's got a gun."

"I know, but we're better off gettin' outta here."

"God, Ace, where have you *been*?" she cried.

"He had me locked up, I only just managed to break out. Okay, here goes," he said, tearing at the boards with his bare hands. "Wish us luck."

Almost two nail-biting hours later he'd made enough space for Max to squeeze through. Once she managed to force her head and shoulders through, he dragged her the rest of the way, scraping the side of her body from thigh to chest. She bit her lip trying not to cry out with pain.

It was still night and the blackness was oppressive. She couldn't see a thing as Ace quickly hugged her. "Let's go," he said, his voice full of urgency.

"Where to?" she asked, shivering uncontrollably.

"Anywhere away from here."

He grabbed her hand and they began to run.

~ ~ ~

Running, breathing, running, breathing, Max thought her lungs were about to explode, but Ace wouldn't allow her to stop, even though they were running in total darkness. She kept tripping and falling as they made their way through what appeared to be a heavily wooded area.

"Shouldn't we try to find the road?" she gasped.

"No," Ace said. "When he discovers we're gone, that's exactly where he'll start looking."

"But if we stay in the woods, we'll be totally lost," she said, experiencing a sick feeling in the pit of her stomach. "Neither of us knows where we are, and he told me this area is completely deserted, nowhere near anything or anybody."

"Don't sweat it," he said, keeping a firm grip on her arm, supporting her when she stumbled.

"I tried to escape," she said, breathing hard. "Kicked him in the balls, it didn't have much effect."

"That's 'cause he hasn't got any," Ace said, stopping for a moment and bending over. "Jesus! I am *so* fucking hungry."

"What? He didn't serve you three-course meals?" she said, squatting on the ground.

"Glad you've still got your sense of humor."

"Trying to keep my spirits up," she said, shivering. "Where were you anyway?"

"Locked in a stinking outhouse. He dumped me in there and never came back. I could've starved to death."

"You haven't had anything to eat or drink all weekend?"

"Nope. Sweet that I took a survival course in school."

"You did?"

"Yeah, we had to survive in the desert on practically nothing for six days."

"Wow!"

"This time I had a coupla packs of gum in my pocket, must've given me enough strength to dig my way out. There was a john over a hole in the ground. That's where I dug. It took me long enough, but I made it."

"Does he still think you're in there?"

"Guess so," he said, pulling her up. "C'mon, we gotta keep movin'."

"But I'm so cold and hungry," she said, still shivering.

"Tell me about it," he said as they began stumbling through the woods again, Max desperately trying to forget the pain she was in with her side and her ankle. "Y'know," she muttered. "He told me he let you go, so I immediately started thinking you were part of it, that he'd sent you to lure me into his trap."

"I might be a bank robber," Ace quipped, "but that doesn't mean I'd get involved in a kidnapping plot."

"He sounded so cool, I thought meeting him would be an adventure."

"One hell of an adventure this turned out to be. You realize we could've both got shot."

"You don't have to draw me a map."

"Listen, Max, I'm not that much older than you, but there's no way you should go running off with strange dudes. He's probably one of those sick pedophiles."

"I'm hardly a child," she said, tripping over a branch and almost falling. "Ow!"

He caught her by the arm. "What's up?"

"It's just that I scraped my side coming out the window, it really hurts."

"You think *that's* bad, wait till you see my hands."

"What's wrong with them?"

"I told you, I had to dig myself out of that place. Then I had to tear those wooden boards off your window. My freakin' hands are nothing but splinters and blood."

"Can I do anything?"

"Just keep moving, we can't afford to stop."

"But I'm tired."

"Max!" he said forcefully. "Suck it up."

"Okay, okay," she answered breathlessly. "But what if he finds us?"

"He's not going to."

"Then if *he* can't find us," she reasoned, "nobody else can."

"We're gonna get out of here," Ace assured her, "so stop with the whining."

"I'm *not* whining."

"You could've fooled me."

49

Monday morning Renee Falcon received a call from a detective. She wasn't surprised—she'd known it was only a matter of time before she was tagged as one of the last people to see Tasmin Garland before her mysterious disappearance. Only it wasn't so mysterious to Renee; she'd had to pay a lot of people big bonuses to make sure they kept their mouths shut. And unfortunately that made her an accessory to murder, thanks to Anthony Bonar.

In retrospect, Renee wished she'd called the cops and busted Anthony's stinking ass. Unfortunately, she was unable to do so on account of the fact that he had too much information about her past, and if she'd given him up, he would've spilled buckets about the money she'd gotten out of Colombia and shifted to Vegas illegally, and the murdered croupier whose body was buried out in the desert, and the amount of drugs she'd purchased for her hotel guests' pleasure over the years.

Damn Anthony Bonar. She wasn't above putting out a hit on him. What a joy it would be to get rid of him once and for all. Good riddance to a misogynous murderous fuckhead.

She agreed to meet the detective in the coffee shop at the Cavendish. Arriving early, she settled into her usual corner booth, ordered coffee, and picked up a newspaper.

When Detective Diane Franklin walked in Renee was surprised. "I wasn't expecting a woman," she said, checking out the black detective, attractive in a no-nonsense way.

"Who did you think you were speaking to on the phone, a secretary?" Diane said, noting that Renee Falcon was an overweight woman with a masculine-style haircut and mannish attire.

"I imagined Detective Franklin was a man."

"As you can see, I'm not," Diane said, sliding into the booth. "I'm a black woman and proud of it."

"I didn't say anything about you being black," Renee said.

"That's all right, I'm sure you noticed."

The two women sized each other up like a couple of heavyweight boxers about to enter the ring.

Shit! Renee thought. *We're off to a fine start.*

Hmm . . . Diane thought. *This one is not going to be easy.*

"Coffee?" Renee inquired.

Diane nodded.

Renee summoned one of the waitresses.

"As I mentioned on the phone," Diane said, "I'm here about Tasmin Garland's disappearance."

"Tasmin has disappeared?" Renee said, managing a look of surprise. "Are you sure?"

"Mrs. Garland hasn't been seen for forty-eight hours, therefore we're starting an investigation," Diane said, producing a weathered notebook from her purse and laying it on the table. "She left a ten-year-old son, an ex-husband, and an excellent job. I understand that the night she vanished she was coming to have dinner with you at your hotel. According to her babysitter, you had told her you were fixing her up with a date."

"No, that's not right at all," Renee said, taking a sip of coffee. "There was no date involved."

"Mrs. Garland seemed to think that's why you had invited her to dinner," Diane said, her eyes watching Renee's face. "She definitely told the babysitter she was meeting a date."

"Nonsense," Renee said briskly. "A friend of mine was in town and he happened to join us for dinner. He's a married man, there was absolutely no date involved."

"You're sure about that?" Diane asked, tapping her pen on the table.

"Perfectly sure. I don't understand why Tasmin would have been under that impression."

"Who was your friend?" Diane asked.

"What friend?"

"The one that Tasmin was under the impression she was being set up with?"

"An out-of-town business acquaintance."

"His name?"

"Does it matter?"

"Yes."

Renee hesitated for a moment. She couldn't lie—too many people had seen Anthony sitting at their table. Besides, she had to act as if she had nothing to hide.

"Anthony Bonar," she said at last.

"What business are you in with Mr. Bonar?"

"He's not really a business acquaintance," Renee said, quickly changing her story. "More of a longtime friend."

"So," Diane said, scribbling in her notebook. "A business acquaintance or longtime friend? Which is it?"

"Longtime friend," Renee replied.

"And where does Mr. Bonar reside?"

"He travels a lot."

"Is he based in Vegas?"

"No."

"I'll need contact numbers."

"Why?"

"Because I'll need to speak to him."

"Very well. My assistant will have to deal with that."

More scribbling before the next question. "Was it just the three of you at dinner? Yourself, Mrs. Garland, and Mr. Bonar?"

"No," Renee said, reluctant to drag Susie into it, but aware that she had no choice. "My significant other was with us."

"And who is that?"

"My partner, Susie Rae Young."

"Any relation to . . . ?"

"Yes," Renee said abruptly. "She's his widow."

"I see." A long beat. "Changed paths, did she?"

"I hardly think that's any of your business."

"You never know when you're investigating a case what details might turn out to be relevant."

"All I can tell you is that Tasmin came to dinner," Renee said. "Then left around ten-thirty, eleven o'clock. That's the last time I saw her. So . . . if there's nothing else, I have a very busy day ahead of me."

Diane had no intention of going anywhere, not until all her questions were answered to her satisfaction.

"You do business with her at the bank, is that correct?" she asked, pen poised.

"I have done so."

"Was everything satisfactory?"

"Of course."

"Of course?" Diane said. "Sometimes people are dissatisfied with their bank managers. You weren't. Everything was copacetic?"

"Yes."

"How was her mood during dinner?"

"Her mood?"

"Was she upbeat? Depressed? Was she in the frame of mind where you thought she could get in her car, drive off, and never be seen again?"

"She seemed to be happy enough, we had a very pleasant dinner."

"And the conversation was about?"

"How the hell am I supposed to remember what we talked about?"

"Movies? Politics? Family? Perhaps she mentioned her ex-husband?"

"I do not recall."

"Very well, Mrs. Falcon. If you have anything else that you consider helpful you can call me on my direct line." She handed Renee a printed card. "And you don't mind me asking a few questions around the hotel, do you?"

"As long as you don't disturb my guests."

"I'll also have to speak with Mrs. Rae Young as soon as possible."

"There's no need for you to do that," Renee said quickly. "I've told you everything you need to know."

"I understand, but it's my job to interview everyone."

"How time consuming," Renee said acidly.

"It is," Diane replied, closing her notebook. "But it's prudent to be as thorough as possible. When can I interview Mrs. Rae Young?"

"I'll have to ask her."

"I'd prefer direct contact. Where can I reach her?"

"I'm not sure where she is today."

"A phone number will do."

Reluctantly Renee gave her Susie's number, and abruptly concluded the meeting by standing up.

"I have an extremely busy day ahead of me," she repeated.

"Thank you for your time," Diane said, also getting up from the table.

"Let me know when she turns up," Renee said.

"*If* she does," Diane said.

"I'm sure she will," Renee said, heading for the entrance to the coffee shop.

Diane watched her go. She'd seen plenty during her seventeen years on the force, especially working in Vegas, but in all the years she'd worked there, she'd never met anyone quite like Renee Falcon. The woman was a force. Big and brash. Gay and proud of it. Forceful and overbearing. With something to hide.

Diane Franklin had a nose for secrets, and Renee Falcon was definitely harboring a secret, Diane would bet her career on it.

50

Alternately running and walking, Max managed to keep on her feet, although she was about ready to give up. She was cold and hungry and everything hurt. Eventually, after what seemed like hours, Ace allowed them to take a rest.

She collapsed under a tree, hugging her knees to her chin, trying to control her shivering.

"What happened to your phone?" he asked.

"He took it. Where's yours?"

"What do you think?"

"I can't tell my mom what happened," she said, worrying about Lucky's reaction.

"Why not?"

"She'd go totally crazy if she knew I let myself get kidnapped."

"You didn't *let* yourself do anything, it was one of those insane things," he said, putting his arm around her and pulling her close. "I'm not coming on to you," he assured her. "I'm keeping us both warm. Body heat, y'know?"

His arms around her felt good, she had no objections. "How about *your* parents?" she asked, snuggling close.

"Don't have any—they died in a plane crash. I live with my older brother. He's a fireman."

"Your brother's a fireman?"

"What did I just say?"

"Sorry, that's one of my bad habits, repeating things."

"You have bad habits?" he teased.

"Shut up."

"I will if you will."

"I don't think I can go much farther," she said. "My ankle's hurting so badly."

"What's up with your ankle? I thought it was your side that hurt."

"He shackled my ankle to the bed, it's all blistered and bleeding."

"Jeez! What a sicko."

"He kept me like that for two days until I finally persuaded him to take it off. Thank God I did, otherwise I'd never have been able to reach the window and get out."

"Sorry this had to happen to you, Max," he said.

"No," she replied. "*I'm* sorry I dragged *you* into this mess, 'cause—y'know . . ."

"What?" he said, squeezing her hand.

"Nothing," she murmured, thinking how incredibly close she felt to this boy she hardly knew. This boy in the Lakers sweatshirt with the cleft in his chin. This boy who'd saved her.

~ ~ ~

Henry didn't often dream, but when he did his dreams were always extremely vivid and graphic. In this particular dream Maria was stroking his forehead and telling him she loved him. He could see her face, so young and serene and innocent, her intense green eyes staring into his, melting into his as if they were one. Then she climbed on top of him and very slowly began to unzip his pants.

He reached for her breasts to feel them, touch them . . .

And he climaxed in his sleep, which awoke him.

He lay there for a minute, disoriented and perfectly satisfied. He might be a virgin, but that didn't mean he did not experience the most earth-shattering orgasms. Usually they were brought on by a trio of girls he visited on the Internet. This time it was different. This time it was real.

After a while he consulted his watch. Five A.M. Monday morning, and only just beginning to get light outside. Maria was asleep in the bedroom. His Maria, so near, so dear.

Yesterday she'd begun to thaw toward him. He'd talked and she'd listened. He'd removed the shackle from her ankle because he'd finally felt he could trust her. She must've sensed—like he did—that it was the beginning of the rest of their lives together. The beginning of paradise.

Feeling exceptionally happy and content, he got out of bed and padded to the bathroom, stopping to listen outside her door as he passed.

Soon he would be in that bed with her. Oh yes, very soon.

But he had no intention of pushing her. As far as he was concerned she could take all the time she needed.

~ ~ ~

"Let me take a look at your hands," Max said as soon as it started getting light.

Ace held out his hands for her to inspect. They were blistered and covered in scratches, his fingernails broken and torn.

"Do they hurt?" she asked, gently touching them.

"'S'okay," he said. "I'll live."

"You want to see my ankle?" she offered.

"It's not number one on my list of things to do, but if you insist," he said, taking a quick peek. "Man, what an asshole!"

"Like you said, he's a sicko."

"At least we got away."

"Thanks to you," she said, looking around and observing nothing but long grass and tall trees. "How long do you think we've been running?"

"I dunno, my watch broke."

"He took mine."

"Do I stink?" Ace asked, sniffing his sweatshirt.

"I'm not exactly Miss Clean, so I wouldn't know."

"No, seriously, do I? I was locked in that place forever. I had to dig through God knows how much crap to get out."

"You're not exactly smelling like a rose, but neither am I."

"She's so sweet."

"No, I'm not," she said, thinking that sweet was hardly the way she wanted him to view her.

"Man," he said, standing up and stretching. "You wanna know what I'm imagining?"

"What?"

"One big fat juicy burger, with fries, and a can of cold beer. Did he feed you?"

"Fruit and cereal, soup and bread. He had a fridge full of stuff."

"That means he was prepared," Ace said thoughtfully. "He must've had it all planned."

"He was definitely expecting me to go off with him for the weekend." She hesitated for a moment. "This might sound weird, but I think he has kind of a crush on me."

"Sure," Ace said disbelievingly. "That must be why he shackled your ankle and held a gun to your head. Some big crush."

"He sounded so cool in his e-mails," Max mused. "I guess he totally faked me out. I feel like *such* a moron. If my mom finds out, she'll kill me."

"So you're telling me that you get kidnapped, manage to make a daring escape, and your mom's gonna kill you?"

"You don't know her."

"Don't think I want to."

"Anyway, I've made up my mind that if we get out of this, I'm not telling her. If she finds out the truth she'll never let me out of the house again."

"Some dragon lady."

"I'll tell her I had a flat tire, got carjacked and dumped off in the woods."

"*That's* a better story than the truth?"

"Maybe."

"Be quiet a minute," he said, standing very still. "I can hear a car, we must be near a road."

"Really?" she said excitedly.

"Yeah, this way," he said, pulling her up. "Let's go hitch a ride."

"Looking like this?" she said, stumbling. "Nobody's going to stop for us."

"Here's the deal—I estimate we're about twenty-five miles outside town, so we need to get a ride otherwise we're screwed, he'll catch up with us for sure. When we hit the road, stay by the side so we can see if it's him coming. I saw his car outside the cabin, he must've taken yours back and made a swap."

"Do you think my car's in the Kmart parking lot?"

"If it is we'd better get to it before he does."

"I'm so cold," she said, shivering uncontrollably. "I think I've had it."

"No flaking out on me now, Max. You'll have plenty of time to collapse when we're safe. Right now you gotta move it. I promise you—we're almost there."

51

"I never want to do that again," Lucky groaned, reaching for a bottle of water on her bedside table.

"What're you never gonna do again?" Lennie asked, rolling over in bed and placing his hand on her thigh. "The sex? The party? The fight?"

"We missed the fight," she pointed out. "And stop being facetious, I'm in no frame of mind to deal with your sarcasm."

"You're not?" he said, stroking her leg.

"No, Lennie," she said, removing his hand. "I have a bitch of a headache, even my eyes hurt."

"It's not a headache, sweetheart, it's a hangover. You were drinking champagne."

"Don't remind me. Champagne *always* gives me a mother of a headache. Why did you let me drink it?"

"Why did *I* let you?" he said, amused. "When have I ever stopped you from doing anything?"

"That's true," she admitted. "Still . . . I'm sorry we missed the fight," she added, stifling a yawn.

"I'm not. Had more fun making out in the bathroom with you. Now, that's *my* idea of a party."

"I guess I'd better get up," she said, sliding out of bed and heading for the bathroom. "Can you call downstairs and check if Max is back?"

Lennie buzzed Philippe in the kitchen and asked the question.

"She's not back," he called out. "Everyone else is assembling for breakfast."

"Son of a *bitch!*" Lucky exclaimed, emerging from the bathroom. "I'm supposed to fly back to Vegas today, but there's no way I can go until I look her in the eye and tell her *exactly* how I feel about her missing Gino's birthday."

"Go to Vegas. I'll deal with Max."

"Lennie, when it comes to our daughter you're a softie and she knows it."

"Listen," he said. "You've got a hotel to open. You can't let Max distract you."

"It's hardly a distraction, more an act of war," she said, pulling on black workout pants and a long-sleeved Nike T-shirt. "Plus I'm worried about her."

"You are?"

"Why do you think she called Gino Granddad on her message?"

"Who knows?" Lennie said, tying his robe. "Could be she was feeling guilty about missing his party."

"I'm starting to have a bad feeling about things."

"What things?"

"We can't reach our daughter. We have no idea who she's with. The whole situation is giving me negative vibes, and you're totally calm about it."

"She's on her way home, Lucky."

"And what if she's *not*? What if she's run off to Vegas and gotten married?"

"Are you serious?"

"I wouldn't put doing something totally crazy past her. Who knows *what* she's capable of?"

"Yeah, but married? Our Max? In Vegas? Forget about it."

"I hope I'm wrong, but my instincts tell me we shouldn't be hanging around waiting for her to show. We should be doing something."

"Such as?"

"Looking for her, Lennie. How about that?"

"And where do you suggest we start?"

"I wish I knew, but I don't, so I'm calling Cookie. She might remember something she's not telling us."

"What about your trip?"

"Vegas will have to wait."

~ ~ ~

"I think Billy's adorable," Brigette said, helping herself to a plate of scrambled eggs and bacon from the buffet Philippe had set up in the breakfast room. "And Alex is nothing but a big old bully."

"Hey," Bobby said, drinking a large cup of black coffee, "are you forgetting it was Billy who took the first shot? What was Alex supposed to do, just stand there?"

"He didn't have to pound Billy into the ground," Brigette retorted, sitting down at the table.

"Got a little crush, have we?" Bobby said, teasing her. "If Venus finds out—"

"Oh, yes," Brigette said quickly. "And talking of crushes, I couldn't help noticing that you were all over Venus like a cheap suit!"

"Nothing cheap about me," Bobby responded, cracking a grin. "And isn't she a bit *old* for me?"

"You know what they say, *Uncle*—a woman in her forties is in her sexual prime, and a man in his twenties has it all going on. So . . . get her to dump Billy and the two of you can swing from the chandeliers!"

"C'mon, Brig," he objected, "she's my *mother's* best friend."

"All the better," Brigette said crisply. "That way you can keep it in the family."

"Man, you've got a mouth on you," Bobby said, shaking his head. "From little Miss Shy to the mouth that roared!"

"I wasn't always sweet little Brigette, sitting in my apartment quiet as a church mouse," she said. "No, there was a time I was out there being used and abused by a series of assholes."

"Hey, listen, whatever turns you on."

"But that's exactly the point, it *didn't* turn me on. The last one almost killed me. Left me to die in some ramshackle farmhouse outside of Rome, pregnant. I lost the baby and practically bled to death."

"I guess an experience like that would turn anyone into a shut-in."

"Thank God for Lucky, she was the one who saved me. Without her intervention who knows what would've happened."

"That's my mom," Bobby said, going over to the buffet table and helping himself to a bagel. "She's pretty adept at saving people."

"You're so fortunate having her as your mother," Brigette sighed.

"An' don't I know it," Bobby agreed, sitting down next to her.

"Anyway," Brigette said. "I enjoyed coming to L.A. with you, and last night was a fun party. Seeing all my old friends was quite a kick. Did you know that Lina and I used to model together?"

"Wow!" Bobby exclaimed, whistling admiringly. "The two of you must have been some hot combination."

"We were," she said, smiling at the memories. "Between us we ruled L.A., New York, Milan, Paris."

"I bet you did."

"Good times while they lasted."

"Hey, Brig, here's an idea," he said, chewing on his bagel. "When we get back to New York, you should start hanging out with me. I've decided to make it my mission to find you a guy who's not an asshole."

"No thanks, Bobby."

"Why not?"

"'Cause I'm perfectly content being man-free," she said firmly. "One of these days you'll learn. Love is a tough road, and believe me, the highs are not worth the lows."

"*Very* philosophical."

"I try."

"And so pretty while she's trying," he said, making major eye contact.

"If you weren't my uncle, I'd think you were flirting," Brigette said, half smiling.

"Who, *me?*"

"You're a dog, Bobby. The kind of guy I would've been attracted to before I learned better."

"That's insulting," he said, not insulted at all.

"How many girls did you sleep with and not call back last year?"

"Hey," he objected.

"I thought so," she said triumphantly. "You're a dog."

"Who's a dog?" Lucky asked, entering the room.

"Your son."

"That's okay," Lucky said, pouring herself a glass of freshly squeezed orange juice. "He's twenty-three, he's entitled to enjoy himself."

"Not if he treats women badly."

"Who said I treat women badly?" Bobby spluttered. "I take 'em out to dinner, buy 'em presents—"

"Sleep with them, then run like thunder," Brigette said, finishing the sentence for him.

"Nice opinion you have of me," Bobby said cheerfully.

"Took me years to figure out men," Brigette said. "I think I've finally got it down."

"So cynical for one so young," Lucky said, sitting at the table.

"Yes," Brigette agreed, quite enjoying the banter. "And you, Lucky, better than anyone, know why."

"That's true," Lucky said.

Philippe entered the breakfast room looking quite flustered for once.

"Everything all right?" Lucky asked.

"There's twenty men dismantling the tent," Philippe said. "May I suggest everyone stays out of their way until they're finished."

"Why? Is someone in their way?" Lucky asked.

"Gino Junior and his friends."

"I'll talk to him, Philippe."

"Thank you, Mrs. Golden. Oh, and this was in the mailbox," he added, handing her the now-familiar envelope.

"What's that?" Bobby said, pouncing.

"Just another one of those stupid invitations," she said, tearing it open.

Bobby grabbed it from her. The same three words were scrawled on the card: *Drop Dead Beautiful.*

"We need to get someone on this," he said.

"No we don't," Lucky said.

"At least put in extra security cameras by the mailbox so we can see who's delivering the envelopes."

"Okay, if it'll make you happy I'll have Philippe arrange it."

"*I'll* tell him."

"That's fine."

Satisfied, Bobby poured himself another cup of coffee. "Max back yet?" he asked. "Be nice to see her before we take off."

"She'll be back today," Lucky said, not prepared to share her daughter's bad behavior with everyone.

"Thought she was coming back for Gino's party," Bobby said.

"So did I. But you know Max . . ."

"Yeah, *right.*"

"What time are you leaving?"

"Around two. Thought I'd hang out with Gino before he heads off to Palm Springs. He told me he's taken up golf."

"Gino? Golf?" Lennie said, strolling into the room and heading straight for the coffee. "Now, *that* I'd like to see."

"I wouldn't," Lucky said. "The thought of Gino on a golf course with a bunch of old-fart buddies hitting a ball around is *not* the Gino I know and love."

"Ha!" Bobby said. "You'd like him to be all Brando-like, sitting in a room handing out favors to the neighborhood peasants!"

"You have a brilliant imagination, Bobby," Lucky said coolly.

"Didn't Gino used to—"

"Okay," Lucky said as Gino Junior came in with two of his friends. "That's enough."

"But Mom—"

"Enough, I said. And you," she added, talking to Gino Junior, "leave the people dismantling the tent alone, they've got a job to do."

"We were only goofing around, Mom."

"Then don't. Okay?"

Since when had she become the mother figure? The disciplinarian?

Well . . . having kids did that to a person.

She couldn't wait to get back to Vegas and her hotel. Right now that's where she belonged.

They were opening in two weeks and she *had* to be there, *wanted* to be there.

As soon as she tracked down Max she'd be on her way.

52

After making himself a cup of tea, Henry returned to his rollaway bed, where he attempted to go back to sleep and summon up the magnificent and magical dream he'd experienced earlier.

Ah . . . Maria. All over him. So young and innocent.

Maria, his dream girl.

The title he'd bestowed on her excited him, making him more anxious than ever to see her.

Once more he got out of bed, wondering if it was too early to wake her. Today he would fix her a proper breakfast, eggs and bacon with toast and strawberry jam.

Yes, he decided, she would like that, unless she didn't eat bacon. Perhaps she was a vegetarian. He needed to know more about her. He needed to know everything about her.

He wondered what his mother would have to say on the day he brought Maria home. He rehearsed the scene in his head, imagining the look of surprise on Penelope's face.

"Good morning, Mother."

"Good morning, dear."

"I would like you to meet Maria, the girl I'm going to marry."

"She's very pretty, dear. And she looks smart too. Are you sure she's not too pretty and smart for you?"

Dammit! That was not the way the scene was supposed to go. Penelope Whitfield-Simmons even controlled his daydreams with her caustic remarks.

Ever since he could remember his mother had put him down, belittled him, treated him with no respect. She'd never told him he was clever or handsome or any of the things a son wants to hear from his mother. She'd never hugged him or kissed him. It simply wasn't fair.

He steamed about his mother for a moment or two, then realized she wasn't there to annoy him with her nasty spiteful remarks. He was on his own, free to do whatever he wished.

And he wished to see Maria.

He got out of bed, dressed, and carefully began to prepare his loved one her breakfast.

~ ~ ~

"You got your car keys?" Ace asked.

"What do you think?" Max snapped back. She knew she shouldn't be taking her bad mood out on Ace, since he'd basically saved her, but she couldn't help herself.

They were sitting in the back of a battered Chevrolet Impala driven by an elderly man with his redheaded thirteen-year-old grandson in the passenger seat beside him.

Fortunately, the old man couldn't see that well, so at the behest of his grandson, who'd spotted Max in her torn jeans and tight tank top standing by the side of the road, he'd stopped for them and was giving them a ride into town.

Max slumped against the seat in the back. She was exhausted, everything hurt, and she was scared of going home. She was certain that if Lucky ever found out the truth, she'd ground her forever. She'd missed

Gino's big party, and in Lucky's eyes there would be no excuse for that, especially as she'd faithfully promised to be there. Her life was about to turn into pure crap.

"It's okay if you don't have keys," Ace said. "I can hot-wire it."

The thirteen-year-old swiveled his head, staring at Max's boobs, his teenage lust bursting out all over. "You know how to hot-wire a car?" he asked, still staring at Max's chest. "Awesome!"

"He knows," Max answered, indicating Ace. "He robs banks, hot-wires cars, he's a regular man of all trades."

"Awesome!" the boy repeated.

Ace took a swig from the water bottle the old man had offered, then passed it to Max. She took a couple of gulps. Now that they were almost safe, her nerves were beginning to kick in. What was she going to tell Lucky? Definitely not the truth, it was too stupid and humiliating, plus Lucky would never let her forget it.

She decided to go with the carjacked story. That was her safest bet.

"You happen to have a phone?" Ace asked the kid.

"I wish," the boy said. "Grandpa thinks cell phones rot the brain."

"Who do you want to phone?" Max asked, shooting Ace a sideways glance. He was still a major hottie, in spite of his bedraggled appearance.

"My brother."

"You're not going to tell him, are you?"

"Not if you don't want me to."

"No, I don't."

"So we're just gonna let that freak get away with it?"

"What freak?" the boy asked.

"Nobody you ever wanna meet," Ace said.

The old man, hunched over the wheel, launched into a nasty coughing fit. The boy took the water bottle back from Max and handed it to his grandfather. The car swerved on the dusty road as the old man drank.

"How about I drive?" Ace suggested, leaning forward. "You look like you could use a break."

The old man acquiesced. He was tired and his arthritis was playing up, his hands bent and misshapen. "Wouldn't mind that a bit, son," he said, clicking his teeth. "You got a license?"

"Yes, sir," Ace replied politely.

The old man pulled the car over. Ace got out. The boy slithered over the passenger seat and into the back next to Max.

She shied away—he reminded her of Gino Junior's friends with their horny eyes and leering stares. The old man settled into the front passenger seat while Ace got behind the wheel.

"How long before we reach Big Bear?" Max asked.

" 'Bout half an hour," the old man said, and promptly fell asleep.

53

"A detective will be calling you," Renee informed Anthony over the phone.

"What the fuck you talkin' 'bout?" Anthony replied, a ferocious scowl covering his face.

"Detective Franklin from Vegas. She might even send someone to interview you if she's not satisfied with your answers, so I suggest you try and repeat exactly what I've already told her."

"You must be fuckin' shittin' me?" Anthony exploded. "You gave the cops my name?"

"I *had* to, you were sitting at the table with us for over two hours, everyone from the busboys to the guests in the hotel saw you. I can't pretend you weren't there."

"Why the fuck not?" he said, marveling at Renee's stupidity.

"I've had to pay a lot of people off, but the entire hotel—impossible."

"I don't fuckin' get it," Anthony raged. "That's the dumbest move you've ever made."

"No," Renee said sharply. "My dumbest move was aiding and abetting you. I should've called the cops."

"Don't even think about it," he said, his voice cold. "You know what would've happened to you if you'd made a foolish move like that."

"Are you threatening me, Anthony?"

"Of course not," he said, backing down. "But what the fuck am I supposed to say to this detective?"

"Tell her you're a friend of Susie and mine, we had dinner, and that's it."

"Jesus *Christ!*" he snarled. "Who needs this shit."

"I know," Renee said. "I'm not thrilled myself. I've got a detective snooping around my hotel questioning people—how do you think I like that? I haven't given her your number yet. What number should I tell her?"

"Here's the deal," Anthony said, still pissed off. "I'll call her."

"That won't fly."

"How d'*you* know?"

"Because I do."

"Jesus Christ, Renee! You're a fuckin' moron! Give her my cell, not any of my business numbers."

Renee controlled her own temper. Anthony was the fucking moron and she was starting to think of ways to get him out of her life permanently.

"When will you be back here?" she asked.

"In time for the big event. Everything still in place? No fuckups?"

"Apart from cops crawling all over my hotel, everything's on track."

"You can handle it."

Of course she could handle it. Who did Anthony Bonar think he was, issuing orders as if she were some lowly employee there to do his bidding? Fuck him.

"Right now Tasmin is listed as missing," she said.

"An' there's no way they can come up with more, ain't that so?"

"Yes, Anthony," she said through clenched teeth.

"Your people were thorough?"

"Yes," she said, knowing he was making sure she'd arranged to have Tasmin's body buried where nobody would ever find it, that is unless *she* pointed them in the right direction. "Everything's taken care of," she added.

"It better be," he said, slamming down the phone. "Son of a *bitch!*" he yelled, furious that he had to deal with this shit.

"What's the matter, Papa?" Carolina asked, entering the room wearing a skimpy yellow bikini and flowered flip-flops.

"Nothing, Princess, it's business," he said, distracted.

"What business exactly are you in?" Carolina asked, biting into an apple.

"Import/export, you know that," he replied, noticing that the bikini she had on was showing too much skin. She was thirteen for chrissakes, what moron allowed her to buy a bikini more suited for a Victoria's Secret model?

"Yes, Papa, but *what* do you import?" Carolina persisted. "One of my friends asked me the other day, and I didn't know what to say."

"I import all kinda things, Princess. I buy items from China, ship 'em to America, then they get sold in the stores."

"Oooh," Carolina said, taking another bite of her apple. "Can I go to one of the stores and buy stuff?"

"There's nothing you'd like," he said, wondering where this sudden interest in his business was coming from. "It's all cheap crap, not your style."

"Why do you sell crap?"

"'Cause it makes me big bucks."

"I lika big bucks," Carolina said, giggling.

"Ain't ya got some kinda coverup?" Anthony asked. "You're too young to be walkin' around with everythin' hangin' out."

"Maybe one day *I'll* go into business," Carolina mused, ignoring his criticism.

"No import/export for you," he said sharply. "When you're old enough Papa's gonna find you a nice boy to settle down with so you can give me lotsa grandkids."

"What if I don't *want* to get married, Papa?" Carolina said, pulling a face. "Boys suck."

"Some of 'em do an' some of 'em don't. One day you'll change your mind."

"Why would I do that, Papa?" she asked, her pretty face a picture of innocence.

"Enough with the questions," he said impatiently. "An' go put somethin' on over that bikini."

Carolina looked dismayed.

"Sorry, Princess," he said quickly. "Didn't mean to get on your case. C'mon back over here an' give your papa a big, fat hug."

She ran over to him. He squeezed her a little too tightly. "What you doin' today?"

"We're having lunch at the beach club, then we might go waterskiing."

He enjoyed the fact that he had kids who got to do all the things he'd never had the opportunity of doing when he was growing up. They snow-skied, water-skied, played tennis, rode horses. He was proud that he'd been able to give them so much.

"Where's your mom?" he asked.

"Dunno," Carolina replied.

"Go find her, tell her I wanna see her."

"When are we leaving here, Papa?"

"You know I never make plans ahead. I'm a 'feel it, do it' kinda guy."

"My friends need to know 'cause they have to tell their parents."

"When do you *wanna* leave?"

"Whenever you do."

"Okay, I'll let you know."

"Thanks, Papa," Carolina said, skipping from the room.

His mind was still on the phone call from Renee. He couldn't even relax in peace without being bothered by the Vegas incident.

It was over.

Done with.

Why was Renee behaving like such a stupid bitch?

~ ~ ~

"Papa wants to see you," Carolina said, approaching Irma, who was lying out by the infinity pool soaking up the hot Acapulco sun.

"What does he want?"

"How should *I* know?" Carolina said somewhat rudely.

Irma didn't bother telling her daughter off. She'd relinquished all responsibility. Anthony was in charge now—Carolina was all his.

"Tell him I'll be right there."

"I'm not a *message* service," Carolina said, ruder by the minute. "Tell him yourself."

What a lovely young lady *she* was turning into. Good luck, Anthony.

Irma got up from her lounger and made her way toward the villa. When she got there she found Anthony sitting on one of the outdoor patios smoking an oversized cigar, his two dogs lying at his feet.

"You wanted me?" she said.

"Yeah," he answered, blowing acrid smoke in her direction. "What's up with you?"

"What's up with me?" she repeated. "I'm not sure what you mean."

"I mean, what the fuck's up with you," he said, scowling. "You're acting like a zombie, all zoned out like nothin's gettin' through to you. You on Prozac or one of those antidepressant pills?"

"Why would I be on antidepressant pills?" she said, veering toward being sarcastic. "You've taken my children, left me in a foreign country with no friends. Surely I'd have no reason to be depressed?"

"You got homes all over the fuckin' place, money to shop your ass off, an' now you're complainin'—is that what I'm hearin'?"

"You can hear what you want to," Irma said, feeling quite bold. "I don't care anymore."

"You'd better stop this shit," Anthony raged. "I work like a maniac to keep my family happy, an' this is the thanks I get? A miserable wife who barely fuckin' functions."

"Oh, I function," she said, wishing she could tell him how well she functioned when Luis was in her bedroom going down on her with a passion she'd never felt from her husband.

"Yeah, in Chanel an' Louis Vuitton with my credit card in your hand you function like a fuckin' machine."

"Is that all?" Irma said calmly. "Can I go now?"

Anthony had been straining for a fight, and Irma wasn't giving him one. What the fuck was she on?

"Don't think you're goin' anywhere," he said. "I—" Before he could continue, his cell phone rang. He snapped it open. "Yes?" he barked.

"Mr. Bonar?" a female voice said.

"Who wants t'know?" he said suspiciously.

"This is Detective Franklin from Las Vegas. I'd like to ask you a few questions about Tasmin Garland."

"Hold on a minute." He turned to Irma, waving her away. "Business, gotta take this."

"Permission to leave granted," Irma murmured, infuriating Anthony even more.

He waited until she was out of sight before taking the call. "Yes?" he said, pacing.

"Were you fixed up on a blind date with Mrs. Tasmin Garland last Friday night?"

"Huh?"

"I've spoken to Renee Falcon. I believe you, Mrs. Rae Young, and Mrs. Garland had dinner Friday night at the Cavendish Hotel. Is that correct?"

"Why you askin'?"

"Because Mrs. Garland is missing. She hasn't been seen since that dinner."

"I hardly know her."

"You dined with her, Mr. Bonar. She informed her babysitter that she was being fixed up on a blind date, and since you were the only man present . . ."

"That means shit. I was sittin' there with a coupla muff divers, didn't even catch the other broad's name."

"I see. Well . . . perhaps you can recall the conversation, the mood of the evening."

"Sorry," he said abruptly. "Had a steak, talked business with Renee, an' left town."

"Unexpectedly?"

"Huh?"

"Unexpectedly, Mr. Bonar?"

"No."

"Your pilot says otherwise."

She'd talked to his fucking pilot! This was unbelievable!

"My pilot knows nothin'," he said, a sharp edge to his voice. "I tell him what t'do when *I* decide t'do it."

"I see. And you decided to leave Vegas at midnight. Unexpectedly."

"It wasn't so unexpected. I knew I was going."

"Apparently your pilot didn't. He thought you were staying overnight."

"I don't pay my pilots to think. I pay 'em to get me from A to B."

"I understand."

"Yeah."

"I want to make certain I get this right. You're saying that after the dinner was finished, you never saw Mrs. Garland again, is that correct?"

" 'S'right. So if ya got nothin' else . . ."

"Thank you, Mr. Bonar. Any further questions, I'll call this number."

"Yeah, do that," he said, clicking his phone shut.

Goddammit! Fucking dumb questions.

He summoned The Grill. "Call the main office," he said. "I need 'em to change my cell phone number, an' get me a new pilot—tell 'em to fire the one I got now. Make sure the new one starts pronto, 'cause we're leavin' for Miami tomorrow."

54

The boy in the back of the Chevrolet was chattering to Max about music, telling her who he liked and who he didn't. The old man was snoring. Max lapsed into silence, trying not to think about how much her side and ankle hurt her.

Ace, with one scratched-up hand on the steering wheel, was wondering if there was anything to eat in the car—a chocolate bar, chewing gum, anything. He leaned over to take a look in the glove department, and as he did so the old man woke up.

"What you nosin' around for?" the old man said, his voice quavering. "We got no money. We're hardworkin' farmers. If you're gonna rob us, it ain't your day, sonny boy."

"Not planning on robbing you, sir," Ace said. "I was seeing if you had anything to eat."

"All you hadda do was ask," the old man grumbled. "We got a half-eaten ham sandwich if that's any use to you."

A half-eaten ham sandwich sounded like bliss. "Uh . . . thanks," Ace gulped, overcome by the thought of food.

"Give him the sandwich, boy," the old man ordered his grandson.

"But Gramps," the boy whined. "I was gonna have that later."

"Can't you see these people are hungry?" he said, throwing Ace a suspicious look. "What you two young-uns doin' out on the road so early anyway?"

"Thought I told you," Ace said. "Our car broke down."

"A likely story the mess you're in. I've heard every story from here to Florida," the old man said. "A likely story. Give him the sandwich."

Reluctantly the boy rummaged in his backpack and produced a brown paper bag. "Here," he said, thrusting the bag at Max, his eyes fixed firmly on her breasts.

She opened the bag, took out the sandwich, and passed it forward to Ace. "You have it," she said.

"We'll split it," he answered.

"No, I'm okay. Really. It's all yours."

Ace devoured the sandwich in three quick bites.

"That's the best-tasting thing ever," he said. "Thanks."

The grandfather had fallen asleep again, and the boy was continuing his music conversation. "I got my own radio," he boasted. "Gramps won't get me one of them boom boxes like I want, he says we can't afford it. I'll get it one of these days soon as I start workin'."

Max made a mental note to find out where these people lived and send this boy a CD player. If it wasn't for them they would still be standing on the road hoping that Internet Freak wasn't going to find them and stick a gun in their face.

She wondered what was going on at home. As soon as she got near a phone, she'd call Cookie and find out before driving back to L.A.

Hopefully when they arrived at the parking lot her car would be there, Ace would start it for her, and she'd drive back to L.A. as quickly as possible.

What a nightmare this past weekend had been.

What a story to tell Cookie and Harry!

She couldn't wait.

~ ~ ~

It was a clear day, crisp, cold, and quite invigorating. Henry decided to go outside into the garden and pick some flowers to put on the tray before he took it in to Maria for her breakfast. He was determined to find something pretty to put on her tray.

Making his way around the side of the house, he was startled to see several boards lying on the ground. He couldn't imagine where they'd come from. Then it dawned on him that they'd been wrenched from Maria's window.

For a moment he didn't understand what was happening. It was impossible for her to escape, and yet . . .

Frantically he ran over to the window and peered in. There was no Maria lying in the bed. No Maria in the room. No Maria!

Rage swept over him, a stark cold rage that enveloped his entire body.

Where was she? How had she escaped?

He ran to the outhouse, finding that the big wooden door was still intact. Rushing back into the cabin, he got his gun and the key to the outhouse, then he went back outside and tentatively unlocked the door.

Instead of the body he'd been hoping to see, there was a gaping hole in the ground leading to a tunnel where the cousin had obviously managed to burrow his way out.

Black fury roared in his head. How had this happened? Even more important, how long had they been gone?

He raced back into the cabin, grabbed his car keys, ran out to his car, jumped in, and set off.

Nobody was taking Maria away from him now. Nobody.

~ ~ ~

The old man was snoring loudly.

"Mind if I put the radio on?" Ace asked.

"I don't care," the boy answered. "Gramps listens to them country stations, but I like rock and roll."

"Who's your fave?" Max asked.

"Rolling Stones, they're good."

"You're too young to know anything about The Stones," Max said, turning her head to look out the back window.

"You too," the boy said. "How old *are* you?"

"I'm—" She was just about to lie, but then she thought, what's the point? "Sixteen," she said. "And you?"

"Gonna be fourteen in a month."

"You're both too young to know who the Rolling Stones are," Ace remarked.

"I am so not," Max objected. "I'm into all kinds of music. Rap, soul, alternative rock."

"The Stones must be as old as this kid's grandfather," Ace said, feeling a lot stronger since eating the half sandwich.

"Thing is they're still rockin'," Max pointed out. "Saw their last concert in L.A. They rule!"

"I've got a record of Mick Jagger singing 'Satisfaction,'" the boy boasted.

"Wow!" Max said, giving him a little slack. "You're smarter than you look."

"You bein' rude?" the boy asked, scratching his head.

"Just eff-ing with you," Max teased.

"Now, now, kids," Ace said from the driver's seat. "And I do mean kids," he added pointedly.

"What?" Max said.

"Sixteen, huh?"

"Shut *up* and put on the radio," she said, embarrassed because she'd originally told him she was eighteen, and now he'd caught her in a lie.

He reached over and switched on the radio. Music filled the car—a twangy female moaning about lost love and a husband who'd dumped her with six kids and no money.

Glancing in the rearview mirror, Ace noticed a car coming up fast behind them. He drew over to the side to let it pass.

Then he saw that it wasn't just any car. It was the Volvo he'd seen outside the cabin, and if he wasn't mistaken, sitting behind the wheel was Internet Freak in hot pursuit.

"Shit!" he exclaimed.

"What?" Max asked, leaning forward.

"Believe me, you don't wanna know."

55

They'd argued all the way home. Venus was furious with Billy for getting in a fight with Alex—a fight that had ended only when Steven and Bobby managed to separate the two men. But not before Billy had received a black eye and Alex a split lip.

When they'd finally arrived at her house, Billy had informed her he wouldn't be staying the night due to his early call to the set the next morning. "Speak to you tomorrow," he'd said, barely kissing her on the cheek.

"Fine," she'd said, and stormed inside, angry and frustrated. Billy's childish behavior reflected on her. She was sure it would get reported in the tabloids or on some scurrilous gossip Web site, and once more she would be the brunt of every late-night talk-show host's jokes.

She'd spent the rest of the evening alone in her bedroom, seething.

By the time Cole arrived early Monday morning for their workout session, she was ready to explode.

"You're lookin' angry," Cole remarked. "Beautiful but angry. Think we'll do the gym today, get out some of that aggression."

"Wouldn't *you* be angry if you were in my position?" she demanded. "I'm sleeping with an idiot!"

"My philosophy is never take responsibility for somebody else's bad behavior," Cole said, flexing his arms as they made their way across the courtyard to Venus's fully equipped home gym.

"It's not fair," she complained. "I'll get all the blame for this, y'know."

"How come?" Cole asked, adjusting the weight level on one of the many pieces of Cybex gym equipment.

"Because it'll be in the papers that *I* instigated the fight. They'll say that Alex Woods and Billy Melina were fighting over me. I can see it now: 'Venus's Boy Toy Springs to Her Defense,' something like that. They make up this shit all the time."

"Honey, Billy doesn't get called a boy toy anymore. He's a movie star in his own right."

"Yes, Cole, *I* know that and *you* know that, but it's more fun for the tabloids to give him a label. You know how they get off giving celebrities demeaning nicknames."

"You've got a point, but we're not gonna dwell on it. Now let's get your ass on the treadmill."

"No treadmill today, I don't feel like it."

"Exercise helps."

"It does?"

"You betcha."

"I'm just pissed, you know."

"I understand," Cole said soothingly. "But you can't let it get to you."

"Nice, huh? I can see it now, the two of them working together today. Billy with his black eye and Alex with his split lip. It'll be a fun day on the set."

"I think it's cool they're working together," Cole said. "They'll be forced to interact, then it'll all be history. You'll be the only one thinkin' about it."

"I suppose it *is* my fault," she admitted.

"An' why's that?"

" 'Cause I'm the one who told Billy that Alex said something negative about him to Lucky, and no good ever comes from repeating gossip."

"Okay, that's a positive—you learned a lesson."

"Did you bring me a Starbucks?"

"Do I look like I'm carrying Starbucks?"

"I'll send somebody out to get us two Mocha Frappuccinos—what do you think?"

"I think you're putting off getting on the treadmill. We'll add boxing today, get out all that aggression."

"Not yet. Let's talk about you for a change, I'm bored with me. Tell me about you and Rich. I'm impressed."

"What're you impressed about?" Cole said with a casual shrug. "Rich is a nice guy."

"He's not just a guy, Cole, he's an icon."

"I get off on mixing with icons. Why d'you think I'm with you every morning?"

"Hmm . . . so now that you've got a superaffluent sugar boyfriend—"

"Listen to you, madam, taggin' *me* with a nickname."

"Okay, I shouldn't have said that. I'll try again. Uh, now that you've got this very famous rock star boyfriend, you really don't have to keep working, do you?"

"I train people because I *like* doing it," Cole explained. "Why do *you* keep performing? You've got enough money socked away to stop anytime you want."

"'Cause I love it."

"Then concentrate on what you do an' stop bitchin' about your boyfriend. Career first—weren't you the one who taught me that?"

"You're right," she said, finally jumping on the treadmill in a better frame of mind. "Career first. Assholes second."

"Well," Cole said with a jaunty grin, "let's not get carried away."

~ ~ ~

"It's all over the freakin' news," Kev announced.

"What is?" Billy asked. He was sitting in his trailer at the location, waiting to be called to the set. Kev had arrived with the newspapers, a stack of mail, and a Thermos of decent coffee.

"This fight you had last night," Kev said, dumping a pile of fan mail on a side table. "I wanna hear all about it."

"Jesus!" Billy complained, not in the mood to discuss it with Kev. "You can't do anything in this town without it getting out."

"You actually *hit* Alex Woods?" Kev said. "Punched him in the freakin' face?"

"Take a look at my eye, Kev," Billy said evenly. "*He* hit *me*."

"Can't see anything," Kev said, squinting at him.

"That's 'cause they covered it in the makeup trailer, but I have a mother of a black eye underneath all this crap."

"Who threw the first one, bro?"

"It might've been me."

"Shit!" Kev said, slapping his palms together. "Wish I'd been there to see it. What did Venus say?"

"She's major pissed."

"I bet. You know how she likes to protect her image."

"*I'm* not her fucking image," Billy exploded. "How come you say dumb crap like that?"

" 'Cause one minute you're tellin' me you're a free man watchin' football an' hittin' the clubs, and the next you're Mr. Freakin' Boy Toy."

"Fuck you, Kev. Don't ever call me that."

"I'm only repeating what they're saying on TV. Turn on channel eleven, Jillian and Dorothy are all over it."

Billy frowned. He had an important scene that morning and he wasn't sure how things would turn out when he and Alex came face-to-face. Was he supposed to apologize?

No, why should he? Alex was as much to blame as he was. Alex was the one running around behind his back mouthing shit. *He* was the one who deserved an apology, not Alex Woods.

He had other things on his mind too. The girl who'd given him crabs, who according to her *hadn't* given him crabs. She was threatening to tell Venus if he didn't score her an acting gig on his movie. And how was he supposed to do that now? Alex would not be exactly open to granting him any favors.

There was a knock on the trailer door.

"Who is it?" he called out.

"Maggie."

"What's up, Mags?" Billy said, throwing open the door, thinking that maybe she could help.

Maggie climbed the steps. "There's press hanging around everywhere," she informed them. "Alex is not happy."

"Uh, yeah?" Billy said, wondering what her point was.

"Not the press that was supposed to be here today, press that decided to show up uninvited."

"I wonder why," Kev chortled, quite enjoying the latest drama.

Billy threw him a dirty look.

"They want your take on the fight, Billy. How about making a comment?"

"It wasn't a fight, Mags, it was a minor altercation."

"Alex has already put out a statement."

"What'd he say?"

"That it was a misunderstanding and the two of you are the best of friends."

"I'll make the same statement, then."

"That's what I wanted to hear," Maggie said. "The less you say, the better. The movie is what's important."

"Yeah, I know."

"And regarding your . . . altercation, on my advice, Alex has forgotten about it. I suggest you do the same."

"Wish I had a woman like you in *my* life, Mags."

"You do," she said crisply. "You've got Venus. She's quite a woman."

"Yeah, right."

Maggie turned to leave.

"Hey, Mags," Billy said, stopping her at the door and turning on the baby blues so she could melt right into them.

"Yes, Billy?"

"Uh . . . there's this girl," he said, keeping it vague. "She's a friend of a friend, and, uh . . . I kinda promised I'd get her a bit in the movie. Nothing big, like a walk-on."

"A walk-on," Maggie repeated, raising a cynical eyebrow.

"That's it."

"Billy, you know what Alex is like. He sees every face, casts every role big and small."

"You can swing it, Mags."

"What's her name?" Maggie sighed.

"I'll let you know."

~ ~ ~

After a vigorous workout Venus got on the phone to Lucky.

"Hey," she said. "Great party."

"Thanks," Lucky said.

"Apart from that, I called to tell you how sorry I am about Billy getting out of line. It was so uncalled for."

"That's okay," Lucky said. "It made Gino's night."

"Seriously?"

"Oh yes, there's nothing that turns Gino on like a good fight."

"Billy's sorry it happened too," Venus said quickly, apologizing for her boyfriend, who apparently didn't give a shit.

"It's forgotten."

"Hardly. The press is all over me. They're outside my house in droves waiting for Billy to comment, and he's not even here."

"Where is he?"

"Out on location with Alex," she said, laughing derisively. "That should be a press-worthy scene."

"I would imagine so."

"Y'know, Lucky, I think the time has finally come for me to move on."

"Again?"

"This time I mean it. Oh, and when I do—please, I beg you—make sure I *never* hook up with an actor again. Too much baggage."

"Whatever," Lucky said, her mind elsewhere.

"What's up with you?" Venus questioned. "You sound out of it."

"Max is still not home and I'm mad as hell. Right now I'm on my way out to talk to Cookie again. These kids share secrets—I've got a hunch our little Cookie knows more than she's saying. . . ."

"Anything I can do?"

"Thanks for the offer, but no."

"Well . . . if you think of anything."

"You'll be the first."

"I should hope so."

After speaking to Lucky, Venus realized it was time she got it together. Billy was taking up too much time and energy. Because of him, she was neglecting her career, and her career was what she *should* be concentrating on, not a man. Even worse—a younger man. And on top of everything else—an actor!

What was she thinking? Falling in love was a bitch. Getting over it was even worse.

But she would do it. No more making excuses for Billy's behavior. No more putting herself out for him. He had to grow up and take some responsibility.

And just as she was thinking about ending their affair, he called, apologized profusely, and told her he'd make it up to her and that he'd been thinking about her all day.

She melted.

Damn! She was still in love.

Why not?

~ ~ ~

"Who's this girl you wanna get on the movie?" Kev was desperate to know.

"A friend of a friend," Billy answered evasively.

"What friend?"

"Fuck off with your questions."

"How's your crabs?"

"What?"

"You heard."

The trouble with best friends was that they usually found out stuff, and Kev knew him too well for him to keep up the lie.

"Okay," he admitted. "It was a mistake, a one off."

"Tell me everything," Kev begged, agog with interest. "And don't leave out *any* of the dirty details."

56

Ace hit the accelerator, and the Chevrolet shot forward.

"What's up?" Max asked, alarmed.

"It's him," Ace said.

"Who?" the boy asked, wriggling around on his seat.

"Nobody," Max replied, looking out the back window and seeing the Volvo in close pursuit. Her stomach did a somersault and she felt like she was about to throw up. How could this be happening, just when she'd thought they were safe?

"Don't worry," Ace said, pressing his foot down hard. "There's nothing he can do."

Oh, yes there is, Max thought. *He can shoot our asses.*

She glanced quickly at the boy. "What's your name?" she asked.

"Jed," he said. "Why we speeding? Gramps don't like goin' fast, sez it uses up too much gas."

"Gramps is asleep," Max pointed out. "So what he doesn't know . . ."

"Think I'd better wake him," Jed said, looking worried.

"No," Max said quickly. "Don't do that. We're playing a game with a friend, it's no big deal."

Jed climbed up on his knees and peered out the back window. "If this person's your friend, how come you ain't drivin' with 'im?"

"'Cause it's complicated," Max replied as Ace put his foot to the floorboard and the Chevrolet hit its limit.

Her heart was pounding—they were still in the middle of nowhere.

WHAT IF INTERNET FREAK CAUGHT THEM?

~ ~ ~

He spotted them immediately and gave chase.

So incensed was Henry that he could barely see straight. Not only was he angry, he was also deeply disappointed, he'd had such high hopes for himself and Maria. And now she was running away from him, and it was so wrong.

The problem was her cousin. He should've shot the cousin when he'd had the chance.

Pow! A bullet through the heart.

Good-bye, cousin.

Good-bye, problem.

A muscle in his cheek twitched uncontrollably as he chased the old Chevrolet down the deserted road. Eventually they'd reach the main highway, so it was imperative he stopped them before they got there.

But how? He was not a very experienced driver, he had no idea how to run another car off the road, because if he did, that's exactly what he'd do. Besides, he couldn't take a chance of hurting Maria. It wasn't *her* fault she'd run, it was all to do with the cousin.

Henry was filled with hate against the cousin, just as he was filled with hate against Lucky Santangelo and Billy Melina. They were all unworthy, all three of them.

Only Maria was pure. His Maria.

Somehow or other he had to save her.

~ ~ ~

"Can't you go any faster?" Max yelled.

"We're going as fast as we can," Ace yelled back.

"I'm gonna wake Gramps," Jed whined.

"No you're *not*," Max snapped, thinking it was a miracle that the old man was still asleep.

"You people are weird," Jed sniveled.

"We're not weird, we're like having fun," Max said, trying to convince him that nothing much was going on.

"This ain't *my* idea of fun," Jed said. "I wanna wake Gramps."

"No!" Max said sharply. "Let him sleep."

"But I—"

"Tell you what," Max said, trying to keep it together. "When I get back to L.A., I'm sending you a CD player and all the Stones CDs. What do you think?"

"You'd do that?" Jed said, his face lighting up.

"Yes. I swear," she answered, saying a silent prayer that Internet Freak was not going to catch them.

Ace swerved the car, narrowly missing a coyote that suddenly appeared in the middle of the road.

Max could see he was sweating, but she had to admit he was doing a great job of getting them away from the Volvo, which seemed to be slowing down. She was trying to remain calm for the sake of the kid, but it wasn't easy, since her heart was pounding so hard she thought it might burst right out of her skin.

"When?" Jed asked.

"When what?"

"When I gonna get me one of them CD things?"

"Soon," she said. "Like that's a faithful promise."

~ ~ ~

Henry hit the coyote full on. The animal rose up in the air and came thumping down on the hood of the car with a sickening thud, blood trickling down the windshield.

Henry pressed his foot down on the brake and promptly lost control. The Volvo veered across the road, finally shuddering to a stop in a ditch.

Henry hit his head on the windshield, and then there was nothing but silence.

57

Lucky drove over to Cookie's house all set to catch her off guard. This time she was determined to find out more information. Enough fudging around from Cookie—there was only so much pretending she could get away with. Cookie *had* to know *something* and Lucky was going to find out what that something was.

Once she'd driven through the impenetrable gates and high-tech security cameras—a way of life in Bel-Air and Beverly Hills—Gerald M. himself opened the massive front door. Barefoot and attractive in an "I am a big star and don't you forget it" kind of way, Gerald ushered her in. "Hey, Lucky, you gotta come out to my studio," he enthused, fiddling with a large diamond cross hanging on a diamond-studded gold chain around his neck. "I laid down a track yesterday that's gonna blow your ass from here to the Bahamas!"

Somewhere in the background a beautiful Latina girl clad in a barely-there bikini flitted from one room to another. Gerald M. ignored her.

"Actually, I came by to see Cookie," Lucky said.

"Some party last night," Gerald continued. "You stage that fight thing or what?"

"Sure I did, Gerald," she said patiently. "It was all staged, couldn't you tell?"

"Genius, baby!" he chortled.

"Thanks," she said, fast becoming impatient. This was not a social call, she wanted action. "Is Cookie around?"

"Still sleepin' it off."

"Do you mind if I go upstairs?"

"Sure," he said, fingering his cross. "Then you gotta come by my studio out by the pool."

"I'll do that," she said, heading for the ornate staircase.

"First door on the right," Gerald called out as a petite blonde emerged from the kitchen drinking Diet Coke from the can.

First door on the right was locked. Lucky knocked loudly several times, until eventually a bleary-eyed Cookie opened up. She was clad in an oversized Snoop Dogg T-shirt and nothing else.

"Mrs. Go— I mean, Lucky!" Cookie exclaimed. "What're *you* doin' here?"

Lucky glanced pointedly at her watch. "It's almost noon and no daughter, so I thought you and I should have a little talk. Can I come in?"

"Uh . . . sure," Cookie said, reluctantly backing up to allow Lucky access to her darkened bedroom.

The room reeked of pot and incense and the walls were painted dark brown. Curled up in a sleeping bag on the floor was a male figure.

"Am I disturbing something?" Lucky inquired, black eyes glittering with impatience.

"No, course not," Cookie said, poking the male figure with her foot. "It's only Harry. He sleeps over when it's late."

"Too far to drive to Brentwood," Lucky said dryly.

"Too wasted," Cookie giggled.

Great, Lucky thought. *And these two are Max's best friends.*

"So," she said as Harry surfaced, spiky black hair standing on end, "I need more information about Max."

Cookie rubbed her eyes. "I wish we like *knew* more," she ventured. "But honestly, we don't."

"Come *on,* Cookie. I understand what it's like to be sixteen—loyalty to your friends and all that. Only this is getting serious. I have to speak to Max, and I have to speak to her today."

~ ~ ~

Cookie gave her nothing, and by the time Lucky got back to the house, she was steaming. Paige was outside the house supervising Gino Junior, who was loading their luggage into the car.

"What happened?" she asked. "I thought Gino was all set for a round of golf. Why are you leaving so soon?"

"Gino has decided we should beat the traffic," Paige explained. "And who am I to fight with your father? He's the worst backseat driver in the world, so I try to avoid all the nagging I can."

"You're a smart lady, Paige."

"Living with Gino, I have to be."

"Hey, Mom," Gino Junior said, almost dropping a heavy Vuitton bag. "Granddad says I can go stay. Is that okay with you?"

"If you promise to behave yourself," Lucky said. Gino Junior always had a good time with his grandfather, and that suited her fine since she'd be spending so much time in Vegas.

Gino emerged from the house. "You're back, kiddo," he said. "I wondered where you were."

"Yes, Gino, I'm back, and I'm looking forward to seeing you in Vegas."

"Can't wait! We'll be there. The party was the greatest, kiddo. Now come over here an' give an old man a hug."

She hugged her father, told Gino Junior to behave himself, and instructed Paige to drive carefully.

Once they'd left, she went into the house and looked for Lennie. He was sitting in front of his computer.

"Any new info?" he asked.

"Cookie's stonewalling me," she said, shaking her head. "Says she's sure Max is okay. As if *she* would know. She and Harry are lying around in her room totally stoned."

"What do you want to do?"

"I guess we'll wait until four, then if we haven't heard from her, I'm reporting her missing."

"Isn't that kind of drastic?" Lennie said. "She called yesterday and left a message that she'd be home today. I'm thinking that would hardly put her on the missing list."

"And what if she's not home today?" Lucky demanded, getting more anxious and frustrated by the minute.

"We'll deal with that *if* it happens. And believe me, sweetheart, it won't, she'll be back today."

"I'm glad *you're* so sure."

"I am. Everything's gonna work out."

Sometimes Lennie drove her crazy with his laid-back attitude. Here she was hanging around L.A. waiting for Max, when she should be in Vegas meeting with the heads of all the different departments. The Keys was due to open in two weeks and that's exactly where she should be right now. She had so much to do it was ridiculous. But no. Max was screwing up all her plans, and there was nothing she could do about it except sit and worry that her daughter was okay.

58

Once they'd lost Internet Freak, it didn't take long before everyone realized the old man wasn't merely asleep, there was something seriously wrong. He'd slumped forward in his seat, and when Jed tried to wake him he'd failed to respond.

Jed immediately began to panic. Max attempted to calm him. "Has your grandpa been sick?" she asked.

"He takes pills," Jed said, wiping his nose with the back of his hand.

Max shook the old man's shoulders. No reaction. "I think he might be unconscious," she whispered to Ace.

"Okay, we're almost at Big Bear," Ace said, his eyes fixed firmly on the road ahead. "Keep it together and find out where they live."

Jed mumbled that they lived way back where they'd come from. According to him, they were on their way to visit the old man's sister. Unfortunately, he didn't know her exact address, although he knew that she lived somewhere in Big Bear.

"This sucks," Ace muttered.

Jed looked as if he was about to cry.

Max squeezed his hand. "Your grandpa's going to be okay," she assured him.

"You shouldn't've been driving so fast," he muttered. "That's what did it."

"No, it didn't," she argued. "Going fast had like *nothing* to do with it. Your grandpa might have, I dunno, some kind of heart condition."

"He sleeps a lot," Jed admitted.

"How old is he?"

"Eighty-three."

"Well, *my* grandfather's a whole lot older than that," she said encouragingly. "And he's *really* healthy, so chances are your gramps will be kicking around for years."

Finally they reached a gas station. Ace hurriedly jumped out of the car and rushed to a pay phone.

"Are you calling your brother?" Max asked, putting her head out the window.

"Yes," Ace replied. "He'll figure out where we should take him. The old man needs a doctor right away."

She thought it was pretty cool the way he was taking charge. She imagined how different it might've been if only *he* had turned out to be her Internet guy. Oh yes, they would have gone off and spent a fantastic weekend together, most likely fallen in love and lived happily ever after.

Instead of which . . . what a nightmare!

Ace's brother, Hart, met them in Big Bear. He was taller and older than Ace. He leaned in the car, checked on the old man, then instructed his brother to follow his truck to a nearby clinic where he'd arranged to have an orderly waiting outside with a wheelchair.

At the clinic, the three men managed to get the old man into the chair. Then Hart had to leave for work, so Ace suggested they stay around to see if they could help. Max agreed it was the least they could do.

Once inside the clinic a doctor took over, leaving them in the waiting area while he whisked the old man off.

Max hurried to the ladies' room where she attempted to clean herself up. Staring in the mirror she realized what a lucky escape they'd had. Internet Freak could have done anything to them. He'd had them trapped, or so he'd thought. Ace escaping was pretty darn brave. He could've got himself shot, but he hadn't been scared, he'd stayed around to rescue her like some kind of superhero. Without him doing that . . .

She shuddered. She didn't want to think about what might have happened.

When she got back, Ace went off to the men's room.

She sat down next to Jed, who looked at her forlornly. "Is my gramps gonna be okay?" he asked.

"Sure he is," she replied cheerfully. "Do you live with him?"

He nodded his head.

"Where's your parents?" she asked curiously.

He shrugged. "Don't have none."

"How come?"

"My mom ran off when I was three. Dad went after her. At least that's what Gramps told me."

"Do you know if they're still alive?"

He shrugged again. "Dunno."

Ace came back with a couple of chocolate bars and sodas he'd gotten from the vending machine. Max grabbed a chocolate bar, peeled off the wrapper, and stuffed it in her mouth. "*Sooo* good," she sighed.

After a while the doctor returned and informed them that the old man's condition was not as serious as they'd thought. Apparently he suffered from narcolepsy and had fallen into an extremely deep sleep.

"You can come in and see him now," the doctor said. "He's awake and doing fine."

They all trooped into a room where the old man was sitting in an armchair. "What happened?" he asked, looking quite alert. "Why'd you bring me here?"

"You shouldn't be driving with your condition," the doctor scolded. "Especially long distances."

"Who, me? I'm strong as iron," the old man retaliated. "An' I *gotta* drive, it's my living. Besides, Jed here's gonna learn soon enough—ain't ya, son?"

"You had me worried, Gramps."

"Nonsense. I took a little nap an' you all panicked. Kids today!"

"Well, now that you're okay," Ace said, "we gotta get going. So, uh . . . thanks for the ride."

"Jed," Max said, "I'll send you that CD player. I promise I won't forget."

"What player?" Gramps asked grumpily.

"She's buyin' me a CD player, Gramps," Jed said excitedly. "She's sendin' it to me."

"We'll see about that," the old man huffed. "We've never bin acceptin' of nobody's charity."

"Write down your address," Max said, taking a piece of paper from the table.

Jed looked pleadingly at his grandfather, who reluctantly nodded that it was okay.

Jed scribbled on the piece of paper and handed it to her. "You're nice," he said shyly. "And you're pretty."

"Thanks," she said, almost blushing.

"S'long, everyone," Ace said. "We're on our way."

They left the old man and the boy at the clinic and began to walk the fifteen minutes to Kmart.

"I'm keeping my fingers crossed that my car's there," Max said, walking fast to keep up with him. "What do *you* think?"

"I think this is one weekend neither of us will ever forget," he said, shooting her a long look.

"What did you tell your brother about being gone all weekend?"

"That I was with my girlfriend."

"You've got a girlfriend?" she said, feeling horribly disappointed.

"Yeah," he answered casually. "Didn't I mention her?"

"No, you didn't."

"Sometimes I spend the weekends at her place. He doesn't care what I do, he's a brother, not a parent. Big difference."

She was silent, thinking, *Is this it? When I find my car do I just say good-bye to Ace and that's it?*

"Uh, is there a way I can, y'know, thank you for rescuing me this weekend?" she said, biting down hard on her bottom lip. "Are you on e-mail?"

"Very funny," he said wryly. "You wanna start with *me* now? One Internet Freak wasn't enough?"

"No, seriously," she said, breaking a smile. "What's your e-mail?"

"I'm not into e-mail."

"You're not?"

"Who's got the time?"

"You have plenty of time. The day I ran into you, you were lurking around doing exactly nothing."

"That's 'cause I kinda had a fight with my girlfriend."

"You did?"

"Yeah, she works at Kmart. I hooked up with you to make her jealous."

"So the whole bank robbery thing—"

"It was a story," he admitted.

"I knew that," she said quickly.

"No you didn't."

"Yes I did."

"Okay, and *I* knew you weren't eighteen," he said, squinting at her. "Why'd you lie?"

"It wasn't a lie."

"It was blatant."

"I'll be seventeen soon enough."

"When's your birthday?"

"In about eight months!"

"You're too much," he said, laughing. "And I don't have e-mail. But," he added casually, "maybe I'll call you sometime."

"No you won't," she said, thinking, *No he won't.*

"Yeah, I will."

"Instead of calling, come visit me in L.A.," she answered boldly, stopping for a minute to catch her breath.

"With my girlfriend?" he countered.

"If you want."

They exchanged a long look.

"We could double-date," she added, starting to walk again. "You and her, me and *my* boyfriend."

"Thought you said you broke up with your boyfriend?"

"I was lying. This weekend was all about making him jealous." A long beat. "You know what *that's* like, don't you?"

"Are you trying to one-up me?" he said, grinning.

"Maybe," she replied, thinking how hot he was with the smile and the great white teeth and the appealing cleft in his chin.

"Hey," he said nonchalantly, "the kid was right."

"About what?"

"You *are* pretty."

She held her breath for a moment. *Pretty . . . hmm . . .* And she looked like crap—they both did. Apparently he didn't think so.

"Uh, you should see me when I try," she said, going for flippant.

"Guess I'll havta raincheck that."

They exchanged another look.

Five more minutes and they reached the Kmart parking lot. "Wow!" Max said, quickening her pace. "I think I see my car. How exciting is *this*?"

"Let's hope he hasn't left a bomb under the hood," Ace said.

"Oh, great!" she groaned. "Make me feel secure."

"You're always secure, aren't you? You're that kind of girl."

"How can you say that? You hardly know me."

"Oh, I know you."

"Good, 'cause that means you trust me, and I'll need money for emergencies 'cause the Freak took my wallet with everything in it."

"Rescuing you isn't enough," he grumbled, digging in the back pocket of his jeans. "Now she wants my money."

"I'll pay you back, I promise."

"You'd better," he said, handing her two crumpled ten-dollar bills. "That's all I've got."

"Thanks," she said, taking the bills.

"Y'know," he said thoughtfully, "I still think we should tell the cops.

The dude's a predator, he threatened us with a gun. And if I hadn't gotten out . . . who knows what would've happened to us."

"No!" she said sharply. "We have to walk away. We're safe, that's all that matters."

"You're just scared your mom's gonna be mad at you."

"So?"

"Okay. If that's what you want. But don't forget he's got all your shit. Laptop, credit cards, phone."

"It can all be replaced."

"Whatever."

A few minutes later he'd hot-wired her car, given her a stern warning not to stop until she got to her destination, and said good-bye.

Sitting behind the wheel of her car with the engine running, she was reluctant to take off. Was it her imagination, or had she and Ace developed a real bond? They'd shared a frightening experience and got through it together. Somehow or other she didn't want to leave. But of course, she knew she had to.

Forget about Ace, she told herself. *He's taken. He doesn't even live in L.A. So forget about him.*

"Okay, bye again," she said, leaning out her window and waving.

"Try not to get in any more trouble," he said. "'Cause next time I might not be around to rescue you."

And then it was over and she was on her way home.

59

Irma was dispatched back to Mexico City by commercial jet while Anthony traveled in luxury on his private plane accompanied by his children, their friends, and the nanny.

Standing in the airport with her luggage, Irma was happy to be parting company with her husband. She was returning to her house, her lover, and she was now ready to cement plans for her future.

Spending a long weekend in Acapulco with Anthony and her children had made it a lot easier for her to make a final decision. As she'd watched her family at play she'd realized she had nothing in common with any of them anymore. It was time to get back to the real world, and living in the real world meant leaving the house in Mexico City. First she would help herself to money from Anthony's safe, enabling her to open her own personal bank account, then she'd decide when to go and what to take with her.

Unfortunately, Luis could not be part of her plans. He was a big temptation, but since he didn't speak English, running off with him would be impossible. Sometimes, in her fantasies, she'd daydreamed about the two of them disappearing to Bali or some other exotic island, but it was merely a fantasy.

She smiled to herself thinking that she was still a young, vibrant woman, and there were plenty of men out there. All she had to decide was where she would go. New York was out of the question, so was Miami, but lately she'd been having thoughts about Los Angeles. She certainly entertained no thought of going home to her parents in Omaha—that would be admitting defeat. Besides, her parents were completely self-absorbed, they'd never asked her for anything. They'd no doubt be horrified were she to turn up on their doorstep.

On the flight from Acapulco to Mexico City, she found herself sitting next to an American businessman. He was about forty with prematurely graying hair and a pleasant smile. He wasted no time in starting a conversation.

"I'm traveling to Mexico City on business," he informed her. "How about you?"

"I live there," she replied, folding her hands on her lap. "Or rather my soon-to-be ex-husband does." She paused for a moment. "Actually," she continued, savoring every word, "I'm shortly moving to Los Angeles."

Saying it out loud gave her a thrill.

"You are?" he said, rummaging in his pocket. "Then I should give you my card because L.A. is where I live."

"How interesting," she answered boldly. "Perhaps you can tell me all about the city."

He proceeded to do so, and by the time the plane landed they were old friends.

"You wouldn't happen to be free for dinner tonight?" he asked as they waited for their luggage. "Here I am, a lonely American all by himself in Mexico City, and here you are—a beautiful American woman about to get a divorce. It seems like fate, doesn't it?"

"It certainly does," she replied, twisting her wedding band on her finger.

"Well," he said, pressing for an answer. "Are we on?"

"Yes," she replied after a few moments' indecision. "I'd very much like to have dinner with you."

"Excellent. I'm at the Presidente InterContinental Hotel. Seven-thirty suit you? We could meet in the bar."

Why not? she thought. She had a lover at home and an attractive man to take her to dinner.

Anthony kept two mistresses. It was her time now.

~ ~ ~

Back in Miami, Anthony didn't bother going home—he called Emmanuelle from the airport.

"Where are you?" he asked, none too pleased. "I tried the apartment, you're not there."

"That's 'cause I'm in the middle of a photo shoot," she explained, speaking on her cell while her Puerto Rican hairstylist fussed with her long hair extensions.

"I'm here," he said. "An' I wanna see you."

"I won't be finished for a couple of hours."

"What is it with you an' fuckin' photo sessions?" he growled. "How come you wanna be on the cover of every fuckin' magazine in town?"

"They pay me the big bucks, daddy," she said soothingly. "And get me mucho attention."

"*I* pay you big bucks, an' *I* give you *plenty* of attention," he responded. "An' don't call me daddy."

"But, honey," she purred, "you never put anything in my name and that hurts my feelings."

Feelings? She had feelings? This was a big surprise.

"I'm young," she continued. "I have to make my own money 'cause if we break up, baby doesn't want to find herself out on the street with nothing."

He was silent for a moment, considering what she'd said. Christ! Women and money. Was that all they ever thought about?

"Where's the studio?" he asked.

She told him.

"I'll come by, check you out."

"No, poopsie, you'll be bored," she said quickly, thinking there was nothing she'd like less than Anthony barging into one of her photo shoots. "You know how you like being the center of attention," she added. "You'll hate sitting on the sidelines."

"I wanna see you at work," he said stubbornly.

"Okay," she sighed, realizing he was giving her no choice. "If that's how you really want to spend your day."

"No, what I *really* wanna do is fuck your brains out," he said, flashing on her luscious body.

"Later, honey," she promised.

"You're makin' me wait?" he said incredulously.

"Only a few hours," she murmured, ending the conversation.

Only a few hours. Ha! Emmanuelle was letting her so-called career as a half-naked cover girl go to her head. She'd better start realizing that the car and the apartment and the clothes were perks that went along with making *him* happy, and he wasn't happy when he had to wait.

Anthony Bonar did not wait for any woman.

They waited for him.

~ ~ ~

Flushed with her success on the plane, Irma arrived back at her house and was surprised when the guard at the gate stepped out of his cubicle and stopped her driver.

"Yes?" she said, opening the back window of the car. It was unusual for the guards to communicate with her in any way. They usually spoke only to Anthony.

"Ah, Señora Bonar," the guard said, leaning one hand against the top of the car while bending his head to speak to her. "I was wondering about the dogs. Are they following behind with Señor Bonar?"

"No, the dogs are still in Acapulco," she said, shrinking back from his garlic breath. "Mr. Bonar took the plane to Miami."

"I see," the guard said, not moving.

"Is that all?" Irma asked, eager to get up to the house.

"*Sí*, Señora Bonar," he said, still not moving. "I am Cesar," he added with a lascivious leer. "And might I say you look very lovely today."

Abruptly she closed the car window and Cesar backed away. Was it appropriate for one of their guards to be complimenting her? Maybe she was giving off vibes today, what with the man on the plane, and now the guard throwing compliments her way.

Marta, the cook, greeted her in the front hall. "I hear you have many parties in Acapulco, *señora*. I speak with my cousin, Rosa, she tell me lot of parties, much work, too much work."

"I'm sure it was," Irma said, not about to get into a discussion about Rosa's workload. "Are the gardeners here today?"

"*Sí, señora*, they both outside."

"The dogs are still in Acapulco so you don't have to worry about feeding them. I'm sure you're thrilled about that."

"*Sí, señora*."

"I see no reason why you can't take the rest of the day off."

"Is okay, *señora*, I fix you dinner tonight."

"No, it's not necessary. I shall be dining out."

"Out, *señora?*" Marta said, raising her eyebrows. Everyone knew Irma never left the house at night unless the master was in town.

"Yes, that's right," Irma said quickly. "You may go home early."

"*Sí, señora*."

Irma hurried upstairs and went straight to her bedroom window. She immediately saw that the old gardener was bent over the rosebushes working diligently, but she couldn't spot Luis.

She was desperate to see him, yet in a way she knew it was a bad idea, because getting too attached was a mistake.

And yet . . . the moment she thought about him she was filled with a flurry of sexual longing.

Hmm . . . she thought. *There's nothing to prevent me from having sex with Luis in the afternoon, and dinner with a perfect stranger in the evening.*

Absolutely nothing.

And that's exactly what she intended to do.

60

"Hi, Max," Gerald M. said, opening up the front door of his mansion, munching a tuna sandwich. Standing behind him was a statuesque blonde of indeterminate age. Bland and beautiful with overly full lips, she wore pink shorts, a tankini top, and a blank expression. Gerald M. did not bother introducing her. "Lucky was here looking for you earlier," he said, taking another bite of his sandwich.

"She was?" Max said, out of breath and totally relieved that she'd made it all the way back to L.A. without any mishaps. Thanks to Ace, the nightmare was behind her.

"Yeah. You'd better give her a call, she seemed kinda frantic. She was gonna come out to my studio an' listen to my music. She never made it. Tell her she's gotta come back, she's gotta hear the latest tracks I'm layin' down."

"I'll do that," Max said, wishing he wasn't in such a talkative mood. "Is Cookie around?"

"My little girl's feelin' kinda fragile today—came down for coffee, an' went straight back up to her room."

"She did?"

"Yeah, it was some party last night, you missed out. Where were you?"

"Uh, I kinda got hung up."

"Yeah, well you don't look so good. You want a sandwich? A Coke? Anything?"

"No thanks. I'll run up and see Cookie if you don't mind."

"No problem. Go ahead. An' tell my baby girl I'll be in the studio. You kids should come on out, take a listen."

"We will," she said, bounding up the stairs to Cookie's room and hammering on the door.

"Go away," Cookie mumbled. "I'm tryin' to sleep."

"It's me, Max."

Within seconds Cookie had opened up, still clad in nothing more than an oversized man's T. "Where've you *been*, you freak!" she exclaimed.

"It isn't *me* who's the freak, it's the Internet maniac I hooked up with."

"*Oh . . . my . . . God!*" Cookie said, pulling her into the room, slamming the door shut, and locking it again. "What happened? Tell me everything! We haven't stopped callin' you all weekend, Lucky's freakin' furious! She's questioned me like a billion times!"

"What did you tell her?"

"Nothin' much."

Harry, sitting on the floor smoking a joint, joined the conversation. "You promised to check in," he said accusingly. "Why didn't you?"

"Would've if I could've," Max replied, flopping onto the bed, wondering if she should call Ace to let him know she'd made it.

"What happened to you, girl?" Cookie said. "You look like crap."

"This is the story I'm telling my mom," Max said, finally feeling safe and secure. "I was carjacked, okay?"

"Carjacked!" Harry yelled, expelling a mouthful of smoke. "Whoa!"

"Not really," Max explained. "But that's what I'm telling Lucky."

"So all this time you were getting it on with Internet Guy, right?" Cookie said, sitting cross-legged on her bed, fresh cornrows framing her expressive face.

"No," Max corrected, pausing for effect. "The real story is I was freaking *kidnapped*."

"*What?*" Harry said, dragging on his joint. "Like by an ax murderer?"

"As if I'd still be here if it was an ax murderer," Max said scornfully. "However, people, know this—it was *way* bad. You can't even imagine how bad."

"Seriously, you like got *kidnapped?*" Cookie said, her eyes widening.

"Yeah, an' then I like got rescued by this hottie who was kidnapped with me," Max said, once again thinking about Ace.

"Huh?" Harry said, blowing smoke throughout the room. He was totally stoned.

"It's a long story," Max sighed. "I hurt my ankle and my sides are all scratched up and—"

"Man!" Cookie exclaimed, jumping off the bed. "Are you makin' all this up?"

"No way," Max said vehemently. "We were kidnapped at gunpoint and held hostage."

"For money?" Cookie asked, her eyes growing wider by the minute.

"Not for money."

"Then *what*?"

"I dunno. It was all so weird."

"How about getting laid?" Cookie questioned. "Did you do it? Was it totally great?"

"Aren't you listening?" Max said, noticing that both her friends were stoned. "I got *kidnapped*, not *laid*."

"You'd better call Lucky," Cookie said. "She's *major* uptight."

"I will, but I should clean up first. Can I shower? And borrow clothes?"

"Sure," Cookie said. "But then I wanna hear *everything*. There's no way you can zoom in here, drop that you were kidnapped, an' not give out details."

"I will, after I've done something about my ankle," Max said, rolling up the leg of her jeans.

"Eew!" Cookie exclaimed, taking a peek. "That's gnarly. How'd you do it?"

"Internet Freak chained my foot to a bed."

"This is *so* like a scene from a horror movie," Harry said, spiked hair standing on end.

"No movie," Max said gravely. "Truth."

"Whyn't you call Lucky before you shower," Cookie suggested. "Get that over with. She's crazy mad, apparently she was supposed to go to Vegas today, canceled 'cause you were on the missing list."

"Oh shit!"

"'Oh shit' is right."

"Lend me your phone."

"Where's yours?"

"It's with my credit cards, money, and laptop. Internet Freak took everything."

"That sucks," Cookie said, handing her phone over. Max finally got up the nerve to call Lucky.

"Uh, hi, Mom," she ventured when Lucky picked up. "It's me, Max."

There was a long, ominous silence, until finally Lucky said, "Where exactly are you?"

"Long story," Max said cheerfully. "I'll be home in an hour, tell you everything then."

"You're in L.A.?"

"Uh . . . I'm kinda on my way. Y'see, the thing is I got kind of carjacked."

"Carjacked," Lucky repeated disbelievingly.

"Yeah, so, um—"

"Not another word," Lucky said, her voice icy. "Get your ass home, go straight up to your room, and stay there until I get back from Vegas, where I should've been five hours ago. Do that, and don't even think about leaving the house. You're grounded. Understand?"

"But, Mom," Max wailed. "That's so unfair. It wasn't my fault."

"It never is," Lucky said, clicking off.

"Man!" Max complained, making a face. "She just told me I'm grounded."

"Surprise, surprise," Cookie said, yawning. "You promised her you'd be home for Gino's party an' you bailed. What did you expect? Oh yeah, and for your information, the party was like a *total* blast. You missed an awesome fight an' everything."

"You got any disinfectant and bandages?" Max asked, not interested in hearing about the party she'd missed. "And I'd kill for something to eat, I'm major starving."

"Here," Harry said, groping in his pants pocket and tossing her a pack of M&M's. "Knock yourself out."

~ ~ ~

"*You* can deal with her," Lucky steamed, clicking off her cell phone. "Believe me—she's all yours."

"I've got a production meeting at four," Lennie said, glancing at his watch. "I take it she's on her way home."

"Thank God—yes! And I *have* to get my ass to Vegas, so now that I know she's safe I'm leaving ASAP. It's all down to you."

"What's her story anyway?"

"Some bullshit about getting carjacked, which I do not believe for one single minute, and you shouldn't either."

"That's our Max—she's inventive."

"She sure is."

"What time will you be back?"

"Who knows? There's so much to deal with. We open in less than two weeks and Mooney says it's crazy. I might have to stay over a couple of days. Are you sure you can handle everything here?"

"'And once again his beautiful wife runs off, while he is left in charge of their delinquent daughter.'"

"*Please*, sweetheart."

"Yeah, yeah. Go look after your other baby."

"Now, about Max—"

"You don't have to tell me—she's grounded."

"I mean it, Lennie, do *not* weaken, I'm depending on you."

"Surely you trust me?"

"When it comes to little Miss Green Eyes, *no*."

"That's 'cause I can't help it, she reminds me of you."

"Should I take that as a compliment?" she asked wryly.

"Max is beautiful, wild, and full of adventure. That's you, Lucky, so yeah, take it as a compliment and don't be too hard on the kid."

"Man," Lucky said, shaking her head. "She's got your number big time. Just remember: grounded—G-R-"

"I *know*. Now get moving. You've got a hotel to open."

~ ~ ~

It was such a relief to only have to face Lennie since Lucky wasn't home. It made things way easier. Whew! Her dad was so laid-back and cool and most of all *understanding*. He bought the carjacked story, didn't question her too much, and had one of his assistants arrange to get her a new phone, cancel her credit cards, replace her driver's license, and he even produced a duplicate set of car keys. Lennie was the *best!*

If only Lucky could be so understanding. But no. Lucky would immediately know she was lying. Lucky had a bullshit detector a mile long.

"Sorry, but you're grounded, sweetie," Lennie informed her. "I gotta go to a meeting, so make sure you stay around the house."

"I get carjacked, robbed, and *I'm* grounded," Max protested.

"Your mom's orders."

"Since when did you take orders from *her?*"

"Watch it, Max. Don't screw with my goodwill."

She went upstairs, lay on her bed, and thought about Ace. She'd told Cookie and Harry about him, but neither of them really got it, they were more interested in puffing weed and listening to details about Internet Freak. *Ugh!* Every time she thought of the creep she got the chills.

Now that her ordeal was over and she was safely home, it all seemed so surreal, as if she had dreamed it. Only her ankle—already healing—and her scratched sides reminded her that it was indeed real. The Internet Freak—whoever he was—had been a definite psycho, and once again she realized how very fortunate they were to have escaped.

Ace had wanted them to go to the police and report him, but she simply couldn't face doing that. If Lucky ever discovered how stupid she'd been, she'd *never* live it down. Lucky expected everyone to be strong and invincible, just like she was.

Yes. Carjacked was the way to go. She'd told Lennie a story and she was sticking to it. Carjacked, managed to outwit the would-be carjackers, and somehow or other gotten stuck in the woods—which is why she hadn't made it back for Gino's party.

It was the best she could come up with.

61

Fortunately, they were out on location and not confined to a studio, so Billy felt that it wasn't necessary to confront Alex. Apologizing to the director was not an option—he was adamant about that.

There were extra security guards to control the paparazzi, and several cops doing duty on crowd control.

Billy lounged in his chair on the street way behind the camera, long legs stretched out in front of him.

"She called you yet?" Kev asked, wandering over.

"Who?" Billy said, although he knew exactly who Kev meant.

"The ho who gave you the crabs," Kev said, chewing on a carrot stick.

"Stop mentioning the crabs," Billy said irritably. "According to her, she didn't give 'em to me."

"Then who did?"

"How the frig do I know."

"Maybe you got 'em from Venus," Kev said slyly.

"Get a life, Kev."

"You never know."

"Venus is dead-on faithful."

"For sure?"

"Yes," Billy said. "Disappointed?"

"I suppose she's gotta be, hasn't she?"

"How's that?"

"You're her young stud. She wouldn't want to piss you off, not until she's through with the ride."

"How many times I gotta tell you to quit with the stud jokes?"

"Seems t'me you an' Venus can't last that long anyway. It's not as if you're gonna walk down the freakin' aisle. I mean, have you considered the fact that when you're forty she'll be fifty-three?"

"Is this what you do all day, Kev, sit around thinking up this crap?" Billy said, yawning. "Stay outta my business, okay?"

"Your business *is* my business," Kev said, still chewing on his carrot stick. "You pay me to be your main man."

"Yeah, an' my main man is not gettin' paid to bug the shit outta me."

"Okay, okay," Kev said, throwing up his hands. "I like Venus, but even *you* gotta admit you're not exactly a perfect match."

"Listen to the expert," Billy said. "I'm having a good time, that's all that matters."

Unfortunately, Kev was envious of his relationship with Venus. Before Venus, they'd spent their nights cruising the clubs, picking up girls, bringing them back to the house, and experiencing a slam-dunk party every night. Then Billy had hooked up with Venus, and as far as Kev was concerned, the fun times were history.

Billy still wasn't sure how long it would last between him and his superstar girlfriend. This boy toy crap was getting older every day.

Later his cell phone rang and it was Miss Broken Taillight. He didn't know her name, so when she said, "Hi, this is Ali," he had no idea who he was speaking to.

"Yeah," he said. "Can I help you?"

"Yes, you can help me," she answered, sounding uptight. "I'm the girl who was up at your house last week. Remember me? The one who sucked your cock. You made me a promise and I'm calling to collect."

"Collect?" he said. "That's an odd way of putting it, makes you sound like a bookie."

"You made me a promise," she repeated. "And I made *you* one back. I won't spill to your girlfriend, and you'll swing me a part in your movie."

"I will, huh?"

"That was our deal."

"Then you'd better drive down to the set," he said, telling her where to come. "I'll figure something out."

"You'd better."

Ignoring her implied threat, he said, "When you get here, ask for Kev. Do *not* let on you know me. You're dealing with my friend Kev on this."

"Oh," she said huffily. "So now I'm not good enough to know you, is that it? Why can't I be your out-of-town cousin or something?"

"It's not an option. There's press everywhere, an' I can't be seen talking to you."

"Why?"

" 'Cause we'll end up in *People* or *Us*. Like I said—deal with Kev."

"You're such a prick."

"Thanks. I love you too," he said, snapping his phone shut. He called Kev over and filled him in.

"What's she like?" Kev asked, sounding a little too interested.

"Young, pretty, skillful, and hands off."

"Why? You savin' her for a repeat performance?"

Before he could answer, he was finally called to the set. He couldn't prove it, but he was sure that Alex had changed the shooting schedule so that he was forced to sit around all morning even though his call was six A.M.

The scene he was about to shoot was with a fellow actor, a black ex–football player who was over six feet four and built like the proverbial brick house.

Billy knew he was about to get a beating whether he wanted one or not. Shooting this scene would be Alex's way of getting back at him.

Fuck it! He'd take it like a man. How bad could it be? The crew were all watching; the other actor seemed like a reasonable guy. The only sadist on the set was Alex Woods.

He was right. Alex demanded seventeen takes, and in each take he had to get punched on the jaw, and even though they were supposed to be fake punches, Alex wanted it to look real—so guess what, he got pounded.

It was bad enough that he had a black eye; once they were through, his jaw felt as if he'd been struck a series of blows with a sledgehammer.

"I'm going back to my trailer," he told the assistant assigned to him when Alex was finally satisfied.

"I'll escort you," said the girl. She was overweight and enthusiastic, and any time she could spend with Billy Melina was a bonus.

There was quite a crowd of people on the street straining to see stars. They all wanted to get a peek at Billy. The cops were doing a good job of keeping them back.

His trailer was parked on a side street. The female assistant chattered nonstop about what a thrill it was working with him, and how wonderful he was in the scene, how she'd seen all his movies, how she'd only been working on this particular one for a month and it was the best moment of her life meeting him.

Assistant/fan. Great! Just what he didn't need.

He tuned her out, not in the mood to listen.

"Thanks, hon," he said when they reached his trailer.

He climbed the steps, all ready to collapse on his couch, flung open the door, and there was Miss Broken Taillight giving Kev a blow job.

62

Emmanuelle was posing, showing off in a string bikini that left little to the imagination. She lounged against a tropical background in the studio, Cuban music blasting over the loudspeakers, a wiry photographer dancing around behind his camera.

Anthony was embarrassed for her. She shouldn't be half naked in front of a studio full of people, it wasn't right. He could see her nipples straining against the thin material of her tiny top, the curve of her snatch through the bikini bottom.

In spite of himself, he began to get hard. Goddammit! If he was hard, so were all the other men in the studio—unless they were gay. Emmanuelle always assured him that all the men she worked with were gay, but looking around he wasn't so sure.

The Grill was hovering somewhere behind him. He didn't want the big lug ogling his girlfriend's private parts—it infuriated him.

"Go wait in the car," he ordered.

"You sure, boss?"

"Yeah, I'm fuckin' sure," he replied, scowling.

Emmanuelle hadn't spotted him yet, she was too busy posing, flinging her long legs this way and that, bringing her arms up, seductively touching her breasts, playing to the camera as if it were his dick.

Jesus Christ! Enough already!

He stepped up beside the guy with the camera. "Hey!" he yelled at Emmanuelle. "Over here, sugar."

Emmanuelle barely stopped posing. Putting a finger to her lips, she murmured, "Shush, honey, I'm in the middle."

"The middle of what?" he said.

"In the middle of my shoot," she answered, pouting.

"'Scuse me, we're working here," the photographer said, taking an aggressive stance.

Anthony turned on him, his face dark as thunder. "Ya think I'm fuckin' blind?" he snarled. "I can see that. You're shootin' my fuckin' girlfriend."

"Okay, man," the photographer said, hurriedly backing off. "But do you think you can give us some space here? We'll be ready to break in twenty minutes, then she's all yours."

"Fuck you," Anthony said. "If I wanna talk to my girlfriend, I'll talk to her now."

Emmanuelle jumped up and ran forward, breasts jiggling. "That's okay, Rodriguez," she said, coming between them. "It might be a good idea if we break early."

The photographer glared at her, while the makeup and hair people started gossiping among themselves, shooting Anthony looks as if to say, "Who *is* this thug?"

Taking Anthony's arm, Emmanuelle steered him into her dressing room. "Honey," she said. "You can't pull me out of a shoot like this, it's not fair."

"Is this what you call work?" he snorted. "Look at you—ya got no fuckin' clothes on."

"You know what I do, poopsie," she purred. "You *love* seeing my photos when they're on the cover of a magazine."

"There's only one thing I love," he said, reaching forward and pinching her left nipple.

"What, honey?" she said, trying not to wince because he was hurting her.

He kicked the door shut. "I love it when you suck my fuckin' dick," he said, unzipping his pants.

"Not here, baby," she objected. "Everybody's outside, I can't do it here."

"Oh, yes you can," he said, pressing down on her shoulders. "Now get on your knees an' show me your *real* talent."

~ ~ ~

Unable to lure Luis up to her bedroom, Irma was disappointed. After showering and changing clothes she'd gone out to the garden where Luis was busy mowing the lawn. When she'd approached him and asked him to come into the house he'd shaken his head, indicating the older gardener who was working nearby.

"It's okay," she'd said, giving him a meaningful look. "I need you to come see my houseplants."

"No, *señora*," he'd replied, vigorously shaking his head, refusing to look her in the eye. "No today."

She couldn't believe he was turning her down. But then, perhaps he was merely being careful, or perhaps he was upset that she'd gone to Acapulco with her husband. After a while she'd given up, and gone back into the house.

Now she watched him from the window. She watched him until he left at four o'clock.

Later she ordered a car and driver to take her to the hotel in town. Using her husband's driver would be a mistake, the man probably reported everything to Anthony, and that would be a disaster. Better to be safe than sorry.

~ ~ ~

Cesar stopped Luis at the gate as the younger man attempted to drive out.

"Well," Cesar said, licking his thick lips in anticipation, "when do I get a taste of American pussy?"

"I don't know what you're talking about," Luis replied in Spanish. "You are imagining things, Cesar."

"I am imagining nothing," Cesar responded. "You think everyone doesn't know what's going on? I want a piece, Luis, otherwise I tell Señor Bonar, and I tell your wife."

"You wouldn't dare tell Señor Bonar."

"You imagine you know me, Luis, but you don't," Cesar said. "Either I fuck that American ass, or your fun and games are over."

"You're crazy," Luis said, refusing to play Cesar's sick game.

"No," Cesar fired back. "*You're* the crazy one, because if you do *not* arrange what I want, your life will be over, my friend."

~ ~ ~

During the drive into the center of the city, Irma attempted to compose herself, although her thoughts kept on drifting back to Luis. Why hadn't he come into the house? It was frustrating. Three days away from him and she found herself yearning for his touch.

Am I in love? she thought.

No. Lust. Pure and simple lust.

Her companion from the plane, Oliver Stanton, was waiting at the hotel bar nursing a tumbler of Scotch. As soon as he saw her approaching he jumped to his feet. "You look lovely," he said.

"Thank you," she replied, noting he was tall and well built, although not as well built as Luis.

The name Oliver had a nice ring to it. She decided that she and Oliver would date when she arrived in Los Angeles. She and Oliver might even become a couple.

She wondered what he did. During their conversation on the plane she had not thought of finding out, or maybe she'd forgotten to ask him as she'd been so busy talking about herself and her early days as a beauty queen, so much so that she hadn't given him a chance to talk about himself. It didn't matter, she'd draw him out at dinner.

"I thought we'd eat in the restaurant here," he said. "I checked it out, seems perfect."

"Fine with me," she said, nodding.

They made pleasant conversation over dinner. She enjoyed her food and drank several glasses of red wine. Glancing around the restaurant, she felt like a human being for a change, not Anthony Bonar's wife relegated to the background. Her future stretched before her, and she was ready to embrace it.

They lingered over dessert, until eventually Oliver leaned across the table, took her hand, and said, "How about coming up to my room for a nightcap?"

She was thankful she'd thought of removing her wedding ring as she considered the possibility. She was not naive—she knew exactly what Oliver had in mind. And why not? She was about to be a free woman, and Luis had rejected her—which she did *not* appreciate, and even now Anthony was probably bedding down his Miami bimbo.

"Yes," she murmured, the wine loosening her inhibitions. "I think I'd like that."

"Good," he said, signing the check.

Once they were in the elevator on their way up to his room, Oliver moved in close and kissed her, a dry kiss, unlike Luis's passionate tongue kisses, but it got her juices flowing all the same, and when they reached his room she was ready, and so was he.

He pushed her back on the bed, lifted her skirt, and pulled down her panties. Then he gave her head for approximately one minute, reached up and fondled her breasts for another minute, then unzipped his pants, put on a condom, and was inside her within seconds.

She lay there thinking about Luis, and how he worshipped her body, how he spent time kissing every inch of her body, how different his touch was.

When Oliver climaxed, she didn't.

"That was very, very nice," he announced, rolling off her. "You're quite a woman. Did you—"

"Yes," she lied, searching for the right word. "It was wonderful."

"Now we can enjoy our nightcap," he said, getting up and going over to the minibar. "Brandy? Liquor? What's your pleasure?"

"Do you have wine?" she asked, adjusting her clothes and getting off the bed.

"Anything m'lady wants," he said, opening a half-size bottle of red wine and a miniature bottle of brandy.

She sat at a small corner table as he handed her a wineglass and pulled up another chair. Then he toasted her and told her once again that she was quite a woman.

She didn't feel like quite a woman, she felt empty inside, and it occurred to her that sleeping around was not a very satisfying way to go.

Five minutes of conversation, she'd drink her wine and make a graceful exit. "So, Oliver," she said, remembering that she still had not asked him what he did, "what business are you in?"

"You'll never guess," he said, smiling at her.

"I think I will," she replied, trying not to stare at his crooked front tooth which she'd never really noticed before. "Let me see, you're a lawyer."

"Wrong."

"A doctor?"

No," he said, still smiling.

"Then you're right—I'm unable to guess."

"I don't tell everybody what I do because it's a little daunting for some people," he said, lowering his voice.

"Hmm . . . sounds intriguing," she said, playing with the stem of her wineglass.

"Some people would say it is, and some people would say it isn't." He paused for a moment. "I'm in the drug enforcement business."

"Excuse me?" she said, startled.

"Yes, I'm a drug enforcement agent," he said, obviously proud of his job. "Y'know, we're the ones who chase down the bad guys and throw 'em in jail."

"You do?" she gasped.

"Are you aware that Acapulco is the drug capital of Mexico?" he said, all businesslike.

Was this some kind of cruel joke? Her first date, and he turned out to be a drug enforcement agent.

"I, uh, I need to use the bathroom," she said faintly.

"I'll be waiting," he said, giving her another steady smile.

She got up and almost ran to the bathroom, desperately trying to control her sense of panic.

Oliver Stanton was a drug enforcement agent.

Her husband was a drug lord.

This situation was totally out of control.

63

Throwing herself back into rehearsing for the one-night show to celebrate the opening of the Keys was therapy for Venus. She had every intention of putting on a spectacular show for her friend. After all, Lucky had worked so hard planning and building a magnificent hotel complex in the desert, and Venus, who had never played Vegas, was doing it as a big favor. However, favor or not, she'd decided it had to be the best one-nighter she'd ever put on.

It was quite satisfying getting back to rehearsing with her backup dancers and singers, her director and musical arranger. Spending time with Billy was fun, but climbing up on her pedestal was just as much fun in a different way. Sometimes it was hard for her to realize just how famous she'd become. She'd made it all the way from nothing, now here she was—Venus—known worldwide by only one name, like Madonna or Cher. It was quite an achievement.

During a break she checked her cell and saw that Billy had called twice. He'd also text-messaged her once again saying how sorry he was.

His apologies were sweet, but a bit late in the day. Why hadn't he been sorry last night on the way home?

He's too young for you, she told herself. *This older woman/younger man crap is just that—crap.*

She should be with an older, wiser man—not quite as old as Cooper, maybe somebody around her own age. Yes, a George Clooney.

Although the thought of losing Billy filled her with sadness.

It wasn't time. Not yet.

~ ~ ~

"Jesus Christ!" Billy exclaimed.

"Oh man!" Kev yelled, reaching an orgasm at exactly the same moment as Billy barged in.

Ali jumped up and ran into the bathroom. They could both hear her spitting into the sink.

"Charming," Billy said, disgusted. "What did I tell you, Kev? What the fuck did I say? I told you hands off, remember?"

"She came on to me," Kev said somewhat sheepishly. "I'm hardly gonna turn it down."

"What do you mean, she came on to you? What did she do? Unzip your pants and whip it out?"

"More or less."

"Ah, jeez!"

Ali emerged from the bathroom wiping her mouth with a crumpled Kleenex. "I thought that's what you wanted me to do," she said sulkily. "I thought that's the only way he'd give me a part."

"*He's* not the one giving you the freakin' part," Billy said, exasperated. "He's gonna talk to the director's assistant, who'll try an' fit you in a scene."

"I didn't know that."

"Learn it," Billy said sharply. "Running around this town giving everyone b.j.'s won't get you shit."

"That's what Marilyn Monroe did."

"Yeah, a hundred years ago. Girls don't have to do that anymore."

"Oh, yes they do," she argued. "How do you think I got that waitressing gig at the party the other night? I had to blow the caterer."

"Jeez," Billy said, shaking his head. "Look, I think I've arranged for you to get a walk-on in the next scene, but you'll have to behave yourself. Don't go offering b.j.'s to everyone who asks."

"Nice trailer," she said, flinty eyes checking everything out. "It's bigger than where I live."

"Where *do* you live?" Kev asked, obviously in deep lust, and not at all embarrassed at getting caught with his zipper down.

"Hollywood," she answered vaguely. "In a room with a coupla other people."

"You a runaway?" Billy asked, inexplicably feeling sorry for her.

"What makes you think *that*?" she said, giving him a wary look.

"Just a thought. How old are you, anyway?"

"Old enough," she replied, full of false bravado.

"You got money?" he asked, remembering what it felt like arriving in L.A. with exactly nothing.

"I told you," she said. "I don't want your money. What I want is a part in your movie. I wanna get discovered."

The great Hollywood mantra: *I wanna get discovered.*

"Okay," he said, wondering if Venus had ever uttered those same words when she was young and broke and desperately trying to make it in a town crammed with hopefuls. "Kev'll take you to meet Maggie, the director's personal assistant. She'll see you get a walk-on, an' you'll get paid too. You've got a SAG card, right?"

"Yes," she said proudly.

"That's something."

"I need to get a line," she added.

"Got a feeling Mags can't pull *that* off," Billy said, thinking, *No way!* "Alex's scripts are written in stone, all speaking parts are cast way before he starts shooting."

"I want a line," Ali repeated, her pointed face setting into a stubborn expression. "Otherwise—"

"Okay, stop trying to blackmail me," Billy said. "It doesn't make you look good."

"I'm not here to look good," she said, glaring at him.

"I'll see what I can do."

This was getting ridiculous. What had happened to his simple life before stardom? Before Venus. Before Alex Woods. Although he couldn't really blame Venus and Alex—they'd discovered him. Truth was he owed Alex a lot, and if the director would stop bad-mouthing him all over town there was a good chance they could be friends again.

As for Kev, well, he'd deal with him later.

To add to the joys of the day, Janey, his publicist, knocked on the trailer door and came charging in.

"Hello? Are you on lunch break?" she trilled. "I'm here to remind you that you've got an interview to finish, Billy. With Florence Harbinger. She's here and she's waiting. Can I bring her in?"

Oh, shit! It was one of those days.

~ ~ ~

Venus was sweating, which was exactly the way she liked it when getting back into one of her vigorous dance routines.

Her dancers were young and energetic and thrilled to be back in business. They gave their all to her hit song "Tornado." She loved the feeling of camaraderie it gave her working with her dancers again. They were an enthusiastic mixed-ethnic group with unbridled stamina and a whole lot of energy. They inspired her to do even better. Soon she'd be going out on tour again, and this was a nice way to ease back into the rigors of the road.

During a break she took a call from her daughter, Chyna, who seemed to be having a great time at summer camp. After camp, Chyna was off on a European vacation with her father, and she was very excited about that. Venus missed her cute little girl, but as long as Chyna was having fun, it was okay. There was another text message from Billy on her phone offering to cook his famous chili for her that night.

Hmm . . . Billy was definitely trying to make amends for losing it with Alex. And so he should.

Okay, she'd go along with it. Why not? Billy was obviously here to stay. For now.

~ ~ ~

"Pete," Maggie said to the first assistant director. "There's a girl Billy would like you to place somewhere in the next scene."

"Is she an extra?" Pete asked, chewing on a wad of tobacco.

"She is now," Maggie said. "Our star is asking for a favor, and we don't want to turn him down, do we? After all, he just had the crap beaten out of him."

"Does Alex know about this?" Pete inquired, still chewing.

"Alex trusts *you* when it comes to extras," Maggie said. "You'll know exactly where to place her."

"Okay, but what if he asks me?"

"Why would he do that? She's a slip of a girl, he won't even notice her."

"Are we talking about the same guy? Alex notices it when the camera operator drops a fart!"

"You can swing it, Pete. Have her walking past a car or something."

"Whatever you want, Maggie."

"You're a doll, Pete."

Maggie was very popular on the set. She was the buffer between Alex and his crew. Alex Woods was known for his uncontrollable temper and furious outbursts, and Maggie was the only one who could always be relied on to calm him down.

She hurried back to Billy's trailer and told him the good news.

"How about giving her a line?" Billy suggested.

"Now you're asking the impossible," Maggie said. "I got her into the scene, be satisfied."

"She wants a line," Billy said.

"I don't think I can manage that."

"You can manage anything, Mags."

"No I can't, Billy, I wish I could."

"All right, get her in the scene and see how it goes."

"Where is she?"

"Outside with Kev smoking a cigarette."

"Don't allow them to smoke in your trailer, huh?"

"That's right."

"Who is this girl, anyway?" Maggie asked.

"A friend of a friend from back home," Billy said vaguely. "I'm trying to do a favor."

"Sure," Maggie said, not believing him for a moment. "Are you going to lunch now?"

"Gonna eat in the trailer an' nurse my bruises. Gotta do a second interview with Florence Harbinger for *Manhattan Style*."

"Do *not* talk about the fight between you and Alex," Maggie warned. "Not even off the record."

"You think she's heard about it?"

"Everybody's heard, and according to my spies, it'll be all over *ET* tonight."

"How do people find out these things?"

"A waiter. A parking valet. A paid snitch."

"Great!"

"Okay," Maggie said. "I'll take your girl over to the wardrobe department and—"

"She's not my girl," Billy interrupted, irritated that Maggie would think she was. "Her name's Ali, and she's not my girl."

"Merely a term of speech."

"She's a friend of a friend."

"I know. You told me," Maggie said patiently, used to dealing with actors and their requests, especially when it came to getting random girls walk-ons. "Have a pleasant lunch, and watch what you say—*especially* about Alex."

Maggie left, and Billy sat on his couch texting Venus while preparing himself for the onslaught of Florence.

Five minutes later the journalist swept into his trailer smelling of lavender and booze, a most disturbing combination. "Billy," she gushed. "Such a pleasure to see you again." An obvious lowering of the voice. "Tell me," she almost whispered, as if they were about to share an important secret. "How's everything with you and Venus? Still going strong?"

"I saw you a few days ago, Florence," he said, flashing the charming smile, the one he pulled out whenever it suited him. "Nothing's changed since then. We're very happy together. It all works."

"Really? Even the age difference?"

"We never notice it—only other people do."

"Well," Florence said, disappointed she wasn't scoring a scoop, "if anything *does* change, promise me I'll be the first to know."

"With bells on, Flo."

"Now," Florence said, switching on her digital tape recorder, "I understand you've not talked about this much, but when are the two of you planning on getting married?"

"You know what, Florence," he said, choosing his words carefully. "Venus and I both have commitment phobias, so marriage will not be happening any time soon. That a good enough answer?"

"I'll have to get a quote from Venus on that," Florence said, groping in her purse for a lozenge.

"You should."

"Let me see. What *didn't* I ask you last time?"

Oh shit! He was so right. It was *definitely* going to be one of those days.

64

After spending several frantic days in Vegas, Lucky flew back to L.A. feeling a lot calmer as far as Max was concerned. Her daughter was home, safe, and when she thought about it—as Lennie kept on telling her—that's all that really mattered.

"Don't even bother getting into it with her," Lennie warned over the phone. "She knows she crossed the line and she's sorry."

"So that's it?" Lucky said, perplexed. "*She's* sorry and I'm not supposed to mention anything?"

"What's the point?" Lennie counseled. "You're not about to gain anything by fighting with her."

After thinking it over, she was inclined to agree. There was so much else going on that getting into a long, drawn-out battle with her daughter seemed redundant. The timing was all wrong.

The Keys was almost ready to open, and for the next ten days she would be consumed by details, and making sure everything went smoothly. She had meetings set with everyone from her general manager to the head of the gambling casino and all the other heads of various operations—security, catering, entertainment, and many other departments. Each person mattered. Each one of them had to be ready to perform at the top of their game. Lucky had plans for the Keys to outshine every other hotel on the Strip, and when Lucky wanted something, she usually got it.

She was psyching herself up for another major event. Gino's ninety-fifth birthday party would be nothing compared to the grand opening of the Keys.

There were so many details to take care of, not the least making sure that all her guests flying in for the event would be comfortable. An entire floor of the hotel was reserved for family and friends. Bobby and Brigette were returning from New York with a planeload of New York–based celebrities. Gino and Paige would be coming from Palm Springs. Steven's wife, Lina, the ex-supermodel, was putting on a lingerie fashion show to rival anything Victoria's Secret had to offer. Charlie Dollar was bringing a group of L.A. luminaries via private plane. Venus would be making a special one-night appearance.

And then there was Alex Woods, who since the party had taken to calling her on a daily basis to complain about Billy and Ling and anyone else he could think of.

Alex had issues. And she didn't have time to deal with them, especially as he ended every conversation with, "So . . . when are you leaving Lennie?"

He thought it was funny. She thought it was not. Alex needed to get himself a woman he could respect and forge a real relationship with. It was patently obvious that Ling was on her way out.

Back in L.A. Lucky finally sat down with Max, who informed her she was major sorry about missing Gino's party, and how could she make it up to him, and it would never happen again, and she couldn't help getting robbed and carjacked, but at least she'd held on to her car, so that was good, wasn't it?

None of it made any sense to Lucky. But instead of staying mad, she gave her daughter a stern lecture about not using the Internet to meet strangers and left it at that.

Lennie added his ten cents. "Your mom's got a lot going on," he said.

"We both do, so we're forgetting about your little trip, and you'd better make sure it never happens again."

Oh man, she was sure. She was also furious that Cookie had blabbed about her meeting a guy over the Internet. Was nothing sacred?

The next day Lucky prepared to fly back to Vegas.

"I'm thinking of staying until we open," she told Lennie before she left. "It's kind of insane flying back and forth. Gino Junior's having a great time in Palm Springs, and you're here to watch Max."

"Sure," Lennie said. "I'll try to fly in next weekend."

"That'd be perfect."

"Perfect, huh?" he said, giving her a lazy smile.

"Yes, you and me in Vegas. We can relive the first time we met."

"Oh, like the time you fired me, right?"

"Ah, but this time instead of firing you, we make mad passionate love. We christen the penthouse."

"I like it already," he said, still smiling.

"Oh!" Lucky exclaimed. "We're forgetting about Max. This is not the best time to leave her alone."

"I could bring her with?" Lennie suggested.

"Definitely not. Don't worry, I'll think of something."

~ ~ ~

Wow! Max thought, thoroughly relieved after her face-to-face with her mom. *I got off lightly.*

She knew for sure that Lucky would go totally nuts if she ever found out the real story of what had happened to her. There was no way Lucky would allow Internet Freak to get away with it—she'd track him down and punish him big time. Truth was the creep deserved to be punished, but who could find him now? She'd tried to see if his e-mail address was still in use on the house computer, but just as she'd thought, it was gone. Internet Freak had vanished.

It disturbed her that he'd taken her laptop with all her personal stuff on it. He was probably jerking off over her pictures—that's what freaks did, didn't they?

Lucky had arranged for Leonardo's nanny, Greta, to come back from her vacation early so there would be someone other than Philippe to watch Max when Lennie took off. Max didn't mind; staying around the house for a few days was no great hardship, especially after what she'd been through.

Before Lennie left for the weekend, she tentatively approached him while he was working on the script of his upcoming movie.

"Hi, Dad," she said, hovering beside the computer.

"What can I do for you?" he said, distracted.

"I was wondering, uh . . . am I still grounded?" she asked, going for the innocent approach.

"For a couple more days," he answered vaguely, too busy with his script to take much notice.

"So . . . can I like go out to the drugstore and stuff?"

"Sure. But come right home after."

Lennie's so easy, she thought. *I can get away with anything when it comes to my dad.*

Lately, all she could think about was driving back to Big Bear to see Ace. She wanted to pay him the money she'd borrowed. And she wanted to buy him a new watch since it was her fault the one he had got broken. She also had to buy the kid—Jed—a CD player and send it to him.

She'd called Ace a couple of times on his home phone, and both times she'd gotten an answering machine. Since she'd left the number of her new cell phone and he hadn't called back, it was frustrating. Didn't he care to find out if she was okay after their harrowing ordeal?

Then she thought that maybe he was too busy with his girlfriend, Miss Kmart, and she started wondering if the girl was pretty, and if they were having sex.

Hmm . . . he probably had sex with plenty of girls. He was nineteen and too hot for his own good.

One thing she knew for sure: she had to see him again, even if he *did* have a girlfriend.

~ ~ ~

Lennie made it to Vegas for the weekend, and Lucky couldn't have been happier, even though they were surrounded by total chaos as everyone got ready for the grand opening. The residential part of the complex was finished, every detail down to fully stocked luxury state-of-the-art kitchens and closed-circuit TV in every room.

"This is ours," Lucky announced, giving Lennie a tour of the penthouse she'd had built to her specifications. "It's got one bedroom—*our* bedroom, 'cause this apartment is a no-kid zone, a special place where we can spend time alone."

"You're too much!" he exclaimed, checking out the huge terrace and amazing view—the city sprawled out like a mosaic of twinkling lights.

"I know," she responded. "And don't you love it."

"I love *you*."

"Come," she said, taking his hand. "I want to show you the rest of the apartment."

"The bedroom?" he said.

"No," she said laughing. "First, your room."

"My room? What's that?"

"Somewhere you can create while I keep a watch on the hotel," she said, flinging open the door to a wood-paneled den set up with a big-screen TV, a sophisticated computer editing console, a state-of-the-art sound system, and all of his former movies and scripts leatherbound and stacked high.

"You're an amazing woman, Lucky Santangelo," he said, checking everything out. "How'd you find the time to organize all this?"

"Because," she said, smiling, "it's for you, and I always have time for you. . . ."

~ ~ ~

Ever since Max had gotten back, Cookie and Harry were behaving like major assholes. All they wanted to do was lock themselves in Cookie's room and sit around getting stoned. She was away a few days and suddenly both her best friends had turned into major potheads. Drugs didn't tempt her—she'd tried coke once, hated it, and smoking pot made her sleepy and desperate for chocolate.

At the age of twelve her mother had given her a strong lecture about drugs, and it had obviously stuck. "Only morons and losers enjoy getting high," Lucky had informed her. "If you want to go through life in a daze, then start taking drugs, but if you're smart, you'll soon realize it gets you nowhere fast, so don't fall for that peer pressure crap. And don't smoke nicotine either. I've been an on-and-off smoker all my life and I hate it. It's a filthy habit, but I can't seem to quit for any length of time. So do not start and you won't find yourself in that pathetic position."

The thing that Max really admired about Lucky was that she wasn't really like a mother figure. Sure, she could be stern at times, but she was very up on everything going on in the world and totally open about sex and stuff. At fourteen Lucky had handed her a pack of condoms and said, "You won't be needing these for a couple of years, but when you do, make sure you use 'em. You're a smart girl. You'll decide when the time is right."

Max had already decided.

The time was right and her potential victim was Ace.

All she had to do was get him to call her back.

65

Henry Whitfield-Simmons drove back to Pasadena in a simmering state of frustration and anger. After hitting the coyote and running the Volvo off the road, not only had he lost sight of the car with Maria inside, but the front tire of the Volvo was damaged, forcing him to change it himself. Since he was no mechanic, the mountain road was deserted, and there was nobody around to help him, it ended up taking him hours.

By the time he'd managed to make it to Big Bear, it was much later. He drove into town wary of getting caught in a trap. It was quite possible the two of them could have gone to the cops.

No, he'd immediately corrected himself. *Not the two of them. Maria wouldn't do that—her cousin would.*

Her cousin was a son of a bitch. *He* was the one who'd persuaded Maria to leave. He'd obviously forced her to do so, and she'd left because he'd given her no choice. Maria had wanted to stay with him, he was sure of it. They'd just started getting to know each other and things were going well between them.

Damn the cousin. Damn him to hell.

After checking out the parking lot and discovering her car was gone, Henry had driven back to Pasadena in a white-hot rage thinking about Maria all the way.

He'd arrived at the mausoleum late in the afternoon to find that his mother was in the middle of one of her charity tea parties. Dozens of women were wandering around the mansion in their ridiculous hats and expensive outfits. On top of everything else, Penelope decided to humiliate him. "Here comes Henry, my little computer nerd," she'd informed anyone who would listen as he'd attempted to slink upstairs unnoticed. "Did you have a pleasant time, dear? Did you meet any suitable girls?"

Why did she do this to him, when all he'd wanted to do was escape to his room where he could log on to Maria's laptop and find out even more about her.

That was almost two weeks ago, and after checking out Maria's e-mail, he'd discovered that Lucky Santangelo was opening a new hotel in Las Vegas, the Keys.

Naturally Maria would be there. So would Lucky, Billy Melina, even Alex Woods.

Henry checked out the Keys online and discovered that there was a grand opening party planned. Tickets were expensive, but that was no problem.

Ah . . . this would be his opportunity to reconnect with Maria. And this time he'd be better prepared to take her away forever.

Nobody was coming between him and Maria again. The two of them were destined to be together.

And that was exactly the way it should be.

66

Anthony was not happy. Over the last week he'd fielded three calls from Detective Franklin in Vegas.

He called up Renee to complain.

"There's nothing I can do," Renee said, stoic as usual. She was experiencing her own problems regarding Detective Franklin. The woman was like a bulldog hanging on to a bone with her incessant questions. And Susie was on her case too.

"What *did* happen to Tasmin?" Susie kept on asking. "And why can't I say she left with Anthony?"

"Because you can't. If you do, it will make *me* out to be a liar."

"So where *is* Tasmin?"

"Nobody knows."

This answer did not satisfy Susie, who every so often continued to question her.

"Whaddya mean, nothin'?" Anthony demanded over the phone. "Why's she still callin' me? Askin' the same dumb questions."

"Tasmin's ex-husband is kicking up a big stink about her being missing, apparently he has connections in the police department," Renee explained. "I've been questioned three times, the detective has talked to Susie twice, and half the hotel staff have been interrogated."

"Pay the bitch off," Anthony growled. "Offer her fifty thousand in cash. She'll go for it."

"No, she won't."

"Give it a try, Renee. Money talks."

"It'll look wrong if I even attempt to pay her off. She'll take it as a sign we have something to hide," Renee said, impatient to get him off the phone.

"You think I give a shit?" Anthony responded. "Get the cunt off my fuckin' case, that's all I care about."

Renee hung up the phone. She'd had it with Anthony Bonar. After Tasmin's brutal murder she was done.

There had to be a way to get him out of their life once and for all.

And then it occurred to her. There was.

~ ~ ~

Anthony had been on his plane on and off for the past ten days, flying back and forth between New York, Miami, and Mexico City, with a crucial twenty-four-hour business trip to Colombia thrown in. Anthony always felt like a peasant whenever he visited the ruling drug lords in Colombia. Those men lived like kings in their huge mansions three times the size of his, with an army of guards on call and dozens of servants. But he couldn't complain—he was not exactly suffering.

In New York he'd received a report that Carlita was not cheating on him. He was so pleased that he'd invested another two hundred thousand in her business. Then he'd spent a pleasant couple of days with his elegant Italian mistress visiting all his favorite New York restaurants and clubs. Carlita was a class act; he was definitely keeping her around.

Back in Miami, Emmanuelle was as demanding as ever. Her latest request was that she wanted him to take her on a vacation. "Please, honey," she'd begged. "You never take me anywhere."

"Where you wanna go?" he'd asked.

"Europe," she'd replied, all excited at the prospect. "Paris, London, and Rome."

One thing about Emmanuelle, she always went for the best.

"Tell you what," he'd said. "You'll come with me to Vegas. There's a big hotel opening, it's gonna be quite a scene."

"But sugar pie—"

"Vegas or nothin'," he'd said flatly. "Your choice."

Shortly after he'd invited Emmanuelle, Francesca informed him that she expected to go with him to Vegas.

"You can't fly," he'd said, determined to put his grandmother off. "The doc told you no traveling with your heart condition, ya gotta take it easy."

"My heart is strong enough to witness the downfall of the Santangelo family," Francesca had replied. "I'm coming with you to Vegas."

Stubborn old woman. What could he do? He'd finally decided to take Francesca *and* Emmanuelle. Francesca was a woman of the world, she'd understand that a man had to have a mistress as well as a wife—it was the traditional Italian way. Although he suspected Francesca would have preferred Carlita to Emmanuelle.

Problems, always problems. But first he had to spend a couple of days in Mexico City attending to business.

~ ~ ~

After sleeping with the drug enforcement agent, Irma suffered a panic attack. She couldn't help wondering if Oliver Stanton had known who she was, and by sleeping with her was he attempting to garner information about her husband?

The situation forced her to rethink her plans. She sat at home and worried about what she'd done. And to make things worse, Luis was still refusing to come into the house, which she couldn't understand.

She finally instructed Marta to tell Luis to meet her in the bedroom to check out her houseplants.

"I keep on asking him," she informed Marta. "It seems he doesn't understand me. And my orchids need special attention."

Marta nodded, her face revealing nothing. "*Sí, señora*," she said, wondering if Señora Bonar was aware that several members of the staff suspected that she and Luis might be having sex. If they were, it wasn't right. Marta knew Luis's family; she also knew his pregnant wife. But Marta was not one to gossip, and she couldn't say exactly what was going on behind closed doors, although Señora Bonar was giving her an awful lot of time off whenever Luis entered the house.

Ten minutes later the old gardener knocked on Irma's bedroom door.

When she saw who it was, she was angry. Luis not coming when she'd specifically requested him was most disrespectful.

Gritting her teeth, she showed the old gardener the bedroom plants and her precious orchids.

The grizzled old man spoke very little English. "*Orquidea* no need much water," he informed her.

"Thank you," she said, tight-lipped.

"*Gracias, señora. Orquídea buenas.*"

Later she went down to the kitchen, cornered Marta, and asked her why Luis hadn't come to tend to her plants when she'd specifically requested his presence. She realized she was treading on dangerous territory, but she was determined to find out anyway.

"Luis go home early," Marta explained, busying herself at the sink.

"Why was that?"

"His wife, she expect baby soon," Marta said, wiping her hands on her apron.

"His *wife*?" Irma said, barely able to conceal her surprise. "I wasn't aware that Luis was married."

"*Sí, señora*."

Now she was really upset. Luis was married with a pregnant wife and he hadn't told her. This was unbelievable.

And yet . . . she still yearned for his touch. She still had a burning desire to feel his naked body up against hers.

Several days later Anthony arrived home, insisting on the usual round of parties at the house. Irma endured more evenings of too much rich food, endless karaoke, and adoring sycophants.

After a few days he got bored as usual, and informed her he was leaving for Las Vegas on yet another business trip. She wasn't sorry to see him go.

~ ~ ~

A few days before Anthony was due to leave for the opening of the Keys, one of the guards from his house appeared at his office and badgered his assistant, telling her that he had to see Señor Bonar regarding a matter of great urgency.

His assistant asked what it was in reference to. The guard replied that it was of utmost importance that he speak to Señor Bonar personally.

"Send him in," Anthony said, puffing on a large cigar.

The man entered his office and planted himself in front of his desk. Anthony did not invite him to sit.

"Whaddya want?" he snapped. "Make it quick."

"I am Cesar," the guard said. "I have worked for you two years, Señor Bonar. I come here to tell you something of a delicate nature."

"Spit it out," Anthony growled, leaning back in his leather chair.

"My circumstances are such that I need to buy a new car," Cesar said, his greedy eyes darting around the office.

Was this son of a bitch *blackmailing* him? Information in return for a car. Anthony couldn't believe the stones on this guy. It was outrageous.

"What information you got that gets you a fuckin' car?" he snarled.

"Private information, Señor Bonar," Cesar said, standing up ramrod straight. "Information you would not want to go any further."

"I wouldn't, huh?" Anthony said, expelling a stream of acrid smoke in Cesar's direction.

"No, *señor.*"

"Okay, we'll do it this way. You tell me what's on your mind, an' if it's worth anything I'll give you cash. An' if it's bullshit, you get nothin'. That fair enough for you?"

"*Sí, señor.*"

"Okay, let's hear what you got."

Cesar glanced toward the door. "It is sensitive, Señor Bonar."

"Speak!"

"I regretfully tell you, *señor,* that a person who should be trustworthy is not," Cesar said, clearing his throat. "This man is taking advantage of your wife."

"What the fuck you sayin'?" Anthony said, sitting bolt upright.

"There is a man working on your estate, *señor,* who is doing bad things with your wife."

"Whaddya mean, bad things?" Anthony said, a muscle twitching beneath his left eye. "Is he raping her? Takin' money from her? What the fuck d'you mean?"

"This man enters your house when you are not there. He stays many hours. He spends time in your bedroom with the *señora.*"

"Who is this person?" Anthony demanded, his eyes cold as steel.

"One of your gardeners, *señor.*" Cesar paused, experiencing a moment of deep satisfaction before continuing. "His name is Luis."

"You sure about this?" Anthony said, staring him down.

"*Sí, señor.*"

"Absolutely fuckin' *sure?*"

"*Sí, señor,*" Cesar said, blinking rapidly several times.

Anthony unlocked his desk drawer, took out a wad of cash, and threw it at Cesar. "Take this and get the fuck outta my office. An' if you open your mouth to anyone 'bout this—anyone at all—I cut out your fuckin' tongue with a buzz saw. Get it?"

"*Sí, señor.*" Cesar said, backing out of the office.

The moment he left, Anthony began pacing. This couldn't be true, could it? This couldn't be possible that Irma, his *wife,* and a gardener on his estate were having sex. In *his* house. On *his* bed.

Some other man fucking his wife.

It was unthinkable.

And yet . . . this stupid guard had come to him with the information, and why would the man lie? Why would he put himself in jeopardy?

Anthony thought back to Acapulco and the change in Irma. She was insolent, withdrawn, and looks-wise she was glowing.

Yes! It was true! The bitch was getting fucked! And not by him.

After simmering for a while, Anthony summoned The Grill into his office.

"This is what I want you t'do," he said, issuing instructions. "An' make sure ya take care of it immediately."

~ ~ ~

Several hours after Anthony left the house, he called Irma from his office and informed her he was sending his car for her, and that she was to meet him in the city for lunch.

Lunch? In the city? She'd thought he was on his way to Vegas.

"I'm not sure . . ." she began.

"There's somebody I want you to meet," he said.

"Who?"

"A business acquaintance. The car'll be there shortly."

Irma was ready when the car arrived. She was also apprehensive that somehow or other Anthony might have found out about Oliver. Over the past two weeks she'd received several calls from her dinner date, none of which she'd returned.

What if Oliver called while she was with Anthony? What if she bumped into him in the city?

This was not an ideal situation. Her nerves were on edge, and for now her plans were on hold.

~ ~ ~

Sitting behind his ornate desk, Anthony put down his phone and stared off into space. Who would have thought that his wife would betray him? Carlita? Yes. Irma? No.

Soon he would know for sure. And once he did, Irma would be punished in a way that would hurt her more than she could possibly imagine.

Nobody cheated on Anthony Bonar and got away with it. Nobody.

67

Max came up with what she considered to be a brilliant idea. Once again she ran it by Lennie, who was so into his upcoming movie he would've said yes to anything.

"Uh . . . there's this boy," she informed him. "And when I got carjacked he kind of helped me. So . . ." She hesitated for a moment before continuing. "I was, uh, thinking I could return the favor by inviting him to the Keys opening."

"What did Lucky say?" Lennie asked, barely looking up from his computer.

"She said yes."

"Okay. Go ahead, invite him."

Later she phoned Lucky in Vegas and had the same conversation. Lucky was so into the opening of her hotel she would've said yes to anything. Well—almost anything.

"What did Lennie say?" Lucky asked.

"He said yes," Max replied, cheerfully lying.

"Then I don't see why not."

How cool was this? She'd wrangled an invite for Ace to attend the opening, and she was determined he'd accept. They'd been speaking on the phone regularly since he'd finally called her back. She'd been delighted to hear from him, ridiculously so. And was it her imagination, or did he sound equally pleased to hear from her?

Yes, he did. She was sure of it.

Since they'd reconnected they'd been talking every day. He never mentioned his girlfriend. She never mentioned her nonexistent boyfriend. They talked about everything from their ordeal to music to movies to books. In fact, they talked nonstop.

She found out he was working as a ski instructor and saving up to one day open his own ski shop.

"No college?" she'd asked.

"The most successful people in America never went to college," he'd informed her. "And one of these days I'm gonna have a chain of ski shops in every resort in America."

He was ambitious, and so interesting and different from all the rich kids she'd grown up with. But best of all, he was so *hot!* And she couldn't stop thinking about him.

~ ~ ~

Things seemed comparatively calm on the Venus/Billy front. She was busy with her various projects, plus rehearsing for Vegas. And he was busy finishing up on Alex's movie.

They both decided that for the Vegas trip they would drive up on Venus's tour bus as opposed to flying. Billy's movie wrapped the day before they were due to leave, and Venus opted out of attending the wrap party. "You'll be bonding with the crew, and saying your good-byes," she pointed out. "It's better I don't come."

"If you're sure," Billy said. "'Cause you know I'd love to have you there."

"No, you go. If you feel like it, you can drop by my house later."

"Sounds like an invite I can't refuse."

"I appreciate a man who can't refuse me," she purred.

Ever since the fight with Alex, Billy had been on his best behavior.

Venus honestly felt they were right back on track. It was a satisfying feeling.

~ ~ ~

Billy and Kev went together to the wrap party on sound stage 3. The place was jammed with crew members and their significant others, most of whom were desperate to get their picture taken with Billy. He obliged, until after about twenty minutes he was startled to see Miss Broken Taillight—alias Ali—flittering around in her cutoff denims and skimpy tank top, long sexy legs tanned and appealing.

"What's *she* doin' here?" he muttered to Kev, who looked a bit sheepish and mumbled something about inviting her. "Why'd you do that?" Billy asked.

" 'Cause she's a sweet kid," Kev said, heading for the bar.

"Yeah, and she gives a sweet blow job, right?" Billy remarked, following him.

"Nothing wrong with that," Kev said, requesting a beer. "*You* didn't seem to object."

"I don't wanna see her around," Billy lectured. "If Venus had come with me tonight, it would've been awkward."

"Why?" Kev said, handing Billy a bottle of imported beer. "She's not gonna run up to Venus and say, 'Oh, I screwed your boyfriend,' is she?"

"I don't know, *you* tell me," Billy said pointedly.

"Did you hear that Alex gave her a line?"

"How'd *that* happen?" Billy said, swigging beer.

"Guess Maggie worked her magic."

"At least it gets her off my case," Billy grumbled, still not happy.

"There's somethin' I've been meaning to tell you," Kev began, looking embarrassed.

"What now?" Billy sighed.

"I'm kinda into her," Kev admitted. "Like I'm thinking of taking her to the party in Vegas."

"You fuckin' nuts?" Billy said, frowning.

"No, I kinda *promised* I'd take her."

"Jeez, Kev!"

"She lives in a rat hole in Hollywood with two gay guys and another girl. I feel sorry for her. I was over there the other night—the place is a pit."

"What's *that* got t'do with anything?"

"Have a little heart. She's trying hard to make it, workin' any job she can. It's that same old story—she comes from a broken home, took the bus to L.A. to get away from her stepdad, and ended up livin' on the street until she hooked up with friends."

"So now you're the knight with a permanent hard-on who's gonna save her. Right?"

"Maybe."

"Of all the girls in L.A. you had to pick this one," Billy said, shaking his head. "What's wrong with you?"

"Anyway," Kev said, "thought I should give you a heads-up."

"That's big of you, Kev."

"Oh yeah, an' I made her swear she'll never mention anything to Venus about gettin' it on with you."

"She'd better not, 'cause if she does, your ass is freakin' fired."

"No worries," Kev said confidently.

~ ~ ~

"I know I shouldn't be the one saying this, but my hotel is *amazing*," Lucky raved to Venus over the phone. "Totally amazing and perfect and great. Better than I could possibly have imagined. Gino will *love* it."

"I'm happy for you," Venus said. "Can't wait to get there and check it out for myself."

"We have a luxurious penthouse suite ready for you and Billy with its own pool and an incredible view of the Strip. Massage therapists are on alert, and anything else you want. Put in your requests now."

"I'll ask Billy. Maybe a pool table."

"Already in your suite."

"A Jacuzzi."

"Both inside and out."

"How about a stripper pole?"

"Done!"

"I'm joking."

They both laughed.

"I'm so pleased you're coming up the night before, so is Lennie," Lucky said. "We'll have a great dinner, just the four of us. I've been testing all the restaurants. The food is sensational, world-class chefs everywhere I turn."

"Billy and I are driving up, which means I'm not sure what time we'll get there."

"Driving, huh?"

"We're using my tour bus—thought it might be fun."

"Hmm . . . five or six hours on a bus. Doesn't sound like fun to me. Are you sure I can't send a plane for you?"

"No thanks. I can assure you—five or six hours on my bus with Billy is gonna *rock!*"

"Okay, so travel safely, I'll be thinking of you."

Lucky put down the phone and surveyed her kingdom from the window of her penthouse. It was true. Everything about the Keys was looking awesome and the hotel section was already running like a smoothly oiled machine. Her general manager was a real pro; so were the dozen or so undermanagers.

Since she'd planned and built two hotels before, she was well aware of what mistakes to avoid. Organization was the name of the game, especially for opening night, and especially with planeloads of celebrities flying in, and a ton of press waiting to cover the event.

It was going to be *the* most special and spectacular night Vegas had ever seen.

She couldn't wait.

68

During the car ride to Anthony's office Irma's mind was darting in many different directions. What did he want with her? Was it possible that he'd found out about Oliver?

One never knew with Anthony. He'd become so adept at completely ignoring her existence that being summoned to his office was quite alarming. When had Anthony ever been interested in her opinion of his business acquaintances?

He greeted her with an affectionate hug.

"Where are we going for lunch?" she asked. "And who is it that you want me to meet?"

"That was just my way of gettin' you here," he said. "Is it a crime to wanna have lunch with my wife for a change?"

"Of course not," she stammered, completely thrown.

He took her to the most expensive restaurant in the city for lunch, and all through the meal he was overly attentive toward her.

Something was definitely going on. She felt uncomfortable and horribly guilty about her one night with Oliver Stanton.

"Is everything all right?" she asked when they were almost finished.

"Why wouldn't it be?" he countered, tapping his fingers on the table.

"I thought you were leaving for Las Vegas, and then you call me for lunch."

"You had something else to do?" he questioned, staring her down.

"Not at all," she answered, lowering her eyes.

"I've bin thinkin' that I should spend more time with you."

"Do you mean traveling?" she said hesitantly.

"Yeah, why not? We got the place in Miami, the apartment in New York—there's no reason you can't come with me sometimes."

"I thought you wanted me to stay in the house here," she said, picking at her dessert.

"It might not be such a bad idea for you to spend more time with the kids. Eduardo's a surly little bastard, an' Carolina's growin' up fast. Could be she needs a mother around."

Was there a light at the end of the tunnel? Had she picked the wrong time to leave him? Could it be that Anthony was actually softening?

After they left the restaurant, he led her down the street to a jewelry store, greeted the owner, whom he knew, and instructed her to pick out a gift for herself. "Choose anythin' you want," he said, lighting up a cigar. "Anythin' you think you deserve."

"It's not my birthday, Anthony," she murmured.

"I know that, but I feel like bein' generous. I can spoil my own wife, can't I?"

Was he sick? Did he have a brain tumor?

She stood in front of trays of lavish jewelry, finally picking out a modest gold bracelet.

"Nah," Anthony said, vigorously shaking his head. "You wanna get somethin' with diamonds. You're my wife—you gotta have the best."

The jeweler produced another tray, this time filled with diamond jewelry.

"Did I mention I'm thinkin' of taking you to Vegas?" Anthony said.

"You are?" she said, startled.

"Yeah, there's a big hotel opening. You might get a kick outta bein' there. It ain't healthy you bein' by yourself all the time. Go ahead, choose somethin' flashy, 'cause I wanna show you off." He picked up a pair of flawless yellow diamond drop earrings. "How 'bout these?" he suggested.

"They're *very* expensive," she demurred.

"My wife deserves expensive," he said expansively. "Try 'em on."

She did so. They were quite incredible.

"You like 'em, they're yours," he said.

Anthony was like a changed man. Irma was perplexed, but at the same time secretly pleased because this was the man she'd always hoped he was. Attentive, generous, kind.

She settled on the earrings. The jeweler had them gift wrapped, then Anthony escorted her to the car and instructed the driver to take her home.

"I'm leavin' for Vegas now," he said. "If I think you'll like it, I'll send for you. Okay, sugar?"

Sugar? He was calling her sugar? Wasn't that a term of endearment strictly reserved for his mistresses? She was confused.

"Take good care of this little lady," Anthony said, speaking to his driver. "She's precious cargo. She's my wife."

~ ~ ~

Once he'd put Irma in the car, Anthony returned to his office. The Grill was waiting for him.

"You do it?" Anthony asked, his expression stony.

"All taken care of, boss."

"Give it twenty-four hours, then get it outta there."

"Yes, boss."

~ ~ ~

Irma arrived back at the house clutching her gift-wrapped earrings, which she knew had cost over a hundred thousand dollars. She felt quite light-headed.

When they were first married, Anthony had bought her a few pieces of jewelry, but over the past several years he'd not given her so much as a birthday present. Was he trying to make up for it now?

She went up to her room, immediately heading over to the window to see what Luis was doing. He was present; the old gardener was not.

Maybe she should see him one more time. And after that she could be the faithful wife, because if Anthony was changing, she could do the same and allow him one more chance.

But still . . . Luis was a big temptation, and she didn't like that he'd rejected her. She craved one more opportunity to be in his arms. Just one more time. . . .

She hurried downstairs and out to the garden. "Luis," she said, walking right up to him, "come with me."

He shook his head, wary eyes darting this way and that.

"Now!" she said firmly. "I'm your boss, come with me."

He didn't understand her words, but he certainly understood her tone of voice. Putting down his rake, he followed her into the house and up the staircase to her bedroom.

She locked the door and turned to face him. "Luis," she said, "what *is* going on with you?"

" 'Scuse, *señora*?" he muttered, wishing he was somewhere else.

"Do not call me *señora*," she said sharply. "My name is Irma, you know that."

"*Sí* . . . Irma."

"Why didn't you tell me you were married and your wife is pregnant?"

He shrugged. He understood two words—*pregnant* and *wife*. The American woman knew, but still she'd invited him into her bedroom, so she must not care. The sex with her was so different from the sex with his wife, and Cesar had not mentioned a word lately, so perhaps it was safe to make love to her one last time. It was obviously what she wanted, and even though she was pretending to be angry, her eyes were filled with anticipation and her cheeks were flushed.

He could not resist. If they did it one more time, how would Cesar ever find out? Besides, Cesar was not on duty today, and the *señora* was looking extremely beautiful, unlike his wife who was so big with child that she refused to allow him anywhere near her.

He reached forward and placed his hand on her breast. She did not object. Immediately he felt himself becoming hard.

Next he began undoing the buttons on her blouse, before unhooking the clip at the front of her bra, exposing her small but perfect breasts with the extended nipples.

"Oh, Luis," she sighed, throwing her head back as his fingers lightly brushed the tips of her nipples, before bringing his lips down to slowly suck on them.

"Luis," she sighed again.

Sweeping her up in his arms, he carried her to the bed and proceeded to make tender love to her, promising himself that it would be the last time.

And while she lay back on the bed enjoying his steady kisses and soft caresses, Irma promised herself that this would be the very last time.

69

"I have to make a trip, Mother," Henry said to Penelope, not interested in explaining himself, but realizing that at the present time he had no choice. "I might be gone for quite some time, and I will be needing a substantial amount of money."

"I gave you two hundred dollars last week," Penelope said, arching an imperious eyebrow. "Why would you need more?"

"I know, Mother, but that is not enough."

"Enough for what, Henry?" Penelope said, brushing an imaginary speck off her pristine linen skirt. "We are not a family who fritters money away."

"One day I'll inherit everything," Henry pointed out. "Therefore I do not understand why I cannot have some of it now?"

"Because you are not a responsible person," Penelope snapped. "No, you are not responsible at all."

"Responsible for what, Mother?" he asked, controlling the rage he felt toward this woman who would not give him what was rightfully his—or at least it would be when she was dead.

Dead. The word had a satisfying ring to it. . . .

"You are not responsible for anything, Henry," Penelope said, sniffing her disapproval. "Look at you—you've made nothing of yourself. You sit in your room in front of your computer all day long. It pains me that you have never shown any interest in joining your father's business. We're both on the board of directors and you've never so much as bothered to attend one meeting."

"Father's business doesn't interest me," he muttered.

"What *does* interest you, Henry? I would be intrigued to know."

"Acting, Mother. I wanted to be an actor, but neither you nor Father encouraged me to follow my dream."

"Your dream!" Penelope scoffed. "How ridiculous! Actors have to be handsome with a personality. Look in the mirror, Henry—with your face you had no chance of succeeding, none at all. *That's* the reason we discouraged you."

"I *am* talented, Mother," he said, knowing full well it was impossible to convince her.

"At what, Henry? Sitting alone in your room? You've never brought a girl home, you are not involved in any social or charity activities." She paused, giving him a penetrating stare. "Are you gay, Henry?"

He found the word *gay* coming out of his mother's pursed lips quite disturbing.

"No, Mother," he answered, swallowing his rage at the way she spoke to him. "I am not gay. And you will be pleased to know that recently I met a girl I like."

"Well, that's news," Penelope said, her long thin face expressing surprise. "Do I know her? Is she from a good family?"

"She's from an . . . interesting family."

"Affluent?"

"Yes, Mother."

"Of our stature and social standing?"

"Yes, Mother. Therefore I wish to treat her in a proper fashion." He paused for a long moment, allowing her to digest the information. "She has an event coming up I need to attend."

"What kind of event?"

"She's an architect, she's designed an apartment building in Nevada, and I wish to go there for the opening. I cannot make the trip unless I have money, otherwise her father will conclude that I am not a suitable match for her."

"How much money are you requesting, Henry?"

"Fifty thousand dollars."

"Surely you jest?" Penelope said, unamused.

"I do not jest, Mother. One day it will all be mine as I keep on reminding you."

"Unless I decide to change my will," Penelope said.

Henry experienced a cold chill. Why would his mother say such a thing? Why would she even think it?

"It is imperative I impress this girl," he said, choking back a response to her comment.

"Impress her?"

"I'm considering buying her an engagement ring."

"Nonsense!"

"Excuse me?"

"An engagement is out of the question until I have met this girl and her family. You must bring them here before I even think about granting my approval."

"Very well, Mother," he said, his voice constricted. "You'll arrange for the money?"

"No, Henry, I'll arrange for *five* thousand dollars, which is a great deal of money. One stipulation: you cannot buy this girl a ring, not until I have met and approved of her. Only then will we discuss the purchase of a ring."

"Yes, Mother," he said, thinking that five thousand was a paltry amount, and he needed more to look after Maria, to take her away where nobody could find them. What he needed was his entire inheritance.

He stared at his mother, loathing her. Penelope Whitfield-Simmons was a tightfisted, mean woman, and he hated her with a deep and lasting passion. She'd never shown him any motherly love, never cared about him like a mother should. All she'd ever done was deride him in front of her friends and told him how useless and untalented and ugly he was.

It occurred to him that if she wasn't around, everything would be his and his days of begging would be over.

Now she was talking about changing her will, and that wasn't right.

He had to do something about it. And he had to do something about it fast.

Dead . . . The word had an interesting ring to it.

70

Apart from Philippe, who spent most of his days cleaning silver and taking care of the house, and Greta, Leonardo's nanny, Max had the Bel-Air house to herself. Greta, who'd been summoned back from her vacation to keep an eye on Max, was a certified TV addict who spent her days glued to daytime soaps and her nights glued to prime time. Max considered neither of them a problem, and since she figured she wasn't grounded anymore, she acted accordingly. It was great when both her parents were too busy to notice what she was up to. She wished it was always this way.

After talking her dad into allowing her to invite Ace, then getting Lucky to agree, she'd been told by Lennie that there were rooms booked for her and her friends at the Keys. "Your mom says you and Cookie can share a room, while Harry can bunk in with your new friend."

"His name's Ace, Dad," she'd said, thinking what a bonus! She hadn't been sure if Lucky would even want her at the opening considering her absence from Gino's party. But not only was she invited, she could bring friends!

Ace was driving to L.A. in his brother's truck, staying the night in Bel-Air, and the next day they'd head for Vegas.

Max warned Cookie and Harry that they had to be on their best behavior when they met him. "You can't be like lying around totally stoned," she said. "I have no clue if he's into that, and since I'm not, don't even mention getting high."

"What's the plan for later?" Cookie asked as they sat beside the pool.

"I was thinking dinner first," Max said, "then maybe a club."

"My I.D. is like *so* fake," Cookie complained, rubbing suntan lotion on her stomach. "Besides, all the bouncers know me now, I can't get in anywhere."

"I know a club we can hit," Harry said, sheltering his skinny white body under an umbrella. "Hundred bucks at the door an' no problem—doesn't matter how old we are."

"Perfect," Max said, thinking she couldn't wait to show off L.A. to Ace. He'd told her he'd never been there before, which was kind of crazy.

"What's he like?" Cookie wanted to know.

"A major babe," Max said, thinking she couldn't wait for her friends to meet him.

"As cute as Donny?" Cookie asked.

"Donny sucks," Max said, dismissing her ex. "I'm so over that loser."

"About time," Cookie said, dangling her feet in the pool.

They decided on an Italian restaurant for dinner, then the underground club Harry knew about.

"Harry," Max ordered. "You pick up the check at both places 'cause I'm not sure if Ace has much money. I'll pay you back our share. And whatever you do, don't let him split it with you. Okay?"

"How do I know you'll pay me back?" Harry said, being difficult.

"Oh, pul—*eaze*!"

"She's in love," Cookie giggled. "Our girl's got a major crush."

"No way," Max said, blushing.

"Yeah, way," Cookie teased. "What you gonna wear?"

"Haven't thought about it."

"Liar!"

"I am *so* not!"

"Are you doin' the deed?" Harry asked. "I mean, you'll be all alone in your house."

"Not alone. Greta's here, and Philippe."

"Your house is so big you can get away with anything," Cookie said.

"Yeah," Harry agreed.

"Is Mister New Dude gonna stay in your room tonight?" Cookie asked.

"His name is Ace, and he's got a girlfriend."

"Sure, but he's leaving her and driving to L.A. to see *you*," Cookie pointed out.

"He knows I'm only sixteen. I had to tell him."

"I don't get it," Cookie said. "Is sixteen considered underage?"

"Dunno," Max said, shrugging. "But it doesn't matter."

"He might not wanna do it if he thinks you're underage," Harry said, throwing in his opinion.

"I think fifteen's underage," Cookie said. "Sixteen's a go."

"You're wrong," Harry said. "The age of sexual consent is eighteen in California."

"Whatever," Max said, pretending she hadn't really thought about it, although the truth was that's *all* she could think about.

To have sex with Ace or not to have sex with Ace—that was the question.

They decided to drive up to Vegas in Harry's new SUV early the next morning. It had a souped-up engine and he was desperate to take it on a long drive.

"I guess it'll be okay with Ace," Max said.

"Why are you so bothered by what *he* thinks?" Harry asked. "It's totally unlike you to care. *You* should be telling *him* what we're gonna do."

"You don't understand," Max said. "He's not the kind of guy I tell what to do."

"What kind of guy *is* he?" Cookie questioned, adjusting her Dolce & Gabanna sunglasses.

"Cool," Max replied with a dreamy smile. "Amazingly cool."

71

Waiting for Lennie to join her in Vegas, Lucky could hardly believe that in less than twenty-four hours she would be opening her third hotel in the shimmering city. The Keys was a more exciting project than any of the others. It was bigger and better and more extravagant—a true oasis of calm and beauty in a city known for its sometimes flashy showmanship. The Keys was not another theme hotel pretending to be Venice or Paris or Rome. It was simply there, making a statement. White and stylish—modern architecture combined with old-fashioned warmth and luxury. Even the casino was different, lighter and more welcoming, with a friendly lineup of pit bosses, dealers, croupiers, and attractive casino hosts of both sexes. The grounds were lush and lovely, filled with exotic plants and flowers. There were three swimming pools—one for adults, one for children, and one for the in-betweens. All of them surrounded by swaying palm trees. The children's pool backed up against a glass-enclosed aquarium where exotic fish proliferated. The adults' pool featured a fully stocked bar. And the in-between pool supplied underwater iPods and a choice of sounds.

Lucky realized she could happily move into her penthouse permanently. She didn't miss L.A. at all, and if it wasn't for Max, Gino Junior, and Leonardo, she would take up residence in a flash. But having kids tied a person down, and until they all went off to college, she and Lennie were stuck in one place. Well, not really stuck—soon their Malibu house would be finished and they could move out of stuffy Bel-Air and back to the beach, which they both loved. But she also loved Vegas. There was something about the place—it reminded her of Gino and the early days. Oh God! So many memories. Building the Magiriano and the problems involved—graft, union walkouts, and threats—but she'd built one hell of a hotel. And Marco—oh Marco, how she'd loved him, and when he'd been shot and killed, Vegas had lost its thrill. But now she was back and the Keys was all hers. And now she had Lennie, her husband, her rock. Yes, Vegas was still an exciting city with so much going on.

Venus called to announce that they'd just arrived and that they were totally impressed with everything.

"Our suite is beyond gorgeous," she enthused. "How clever are *you*?"

"Look who's calling *me* clever," Lucky responded, looking forward to showing off her new hotel to her best friend. "Was the drive up fun?"

"Oh yes," Venus said, sounding like she really meant it. "We spent most of it in my bed! Gives a whole new meaning to the mile-high club. Guess we just started the mile-long club!"

"You're incorrigible," Lucky said, laughing.

"Hey, when you've got a young lover, you gotta keep him occupied."

"Seems you do."

"Oh, news flash," Venus announced. "Alex and Billy are on speaking terms, there'll be no more fights."

"That's a relief. I hate it when two grown men beat the shit out of each other."

"Me too. It's the last thing any of us need."

"Okay, so settle in," Lucky said. "Then I thought we'd have drinks at our place around eight. I'll send someone to escort you."

"Are we on the same floor as you?"

"No. You're in one of the hotel penthouses, we're in the apartments."

"Drinks at eight sounds perfect, and after dinner Billy wants to gamble."

"Not at my hotel. I'd feel bad if he lost. Besides, the casino doesn't officially open until tomorrow night."

"Okay, then where?"

"How about dinner here, then we'll go over to the Cavendish. Nothing like checking out the competition."

"No rivalry amongst hotel owners?"

"Not as far as I'm concerned."

Later Lennie arrived, they took a shower, made love, then lay on the bed staring up at the skylight she'd designed above the bed with blackout blinds that could be closed at the press of a button. The blinds were open, revealing a startling expanse of sky and stars. It was beautiful and romantic.

"Man," Lennie observed. "I gotta admit, when you do something . . ."

"You'd better stop telling me that," Lucky said, smiling. "It'll go to my head, and I'll become impossible."

"Not you, sweetheart. When's Gino arriving?"

"Everybody's coming in the morning."

"Excited?"

"Of course I am."

"What time's the party tomorrow?"

"The reception starts at six, then everyone heads to the theater for Lina's event, followed by Venus's show. After that it's outside for the fireworks display. Did I tell you I was able to get these silver fantasy fireworks from Italy? They are *so* fucking beautiful."

"*You're* so fucking beautiful," Lennie said, stroking her hair. "Man, did I luck out finding you."

"Right back atcha."

~ ~ ~

Billy and Venus showed up on time.

"Oh my God!" Venus said, checking everything out. "This place is amazing! I need to buy me a penthouse immediately. It's too damn fabulous. What do you think, Billy?"

"It's pretty great," he agreed, wandering around from room to room, especially loving Lennie's den. "You want me to buy one of these apartments for you?"

"How's your career going?" she teased.

"Very funny."

"I've got a great idea," Venus said. "Let's buy an apartment together, put both our names on it."

"Not good," Lennie said, handing out martinis.

"Why not?" Venus asked, blond and stunning in a simple Roberto Cavalli short silver dress.

"He's right," Lucky agreed, equally stunning in a soft black leather pantsuit that fit her like a second skin. "If the two of you ever split up, who gets the apartment?"

"That would be one hell of a fight," Lennie remarked.

"Thanks, my friends," Venus said, bristling slightly. "What makes you think we're going to split up?"

"I can solve this," Billy said, quickly jumping in. "Either *I* buy it, or *she* does, or *I* buy it for her."

"Maybe I should mention there are only two penthouses left," Lucky said. "Brigette's thinking of buying one, and Bobby's got his eye on the other."

"I'm your best friend," Venus pointed out. "I should get first dibs."

"I've been telling you about them forever," Lucky reminded her. "If you'd come in at the construction stage, you could've had the shell designed exactly to your specifications."

"I didn't realize they were this fabulous."

"Anyway, the two available penthouses are not quite finished, so whoever gets them can choose their own kitchens, bathrooms—"

"Tell you what," Billy said magnanimously. "I'll buy it for Venus as a present."

"Nice gesture, Billy," Lucky said. "But I think I should tell you that the asking price is twelve million dollars."

"Holy shit!" he exclaimed. "Are you *kidding* me?"

"Totally serious."

"Guess I'm not getting a present," Venus said ruefully. "My boyfriend is a cheapo."

"Come *on*," Billy said. "Even *you* have to admit that's freakin' outrageous."

"*How* much did you make on your last movie?" Venus asked, winking at Lucky.

"Not enough," he said, thinking that she couldn't possibly be serious.

"Now, now, you two," Lucky said. "No fighting over millions, it's time for dinner. Let's go."

72

After Luis left, Irma slept peacefully. She was no longer concerned about Oliver Stanton. Sleeping with him had been a mistake, but now he'd stopped calling and gone away. She was sure it was pure coincidence that they'd sat next to each other on the plane, that she'd ended up having dinner with him, and that he'd turned out to be a drug enforcement agent. She regretted it, but at the time she'd thought she was leaving Anthony. The new Anthony was certainly worth giving another chance to. He was acting like a different man, and she was impressed.

She wondered what had happened to change him. Being thoughtful and generous was so unlike Anthony. Maybe his mistresses had started to misbehave, and he'd remembered he had a wife at home. That could explain it.

Anyway, they were merely mistresses, while *she* was Mrs. Anthony Bonar. That had to mean something, and it obviously did, because *she* was the one getting the diamond earrings.

Idly she wondered if she could persuade him to vary his lovemaking technique. Anthony was so rough, and now, for the first time, she understood what making love could be like.

Luis was an accomplished lover, but he was also an uneducated man with a pregnant wife, so she'd definitely decided not to continue their sexual tryst. Last night was the final time. It was memorable and now it was over.

She'd slept with her new diamond earrings on the bedside table, and the first thing she did when she woke up in the morning was to admire them. They were simply the most beautiful piece of jewelry she'd ever possessed.

Marta brought her breakfast on a tray.

"What a lovely day it is today, Marta," she said, smiling at the woman.

Marta nodded, her face surly. She'd seen the *señora* bringing Luis into the house the previous day. She'd seen him follow her up the stairs into her bedroom, then she'd seen him depart several hours later. It wasn't right. Should she warn his wife? But if she did, Luis would be out of a job and she knew his family did not have much money.

One thing she *did* know, and that was as the Bonars' housekeeper the safest thing was to keep her mouth shut.

However, she couldn't help confiding in her cousin, Rosa, the Bonars' cook in Acapulco.

"What the *señora* does is nothing," Rosa spat. "Señor Bonar has mistresses everywhere. It is good she does it back to him."

"Luis is a nice boy," Marta insisted. "I know the family, his wife is pregnant."

"So what?" Rosa responded. "If I was sleeping with a man other than my husband, I'd choose someone young too."

"And *married?*" Marta said disapprovingly.

"You can't blame the woman. Señor Bonar is a pig—he ignores his wife and manhandles me. I'm forced to accept the way he humiliates me in front of his friends. He often threatens to fire me, then he thinks it's so funny. I loathe him."

"Why don't you quit?" Marta asked.

"Why don't *you?*" Rosa responded.

They both knew that neither of them could afford to.

Unaware of the heated conversation going on downstairs, Irma glanced at the morning paper, ate her scrambled eggs and toast, and finally got out of bed. Had Marta noticed the diamond earrings lying on her bedside table? She probably should have put them away; tempting the staff was not wise.

Excited at the thought of Anthony taking her to Las Vegas, she realized he had not taken her anywhere in years. This could be a new beginning. A second honeymoon.

She went into the bathroom and ran a bath.

When Anthony phoned her later she wasn't surprised. She'd been expecting to hear from him.

"My earrings are beautiful," she said. "I can't wait to wear them."

"I haven't left yet," Anthony said. "I'm still here."

"You are? Why?"

"There was a problem with my plane. Didn't wanna bother you, so I spent the night at a hotel."

"You should've come home," she said, thinking of the consequences if he'd discovered her in bed with Luis. It did not bear thinking about.

"We'll have lunch again before I leave," he said. "I'll take you back to the same jewelry store, buy you somethin' else. Wouldja like that?"

"If you're sure."

"I'm gonna send the car for you."

"What about Las Vegas?" she asked hopefully. "Am I still going with you? I can pack and be ready to go with you today."

"Not a bad idea," he said. "Do that. Don't bring much with you—only a small bag."

"But if it's a big opening, surely I'll need a gown?"

"You'll pick up whatever you want in Vegas. An' don't forget t'bring your earrings."

"As if I'd forget."

"See you later," he said, hanging up the phone and calling for The Grill.

"Yes, boss?"

"Go get it now," he ordered. "An' make sure the car bringin' my wife is delayed on the way here."

"Yes, boss."

"Make it fast."

"Yes, boss," the big man said, his wide face impassive.

Anthony rubbed his eyes and thought about what he'd do if the evidence was incriminating.

Someone would end up dead.

That he knew for sure.

73

The funeral of Penelope Whitfield-Simmons was a somber affair. It took place in Pasadena and there were almost a hundred mourners gathered at the graveside. Front and center was Penelope's only son and heir, Henry Whitfield-Simmons.

Henry stood with his head bowed. Later he maintained the same desolate expression as people lined up to offer him their condolences. He recognized most of the women—they were his mother's friends, the pack of vicious gossips she'd surrounded herself with. The same women who'd either laughed at him or ignored him. It was different now that he was about to inherit the Whitfield-Simmons fortune.

"I'm so sorry, dear," one of the women said, gripping his arm with a clawlike hand. "What will you do?"

I will be very happy, he thought. *Very happy and very rich.*

"I'll manage," he said, adding a forlorn, "We'll all miss her so much."

"I know, dear," another woman said, patting his shoulder as if he were a pet dog. "Your mother was so fond of you, Henry. She talked about you all the time."

"She did?" he said, not believing her for a minute.

"Yes," the woman continued. "She was worried that you'd never find the right girl. I was delighted when she phoned me last week and told me that you had indeed met somebody."

"She was right," Henry said. "I have."

"That's wonderful news. The right girl will help you get over this sad occasion. Penelope wanted nothing more than to see you happily married, and perhaps one day have children of your own."

"It'll happen," Henry said, imagining what a beautiful baby he and Maria would produce. "If we have a daughter, we'll call her Penelope."

"Such a precious sentiment," the woman sighed.

Henry nodded. *Yes it is.*

There was a formal reception back at the mansion. It seemed to Henry that most of the people who attended wanted nothing more than to drink and eat and gossip amongst themselves. They were certainly not there to mourn Penelope Whitfield-Simmons, and although some of them mentioned her in passing, it was more of a social occasion.

"She was so young," one woman said. "To think that the poor dear simply went to sleep one night and failed to wake up the next morning."

"Yes," Henry said. "According to the doctor, her heart stopped beating."

"It's so sad," the woman said. "But at least it was a peaceful ending."

His mother's lawyer was there, a heavyset man wearing a suit and horn-rimmed glasses.

"We have a lot to talk about, young man," the lawyer said, approaching him in a blustery fashion.

"We certainly do," Henry replied, getting right to the point. "I understand that I am the sole beneficiary."

"Your mother told you that?"

"She certainly did. We discussed everything, especially my upcoming trip."

"You're going away?"

"Yes. I have an important trip to make that I cannot postpone. I'll be leaving at the end of the week. My mother was arranging for a substantial amount of cash for me to take. Since I *am* the sole heir, I'm sure you will see that it is taken care of before things are officially settled."

"How much did your mother promise?" the lawyer asked.

"One hundred thousand dollars," Henry said calmly. "And also please have your office arrange a black American Express card for me. I'll need it while I'm traveling."

"Where will you be going, Henry?"

"Europe. In the meantime I've decided to put the house on the market, so perhaps you can take care of that too."

"You're putting your mother's house on the market?" the lawyer said, expressing surprise. "Surely you should think about this for a while."

"I do not need to. My mother and I discussed it many times. She didn't want me living here by myself surrounded by memories. She was adamant that when she died I must sell the house."

"How long will you be gone?"

"I'm not sure, but I'll be in touch. And I wish to have the money and the credit card before the end of the week."

The house was delightfully peaceful when everybody finally left and he was alone. The live-in couple retired to their apartment above the garage, while Markus went home at night.

Before Markus left, Henry had informed him that he would shortly be going on a trip. "Prepare the Bentley," he'd ordered.

"Mrs. Whitfield-Simmons's Bentley?" Markus had said, acting as if she were still alive and likely to object.

"The Bentley is mine now, Markus, so make sure it's gassed up and ready, because last time I took the Volvo it ran out of gas. That was your fault. Isn't your job to see that each one of the cars are fully gassed at all times?"

Markus had shied away from Henry Whitfield-Simmons, who seemed to have developed a new aggressive personality overnight. "Yes, Mr. Henry," he'd muttered.

"Then if you wish to keep your job, make certain it's done."

Alone in the house, Henry wandered around, realizing that the only part of the house he was really familiar with was his own room. Now he could go where he wanted, touch whatever he felt like touching. As a child the only words he remembered his mother saying over and over were, "Don't touch that, Henry, you're so clumsy, you'll break it."

Now he could break anything he felt like, because everything was his.

He sat in Penelope Whitfield-Simmons's bedroom and read her obituary in the *Times*. Then he carefully cut it out and placed it in his wallet.

Penelope Whitfield-Simmons was dead.

It was her own fault.

74

"Jeez," Ace whistled. "You didn't warn me that you lived in a freaking palace."

"This is just a rental place," Max said casually, greeting him at the door. "Our real home's in Malibu."

"A rental?" he said, shaking his head in wonderment. "More like a hotel, I've never seen anything like it."

"Now that you're here, come on in," she said, taking his arm, trying to conceal her excitement at seeing him.

"I dunno why I said yes to this," he mused.

"Oh, *I* do," she said teasingly. "You were *desperate* to see me again. You couldn't *wait!*"

"You're a cocky little thing, aren't you?" he said, a slow grin spreading across his face.

"So I've been told," she replied, leading him into the grand entry hall.

"I feel like I'm in the lobby of a Hilton," he said, gazing around.

"Mom would *love* to hear that," she said, laughing.

"Is the dragon lady around?"

"She'd freak if she heard you calling her that. And no, she's safely in Vegas awaiting our presence."

"Does that mean I get to meet her?"

"Of course," she said, still holding on to his arm. "C'mon, let's go upstairs, I'll show you your room."

"I have a room?" he said, raising his eyebrows. "I thought the whole point of my coming here was that we were heading straight to Vegas."

"We're leaving first thing in the morning," she assured him. "Tonight you get to see L.A."

"It wasn't what we planned, Max."

"Plans change, and Harry's got a new SUV, so—"

"Who's Harry?" he interrupted.

"I told you about Harry, he's my gay friend. You don't mind that he's gay, do you?"

"Why would *I* mind?"

"Just thought I'd fill you in."

"You think he'll try to jump me?"

"Sure," she joked. "*Scared?*"

"Shaking," he deadpanned.

"My other friend, Cookie, is meeting us later with Harry," she said, opening the door to the guest room.

"Is she gay too?"

"No. Now *stop* it," she said, laughing again.

"Am I supposed to sleep here?" he said, throwing his duffel bag on the floor. "It's bigger than my entire house."

"It's not *that* big. By the way, did you bring a tuxedo?"

"Do I look like the kinda dude who *has* a tuxedo?" he said, giving her a quizzical look.

"No," she said, hardly able to take her eyes off him. "But I told you the opening was like, black tie, didn't I?"

"How do *I* know what black tie means? I brought a suit and I brought a tie. Sorry—neither of them are black."

"We could rent you a tuxedo," she suggested.

"No thanks."

"Why not?"

"The penguin look doesn't suit me."

"Are you hungry?" she asked.

"Kinda," he replied.

"Let's go down to the kitchen then."

He followed her downstairs where she asked Philippe to make them a sandwich. Then she led him out to the pool.

"This place is like something out of a movie," he marveled. "It's so big."

"Our house in Malibu is much nicer. I love the ocean, don't you?"

"Philippe brought them out toasted-cheese-and-tomato sandwiches and a selection of soft drinks.

"You really live the cushy life, don't you?" Ace said.

"Uh, how's your girlfriend?" She couldn't stop herself from asking.

He threw her a penetrating look. "If I was still with her, do you think I'd be here?"

"You mean you broke up?" she said, attempting to sound casual, but desperate to find out everything.

"You got it."

"What happened?"

"She dumped me."

"*She* dumped *you?*"

"Yeah."

"Why'd she do that?"

"'Cause I was supposed to meet her the night we got kidnapped, and when I never turned up she was pissed, so she went off with one of my friends."

"Wow! That's not nice."

"This is even not nicer—they both got drunk and got it on. When I found out, it was my turn to be pissed, so I guess you could say we kinda dumped each other. End of story."

She was dying to ask him a ton more questions, but then she figured it wouldn't be cool if she showed too much interest.

"What's going on with you an' your boyfriend?" he asked, springing open a can of Coke.

"Uh . . . we broke up," she mumbled.

"Who did the dumping?"

"Who do you think?"

"You?"

"I caught him out with another girl, so I said good-bye."

"We're some pair."

"*Are* we a pair?" she asked hopefully.

"No, we're two people who just got caught up in a bad scene and now we're friends."

"Sure we are."

"Hey, Max, I'm not forgetting how old you are, so don't go reading anything into this trip."

"What's my age got to do with anything?" she said, irritated.

"You're sixteen, Max. I'm here as your friend an' that's all."

"Ooh," she said with an exaggerated eye roll. "And there was little old me thinking you came to ravish my teenage body."

"I came 'cause I needed to get away," he said, quite serious.

"Not to see me?"

"To see you too. Oh yeah," he added, lightening up, "an' to get that twenty bucks you owe me."

"Like I'd forget," she said, digging in her jeans pocket and handing him a couple of crumpled tens. "See, I had it all ready for you."

"I was kidding."

"It's your money, take it."

Later they met up with Cookie and Harry at the Cheesecake Factory in Beverly Hills.

Cookie took one look at Ace and liked what she saw. "Definite babe magnet," she mouthed to Max behind his back.

"Ace just broke up with his girlfriend," Max announced as they sat down.

"That's convenient," Harry said, paler than ever. "Now you two can get it on."

Max threw him a furious look.

"My dad's taking a plane up to Vegas tomorrow, so if we don't feel like driving, we can fly with him," Cookie said, ordering a Diet Coke. "Anyone wanna do that?"

"I thought we were testing out my new car," Harry interjected. "Got a few records I wanna break."

"What do *you* feel like doing?" Max asked, turning to Ace.

"You people are unbelievable," he said, wondering what he was doing hanging out with this bunch of rich kids with whom he had nothing in common. "Planes, new cars—I'm not used to this."

"Yeah, well, since you and Max are hooking up, you'd better get used to it," Harry said, picking up the menu.

"Nobody's hooking up," Max replied, glaring at him. What was wrong with Harry? He was behaving like a dick.

"That's right," Ace said. "We're just friends."

"Really?" Cookie said disbelievingly.

"I guess Max told you what happened to us?" Ace said. "It was some screwed-up experience."

"Yeah, like *major* spooky," Cookie said. "I warned her about weirdos online, but Max never listens to anyone."

"Please don't talk about me as if I'm not here," Max said quickly.

"I was all for going to the cops," Ace said. "She wouldn't let me."

"Good boy," Harry sneered. "You'll find it pays to be obedient around our Max, she's a total control freak."

"Shut *up*, Harry," Max warned. "What's up with you?"

"Nothing," he answered sulkily.

"Max told us you were kinda like a superhero," Cookie said. "Y'know, rescuing her, getting her outta there."

"I did what I had to," Ace said modestly, while Harry made a face and pretended to throw up.

During the course of the dinner, Max discovered several things about Ace. He did not smoke, he did not do drugs, and he went to church with his brother every Sunday. He was so unlike most of the boys she knew, and she was fast becoming totally crazy about him. By the time they'd finished eating and had made their way to the club Harry was so sure they'd get into, she was feeling quite dizzy, and not in a bad way.

Harry circumvented the line outside the club and marched up to the burly doorman, who was unimpressed—especially when Harry started yelling and waving hundred-dollar bills around. It made no difference. Underage was underage, and they couldn't get in.

"This is bullshit," Ace said, grabbing Max's arm. "Let's split."

"Sure," she said, nudging Cookie, who got the message and dragged Harry away from the entrance to the club and back to his car.

"I'll drive," Ace said.

"No way," Harry objected, swaying slightly.

"You're stoned," Ace accused.

"No way," Harry repeated, glaring at him.

Crap! Max thought. *So this is why Harry is acting like such a prick. Ace is right. He's totally stoned.*

"Hey," Ace said forcefully. "Either *I* drive or we're getting a cab."

"Go ahead," Harry said belligerently, spiky black hair standing on end.

"Cool it, Harry," Cookie said, stepping between them. "Let Ace drive. What's your problem?"

"It's *my* car and I'm driving it," Harry shouted. "So you can all go fuck off."

"He's not usually like this," Max whispered to Ace. "I don't know what's up with him."

"Listen," Ace said. "He's your friend, and I'm sorry, but neither of us are getting in a car with him."

"What about Cookie?"

"She shouldn't drive with him either. Tell her."

"Cookie, come with us," Max said.

"I'll stick with Harry," Cookie decided. "He's not *that* stoned. You two take off, we'll see you in the morning."

"I'm so sorry about Harry," Max said as she and Ace walked off down Hollywood Boulevard.

"Those two are your best friends?" he said.

"They're normally great, but lately they're into this whole getting-stoned mind trip. It's not *my* idea of a fun time."

"Glad to hear it. I went through that phase when I was sixteen, but I didn't drive. Truth is I didn't have a car."

"My mom thinks doing drugs is totally uncool. That's one thing we agree on."

He took her hand as a couple of suspicious-looking guys walked toward them.

"I'm really glad you're here," she said, loving the way her hand felt in his.

"I'm not getting in a car with Harry tomorrow," he said. "We'll take my brother's truck."

"Really?"

"Your friend is on a roll, Max. I don't want to be around when he crashes and burns."

"Isn't that like rather dramatic?" she said, looking up at him.

"Maybe, but it's what happens."

"Harry's going through a tough time. His dad is some kind of mogul, and his mom's a born-again. They went through a bad divorce, plus he's stuck in the closet, so he's major screwed up. Cookie, Harry, and me have been best friends since we were like five years old."

"I understand, an' I'm not being difficult, but you don't wanna get in a car with somebody when they're high."

"Okay, we'll take your truck, and they can either go in Cookie's dad's plane or drive."

"Who's Cookie's dad?"

"He's a famous soul singer. Gerald M. You heard of him?"

"Nope."

"You really do live in the boondocks, don't you?"

"You sound like a Beverly Hills brat when you say things like that."

"Well, I'm not," she said defensively. "You should meet my grandfather, he's a real character, he built hotels in Vegas way back. He's ninety-five now. My parents were way pissed I missed his party."

"Your parents sound interesting."

"My dad's the greatest. He started out as a comedian, then he became a movie star, now he writes and directs movies."

"I know, I looked him up on my brother's computer."

"Oh, so you *do* have e-mail at your house. How come you didn't tell me?"

"Max," he said, giving her another one of his penetrating looks. "There's a lot I haven't told you."

"Like what?"

"Like one of these days—if we stay friends—you'll find out."

75

The Grill was a speed demon. It would have taken a normal person an hour to get to the house and back, but The Grill managed to make it in half the time.

He entered Anthony's office and handed him the small hidden camera that he'd installed in the master bedroom at his boss's house the day before.

"You arranged for the car bringing my wife here to be delayed?" Anthony asked.

The Grill nodded.

"Get out," Anthony ordered. "And tell my secretary nobody's to disturb me."

"Yes, boss," The Grill said as he left the office.

Anthony connected the small spy camera to the TV before switching it on. He wasn't sure what he was about to see, but whatever it was it would either validate what Cesar had told him, or it would make the man out to be a liar, in which case Cesar would be severely punished before his ass was fired.

Working the remote, Anthony sped through the scenes of the empty bedroom, stopping when Irma appeared. He observed her enter the room and walk straight over to the window.

What was she doing at the window? He couldn't tell.

She looked out of the window for a few minutes before turning around and leaving the room.

He fast-forwarded again until she returned. Only this time she was not alone—this time there was a man with her.

Anthony's back stiffened as the man followed Irma into their bedroom. Then the bitch locked the door, she locked the fuckin' door!

Anthony sat very still watching intently as his wife began talking to the man, saying something Anthony couldn't hear. He adjusted the sound and rewound to make sure he missed nothing.

"Luis," Irma said, "what is going on with you?"

" 'Scuse, *señora*," the man muttered.

"Don't call me *señora*," Irma said. "My name is Irma. You know that."

"*Sí*, Irma," the man said.

Anthony pressed Pause and rewound again, just to make sure he was catching every word.

"Why didn't you tell me you were married and your wife was pregnant?" Irma said as the tape continued.

The man shrugged and looked away. But then to Anthony's fury, the son of a bitch turned toward her, and in a most familiar fashion placed his fuckin' hand on her right breast.

Anthony leaned forward, hardly believing his own eyes. That Irma would *dare* to do this was beyond his comprehension.

Within seconds the man began undoing the buttons on her blouse. Next he unhooked the clip on the front of her bra, exposing her breasts.

Anthony attempted to keep his breathing even, but the anger that was building inside him was getting ready to explode.

"Oh, Luis," Irma sighed, throwing her head back in abandon.

The man, or Luis, as that was obviously the bastard's name, lightly brushed her nipples with his fingertips before bringing his lips down to suck on them.

She did *not* object. *His wife did not object!*

"Son of a mothafuckin' *bitch!*" Anthony screamed, his face reddening. "Cheating fuckin' WHORE!"

Irma sighed the name "Luis" again before the prick swept her up in his arms and carried her over to the bed where he proceeded to make love to her.

ANOTHER MAN WAS FUCKING HIS WIFE. ANTHONY BONAR'S WIFE! AND THE CUNT WAS ENJOYING IT!

Anthony could feel the bile rising in his throat. This was the woman he'd married, the woman he'd given his name to, the *mother* of his children.

This woman was nothing but a prostitute, a douche bag, an unfaithful cheating CUNT.

Abruptly Anthony switched off the TV and summoned The Grill.

The big man entered his office and stood at attention.

"I have a job for you to take care of," Anthony instructed. "A job that needs to be executed immediately."

~ ~ ~

The driver took Irma to the same restaurant where she and Anthony had lunched the day before. She was not happy because the driver had insisted on making several stops along the way, claiming he was running errands for Señor Bonar. After the third stop she complained bitterly that she would be late for lunch and Señor Bonar would be very angry if she was late.

The driver shrugged and informed her that he was only following Señor Bonar's orders.

Irma decided she would tell Anthony she did not wish to use this particular driver again—he was insolent.

When she finally arrived at the restaurant Anthony was not there, even though she was at least twenty minutes late. She requested a glass of wine and looked at the menu, then after fifteen minutes she called for the head waiter and asked if Señor Bonar had left a message for her.

"No, *señora*," the man said. "Perhaps you would care to order?"

No, she wouldn't care to order, not until Anthony got there.

Another ten minutes passed and she wasn't sure what to do. She requested a phone and connected with Anthony at his office.

"Where are you?" she said. "I've been sitting here for over half an hour."

"Something came up," he said.

"Will you be here soon?"

"Go ahead and order."

"Without you?"

"I'll try to make it. Otherwise come to the office when you're finished."

"But I hate sitting alone in a restaurant," she complained. "It's uncomfortable. I feel awkward."

"Sometimes we gotta do things we don't want to. This is one of them."

He did not sound as friendly as he had the day before, but she understood that when Anthony was immersed in business he became distant.

"Am I still coming to Vegas?" she asked, hoping that he hadn't changed his mind.

"Wouldn't want you to miss out, would I?"

"I'll go ahead and order. Should I get something for you in case you make it?"

"It's unlikely," he said. "Take your time, I'll be at my office waitin' for you."

"Can I bring you anything at all?"

"Funny thing," he said slowly. "Seems like I lost my appetite."

She ordered a salad and another glass of wine. She lingered over the wine. Anthony did not appear.

After a while she asked for the check, paid it, and was on her way out of the restaurant when who should she run into but Oliver Stanton.

"Irma," he said, stopping and blocking her path.

"Oliver," she replied, thanking God that Anthony wasn't with her.

"I called you," Oliver said, giving her a hurt look. "More than once, and you haven't returned my calls."

"I know," she answered, trying to come up with a reasonable excuse. "I've been very busy."

"Was it something I said? Did? Because I was under the impression that we really hit it off."

"No, no, Oliver, our evening together was most enjoyable."

"But you never called me back."

"I will," she said quickly. "I've got your number."

"Is that a promise?"

"Yes," she said, hesitating for a moment. "It's just that things have changed since we were together."

"They have?"

"I can't explain right now," she said, eager to get away from him. "I'll call you later."

She hurried from the restaurant without looking back. The driver was waiting by the car.

"Señor Bonar's office," she said, getting in the car. "And this time no stops along the way."

"*Sí, señora.*"

She reached in her purse, took out her compact, and applied powder and lip gloss. Running into Oliver Stanton was quite a surprise. What if Anthony had been with her? How would she have explained it?

Anthony's suite of offices was on the top floor of the building. His assistant was not at her desk and there seemed to be nobody else around, so Irma made her way to his office.

Anthony was sitting behind his desk smoking an expensive cigar.

"I thought you were so busy," she scolded. "I didn't enjoy lunching by myself. Sitting alone in a restaurant is embarrassing."

"Embarrassing, huh?" he said, puffing away on his cigar.

"Is everything all right?" she asked. "Are the children okay?"

"Why wouldn't they be?"

"It's simply that you seem so different from yesterday."

"Different. In what way?"

"I don't know, Anthony. Yesterday I thought that things were getting better between us. Now you're acting toward me as if—"

"As if what, Irma?"

"As if I've done something wrong."

"Have you?" he asked, blowing smoke in her direction.

"Have I what?"

"Done something wrong."

"Of course not," she said, adding, "I'm so looking forward to Vegas."

"Yeah, I'm kinda lookin' forward to it myself," he said. "But first there's a few things I gotta take care of, so whyn't you sit down 'cause I got somethin' t'show you."

"What do you want to show me, Anthony?" she asked, sitting on a leather chair, folding her hands neatly on her lap.

"A movie," he said mildly.

"A movie?"

"Yeah. It's not exactly a love story, more a kinda porno."

"Anthony," she said sternly, "you know I do not enjoy porno films."

"I believe you mentioned that when we were first married. Only things change, don't they?"

"No, Anthony," she said primly. "I refuse to watch porno. I find it demeaning to women."

"You might get a kick outta watchin' this one, 'cause it stars someone you know."

"Who?" she asked, immediately thinking that perhaps it was one of his entourage's wives. Wouldn't *that* be something.

"Sit back, Irma, an' enjoy the show. I gotta hunch you're gonna find it more than interesting."

THE KEYS

76

"Good morning," Lucky said, kissing her husband on the lips.

"Man," Lennie groaned, waking up with a lazy smile on his face. "So cheerful for a dawn wake-up."

"It's six A.M., the sun is shining, and today's my big day."

"Yeah, an' last night was my big night trading shots of tequila with your friend Billy. Why'd you let me do it?"

"I seem to recall us having the same conversation when I overdid the champagne at Gino's party. Wasn't it me saying to you, 'Why'd you let me drink champagne?' And you saying to me, 'When have I ever stopped you from doing anything?' "

"She has a memory too."

"She sure does. So I suggest that you haul your lazy ass out of bed and come with me."

"Where're we going?"

"Who knows? I've got this urge to walk around my hotel and take it all in before chaos."

"Chaos, huh?"

"I guess I'm experiencing that feeling you get just before the opening of one of your movies."

"Extreme stomach cramps and a desperate need to hide?"

"No," she said, laughing. "Excitement. Pure unadulterated excitement."

Lennie looked at his wife, marveling at how beautiful she was. Lucky Santangelo. Mother of his children. Powerhouse. Businesswoman. Tough. Vulnerable. Wildly sexy. His true partner in every way.

What a woman!

"Let's go," he said, jumping out of bed.

"You're naked," she pointed out. "Put your pants on."

"First time you've asked me to do that," he said, grinning.

"Don't piss around with me today, Lennie, 'cause nothing you do is going to upset me."

"Okay, then I won't bother putting on pants."

"Ha ha! This is *not* a nudist camp—pants on and let's hit it. Okay, lover?"

"Okay, wife."

~ ~ ~

Venus was up early too, in spite of the fact that they'd all ended up at the Cavendish and gambled until three A.M. Billy had been on a winning streak, which had put him in an excellent mood.

"I had no idea you were such a big gambler," Venus had said. "Vegas agrees with you."

"When I win it does," Billy had said. "Last time I was here was for a bachelor party, had a wild time."

"I bet you *did*, what with all the strip clubs, not to mention the convenient whorehouses."

"Baby," he'd said, laughing, "if there's one thing I've *never* had to do, that's pay for it."

Now it was morning and she was ready to rehearse. "How are you going to occupy yourself today?" she asked.

"Don't worry about me. I'll find something to do."

"Yeah, if I know you, you'll be heading back to the tables to lose it all."

"Don't knock it. Besides, there's nothing else to do in Vegas."

"Yes, there is," she said crisply. "Shopping."

"Shopping is a girls' thing."

"Since when? You love to shop."

"Not today. Anyway, Kev's arriving this morning, he'll keep me company."

"Is he coming by himself?"

"Uh, no," Billy said, dreading the moment he might have to introduce Venus to Ali. "Think he's bringing one of his girls."

"You make him sound like a pimp."

"He wishes."

"Well," Venus said, preparing to leave, "if you need me, I'll be at rehearsal. I should be back around three. Then I plan on having a full-body massage and taking it easy until my makeup and hair people arrive at four."

"Got it, babe."

"Oh yes, and if you feel like buying me that apartment, go right ahead."

"Never knew you were a comedienne too."

"Thanks, darling," she drawled. "A girl's got to try."

~ ~ ~

Renee Falcon was always up early, unlike Susie who most days lazed in bed until noon. Renee didn't mind, she genuinely loved her partner. Susie was all the things she wasn't—soft and loving and kind and quite astute in her own way.

The previous night Renee had found to be quite disturbing. Her casino floor manager—always on celebrity alert—had called and informed her that Billy Melina and Venus were in the house. Naturally she'd gone into the casino to personally welcome them to the Cavendish. She had not been expecting to find Lucky Santangelo and Lennie Golden with them. She'd never met Lucky, nor had she wanted to in view of what was to take place the following day.

"We're about to be neighbors," Lucky had said with a warm smile. "Anytime you want to come over to the Keys, you'll be my guest. Call first—if I'm around, I'll make sure to give you a personal tour."

Renee was surprised to note that not only was Lucky Santangelo a true beauty—stunning, with her slim figure, wild profusion of jet-black curls, and penetrating dark eyes—she was friendly too. This was a shock after all the vitriolic things Anthony had said about the Santangelo family, Lucky in particular. He'd called her a bitch and a cunt and a murderer. And he'd given Renee the impression there was no more evil woman on earth. Obviously he was lying, or Lucky was the best actress in the world.

Later Susie had joined her in the casino and then they'd all ended up in the lounge having drinks together. Susie had also liked Lucky, and she'd especially enjoyed talking to Lennie, who she soon discovered had once worked with her deceased husband on a movie.

"I'm inviting you both to our opening tomorrow," Lucky had said before they all left. "There's a reception on the terrace at six, followed by a lingerie show, then Venus's special appearance. I'd be delighted for you both to be my guests."

"We accept," Susie had said with a happy nod.

Renee considered Anthony's reaction had he witnessed this cozy little scene. He would've thrown one of his explosive temper tantrums. But who cared about Anthony? Ever since Tasmin's murder, Renee fervently wished she could sever all connections with him. Yes, the Keys would be competition, but what Anthony had persuaded her to put in place was extraordinarily drastic and now she was starting to regret it. Thank God Susie knew nothing, for she'd put an immediate stop to it.

Lately Renee had spent too much of her time keeping Detective Franklin at bay. The detective had a nose for details, and kept on returning to the hotel with more and more questions. She seemed very interested in speaking to Anthony in person.

Renee managed to stonewall her.

"You're wasting both our time," she'd said. "I've answered all your questions more than once. You've spoken to Mr. Bonar on the phone. I don't understand why you keep coming back."

"Because this is where the trail ends," Detective Franklin had answered. "Doesn't it concern you that after Tasmin spent the evening with you and your guests in *your* restaurant at *this* hotel she was never seen again?"

Renee had shrugged. "Sorry, but I can't help you."

Secretly she wished she could, for her thoughts often turned to Tasmin's body buried in the desert where nobody would ever find it, unless she guided them in the right direction. Then she thought about what a smart and beautiful woman Tasmin had been, and how unnecessary her murder was. A true waste of a decent human being who happened to enjoy sex—and thanks to Renee, had gotten herself fixed up with the wrong one-night stand.

Deep down Renee felt responsible. Even though Anthony Bonar had helped her flee Colombia and set her up in Vegas, she wished she'd never set eyes on the murderous son of a bitch. He was a danger to himself and everyone around him.

Too late now. Or was it? Anthony was heading to Vegas and he expected action.

~ ~ ~

Sitting next to Ace in the passenger seat of his truck on their way to Vegas, Max felt content—a feeling she wasn't used to. Last night they'd stayed up late, talking. Unfortunately for her *just* talking, because she'd desperately wanted him to kiss her, willed him to do so, but he hadn't. Around midnight he'd said, "I'm gonna catch some sleep, we should try to leave early in the morning."

She'd gone to bed vaguely disappointed, only to be awoken at three A.M. by a call from a hysterical Cookie, who'd informed her that Harry had crashed his SUV, totally wrecked it, failed a sobriety test, and subsequently been arrested.

"But he wasn't drunk," Max had said, struggling to wake up.

"By that time he was," Cookie admitted. "After you left, we bribed our way into another club where Harry made it his mission to see how many vodka martinis he could chug. You know Harry when he's on a roll."

"Weren't you *supposed* to be watching out for him?"

"Since when did *I* turn into like a *nursemaid*?" Cookie grumbled. "Y'know, *I* was in the car too. I could've been killed."

"Are you hurt?"

"A few bruises, nothing major."

"That's good."

"Harry's dad was *way* mad—like *totally* pissed. He sent his big-time lawyer to bail number-one son out, so now Harry's grounded, can't come to Vegas."

"How about you?"

"I figure I'll hitch a ride on my dad's plane an' see you there."

"Sounds like a plan," Max had said, contemplating whether she should wake Ace, but deciding against it. The next morning she'd filled him in over breakfast.

"That's one screwed-up dude," Ace had said, not at all surprised. "He was an accident waiting to happen."

"Guess you were right about not getting in the car with him."

"It's called instincts," he'd replied. "Always gotta follow 'em."

Now they were on their way to Vegas, and as far as she was concerned everything was cool, *especially* as Ace had broken up with his girlfriend. What a bonus!

She stole a sideways glance at him. He was *so* damn handsome, and that cleft in his chin . . . wow!

Donny, once her reason for getting up in the morning, had faded to a distant memory.

Maybe tonight she'd get that kiss she'd been waiting for.

A girl could hope, couldn't she?

~ ~ ~

And on the same highway, several hours ahead of them, Henry Whitfield-Simmons drove his mother's sleek royal blue Bentley, estimating that he should be arriving in Las Vegas in less than an hour.

He hummed softly to himself. Everything had turned out exactly as he'd predicted. His mother's lawyer had been wary about not getting on his bad side. The man was a trustee of the estate, and as such he would be making himself a hefty percentage of billions of dollars, so his main desire was to keep Henry happy. He'd come up with the credit card and cash Henry had requested.

Once Henry had the black American Express card in his possession, he'd driven straight to the Beverly Hills Neiman Marcus and purchased an entire new wardrobe of clothes, all the better to impress Maria. Not that he felt she was the type of girl attracted by appearances, but it was only polite to look smart for her.

Now he was in the Bentley on his way to Vegas to claim his rightful prize.

And his prize was Maria.

He knew that once he convinced her it was the right thing to do, she would be happy that he'd come to take her away from the life she was forced to lead with Lucky Santangelo as her mother.

Very happy indeed.

77

Irma could not stop shaking—she was in shock—and nobody aboard Anthony's plane cared as it winged its way toward Las Vegas. Not Francesca, her husband's witch of a grandmother, who sat next to her grandson drinking endless cups of black coffee and chain-smoking. Not The Grill, Anthony's giant psycho bodyguard with the blank glassy eyes and expressionless face. Not Emmanuelle, her husband's blond mistress who kept on shooting her filthy looks as she thumbed through a selection of trashy magazines. And certainly not Anthony himself. Her vicious husband. Her worst nightmare.

Yesterday's events were etched into her brain forever. How could she forget the horror of what Anthony had put her through.

It had all started with the movie. . . .

She'd watched in disbelief as her image had appeared on the screen. Her words. Her gestures. Luis.

Anthony had *everything* on film. Luis touching her, undressing her, making love to her.

Oh God! Every moment of her last assignation was captured in excruciating detail.

She'd watched and cringed and begged Anthony to stop the film. But no, he was having none of it.

"Shut the fuck up, you whore!" he'd screamed at her. "Keep on watchin' that motherfucker's cock rammin' into *my* wife, the *mother* of *my* kids."

There was a moment when she'd tried to get up and run from his office, desperate to escape the fury she had no doubt would erupt. But as soon as she'd attempted to do so, Anthony had violently slammed her back into the chair, where she'd stayed, watching, until Luis got off the bed, tenderly kissed her, put on his clothes, and left the bedroom.

At last it was over. The TV screen went blank, and there was an ominous silence.

"I'm sorry," she'd begun, choking over the words.

"You'll be a lot sorrier than this," he'd warned. "Where'd ya get the balls to cheat on *me*, Anthony Bonar? You fuckin' *puttana whore*."

"Anthony," she'd pleaded, hoping that somehow or other she could make him understand. "There was a reason I did it. You haven't touched me in years. I was—"

"Shut the fuck up," he'd ordered. "Do not say one more fuckin' *word*."

She'd sat in silence and shame, until the door to his office opened and in walked The Grill.

The big man was not alone; he was dragging Luis with him. *Her* Luis. Her lover, so badly beaten he could barely stand. Both his eyes were blackened, his nose looked like it was broken, his lips were puffed up and split, and there was blood all over his shirt.

Their eyes met for a brief second. "Oh God!" she'd moaned. "What have you done to him, Anthony? It wasn't his fault, it was mine, all mine. *I* seduced *him*. If you have to punish anyone, punish me."

"You," Anthony spat. "Why would I punish *you*? Your punishment is watchin' what happens to your fuckin' boyfriend."

"He's not my boyfriend!" she'd screamed hysterically. "You've done enough. Look at him—he's beaten to a pulp."

"You think I give a shit? You think I'd allow someone who *works* for *me* to run around sayin' he's fuckin' my wife? You think *that's* the kinda man you're married to? I got news for you, *bitch*. Nobody fucks Anthony Bonar's wife and gets away with it."

The shaking had started then and it hadn't stopped since.

"You got a choice," Anthony had said, staring her down. "An' I'm gonna let you decide, Irma, my dear wife, my favorite *cunt*. His cock or his balls—whaddya wanna cut off?"

"Anthony, don't do this," she'd pleaded.

"I'm givin' you a fuckin' choice, which is kinda big of me," he'd crowed, fully pleased with himself. "Cock or balls? You pick."

"You're insane," she'd moaned.

"Insane? Me? Listen, whore, *I'm* not the one who's bin screwin' another man's wife. This asswipe's the insane one."

"No," she'd said, desperately trying to keep it together and fight back. "*You're* the one who has mistresses everywhere. Three, four, I don't know how many women you sleep with. What was I *supposed* to do?"

"I got a suggestion," he'd said. "Whyn't you fuck the gardener? How's that?"

"If you do anything more to him, I'll go to the police," she'd gasped.

"You'd do that wouldja? You'd go to the cops 'cause your husband caught ya fuckin' another man." He'd shaken his head as if he couldn't believe she'd come out with something so dumb. "This is Mexico, whore. In this town they'd give me a fuckin' medal for beatin' up this prick."

"It's not just a beating, Anthony, you're threatening more."

"You bet your cheatin' ass I am. Now make up your fuckin' mind. What's it gonna be? Balls or cock?"

"I swear I *will* go to the police, Anthony," she'd said, panicking. "You can't stop me."

"Do that, an' I promise you you'll never see your kids again. Or your mother, or your father, 'cause I'll have somebody go to their house an' burn it to the ground. You got no fuckin' clue who you're messin' with, do you?"

The rest of it was a blur. She remembered the knife, she remembered Anthony putting it in her hand. She remembered lifting her arm and attempting to stab him. He'd laughed, snatched it away from her, and handed it to The Grill.

Above all she remembered the expression on Luis's face. Pure terror.

She could still hear his screams.

Later she'd been bundled into a car and taken to the airport where she'd been put on the plane by The Grill. Anthony had boarded the plane after her, and they'd flown to Miami, where he'd picked up his grandmother and his blond mistress.

"You say one fuckin' word to anyone and you're a dead woman, along with your parents," he'd warned her.

She sat on the plane, dazed, shaking, and numb.

There was nothing she could do about it. Not one damn thing.

78

By the afternoon most of the invited guests had arrived and the Keys was buzzing with activity.

Lucky was running around, greeting family, making sure they were all taken care of, dropping by Venus's rehearsal, and—the best moment of the day—giving Gino a personal tour.

The old man was impressed. "You did it, kiddo," he said, full or pride. "This place is somethin', an' you made it all happen by yourself."

"With a little help from my investors—including you," she said modestly. "Learned everything I know from you."

"You learned it well."

"I had to, didn't I? You'd've kicked my ass if I hadn't."

"You got that right," he said nodding. "You make me proud, kiddo, you did everythin' for this family a son would've done."

"Ha!" she said, pouncing triumphantly. "I *knew* you wanted a boy when you had me."

"Whatever I wanted, you turned out to be a winner. Couldn't've done better than you."

"Dario would've been a winner if he'd had the chance," she said softly.

"Yes he would," Gino agreed, shaking his head as his thoughts turned to the man who'd arranged for the murder of his son. "That dirty bastard Enzio Bonnatti, that two-timing motherfucker—'scuse my French. An' you, Lucky, you took care of him like a true Santangelo. You're my daughter all right, a Santangelo all the way."

"An eye for an eye," Lucky said, pushing back her long dark hair. "That's what you taught me, and that's the way I've always lived. Don't fuck with me and I won't fuck with you. *Capice?*"

"My daughter. My goddamn pride," Gino said, cracking a grin. "I came to America over eighty years ago, it's the greatest country on earth. In America you can achieve any dream you want."

"I know," she murmured. "You did it all, Gino. Everything."

"I certainly did. I got you, Lucky," he said, becoming more prideful by the minute. "I got grandchildren, a wife I love, an' loyal friends. I got it all, an' y'know what, kiddo, if I died tomorrow, I'd die a happy man. All you gotta do is look at me."

"I am looking, Gino," she said softly. "And I like what I see."

"Y'can call me Daddy if you want, you've earned the right."

"Oh, really?" she said, raising a skeptical eyebrow. "*Finally?*"

"Go ahead," he said with a magnanimous shrug. "I'm givin' you permission."

"Gee, thanks, Gino. But it's a little late for me to revert to calling you Daddy."

"It is?"

Now it was her turn to grin. "Bet on it, old man."

~ ~ ~

Just as Venus had predicted, Billy hit the Strip and went gambling, successfully losing back all his winnings from the night before. Since he was by himself—Kev had not yet turned up—he was constantly hassled by adoring fans, until he was finally forced to return to the Keys, where everybody seemed to be somebody, so it was no problem sitting out by the pool without being bothered. The hotel did not open to the general public for another week, so the only guests were VIPs, and civilians willing to pay fifteen hundred bucks for a ticket to Venus's one-night show.

He felt kind of psyched that his girlfriend was the hottest ticket in town. If he could only get over the feeling of coming across as second best in her company, they could be very happy together. Venus might be a superstar, but she was *his* superstar, and he was beginning to realize that in spite of everything he genuinely loved her. He also regretted cheating on her; it was such a dumb thing to do. A stupid move he could only blame on his youth.

By four o'clock Kev had still not shown up and Billy was starting to worry. Kev was driving his Maserati, and Kev was kind of a reckless driver, so he began imagining all kinds of bizarre accidents.

At four-thirty Kev finally called.

"Where the hell *are* you?" Billy demanded, accepting a piña colada from a statuesque poolside waitress. "This is the kind of event I need you at to run protection."

"Protection?" Kev snorted. "What am I, a friggin' bodyguard?"

"Yeah, you're supposed t'do everything for me, Kev. That's our deal. I pay, you do."

"Nice," Kev said disgustedly. "What happened to friendship?"

"C'*mon*, you know you should be here, so once again—where are you?"

"The truth?"

"No, lie to me."

"You're gonna get mad . . ."

"Why's that, Kev?" Billy said, thoroughly fed up with Kev's antics. "'Cause if you tell me you smashed up my Maserati, I'll get so freakin' mad you won't even know what hit you."

"Your precious car's fine. In fact, we're in it now."

"Who's we?"

"Ali and me," Kev said, his voice muffled.

"You brought Ali, huh?"

"Yeah, an' before you go off on a rant, here's the news of the day. We, uh . . . we got married."

"You did *what?*" Billy exploded, almost spilling his drink.

"Married. Hitched. Ain't that something?"

"Oh jeez!" Billy exclaimed. "You really are a piece of work."

~ ~ ~

"How much money did you invest in this hotel?" Ling asked Alex as they checked in.

"Enough," he replied, signing his name on the register.

"And how long before your investment pays off?"

"With Lucky in charge, not too long," he answered, irritated that she felt free to question him.

"Lucky, Lucky, Lucky," Ling muttered. "You're obsessed with that woman."

"Stop with the bitching," Alex groaned. "Otherwise I'll be sorry I brought you along."

"I'm your girlfriend, Alex," Ling said. "Of course I should be with you."

"Then quit making me crazy."

"Easy. If *you* quit lusting after Lucky Santangelo."

"Oh, for God's sake!" he muttered.

"This way, Mr. Woods," said a helpful manager. "I'll be escorting you to your suite."

~ ~ ~

"I was thinkin' I could go play tennis, Mom," Gino Junior said.

"Go ahead," Lucky said, delighted that her youngest son showed such a passion for sports. Lennie insisted it kept him out of trouble, and Lucky often wished that Max was into sports—it would probably make things a lot less explosive.

"D'you think Bobby'll play?" Gino Junior wanted to know.

"Go ask him. There's eight courts and a championship pro just waiting."

"I will. And, oh yeah, your hotel rocks, Mom."

"Yes?"

"Totally."

Yes, she thought, *my hotel rocks. And why not? I put my heart and soul into it.*

Gino Junior ran off just as she got a call from Max informing her they were minutes away. Lucky wanted to check out this new friend of Max's, so she headed for the front of the hotel to greet them.

~ ~ ~

After Venus finished rehearsing she returned to the penthouse suite where she was not thrilled to find Kev, some young girl, and Billy, all drinking champagne. Exactly what she *didn't* need.

She'd never really discussed it with Billy, but she considered Kev to be a bad influence. She and Billy's best friend had never warmed to each other—they'd always kept their distance—and she was certain that Kev put her down behind her back. Before she and Billy had become a couple, Kev was always talking about the parade of gorgeous girls Billy had had, and the amazing events, clubs, and parties the two of them had attended on a nightly basis. Obviously Kev did not appreciate her putting a stop to all the partying. Now *she* did not appreciate him lounging around in their suite swigging champagne with a young blonde.

"What's going on?" she asked, shooting Billy a look. "Are we celebrating something?"

"Hi, babe," Billy said, getting up and giving her a hug. "'S'matter of fact we are."

"We are?" she said coolly.

"Yeah, um, this is Ali. Kev and Ali just got married."

"Wow!" Venus said, quite surprised. "And how long have you known this young lady, Kev?"

"We go way back," Kev said, a bit sheepishly.

"Actually," Ali said, quickly joining in, "we only met a couple of weeks ago, but Kev's so great, I feel as if I've known him forever."

"Yeah," Kev agreed. "Getting married was a spur-of-the-moment thing. Y'know, bein' in Vegas an' all. I said, 'Let's do it,' an' Ali was way into it."

"How nice," Venus said. "Congratulations to the two of you. I guess that's what the champagne is all about."

"Have a glass," Billy said.

"Not right now," she answered, shooting Billy another look.

"Kev, you should go find your room," Billy said, catching Venus's disapproving vibe. "We'll get together later and celebrate properly."

"Sure," Kev said, getting the hint. "C'mon, Ali, we gotta go."

Ali was busy staring at Venus, which totally alarmed Billy. Was she about to say something incriminating, such as, "I fucked your boyfriend. Oh yes, and I went down on him too"?

No, she wouldn't do that.

Or would she?

"Okay, guys," Billy said, hustling them out the door. "Later."

~ ~ ~

And somewhere in Vegas, Tucker Bond was busy putting everything in place. Two days earlier he'd driven his large truck into the city and settled himself and his two-woman crew at a convenient motel.

Tucker was a heavyset man in his late forties with weather-beaten skin, sunken eyes, and a thrice-broken nose. Australian by birth, Tucker had lived in America for more than thirty years, although he'd never lost his strong Australian accent. Tucker was a man for hire, and over the years he'd developed quite a reputation for getting things done. Anything.

Tucker didn't care what he did or who he did it for, as long as the price was right.

Destroying the Keys was costing someone a million bucks. Tucker had already made sure the job would take place without a hitch.

Paying for Tucker Bond meant getting the best. Whatever the client wanted, he made sure it happened.

Tucker Bond never failed to deliver.

79

"Hi, Mom," Max said, leaping out of Ace's truck, long dark hair flying, green eyes sparkling.

"Hey, Max," Lucky said warmly. She'd made up her mind to put Max's bad behavior behind her and try for a stress-free weekend.

"Uh . . . this is Ace," Max said, hanging tightly on to his arm, her multiple gold bracelets jangling.

"Nice to meet you, Ace," Lucky said, immediately realizing that her daughter was suffering from a major crush. And why not? Ace was tall and lanky with an almost surfer-dude look. He had mesmerizing blue eyes that almost matched his light blue denim work shirt, and an appealing cleft in his chin. He was also older than Max by several years. Lucky had to stop herself from asking exactly *how* old he was.

"Your grandfather really wants to see you," she said. "And don't forget to wish him a happy birthday."

"Like I would forget," Max said a tad scornfully.

"Oh, yes," Lucky added, "and you'd better apologize for not being at his party. You'll find him in the Santangelo Lounge."

"The *what?*" Max asked, stifling a giggle.

"Don't start with me, Max," Lucky said, walking them into the lobby of the hotel. "It's called the Santangelo Lounge in honor of Gino."

"Of course it is," Max said, shooting Ace a quick look.

"You can go check in at the front desk first," Lucky said. "Everything's arranged. Max, you're sharing a room with Cookie, and Ace, you're in with Harry."

"Thanks, Mrs. Golden," Ace said. He was shell-shocked by Max's mom—a stone-cold fox—not to mention the opulence of the hotel.

"The reception starts at six on the main terrace," Lucky said. "Try not to be late."

"Do we get a tour of the hotel?" Max asked, not bothering to mention that Harry wouldn't be coming. "It looks totally awesome!"

"Go find Bobby," Lucky said. "He'll show you around."

"Oh great! He's here!" Max exclaimed, turning to Ace. "Bobby's my older brother," she continued, excited by the thought of seeing him. "Bobby's *major* cool, you'll *so* like him."

"Yes, you will," Lucky said. "Bobby's a trip."

"Where's Dad?" Max asked.

"Playing golf with Charlie Dollar."

"I want to see him."

"You will," Lucky said. "So . . . I have a million things to do. Are you two all set?"

"Uh, thanks, Mrs. Golden," Ace said again, trying hard not to stare, for Lucky was not what he'd expected at all. "It's an honor to be here."

At least he's polite, Lucky thought. *And he seems like a nice enough kid, although they all do until they have your daughter half undressed in the back of a parked car. And Max is only sixteen. A wild little sixteen-year-old with a mind of her own and a major rebellious streak.*

Hmm . . . polite and hot. Her teenage daughter was in heaven.

~ ~ ~

"How long have Kev and that girl really known each other?" Venus asked once Kev and Ali had left.

"I'm sure they go way back," Billy said, keeping it as ambiguous as possible. "You know Kev, he's always hanging with a different girl."

"Yes, I do know Kev. That's why I find it so surprising he should get married. Where exactly did he meet this one?"

"Dunno," Billy said vaguely. "She might've been an extra on the movie."

"Hmm . . ." Venus sighed, rapidly losing interest. "I don't know about you, but I'm exhausted." She flopped onto the couch, stretching languorously. "Although I do have to admit it's quite invigorating getting back into the swing of things. My backup dancers are full of amazing energy, and so they should be, considering they're all ten years younger than me."

"Ten?" Billy teased.

"Okay, *twenty* years younger than me," she admitted, laughing. "God, that makes me feel so *old*."

"You? Old? *Never*," Billy said gallantly. "I'm gonna be thirty in two years—guess that'll be *my* time to feel old."

"It's different for men."

"No it's not."

"You're right. Why'd I say such a stupid sexist thing? Me—who's never bought in to that Hollywood bullshit. It's not different for men at all. Women can screw from thirteen to a hundred and thirteen. Men have the problem of getting it up, only now they've got Viagra to do it for them."

"Never tried Viagra."

"Oh, baby, believe me, you don't need to."

He yawned, relieved that Kev and his new bride were long gone. "How about we take a little siesta?" he suggested.

"How about I can't. My makeup and hair people will be here any minute."

"Tell 'em to come later. You don't need to spend *that* much time getting ready."

"Lucky wants us to go drop by the reception—we can't let her down—and later the place will be jammed with press and camera crews, so yes, I've got to get all glammed up."

"Whatever you do, you're always the sexiest woman in the room, glammed up or not."

"I am?"

"You know it, babe."

"So," she said, basking in his compliments. "What did *you* end up doing today?"

"Craps. Poker. Blackjack."

"My own Mister Predictable. Did you lose it all back?"

"What do *you* think?" he said, grinning.

"Yes."

"Easy come, easy go, an' tonight I'll be a winner again."

"Oh, Billy," she sighed. "What *am* I going to do with you?"

"Follow me into the bedroom, my sexy little superstar, and allow me to show you."

"I'm right behind you," she said, jumping up.

~ ~ ~

"So," Max said as they walked around the edge of the main swimming pool after spending time with Gino, Bobby, Brigette, and the rest of the family. "What's your take?"

"On what?" Ace replied.

"Everything. The hotel. My mom. My granddad. And especially Bobby."

"I think you've all led a charmed life of money and privilege."

That was not the answer she'd wanted to hear. She refused to be viewed as a spoiled rich kid with famous affluent parents and rich relatives. She was her own person. Max. And more than anything she wanted Ace to see that.

"Charmed life—not so much," she said defensively.

"C'*mon*, Max," he said, giving her a quizzical look.

"What?" she said. "You think it's *easy* having parents who've achieved so many things?"

"Better than having no parents at all," he pointed out.

"You've got me there," she said, realizing how tough it must have been for him losing his mom and dad.

"Lucky doesn't seem like a dragon lady," he observed. "If you want my opinion I think we should've told her about the kidnapping thing."

"Why's that?"

" 'Cause it was bad, Max," he said, frowning. "The freak had a gun. He had *you* chained like a dog, and me locked up. What if he's still out there trying to do it to somebody else?"

"You don't understand," she said, agitated. "Lucky would've blamed *me*. She'd think I was weak and unable to look after myself."

"No she wouldn't."

"You met her for five minutes," Max said sharply. "That doesn't mean you *know* her."

"Okay, okay," he said, realizing he'd hit a sensitive spot. "I get it."

"No you *don't*," she said sulkily. "You've fallen under Lucky's spell. Everyone does. Whenever I'm around her it's like I become invisible."

"In *your* mind."

"Whatever. She's so clever and beautiful and smart. It's crap trying to live up to all of that."

"Hey, Max," he said, stopping and taking hold of her shoulders. "You got *any* idea how hot you are?"

"Me?" she said, staring into his blue eyes.

"No," he deadpanned. "That girl over there."

"I'm so hot that you didn't even kiss me last night," she said, regretting the words as soon as they left her mouth. She probably sounded like dork of the month.

"You're sixteen," he pointed out.

"So was Lucky when she got married the first time."

"Get over it, you're not in a competition with your mom."

"Says who?" she said, moving away from him and sitting on the end of a lounger.

"Says me," he said, squatting down next to her.

"Do y'know why I tried to hook up with that freak from the Internet?" she said, gazing at the ripples in the pool.

"Go ahead, surprise me."

"It's 'cause I wanted to show my ex-boyfriend that he lost out."

"And how were you going to do that?"

"My plan was to sleep with the creep—although when I decided that's what I'd do I thought I was like meeting up with this totally interesting smart dude. Then psycho man appears. Ugh! Gross!"

"So you're a—"

"Virgin. Yes! I admit it," she said, blushing. "How lame is that?"

"Shows you're selective."

"More like retarded," she mumbled.

"Not retarded, Max, cute."

"Cute!" she exclaimed in horror. "I hate that word, it's totally . . ."

"What?"

"I dunno, but I'll think of something."

"Yeah," he said, starting to grin. "You'll think of something, you always do."

~ ~ ~

Henry Whitfield-Simmons checked into a luxury bungalow at the Cavendish under a false name. Lord Grant was the name he'd chosen. It had a ring to it, suggesting that he could indeed be an English Lord.

He'd changed the plates on Penelope's Bentley, and he was paying for everything with cash.

Being anonymous was quite freeing. Nobody knew who he was or anything about him, and that suited him just fine. All they knew was that he tipped lavishly, wore the best Brioni had to offer, and drove a Bentley.

It was enough.

80

Anthony demanded two premier bungalows, which infuriated Renee because she had not realized he would be arriving with an entourage. He turned up with his wife, grandmother, mistress, assistant, and bodyguard. Damn him. The hotel was overbooked as it was, and she'd reserved him his usual suite. But no, that wasn't good enough, he wanted two of the best bungalows, forcing her to move a couple of high rollers who threatened never to return.

"I had to throw people out to accommodate you," she complained. "You're a pain in the ass, Anthony."

"You have no idea," he responded.

Yes I do, she wanted to say. But she kept her silence because she knew it would be foolish to speak her mind. Instead she went back to her house on the hotel grounds and bitched to Susie about Anthony's arrival.

"Why is he here?" Susie was curious to know.

"I presume to spend leisure time with his grandmother," Renee said, not revealing the true purpose of Anthony's visit. The less Susie knew, the better. Susie would not understand why certain things had to be done, and if she ever found out she'd try to put a stop to it. Susie did not approve of anything illegal. To say she was naive was an understatement—she honestly believed that Tasmin had disappeared all on her own and that Anthony had nothing to do with it, although she still asked the occasional question.

"Anthony has a grandmother that he actually takes around with him?" Susie asked, her eyes widening.

"He's very Italian when it comes to family," Renee explained. "His wife is with him too."

"Anthony has a wife?"

"Yes, Susie. He has a wife *and* a grandmother. He didn't just crawl out of a hole in the ground."

"You could've fooled me."

"Here's the kicker," Renee said. "His bimbo mistress is also along for the ride."

"Oh my goodness," Susie exclaimed. "How does *that* work? Do you think they're having a threesome?"

"Hardly," Renee said. "The wife looks shell-shocked while the mistress is all perky and ready to party."

"Not with you I hope," Susie said, her jealous streak surfacing at the slightest provocation.

"Of course not with me," Renee assured her insecure partner.

God! If Susie ever found out she'd once slept with Anthony, her life wouldn't be worth living.

"You know," Susie said thoughtfully, "I've been thinking about it, and although I know you're unsure, the Keys opening next door to us is a bonus."

"Excuse me?" Renee said. "Why do you think that?"

"I know you imagine it'll take business away from us," Susie said. "But you're wrong. The Keys being so near to us will enhance our hotel. You'll see. It's all about synergy. We're the two classiest hotels on the Strip, and it'll all work out. I'm happy they're opening, and I also think Lucky can be a good friend to us."

Susie was right. Susie was always right.

Renee's mind began ticking. Yes, now she was sure she had to get Anthony Bonar out of their lives once and for all.

~ ~ ~

Irma was in turmoil. How was she supposed to make sense of the situation she found herself in? It was all so unbelievably horrifying.

Her husband was a cruel and repugnant man, a vindictive inhuman monster. The very thought of what he'd done to Luis would haunt her forever, and worst of all, *she* was responsible, for it was she who'd lured Luis into her bedroom the first time, and if she hadn't done so, none of this would have happened.

Yes, the sad truth was that she was to blame.

Now she was trapped with Anthony, who'd informed her that she was not allowed to speak to anyone or go anywhere without his permission. "You're gonna do exactly what I say," he'd told her. "An' doncha open your fuckin' mouth to anyone, or your parents gonna feel the heat. Understand what I'm sayin'?"

Yes, she understood, and she had no doubt his threats were authentic. After the things she'd witnessed she was genuinely frightened. Anthony was not a bluffer—her psychotic husband was capable of anything. He'd proved that.

"Tonight we're goin' to a party, so go buy a dress an' be prepared t'look like you're enjoyin' yourself," Anthony announced, strolling into the bedroom where he'd made sure she was a prisoner. He'd instructed The Grill to remove the phones and make certain any doors leading outside were locked. There was no escape.

"How can I go shopping?" she cried out. "After everything you've done, how can you expect me to do that?"

"Who gives a shit," he snarled. "S'long as you're ready at six. Buy a decent dress, an' wear your new earrings."

She was forced to visit the shopping mall with The Grill, who stood guard outside a fitting room while she reluctantly chose a plain black dress to wear.

It was all so surreal. Here she was in Las Vegas buying a dress, while back in Mexico City her lover had no doubt bled to death.

Poor Luis. Poor dear, sweet Luis. She remembered his gentle touch and suddenly she was overcome with grief. She sank to the floor of the fitting room and began quietly weeping.

After a while she pulled herself together. Above all else, Anthony had to be punished for his sins.

There must be a way, and she was determined to find it.

~ ~ ~

After arranging invitations to the opening reception at the Keys, Anthony had gone ahead and bought tickets for the concert event, although he wasn't sure if he'd stay around that long. Emmanuelle had informed him she was desperate to see Venus perform. Little did she know that there would be a lot more to observe than an aging blond singer, although the real action would take place to coincide with the fireworks display.

He decided to stay long enough to watch the fun begin, then he'd gather his entourage and get the hell out. A timely exit was one of the advantages of having his own plane.

According to Renee, everything was in place, and by God, she'd better be right. He was expecting results. They were spending a million bucks to make sure the Keys burned to the ground. Tucker Bond was expensive, but according to his reputation he never failed.

Destroying the Keys and making Grandma happy was worth every dollar. Anthony did not regret one red cent.

Not that he planned on paying Renee back—it was *her* responsibility. She could whistle for him to come up with his half.

~ ~ ~

Emmanuelle danced happily around the bungalow, quite taken with the Elton John–style white piano, indoor Jacuzzi, and luxury furnishings. Boarding the plane in Miami, she'd been startled to notice Anthony's wife huddled in one of the seats. "What's *she* doing here?" she'd whispered to Anthony, thinking that if he planned on a cozy threesome, she was a definite no.

"Take no notice of Irma," Anthony had said. "We got an understanding. Ignore her."

So Emmanuelle had done exactly that, playing up to Anthony's grandmother, who was quite a colorful character with her nonstop smoking, incessant coffee drinking, and raspy voice.

As soon as Francesca spotted Emmanuelle, she'd taken Anthony to one side. "Why you do this?" she'd demanded, spoiling for an argument. "Why both women here?"

"One's my wife, one's my mistress," Anthony had explained. "That's the Italian way, right, Grandma?"

"You leave those two together, they'll tear each other to pieces," Francesca had muttered.

"I promise you Irma's gonna do nothin'. She knows t'keep her mouth shut an' stay in her place."

"You and Irma fighting?" Francesca demanded, narrowing her eyes.

"No fight."

"You bloody sure, Anthony?"

"Would I lie to you?"

~ ~ ~

Detective Franklin had cultivated quite a few spies at the Cavendish, and it wasn't long before one of them reported that Anthony Bonar was back in town. This was the news she'd been waiting for. She got in her car and drove straight to the hotel.

For the past few days she'd been contemplating a trip to Miami, where it seemed Anthony Bonar spent most of his time. Now that he was actually back in Vegas he'd saved her the trouble. She had more than a strong hunch that Anthony Bonar knew a lot more about Tasmin's disappearance than he was saying. And Detective Franklin was famous around the department for hunches that usually paid off.

She'd checked Anthony Bonar out. He'd been arrested once many years ago when he was a teenager on a possession-of-drugs charge. A lawyer had sprung him within twenty-four hours, and he'd managed to stay out of jail ever since, although he'd certainly been investigated many times. He was known to be involved in major drug trade activities, but the FBI had never been able to find enough evidence to put him away.

"I'm here to see Mr. Bonar," she informed the desk clerk at reception.

"Do you have an appointment?" the clerk asked.

"No, I do not," Diane Franklin said, flashing her badge. "But somehow I imagine this is appointment enough."

"I'll let him know you're on your way."

~ ~ ~

Tucker Bond worked with two assistants, both female, both adept at whatever job he assigned them. He'd found that women were easier to control than men, and attractive women blended in. They were also a great deal more trustworthy and loyal.

These two had worked for him for more than ten years. They did whatever he told them to do, and no arguments. On this job he was paying them a hundred grand each. Not bad for a few hours' work.

Not bad at all.

~ ~ ~

"Fuck!" Anthony steamed. The last thing he needed was a small-town detective questioning him about Tasmin Garland. He'd answered a shitload of questions over the phone, so what was this about, and why hadn't Renee warned him?

Bitch! They were all bitches. Especially his cheating whore wife, whose fate he had all planned. Watching her boyfriend lose his manhood in front of her was not punishment enough. Oh no. He had more delights in store for her.

Tonight she'd be humiliated.

Tomorrow she'd be shipped off to Bolivia where he'd made arrangements for her to be placed in a facility that craved blond American whores. She'd asked for it. Any woman who screwed another man in the marital bed was asking for it.

If Irma wanted to fuck around, who was he to stop her?

Detective Franklin was full of more dumb questions. Anthony resented her intrusion into his life. Bad enough he had to deal with a detective, but a black female one at that. Shit! What was the fuckin' world coming to?

He answered her questions fast and hustled her out in record time.

The bitch would never get anything on *him.*

81

The opening of the Keys was a much coveted event. Celebrities were jetting in from all over the world, delighted that they'd been invited. Lucky Santangelo and Lennie Golden were a power couple with friends across the globe, and everyone wanted to be there to help them celebrate.

The world press were also assembling. Journalists, camera crews, photographers. *ET, Access Hollywood, Extra, E! News*—they were all there to cover the event.

Security was a top priority—every member of the press had to display a laminated name tag and a red-carpet pass.

Henry Whitfield-Simmons had acquired both. With money, anything was possible.

~ ~ ~

Detective Franklin returned to the precinct more convinced than ever that Anthony Bonar had something to do with Tasmin's disappearance. Now that she'd actually met the man face-to-face he struck her as a lying scumbag in an expensive suit. She'd come across his type before. Anthony Bonar was the kind of man who imagined money could buy him anything and anybody. He was involved with Tasmin's disappearance, she would bet her life on it. And as for Renee Falcon, she knew a lot more than she was saying, that was for sure. Her girlfriend had given her away. Her girlfriend had more or less accused Anthony of having something to do with Tasmin's disappearance.

The way Diane Franklin saw it, Renee had fixed Anthony Bonar up on a date with Tasmin and something had gone horribly wrong.

But what? That was the big question.

~ ~ ~

"What do you think?" Lucky asked, emerging from her dressing room in a floor-length scarlet Versace backless gown, Jimmy Choo stilettos, diamond earrings, and Neil Lane black-and-white Art Deco diamond bracelets decorating both wrists.

Lennie whistled as he checked out his wife. "I swear I've never seen you look so staggeringly beautiful," he exclaimed. "You're incredible."

"I mean what do you think of my dress?" she said modestly.

"It's not the dress I'm concerned with, it's the body underneath."

"Lennie!" she said, smiling. "Be serious."

"The dress is a smash."

"Not too revealing?" she asked, twirling for him.

"If I had my way you'd be hidden under a burka. I don't enjoy other men ogling my woman."

"I'm your woman, am I?" she teased.

"Now and forever."

"Good, 'cause that's the way I like it."

"Can I fix you a drink?" he asked.

"How about a martini," she said, walking out onto the spacious terrace overlooking the sparkling lights of the city.

"Coming right up."

As she stood gazing out at the spectacular view, her thoughts drifted back to the opening of the Magiriano, her first Vegas hotel. This time it was better, because this time she had Lennie and her family beside her.

It was exciting. More exciting than owning and running a major movie studio. More exciting than all the other businesses she'd been involved with.

Yes. The Keys was her ultimate prize.

She often wondered why she felt such close ties to Vegas, although deep down she knew why. It was the place it had all begun for her when she'd taken over from Gino and finished building the Magiriano. It was the place where she'd become a woman of substance, a woman capable of doing anything.

Now here she was, opening her dream hotel, and everything was perfect.

Well . . . almost . . .

Something was bothering her. Something that she'd dismissed over the past few weeks as a frivolous invitation to a party or event. Bobby had been concerned, and maybe rightfully so, because over the last twenty-four hours she'd received two more handwritten hand-delivered notes, similar to the ones she'd received in L.A. Only now, instead of saying *Drop Dead Beautiful*, the word *Beautiful* had been replaced with *Bitch*.

Drop Dead Bitch. And the word *Bitch* was scrawled in what looked like blood.

This was no invitation. This was a threat.

And since Lucky was not the kind of woman to be intimidated, she'd decided to deal with it after the opening.

Nothing was about to spoil her night of triumph.

~ ~ ~

Emmanuelle appeared in the living room of their bungalow wearing a shiny gold sequin number, short to show off her legs, low-cut to show off her tits, and dipping at the back to show off the beginning of her ass crack.

Her blond hair was piled high, and her lips were pouty and full. Francesca informed Anthony in a hoarse stage whisper that his mistress resembled a street hooker. Anthony didn't care, Francesca had no idea what girls looked like today, and as far as he was concerned, Emmanuelle was every man's walking wet dream, a cover-girl fantasy in the flesh.

"Irma!" Anthony yelled, prowling around the living room. "Get your ass out here."

Irma appeared from the bedroom. She was twelve years older than Emmanuelle and tonight she looked it. Though she'd once been a glowing beauty queen, Anthony had managed to turn her into a tense and unhappy woman wearing a black dress and the diamond drop earrings he'd insisted she put on.

She refused to even glance at Emmanuelle, which suited Emmanuelle, because she'd already decided that the only way to deal with the wife situation was to ignore her. If Anthony was playing games it was all right with her, as long as *she* wasn't involved.

"Take off your earrings," Anthony commanded his wife. "Take 'em off an' give 'em to Emmanuelle."

Irma stared at her husband, unbridled hatred in her eyes.

"Take 'em off," Anthony repeated, "before I rip 'em off your fuckin' ears."

Irma reached up and removed her diamond drop earrings.

"Give 'em to Emmanuelle," Anthony instructed, enjoying this little scene. "They're hers now."

"You think I care?" Irma said, through clenched teeth. "You think I give a damn?"

"Shut the fuck up an' hand 'em over," Anthony said, annoyed that she still had some fight left in her.

Irma took off the earrings and threw them on the floor, infuriating Anthony even more.

He jumped forward and slapped his wife across the face, his pinky ring cutting into the delicate skin on her cheek, drawing blood.

Fortunately, Francesca chose that moment to walk back into the room. Her flinty eyes took in the scene, and she began screaming at her grandson in Italian.

Anthony glared at her, but he backed off and walked over to the bar where he poured himself a hefty tumbler of Scotch.

Emmanuelle picked up the earrings from the floor—she wasn't allowing *them* to go to waste—while Irma retreated to the bedroom.

Anthony downed his drink and stared at his blond mistress as she put on the earrings and paraded in front of him.

On Emmanuelle they looked fake. Stupid, fake baubles, like her stupid, fake tits.

Sometimes everything wasn't enough.

~ ~ ~

"Can you believe she put Ace on a different floor?" Max complained. "It's like she *totally* doesn't trust me."

"Wise woman, your mom," Cookie said, rolling her eyes as they both stood in front of the bathroom mirror applying gloss and mascara and gold shimmer and all other kinds of makeup enhancements, readying themselves for the night ahead.

"Whose side are you on, anyway?" Max asked, smudging black eyeliner to give her eyes a smoky look.

"I'm on the side of anyone who can find me a hottie of my own tonight," Cookie replied, picking up the curling tongs and attacking her hair.

"There should be plenty around," Max remarked. "She's got most of young Hollywood putting in an appearance. I took a peek at the list."

"You did?" Cookie said, trying not to appear too excited. "Any sexy young Will Smiths on it? He's *sooo* hot for an old dude."

"Not my type."

"Course he isn't," Cookie grumbled. "You've got your own personal hottie stashed in a room he's *not* sharing with Harry. Man, you're gonna have a wicked time!"

"I can only hope," Max said, applying blusher. "Thing is, I'm not so sure he's into me, he kinda thinks I'm too young."

"You gotta *play* it, girl," Cookie advised. "You know how to do that, don't you?"

"Kinda. Sorta."

Cookie piled on the lip gloss. "What did Lucky say about him?"

Max shrugged. "Dunno. She was all over the place."

The phone rang and Max picked up.

"Miss Golden, this is the front desk."

"Yes?"

"Your cousin requested that you meet him outside the spa in fifteen minutes."

"My cousin?" Max said, frowning.

"That is correct, Miss Golden."

"Oh, my cousin!" she said, giggling as she put the phone down.

"What's going on?" Cookie asked.

"It's Ace," Max said, a grin spreading across her face. "Y'see, Internet Freak thought that Ace was my cousin, so now Ace is into the game. He wants me to meet him outside the spa."

"I thought we were all going to the party together."

"Is it okay if we see you there? You don't mind, do you?"

"Why would I mind?" Cookie said sarcastically. "I'm totally psyched walking in by myself."

"Not to worry, we'll get there before you," Max said, excited at the thought of seeing Ace. "Quick, pass me the tongs, I've got to get downstairs pronto!"

"Okay, go have fun."

"I will," Max said, pulling on her favorite Seven Jeans and a slinky red silk tank. "Do I look hot?" she questioned, staring at herself in the mirror.

"Sizzling!"

"Really?" she said unsurely.

"Go get him, girl. It's time."

~ ~ ~

Detective Franklin was still sitting at her desk thinking about her meeting with Anthony Bonar when a male colleague dumped a package on her desk.

"This came addressed to you," he said.

"What is it, a bomb?" she joked.

There was a running gag at the precinct that anytime an unidentified package appeared, it had to be a bomb.

"No chance. It's kinda soft."

"Hmm . . . like you were last night on your hot date," Detective Franklin said.

The other detectives in the room roared with laughter.

"Who's opening it?" she asked.

"Your turn," the male detective said.

"Am I the only one with stones around here?" she asked, ripping open the package.

"You said it," the guys chorused.

The package contained a bloodstained white bathrobe from the Cavendish Hotel. Pinned to it was a crude hand-drawn map, and a piece of paper with cut-out letters from a newspaper spelling out TASMIN and ANTHONY BONAR.

"Someone get this to the lab immediately and have tests done right away," Detective Franklin said, adrenaline coursing. "Blood, semen, hair, and anything else they can come up with. I think we got us a body and a killer. Let's go!"

82

"How come *I* didn't get to meet Max's latest victim?" Lennie asked as their private elevator descended to the terrace level.

"Because," Lucky replied, holding tightly on to his hand, "you were out on the golf course having a great time with Charlie Dollar when they arrived."

"Is this the boy Max was in Big Bear with?"

"Apparently so. According to her, he saved her ass from a gang of carjackers—or so she says. Personally, I think she came across him online, met up with him in Big Bear, and fell in first love."

"First love?" Lennie questioned.

"Oh, you know. Or maybe you don't—you're not a girl."

"Gee, you noticed!" he drawled.

"Anyway, first love is special," Lucky said, matter-of-factly. "It's all-consuming and usually involves rejection. My opinion is that this boy isn't as into Max as she is into him. He's older and killer handsome, so he'll break her heart, forcing her to realize that all men aren't perfect, and that'll prepare her for the reality of life, so it's all good."

"Jeez!" Lennie whistled. "My wife the cynic."

"It's called training."

"And who trained *you?*"

"I had to learn all by myself."

"You're a hard woman."

She reached up and softly caressed his cheek. "Did I tell you how handsome you look in your tux?"

"No. You take me for granted."

"Lennie," she chided, "you are the one man I will *never* take for granted."

"Promise?"

"Bet on it."

~ ~ ~

Lord Grant, aka Henry Whitfield-Simmons, left the Cavendish and drove his Bentley to the Keys. He had passes for the reception and tickets for the lingerie show and concert. Tickets he had no intention of using, for by the time the show started, he and Maria would be busy getting reacquainted.

~ ~ ~

"We should get married, Alex," Ling said, surprising him in the shower.

"You're not bringing *that* up again," Alex responded as his beautiful naked Asian girlfriend with the straight pubic hair and inappropriate fake tits sunk to her knees and began doing things to him he could never resist.

He leaned back against the side of the shower as Ling went to work. She was an excellent lawyer, but her real talent lay in her delicate tongue—a tongue that could perform feats resulting in extraordinary sexual pleasure.

"Jesus, honey," he groaned, giving himself up to the moment. "I don't want to be late . . ."

Oh no, Ling thought, *mustn't be late for Lucky. That would never do. Lucky always has to come first. Lucky! Lucky! Lucky!* She was so sick and tired of his obsession.

Soon she had his full attention as she employed her talents to their best advantage. Ling had learned at a very young age how to bring a man to the brink of orgasm and then take him back, just a tad, so that by the time he actually came, it was an orgasm of mammoth proportions.

Alex knew nothing of her early life in China where she'd been raised in a house of ill repute, before managing to escape at the age of fourteen, thanks to a married American businessman fifty years her senior. The man had brought her to America, set her up in an apartment, and financed her education. In return she'd given him the best sex of his life.

He'd died ten years ago a happy man. She'd gone on to pass the bar and become an extremely accomplished divorce lawyer at one of L.A.'s most prestigious law firms.

Meeting Alex Woods was the finest moment of her life. She admired his blazing talent and unbridled masculinity—she'd always been a big fan of his films.

Shortly after moving in with him she'd decided she wanted to marry him, but Alex was forever resistant, in spite of her unusual sexual prowess.

Over the two years they'd been together she'd convinced herself that Lucky Santangelo Golden was the reason for his reluctance to make the ultimate commitment. Without Lucky, there would be no problem.

In Ling's eyes Alex Woods harbored an obsessive love for Lucky Santangelo Golden that was not healthy. It was up to her to do something about it.

Tonight she might get the opportunity to do just that.

~ ~ ~

The grand terrace of the Keys was the perfect setting for a party: creamy limestone floors and towering Italian marble columns, giant urns filled with a profusion of purple bougainvillea, and thousands of white candles in silver holders.

As Lucky entered, still holding Lennie's arm, the sight of everything took her breath away. She felt an enormous surge of adrenaline as she looked around, realizing that all the hard work of putting this project together had been worth it. Five years ago she'd had an idea. Now, here it was—the Keys. Her hotel. Her palace. She was queen of her kingdom.

"Amazing!" Lennie whispered in her ear before they were separated and she was swept up in a sea of people congratulating her. She went with the flow, accepting the many compliments coming her way, graciously kissing cheeks and shaking hands. It was a whirlwind of activity, and no press. The press were not allowed into the reception—they were stationed outside on the red carpet, which would serve as a pathway to the lingerie show and Venus's appearance.

Lucky had an army of people working for her, and they were all doing a fantastic job. From the P.R.'s to the caterers, security, and management, everyone was in top form, making sure there wasn't a glitch in sight. Spotting Gino, she attempted to make her way toward him, but before she could get very far, Alex blocked her path. "Hey, you," he said. "I see you got yourself quite a turnout. Shame you're not popular."

"We're in business," she said, smiling. "Now I'll have to concentrate on paying back all my investors in record time. Think there's a chance?"

"No hurry on my account," he said, leaning in.

She took a step back just as Ling appeared, sleek in a white Valentino suit.

"Don't *you* look lovely," Lucky said to the Asian woman. "How come you're still hanging around with this old fart?"

Ling lacked a sense of humor, especially when it came to Alex. "Good evening, Lucky," she said, her expression tight and unfriendly. "Please do not call Alex names. He may look like he gets the joke, but I can assure you he doesn't. Later, *I'm* the one who has to deal with his bad mood."

"Now *wait* a minute—" Alex objected.

"Hey, hey, hey, here's my Lucky lady," Charlie Dollar, movie icon supreme, drawled, sweeping in between them. "Gotta big fat boner this joint's gonna make it."

"Charlie!" Lucky exclaimed, relieved to move away from Ling's icy demeanor. "I'm so glad you could come."

"Wouldn't miss a Lucky Santangelo event," Charlie said, Cheshire cat grin firmly in place. "Gotta tell ya, nobody does it better."

"Thanks, Charlie, that means a lot coming from you."

"Gotta give props where props are due," he said, stoned eyes checking out the possibilities.

"You are *the* most supportive friend, and I love you for it," Lucky said, kissing him on the cheek.

"Calm down, chickadee, don't go gettin' all sentimental on me. I cry at the sight of emotion."

Charlie always made her smile. "I'll try not to," she said.

"Just came from the lingerie rehearsal. Wowee! Hot bods in Technicolor action. Excellent move not bringin' a date."

"I'm sure you'll have fun tonight, Charlie."

"Don't I always?" he said, another enormous grin crossing his weathered face.

"Oh yes," she agreed. "Got no doubts on *that* score."

Finally she made it over to Gino, who was surrounded by family and friends.

"I'm feelin' the excitement, kiddo," Gino rasped. "You got yourself another hit!"

"I hope so."

"I *know* so."

~ ~ ~

Anthony Bonar wore Armani. Emmanuelle wore Tramp of the Day. Irma wore a dazed expression. Francesca wore a faded black dress and an embroidered shawl. The Grill wore an ill-fitting suit and a threatening expression.

As a group they stood out.

Irma could not understand why Anthony was doing this to her. Surely he would prefer *not* to see her? Yet he was keeping her close, with The Grill always hovering.

The image of Luis being mutilated refused to go away—it was constant. She could see his face, hear his agonizing screams, while she'd been forced to sit there watching helplessly as her lover was butchered.

Anthony was evil, and the second the opportunity arose she was running.

It didn't matter that she had no money and nowhere to run to. Anything was better than staying with Anthony Bonar. He was a true monster.

~ ~ ~

Susie wanted to attend the reception at the Keys. Renee wasn't so sure it was a good idea to go, but Susie was insistent, so they went.

The first person they bumped into was Anthony Bonar, swaggering around with his trampy-looking girlfriend in tow, while his wife and grandmother trailed behind him with the hulking bodyguard he was never without.

"What the fuck you two doin' here?" was his opening comment.

"Why shouldn't we be here, Anthony?" Susie replied, speaking up for once, because usually in Anthony's presence she never said a word.

"Renee knows why," Anthony said. "It don't look right."

"Nonsense!" Susie replied. "This hotel opening next to us will be excellent for business."

"Are you fuckin' stupid?" Anthony growled.

"As far as I'm concerned," Susie retaliated, "there's only one stupid person around here."

Renee quickly jumped between them. Since when had Susie decided to take on Anthony Bonar? That was *her* job.

"Susie, dear," she said. "Can you do me a favor and go talk to the mayor? He's over there. I'll join you in a minute."

Susie threw Anthony a baleful look and walked away.

"Dumb cunt," Anthony muttered.

"Excuse me?" Renee said.

"Dumb cunt," Anthony repeated.

"That's my partner you're talking about."

"Yeah. I know. She's dumb an' she's a cunt."

Renee stared at the man she'd had so many dealings with over the years. The man who'd bled money from her hotel and given nothing back. The man who'd always made her feel that she owed him everything. The man who'd murdered a woman and showed nothing but a cold indifference.

Payback was a bitch. A bitch Anthony Bonar was about to meet head-on.

83

"I want to go over to Gino Santangelo, see if he remembers me," Francesca said, pulling on Anthony's sleeve. She'd spotted her old love across the terrace and was all set on facing him.

"Are you fuckin' *crazy?*" Anthony responded. "You're not doin' any such thing."

"*Sí*, Anthony," Francesca replied, a stubborn gleam in her faded eyes. "You and me, we go over *now*."

"Aren't you listening to me?" Anthony said, raising his voice. "Read my fuckin' lips: No fuckin' way."

"Don't you tell *me* what to do, Anthony," Francesca raged, pointing a bony be-ringed finger at him. "*I'm* the one took you out of Italy, gave you a life, a business. *You* don't tell *me* what to do, *I* tell *you*."

"Jesus Christ, Grandma."

"Come," she said authoritatively.

"Keep an eye on these two," he muttered to The Grill. "Don't let either of them outta your sight, understand?"

"Yes, boss."

"And you," he said to his mistress. "Stay put."

"Sure, honey," Emmanuelle purred, although she had no intention of doing so. She was in heaven—she'd never seen so many stars gathered in one place. She already had her eye on Charlie Dollar. Oh yes, Charlie Dollar might be ancient, but he was still raging hot in a Jack Nicholson kind of way. And to Emmanuelle he was a sizzling superstar. She'd seen every movie he'd ever made and she considered herself his biggest fan.

Tonight Emmanuelle was determined to score a piece of Mr. Dollar. Absolutely determined.

~ ~ ~

"Wow!" Billy said, looking around. "This is quite a star-studded event. Even *I'm* impressed."

"I told you," Venus replied. "Lucky sure knows how to pull 'em out."

"Yeah, and the fact that you're performing later has a little something to do with it too," Billy pointed out.

"Yes?"

"Yeah, baby," Billy said, feeling exceptionally close to her. "Face it—you're an icon, a living legend."

"I'm glad you said 'living,'" she joked.

"You're living, you're breathing, you're beautiful, and I've been thinking—"

"I know," she said teasingly. "You've been thinking that you can't wait to get back to the craps tables as soon as possible. How well I know you!"

"That wasn't what I was thinking at all."

"Hmm . . . let me see. You want to throw Kev a day-of-the-wedding bachelor party with strippers and lap dancers and—"

"Wrong," he interrupted.

"Okay, I'm stumped. What *were* you thinking?"

"I was thinking if Kev can do it, why can't we?"

"Excuse me?"

"You an' me, babe. Why don't *we* get married?"

She took a deep breath. *This* was a surprise. "You're not serious?"

"Your divorce is final, right?" he said, thinking that he was expecting a more enthusiastic response.

"Yes."

"Then there's nothing to stop us."

"Nothing to stop us from doing what?"

"You know, getting married."

"Oh, *wow!* You really are serious, aren't you?"

"Yes, Venus, I am. We've been together almost a year, and I've got a strong vibe we should give it a shot. Whaddya say?"

Before she could say anything at all, Bobby and Brigette descended on them.

"Some party, huh?" Bobby said. "Fantastic turnout. Looking forward to your show, Venus. Hope you're planning to sing all my favorites."

"I'll try, but you'll have to tell me what they are," she replied, still trying to process Billy's sudden desire to get married.

"You got three hours?" Bobby said. " 'Cause if you have, I'll tell you. By the way, you look spectacular, as always. Billy, I hope you realize you're one *very* fortunate guy."

"Don't I know it," Billy agreed.

"Y'know," Bobby continued, "when I was twelve—"

"Stop it!" Brigette interrupted. "Venus is not interested in hearing about your teenage fantasies."

"They were hot," Bobby assured her. "Very, very hot!"

"Quiet!" Brigette scolded.

"Uh, Billy," Venus said, turning to her boyfriend. "Remember that question you asked me?"

"*The* question?" he said, gulping down a glass of champagne.

"Well," she said slowly, "I've been considering my answer."

"You have?" he said, swapping glasses with a passing waiter.

"Yes," she said, smiling. "I have."

"And?" he said, nervous as hell, for what if she said no? If she rejected him he'd be gutted, his ego would take a giant nosedive. Christ! He'd actually proposed.

"My answer is . . . yes," she said, putting him out of his misery.

"It is?" A huge grin spread across his face. "You're sure?"

"I couldn't be more sure."

"What's up with you two?" Bobby asked curiously. "Something you want to share?"

"Maybe we'll all meet up later," Billy said, keeping it casual. "We'll share then."

"Suits me," Bobby said. "I'll be hitting the tables right after the show."

"So will I," Brigette said, joining in. "What's the point of having all this money if I can't lose it!"

"You're my kind of heiress," Billy quipped, still feeling nervous but in a kind of ecstatic way. She'd said yes! Venus had said yes! He was marrying a superstar!

No. Big correction. He was marrying the woman he loved.

"Is that an offer?" Brigette joked. " 'Cause I'm available."

"*Now* she tells me," Billy said, still grinning.

"Venus, is he making me an offer?" Brigette asked, all big blue eyes and innocent expression.

Venus smiled. "Right now I truly suspect that it's highly unlikely."

~ ~ ~

"I'm going back to the suite before the show," Alex said. "Forgot my watch."

"I'll come with you," Ling said.

"You don't have to."

"I want to."

"No, you go ahead, save our seats."

"But Alex— "

"Ling. I am perfectly capable of going to the suite by myself."

"Very well," she said, giving him the pissy look he couldn't stand.

"Where's Lucky?" he asked.

"Why?" Ling sniped. "You wish *her* to go with you?"

"Oh, for chrissakes!" he snapped. "Get over this thing you have against Lucky. I merely need to ask her how the fuck I get out of here without doing that red-carpet press shit."

"I'm sure someone else can help you with that," Ling said. "It doesn't *always* have to be Lucky." She paused, glared at him, then added, "Or maybe it does."

"Piss off, Ling," he said, stalking away from her.

~ ~ ~

"Gino Santangelo," Francesca crowed, wrinkling her forehead. "So many years, so much time. Surely you remember me?"

Peering at the old woman, Gino realized there was something vaguely familiar about her. "Sorry . . ." he muttered. "You're gonna havta remind me."

"Francesca Bonnatti," she said, tilting her chin. "And this my grandson Anthony Bonar."

Gino felt the hairs on the back of his neck stand up. Of course, Enzio's wife, and now widow. What the hell was *she* doing at the opening of Lucky's hotel? And he'd never heard of Enzio having a grandson named Anthony.

Why was Francesca here? And even more important—what did she want?

"Long time, Gino," she said, her eyes vindictive and glittering with hate. "Long time—much water under the bridge, *sí*?"

He had nothing to say to her.

"And your daughter, Lucky, she the one built this hotel, *sí*?"

Gino's mind started racing. His onetime partner and Lucky's godfather, Enzio Bonnatti, had arranged for the murder of his wife and son, and in retaliation Lucky had shot Enzio.

Francesca and he were both well aware of these past events. They were two families pitched against each other forever. Two endless vendettas. The Santangelos and the Bonnattis. They hated each other.

Now Francesca was standing in front of him as if nothing had happened in their dark and ominous past.

"You and me," Francesca mused. "We go back *molti* years, Gino."

"What do you want?" he said guardedly. "What are you doing here?"

"I come to see."

"See what?"

"To see the end of the Santangelos," Francesca said with a hoarse cackle. "You and your family are cursed—*maledetto*. This hotel is *maledetto*. May the ghost of—"

"Grandma, we gotta go," Anthony interrupted, pulling her by the arm, refusing to even look at Gino.

Gino's black eyes checked out Anthony Bonar. The man was not good news, he sensed it immediately. Gino had always possessed dead-on instincts when it came to summing people up, and this one was a bad human being, he had no doubt of it.

What the hell are the two of them doing here? he thought for the second time.

Whatever the reason, it wasn't good.

He should warn Lucky. Francesca Bonnatti and Anthony Bonar were unwelcome guests. It was obvious that as far as the Bonnattis were concerned, the Bonnatti/Santangelo vendetta was still very much alive.

84

"Hi," Ace said as Cookie opened the door to their room.

"Hey," Cookie responded.

"Uh, is she around?" Ace asked, hovering in the doorway.

"Is who around?" Cookie asked, thinking that Max had found herself a *real* hottie, this dude was majorly *handsome*.

"The queen of England," Ace deadpanned.

"Oh, you must mean Max."

"Yeah, that's exactly who I mean. I was supposed to pick her up and here I am. I put on a white shirt for the occasion. I feel like an idiot. Does it look okay?"

"It's totally happenin', dude, but I thought you were meeting her outside the spa."

"Why would I be meeting her there? I arranged to pick her up here."

"You left a message half an hour ago that she should meet you outside the spa," Cookie said, wondering how he liked the skimpy purple dress she'd decided to wear.

"I didn't leave a message," Ace said.

"Yeah, the guy at the desk called and said her cousin wanted her to meet him."

"Did you say 'cousin'?" he said, getting concerned.

"Yeah. Max explained that you were playing some game pretending to be her cousin."

"Fuck!"

"Wassamatter?"

"This is bad," he said. "It could be that maniac."

"*What* maniac?" Cookie asked, her eyes widening.

"The dude who kidnapped her in Big Bear."

"*Whaaat?*"

"Yeah," he said urgently. "Let's go. We gotta find her before he does."

~ ~ ~

"I have to talk to you," Venus said, cornering Lucky. "Alone. Now."

Excusing herself from Cole and his rock star boyfriend, Lucky concentrated on Venus. "What's on your mind?" she asked. "What's with the 'alone' and 'now' bit?"

"We're getting married," Venus confided, somewhat breathlessly.

"*Excuse* me?" Lucky responded with a look of surprise. "Did I just hear you say the M word? I mean, isn't that the word you swore you'd never use again after Cooper?"

"Yup," Venus confessed. "You're right. But Billy finally asked me."

"I don't believe this!" Lucky exclaimed.

"Believe it," Venus responded.

"Is it what you want?" Lucky asked.

"I think so."

"You *think* so?" Lucky said, shaking her head. "You'd better be sure."

"Well, I've said yes, so it's too late to *not* be sure."

"Man!" Lucky grumbled. "Like I don't have enough going on, now I've got a wedding to plan. When we get back we'll—"

"No!" Venus interrupted. "You don't understand. We're doing it tonight, after the concert. So if you're planning anything, you'd better do it fast!"

~ ~ ~

"Mr. Dollar," Emmanuelle said, sidling close to the famous movie star, thrusting out her considerable assets. "I'm your biggest fan."

Charlie Dollar checked the young blonde out. She was certainly succulent, and he was certainly into succulent. Young too. Yes, this one was just his type.

"Hi, there, chickadee," he said. "What's your name?"

"Emmanuelle," she answered, reaching up to touch one of her recently acquired diamond earrings.

"Oh," Charlie said with a knowing chuckle. "Like one of those dirty movies from the seventies."

"I don't know what you're talking about."

"You wouldn't. Too young. Are you even legal?"

"I'm twenty, and I've been on sixteen magazine covers," she boasted.

"No shit?"

"Sixteen covers," she said proudly. "But I bet you've been on more than that."

"Well, little lady," he drawled, "I'm mucho older than twenty."

"I just wanted to say how much I admire you," she gushed.

"That's very smart, young lady," he said, scratching his stubbled chin.

"I'm here with somebody tonight," Emmanuelle continued. "But I was wondering if you'd give me your number so that when I come to L.A. I can call you."

"You're with somebody tonight, huh?" he said, peering at her over the top of his tinted shades.

"That's right."

"A guy?"

"I'm not a *lesbian*, Mr. Dollar," she said coyly.

"Shame."

"Excuse me?" she said, toying with her necklace nestled cozily in her cleavage.

"Uh . . . nothin'. Where's your boyfriend?"

"Somewhere around. I'm sure he'll find me in a minute."

"*Then* what's he gonna do, beat my ass?"

"He might," she giggled. "He *is* kind of the jealous type."

"Why is it that you jailbait little hussies always manage to target Charlie," he complained. "You got any clue how many times I've had one of you poptarts come on to me, an' then some asshole boyfriend or husband appears ready to beat the shit outta me?"

"No," she said, fluttering her eyelashes.

"It happens, sugar-tits, so here's my suggestion—take your pretty little ass an' go peddle the goods elsewhere."

He walked away, leaving Emmanuelle nonplussed.

Irma and The Grill standing nearby observed the entire scene.

Irma felt a tiny frisson of satisfaction. Anthony was going to get what he deserved from this one.

~ ~ ~

"I should leave," Venus sighed, holding Billy's hand. "I need time by myself before my show. I have kind of a ritual I put myself through."

"I understand that you want to be alone," Billy said, "but you're not changing your mind, are you? You wouldn't do that to me, would you?"

"Now why would you think that?" she said softly. "I'm as excited as you are."

"Just checking," he said with a nervous laugh. "I mean, I know it's sudden and all, but we're doing the right thing—I'm sure of it."

"So am I, baby, otherwise I wouldn't've said yes."

"Okay," he said, taking a deep breath. "After the show we're gonna do it, an' we're not telling anyone except Lucky and Lennie, right?"

"Lucky's promised to get it all organized. All she's asked is that we wait until after the fireworks display. Then we show up at the chapel, and *voilà*!"

"Sounds perfect."

"What about Kev?"

"What *about* him?"

"He's your best friend. Surely he'll be hurt if he's not included."

"Since when did you care about *Kev's* feelings?" Billy said, thinking that the last person he planned on telling was Kev—who'd immediately share the news with Ali, and Ali was the kind of girl who would most likely alert the media and maybe even sell her story about her afternoon of sex in the pool with Billy Melina, movie star.

Oh shit! Why had he ever banged her? Shit! Shit! Shit!

"I don't hate Kev," Venus explained. "I think he always resented me for taking you away from him."

"You're wrong, babe."

"No I'm not. So here's what I think we should do."

"What?"

"Make a new start and invite him."

"No!" Billy said sharply. "He didn't invite *me* to *his* wedding."

"Don't be so petty," she chided. "That's not like you, Billy."

"I do not want him there, baby. Okay?"

"Whatever you say."

"Hey, I kinda like it when you're subservient."

"And I like you," she said, reaching up to touch his cheek. "I like you so much I'm even marrying you."

"That's right, we're getting married, babe, so I think you can use the L word."

~ ~ ~

The spa was located in a separate building near the main swimming pool at the back of the hotel. The setting was idyllic—fountains and exotic fish ponds surrounded by lush greenery and tall palms. Since the spa did not open until the following day, and with everyone's attention focused on the reception and concert, the area around the spa was quite deserted.

Max, who'd thoroughly explored the hotel earlier with Ace, raced to meet him. She felt comfortable and excited in his company. Once again she marveled at how different he was from the kids she'd grown up with in Malibu and Beverly Hills, her so-called peers—all with rich, famous, or powerful parents. Cookie and Harry were the only two she'd bonded with. They were different, and so was Ace—he didn't have that rich-kid vibe, he was genuine and nice and most of all HOT!

Just thinking about him made her shiver with the anticipation of seeing him. Was it possible to have a relationship with someone who didn't live in L.A.?

Yes! Yes! Yes! They could drive to see each other on alternate weekends. One weekend she'd go to Big Bear, the next he'd drive to L.A. It was a workable situation.

Then it occurred to her that she was getting way ahead of herself since Ace hadn't even kissed her. Hmm . . . she definitely had to do something about *that*.

And just as she was thinking he was late, a figure began walking toward her, and to her utmost horror she realized it was the Internet Freak himself.

For a moment she froze. Then she turned to run.

"Wait!" he yelled, leaping toward her. "Maria, wait! It's me. I've come back for you. Please wait!"

~ ~ ~

Reaching in her purse for a Kleenex, Irma discovered that she still had Oliver Stanton's card. She stared at it for a moment, studying the numbers. What if she called him? And in exchange for information about Anthony's drug dealings asked him to rescue her? It was a thought. A very welcome thought.

She had plenty of information about Anthony's drug activities. He'd taken her to Colombia on more than one occasion, and she knew some of the names of the people he dealt with. She'd also witnessed many of his late-night business transactions in Acapulco.

Yes, she knew more than enough. But how to get to a phone, that was the problem.

"I need to use the bathroom," she informed The Grill.

"You wait," the big man said, glowering.

"I can't wait," she said sharply. "I need to go now."

"No!"

"Yes!"

Reluctantly The Grill escorted her to the ladies' room, where he stationed himself outside.

The moment she got inside the restroom, she quickly looked around to see who else was in there.

A redheaded woman was standing at the sink washing her hands.

"Excuse me," Irma said, approaching her. "Would you happen to have a cell phone I can use? I left mine at home and it's kind of urgent."

"I don't, dear," the woman said, drying her hands. "Damn thing wouldn't fit in my purse. My friend might have one, though."

"Where's your friend?"

"Making a tinkle."

Irma stared at the closed stall door, willing the woman's friend to emerge.

"Are you all right?" the redheaded woman asked. "You look awfully pale."

No, I am not all right. Earlier today I watched my husband cut off my lover's balls in front of me. And now my insane husband is threatening to kill me and my parents.

"I'm fine, thank you," she managed. "But I do need to make this call, it's very urgent."

"We should go outside," the woman suggested. "I'm sure my husband has his phone."

Before she could think of an excuse, the other woman, a petite brunette, emerged from one of the stalls.

"Ah, Doreen," the redhead said. "Do you have your phone on you?"

"Yes, why?" Doreen asked.

"I promised this lady she could use it. She has to make a quick call."

"The battery might be low," Doreen said, reaching into her purse. "I'm always forgetting to charge it." She handed Irma a pink sequined phone.

Irma pulled out Oliver's card and squinted at the numbers again. Office. Home. Cell.

She chose cell and quickly punched out the number, moving away from the two women who were now chatting about the reception and how much they were enjoying it.

Her hands were trembling, any moment now Anthony might return and come busting in.

She misdialed, tried again, and finally the number rang.

Please God, let Oliver pick up.

Please God, let him answer.

"Hello?"

"Oliver," she gasped. "It's Irma. I need your help."

85

The reception was winding down. A series of assistant P.R.'s were attempting to usher the most famous guests to the red carpet pathway where they would be photographed and interviewed by the many photographers and TV crews as they made their way to the lingerie show.

Lucky was swamped, what with everyone attempting to speak to her, members of her staff giving her a series of updates, Gino trying to attract her attention, and now a wedding to get together in a matter of hours.

She elicited the help of Mooney, who knew everyone in Vegas, to arrange the wedding chapel and keep everything quiet. If the news of Venus and Billy's impending nuptials got out to the press, it would be chaos.

Next she spoke to her catering and entertainment directors about organizing a small, extremely exclusive private reception in her penthouse later that night.

"A very close friend of mine is getting married," she informed them, revealing no names. "It has to be special."

They assured her it would be. Everyone who worked with Lucky loved her—she had a way of inspiring great loyalty and enthusiasm.

"Have you seen Max?" she asked Lennie when he appeared to accompany her down the red carpet.

"No," he said, shaking his head. "And I was looking forward to meeting the new boyfriend."

"Don't say 'boyfriend' around her, she'll kill you."

"Something wrong with 'boyfriend'?"

"She wouldn't like it."

"Then I won't say it."

"That's wise."

"Gino's waving at you."

"I know. Let's try to get over to him. I can't seem to make a move without a dozen people attempting to stop me."

"In that case, grab hold of my arm and hang on. Smile a lot, I'll get you there."

"You're so macho."

"And handsome, right?" he quipped. "Isn't that why you married me?"

"Oh yes!" she said, laughing as he propelled her through the crowd until they reached Gino.

"What's up?" she asked her father.

"Somethin's not right," Gino replied, rubbing the scar on his cheek.

"Not enough ice in your drink?" she said flippantly. "Music too loud? *What?*"

Gino's face was serious. "Enzio Bonnatti's widow is here with a supposed grandson," he said. "I don't like it, Lucky, they're up to somethin', an' you'd better find out what it is. She had a crazy hostile look in her eyes. Kept on muttering about the hotel being cursed. They're here for some kind of revenge—you can bet on it."

~ ~ ~

When Anthony came back with an angry Francesca lagging behind him, he was perplexed to find Irma missing.

"Where the fuck is she?" he demanded of The Grill.

"In the ladies' room," the big man muttered.

"What the fuck you let her go there for?"

"She told me she had to go."

"Jesus Christ!" Anthony steamed, walking over to the door of the ladies' room. "Irma!" he yelled. "Get your ass out here."

Irma came out immediately.

He glared at her. "I told you not to go anywhere. When I tell you somethin', you'd better fuckin' listen."

She refused to look at him.

"Where's Emmanuelle?" he demanded, turning back to The Grill.

"Over there, boss," The Grill said.

Anthony observed Emmanuelle talking to a man. He'd told both women to stay next to The Grill, not to go running around all over the place. Amazing wasn't it, that he had to control everything.

Taking hold of Irma, he pulled her over to Emmanuelle, who was in midsentence. Anthony grabbed Emmanuelle's arm, yanking her away from the man.

"That was so rude," Emmanuelle objected, her cheeks flushed. "That man is a *very* important producer. He told me I should be in movies."

"I don't give a shit who he is," Anthony snapped. "When I tell you to stay somewhere, you stay there. Got it?"

Irma met the girl's eyes.

Emmanuelle stared back at her defiantly before turning to Anthony and saying, "You shouldn't speak to me like that. I'm not your wife."

Anthony controlled an overwhelming impulse to slap her across the face. Emmanuelle was getting too lippy for her own good. It was time to do something to put her in her place.

~ ~ ~

"Are you sure your heart can take this?" Lucky teased Gino as she escorted him to the front row of the lingerie show.

"Think I'll survive, kiddo."

"Oh yes, I almost forgot," she said, smiling. "Your nickname used to be Gino the Ram, right?"

Gino's mind was elsewhere. "What didja do 'bout the Bonnattis?" he said, frowning. "Didja get 'em outta here?"

"Not yet. There's press everywhere, it wouldn't be smart to cause an incident."

"Whaddya think they're doing here?" he mused.

"They're probably just checking the place out."

"You don't know Francesca like I know that witch," Gino said, still worrying. "She had balls when she was married to Enzio, big brass balls. I'll never forget her sittin' in the courtroom when you were on trial for Santino's murder. She sat there every day, glaring at you, vowing revenge. You don't remember?"

"That whole trial is a blur."

"*I* remember it, kiddo. They're here for a goddamn reason. I can smell it."

"You're wrong, Gino. All that stuff happened so long ago."

"Listen to me, Lucky: she's Sicilian. It don't matter how long ago shit happened, Sicilians never forget an' they never forgive. Have your security people watch 'em, okay?"

"I'll do that. Where are they anyway?"

"Last time I saw 'em they were at the reception."

"I'm leaving you here, but I'll be back. The show's starting in five minutes. I only hope you survive it!"

"Oh, he'll survive it all right," Paige said, leaning forward. "He'll love every minute of it. He might be ninety-five, but believe me, he's still breathing."

~ ~ ~

Alex did not care how adept Ling was in the bedroom—it was over, her constant jealous bitching about Lucky had finally taken its toll. When they got back to L.A. he was definitely telling her to move out. He'd sooner be by himself than stuck with a woman who really didn't understand him at all. Ling should be with somebody who enjoyed getting the shit nagged out of him.

Besides, he had his movie to edit, no time for Ling. Being in the editing room seventeen hours a day was relationship enough.

Upstairs in their suite, he conducted a search for his watch. It was a special gold Patek Philippe watch given to him by Lucky at the end of the movie they'd produced together. Lucky had inscribed on the back, *I'll always remember our time together. Lucky.*

It was an ambiguous inscription that could mean anything. He chose to think it meant their one night together long ago. Only realistically he knew it didn't. Because of Lennie. Because Lucky was not a cheater, she was a woman of principle. It was one of the things he loved most about her.

It occurred to him that maybe Ling had hidden the watch somewhere. He wouldn't put it past her—once she'd read the inscription, she'd gotten very uptight, claiming the watch was too flashy for him to wear. Flashy! It was a Patek Philippe, for Christ's sake.

He knew the real reason she hated it. It was a gift from Lucky, and that was enough to set her off.

He was getting more livid by the minute, convinced Ling had stashed it away. Unzipping her suitcase he started rooting around, finding no watch, but coming up with an envelope that he took out and opened. Inside were several Cartier cards, and on each card were written the words *Drop Dead Bitch.* The word *Bitch* looked as if it had been scrawled in blood.

What the hell was *this* all about?

Then he remembered Lucky over lunch in Vegas telling him about the odd notes she'd been receiving.

Jesus *Christ!* Had Ling been sending Lucky hate mail? He couldn't believe it. What kind of psycho was his live-in girlfriend turning out to be?

This was most definitely a reason to get rid of her permanently.

~ ~ ~

The woman's body buried out in the desert, wrapped in plastic like a shroud, was dug up and taken back to the city where she was immediately identified by her former husband.

Tasmin Garland. Murder victim.

And Detective Franklin had no doubt who did it.

86

Before Max could run too far, Henry caught up with her, tackling her to the ground, where he pinned her with a steel-like grip on both her arms, his body half over hers.

For a man with a gimpy leg he could sure move fast, and he was surprisingly strong.

"What do you want with me?" she shouted, determined not to give in to this creep again whether he had a gun or not. She was Lucky Santangelo's daughter and she realized she'd better start fighting back. *Girls can do anything*—Lucky had taught her that ever since she could remember. It was time for action.

"Maria," he crooned, his disgusting breath in her face. "Why are you trying to run away from me when surely you have realized by now that we belong together?"

She lay very still on the damp ground. It was patently obvious he was a total whacko, and how best to get herself out of this situation? She had to think fast.

"What's your name?" she managed. "Your real name."

"Lord Grant," he said grandly.

"Lord Grant," she repeated.

"Yes. And I came here today for *you,* to take *you* to a place where people will leave us alone."

"What people?"

"Lucky Santangelo," he said, his voice full of animosity. "That woman is not a fit woman to be your mother, she will do nothing but corrupt you. God has sent *me* to save you, Maria."

How did God get into this? Was this guy a Jesus freak on top of everything else?

"Do you *know* Lucky?" she asked, trying to move out from under him.

"Yes, I know Lucky," he said, spitting venom. "Lucky Santangelo ruined my life. However, out of bad comes good, and now I have you."

She shifted on the ground, thinking that at least she finally knew why he was targeting her. This whacko had some kind of grudge against her mom, and somehow or other she'd been dragged into it.

Where was Ace when she needed him?

~ ~ ~

Before the lingerie show started, Renee excused herself from Susie and went off to make a phone call. She reached Tucker Bond on the designated number he'd given her to be used only in emergencies.

"I'm calling it off," she said.

"You're doin' *what?*"

"Stopping the action."

There was a long silence. Tucker was used to clients changing their minds, but not at the last moment, not when everything was set up and ready to go.

"Can you do it?" Renee asked.

"I can do anything," Tucker replied. "S'long as I get paid. In full."

"I understand," Renee said. "Our financial arrangement still stands. You'll get your final payment."

"Oh yes, I will."

"Then we're agreed? It's off."

"You're the client."

~ ~ ~

Emmanuelle was in her element sitting amongst an audience dotted with famous people. They were all waiting to view the lingerie show, and she was proud to be one of them.

Anthony had shoved his way into front-row seats. He was confident they had plenty of time before anything happened. The destruction of the Keys would not take place until after Venus's concert, when everyone was outside for the fireworks display. How fitting that everything Lucky Santangelo had worked so hard for would go up in smoke.

He'd sent his grandmother back to the Cavendish with The Grill to watch over her. She'd claimed she wasn't feeling well, but he wasn't sure he believed her. She was putting it on because she was pissed at him for dragging her away from Gino Santangelo. To make him feel bad she'd begun muttering about heart palpitations.

"Stay with her," he'd instructed The Grill. "If you think she needs it, call a doctor. I'll be back soon."

He hadn't wanted to miss out on humiliating his wife even further. How galling it must be for her having to walk around with him and his sexy mistress. How mortifying and degrading and fuck the cunt! He didn't care. It was over between him and Irma. Tomorrow she'd be history, and if Emmanuelle kept on talking to other men, she'd be history too.

~ ~ ~

"We're going in the wrong direction," Ace said. "The spa isn't this way."

"I'm sure it is," Cookie argued. "I passed it earlier."

"No!" he said urgently. "It's at the *back* of the hotel. Come on, move it."

"Uh . . . if this freak had a gun last time, don't you think we should maybe like call security?" Cookie ventured, trying to keep up with him.

"Good thinking," he said, realizing she was scared. "You go inside the hotel and alert security, I'll find Max. And hurry up."

~ ~ ~

Lucky had no idea who to look for. Gino had said Francesca Bonnatti and her grandson were trouble, but where the hell were they?

Hundreds of people were at the lingerie show. How was she supposed to pick them out?

Her eyes scanned the rows of guests, but she couldn't spot an old woman dressed all in black. On the contrary, everyone seemed to be young and beautiful. Such a glamorous turnout!

She spotted Renee Falcon and Susie.

"Hi," she said, going over to them. "I'm so glad you could make it."

"We wouldn't dream of missing out," Susie said. "Only I'm putting a blindfold on this one during the show."

"*Puleaze!*" Renee said, feeling delightfully relaxed.

For once she'd done the right thing, and it was a good feeling.

~ ~ ~

Ling was sitting in a front-row seat alongside the catwalk. Alex made it back just before the lingerie show started.

"What took you so long?" Ling asked as a couple of hovering photographers spotted Alex and to his annoyance began snapping his picture.

"I was catching up on some reading," he said, sliding into his seat. "Interesting stuff, take a look." He dove into his jacket pocket and passed Ling one of the Cartier cards.

Her face remained impassive as she glanced at it. "Have you been going through my things?" she asked in an accusatory tone.

"I was searching for my watch, and look what I came up with," he said. "Care to comment?"

"Going through someone else's belongings is low," Ling said, refusing to address the issue of the Cartier card with *Drop Dead Bitch* scrawled on it. "I would never go through your things."

"Have you been sending these cards to Lucky?" Alex demanded. "Have you been *threatening* her?"

"Shush," Ling said, "the show is starting."

And indeed it was, as a parade of models, each one more statuesque and gorgeous than the last one, began stalking down the runway wearing nothing much at all except a plethora of hair extensions, five-inch heels, and "I am so much better than you" disdainful expressions.

~ ~ ~

"You've got to let me stand up, I promise I won't run," Max said, determined that this time there was no way she was becoming a victim.

"It doesn't make any difference," Henry replied. "Because wherever you run to I will find you. We are destined to be together, Maria, and I will make you very happy and content. I wish you would believe me."

"Yeah, I get it," she said as he moved off her, allowing her to stand up. This creep was definitely psycho city. Nutty as a loon. "So . . . uh . . . the reason you think we should be together is because of my mom—something she did to you—right?"

"Lucky Santangelo took my chance of stardom and handed it to Billy Melina," Henry said, spewing his anger and frustration. "But it doesn't matter now, because God works in a mysterious fashion, and because of what Lucky did to me, it has brought *us* together, and that is a magical and wonderful thing."

"Oh sure, wonderful," she muttered sarcastically, brushing off her clothes. "Especially when you've got to throw me on the ground to tell me this."

"I hope I didn't hurt you," he said with a solicitous expression. "I had no intention of doing so."

"I'm okay," she answered, wondering if it was wise to make another run for it. Did he have his gun with him? That was the question. He was lunatic enough to shoot her in the back if she tried to escape again, so instead she decided to humor him. "Uh . . . what's your plan this time?" she asked. "We're not going to that gross cabin of yours, are we?"

"My mother recently passed on," he said, not sounding at all upset. "Unfortunate for her. Fortunate for us."

As he spoke, Max spotted Ace stealthily approaching from behind where the freak couldn't see him.

Oh, wow! Ace never disappointed.

Taking a deep breath she kept him talking. "Why is it fortunate for us?" she asked, feigning interest.

"Because I am an extremely affluent man," Henry informed her. "I inherited everything, and now I have more than enough money for us to go anywhere and do anything we wish. Nobody can stop us," he boasted. "Not even Lucky Santangelo. This time *I* am in control."

"That's incredible," she said, her heart pounding as she watched Ace edging closer by the second. "Tell me more."

"Oh, I will. I have so much more to tell you, Maria. I—"

Before he could finish the sentence, Ace pounced, knocking him to the ground.

Henry let out a primal scream of pure fury, rolled over, and sprang to his feet. Whereupon he and Ace became embroiled in a fight while Max raced to get help.

This time she wasn't letting him get away with it.

Oh no, she was a Santangelo—this time she was going to nail his ass.

87

Irma sat extremely still, her hands clasped on her lap. She was on one side of Anthony, Emmanuelle on the other.

The Grill was back at the other hotel with Francesca and Anthony was busy ogling the models.

What could he do to her if she got up and walked out? He couldn't cause a scene, the place was too packed. He couldn't stop her. In fact, there was nothing he could do.

Yes, exactly nothing, except have her parents murdered and their home burned to the ground, and after he'd arranged that, come after her with a vengeance.

She was trapped with this despicable man, unless Oliver came through for her. She'd spoken to him briefly, managed to tell him what she'd witnessed regarding Luis, and he'd promised to get in touch with the police in Mexico City to see if they could track anything.

She'd told him where she was and then offered him information in return for her rescue, but before he could reply, the battery on the cell had given out. Then she'd heard Anthony yelling for her outside the ladies' room, and she'd quickly handed the phone back to the woman she'd borrowed it from and hurried outside.

Now she was being forced to watch a lingerie show with her psychotic husband and his tramp mistress.

~ ~ ~

The models paraded down the runway, strutting their goods, twirling and turning in the briefest of teddies and sexy little numbers, the music blaring. Every man in the place was mesmerized—every man except Alex, who couldn't give a rat's ass about a parade of half-naked models. He was more interested in finding out what Ling had in mind sending Lucky a series of sick notes. How *dare* she.

"Give me your purse," he said, trying to jerk it away from her. "I want to see how many of these pathetic notes you've got hidden away."

"No!" Ling responded, making him all the more anxious to take a look. "I will not."

"Oh, yes you will."

"Stop bullying me, Alex."

"When you start telling me what the hell you hoped to achieve."

~ ~ ~

As Max raced for help, she ran into Cookie and two beefy security guards.

"Quick!" she gasped. "Hurry! I think he's got a gun."

"Who's got a gun, miss?" asked one of the security guards, pulling out his own weapon.

"The freak who tried to kidnap me," she said, starting to run back in the direction of the spa.

"Kidnap you?" the other guard said disbelievingly.

"This is Lucky Santangelo's daughter," Cookie interjected. "So unless you're all planning on getting fired, let's move it, guys."

Both guards began to run, and within moments they arrived outside the spa to find Ace and Henry wrestling on the ground trading punches.

Security guard number one trained his weapon on them. "Quit it, *now!*" he commanded, as Ace got in one last punch, a satisfactory blow to the freak's jaw.

And then it was over.

Henry stood up. "This boy jumped me," he blustered. "The two of them were trying to rob me."

And while he was speaking, Max mustered all her strength and kicked him in the balls.

"That's for everything," she said as he crumpled to the ground. "And my name is Max. M-A-X. Don't ever forget it."

~ ~ ~

"Enjoy the show," Anthony whispered in Irma's ear. "'Cause tomorrow I'm sendin' you to a place where the only show's gonna be *you*."

Irma stared at her vile husband. "You're a bloodthirsty monster, you know that?" she said, loathing him with a hatred she had not thought herself capable of. "You took away a man's life for doing something *you* do every day. You're no better than a savage."

"Tomorrow," Anthony taunted as a six-foot blonde in revealing leopard-print lingerie sashayed past on the runway, "I'm sendin' you to a place where you'll get to fuck ten men a day. An' you're gonna get off on it, Irma, 'cause you're a born fuckin' whore."

Before she could process what he was saying, a big commotion started happening with the people sitting on the other side of her—an Asian woman and her male companion.

The scuffle was over the woman's purse, which the man was attempting to wrest from her grasp.

Suddenly a gun fell out of the purse onto the ground.

Without thinking clearly, Irma bent down and quickly picked it up.

She held it for a moment, the image of Luis being tortured flashing before her eyes. Then she turned to Anthony, who started to say, "What the fuck—"

Raw fear flicked across his face as she raised the gun and pointed it straight at him. He knew what she was about to do before she knew it herself.

Quite calmly she flicked off the safety catch, and shot her husband right between the eyes.

Anthony Bonnatti died within seconds.

At last Irma was truly free.

EPILOGUE

Six Months Later

Detective Franklin got her man. Only he happened to be dead at the time—shot in the face by his distraught wife, whom he'd forced to watch the torture and murder of one of his employees.

Detective Franklin didn't know who'd sent her the bloodstained bathrobe and a map leading to Tasmin Garland's body, although she had her suspicions.

What she *did* know was that it was a good thing. Anthony Bonar was guilty. Dead or alive.

~ ~ ~

Oliver Stanton almost got his man too. But his man was dead on arrival. By the time he arrived in Las Vegas, Anthony Bonar was lying on a slab in the police morgue.

Unfortunate for Oliver, because he'd finally gotten the one break he'd been hoping for regarding the man he'd been tracking for two long and tedious years.

And now it didn't matter. Now all his hard work was for nothing.

~ ~ ~

Francesca Bonnatti expired within moments of her grandson being shot. She was lying on her bed in the bungalow at the Cavendish, and she went peacefully with a satisfied smile on her face.

Anthony had been with her since he was twelve. She was not allowing him to go anywhere without her.

~ ~ ~

Emmanuelle returned to Miami, but since nothing was in her name, she was forced to relinquish her car and vacate her apartment. Her jewelry she kept—she wasn't giving *that* up.

She called the producer she'd met at the Keys party, and he offered her a job in L.A. Little did she know he was the biggest producer of porn on the West Coast.

Emmanuelle was determined to become a star—one way or the other.

~ ~ ~

Carlita stayed in New York. She was a savvy businesswoman, and everything Anthony Bonar had invested in her design business was all hers. She gave The Grill a job as her head of security. He was eternally grateful.

Carlita was a woman who knew how to look after herself.

~ ~ ~

Irma Bonar was arrested and charged with murder. After all the evidence was reviewed and the lawyers got together with the D.A., the charge was eventually reduced to manslaughter. Luis's mutilated body had been discovered buried under the rubble of a building site in Mexico City, along with a security guard from the Bonar estate. The security guard's name was Cesar.

Irma was given three years' probation.

As soon as she was able, she presented the house outside Mexico City to Luis's family as a gift, then she signed over the Acapulco villa to Rosa and Manuel.

Irma knew that both gestures of generosity and kindness would have driven Anthony insane. The thought comforted her.

She put the rest of Anthony's fortune into trusts for her children, and bought herself a house in Omaha, near her parents. She moved there with Carolina and Eduardo, both of whom objected furiously.

She didn't care, she knew they'd soon settle into a normal life. And so would she.

~ ~ ~

Needless to say, Alex Woods and Ling did not stay together. His fury about the notes she'd been sending to Lucky was palpable. And what the hell had she been doing with his unlicensed gun in her purse? That was not easy to explain.

He'd always known Ling was envious of the strong bond he shared with Lucky, but it was too bizarre to imagine she'd been planning to *shoot* her.

No way. Not even Ling was *that* crazy.

Ling moved out and he was happy about it. No more nagging, no more flowers in his house or a fridge full of food.

Once more he was a free soul, and that's the way he liked it.

Nothing could change the way he felt about Lucky. She was his friend. She would always be his friend.

And while Lennie was around, that's the way it had to stay.

~ ~ ~

To Renee's surprise, Susie was right, and the Keys opening next door to the Cavendish turned out to be excellent for business. Receipts at the Cavendish were up twenty percent on the year before.

Renee did not mourn Anthony Bonar. He'd got what he'd been asking for. After all, one bad turn deserves another.

Renee vowed to clean up her act and be more like Susie. Good karma was important.

So far it seemed to be working.

~ ~ ~

Venus married Billy back in L.A. several weeks after the drama at the Keys. They both decided their wedding should not take place on the same night as a violent shooting.

Two days before their wedding, Kev got his marriage annulled. Ali was not exactly a girl to settle down with. Neither Venus nor Billy was surprised.

Billy bought Venus an eight-carat diamond ring, and she bought him a two-hundred-thousand-dollar Ferrari he'd been coveting.

Together they purchased the last available penthouse at the Keys.

Billy got off on being married to Venus—he'd never felt so complete.

Venus loved being married to Billy—he was funny and loving and, most of all, he was hers.

The age difference didn't matter to either of them. Like Lucky and Lennie, they both finally felt they'd found their soulmate.

The tabloids existed in a state of ecstasy. Now that their favorite twosome were married, they could speculate about when the divorce would take place. Or even better—when would Venus get pregnant?

The headlines never stopped.

~ ~ ~

Gino returned to Palm Springs with Paige. Funny how things worked out. He'd sensed that Anthony Bonar was trouble, but he'd never imagined he'd get shot by his own wife.

The Bonnatti family had never had much luck. Too bad. Or not.

At ninety-five Gino felt fortunate to be a survivor. Getting old was a bitch, but it was better than the alternative.

~ ~ ~

The Santangelo-Golden family declined to press charges against Henry Whitfield-Simmons. Both Lucky and Lennie decided that Max had endured enough, and they did not want to see her dragged through court testifying against him.

So Henry was released, and he drove back to the Pasadena mansion where he was promptly arrested for the murder of his mother. An autopsy, which he had not realized had taken place, had revealed that Penelope Whitfield-Simmons had been suffocated to death. The prime suspect was Henry. Proving that he'd done it was not difficult.

~ ~ ~

Max confessed everything to her parents. They weren't mad, they were concerned and relieved.

"Family is everything," Lucky told her. "And even though you didn't tell us the truth, we still love you very very much. But if anything like this *ever* happens again and you don't tell us, that's it, you'll be grounded forever!"

Max loved her mom. Lucky was tough, but she always came through when it mattered.

Ace stayed around. He wasn't mad about the L.A. lifestyle, but as he said to Max, "You need me to watch out for you, so I guess I'm gonna have to spend more time here."

"Cool with me," she'd said, trying not to sound too happy about it.

And finally she got the kiss she'd been hoping for.

Yes. It was worth the wait.

~ ~ ~

Lucky and Lennie continued their life of married bliss. Even when they were apart, it felt as if they were together.

Lennie went off and made his movie in Canada. Lucky spent several days a week in Vegas overseeing the Keys, which was an enormous success.

She spoke to Bobby almost every day, and he assured her he was keeping in touch with Brigette—in fact, he'd introduced her to one of his friends and they seemed to be getting involved.

The club business was booming.

"I'm opening in L.A.," he warned Lucky. "So you'd better watch out, I'm getting closer every day!"

"I'm shaking!" she joked.

Finally the family house in Malibu was ready to move back into. Lucky and Lennie drove there together.

Lucky Santangelo and Lennie Golden. Two of a kind.